Opening a Chestnut Burr

Edward Payson Roe

Contents

OPENING A CHESTNUT BURR

BY

Edward Payson Roe

PREFACE

In sending this, my fourth venture, out upon the uncertain waters of public opinion, I shall say but few words of preface. In the past I have received considerable well-deserved criticism from the gentlemen of the caustic pen, but so far from having any hard feeling toward them, I have rather wondered that they found so much to say that was favorable. How they will judge this simple October story (if they think it worth while to judge it at all) I leave to the future, and turn to those for whom the book was really written.

In fancy I see them around the glowing hearth in quiet homes, such as I have tried to describe in the following pages, and hope that this new-comer will be welcomed for the sake of those that preceded it. Possibly it may make friends of its own.

From widely separated parts of the country, and from almost every class, I have received many and cordial assurances that my former books were sources not only of pleasure, but also of help and benefit, and I am deeply grateful for the privilege of unobtrusively entering so many households, and saying words on that subject which is inseparable from happiness in both worlds.

I think the purpose of the book will become apparent to the reader. The incidents and characters are mainly imaginary.

Observation has shown me that there are many in the world, like my hero, whose condition can be illustrated by the following lines:

Were some great ship all out of stores,   When half-way o'er the sea, Fit emblem of too many lives,   Such vessel doomed would be.

Must there not be something fatally wrong in that scheme of life which finds an heir of eternity weary, listless, discouraged, while yet in the dawning of existence? It is not in perishing *things*, merely, to give back the lost zest. But a glad zest and hopefulness might be inspired even in the most jaded and ***ennui***-cursed, were there in our homes such simple, truthful natures as that of my heroine; and in the sphere of quiet homes--not elsewhere--I believe that woman can best rule and save the world.

Highland Falls, N.Y., September, 1874.

CHAPTER I
A HERO, BUT NOT HEROIC

"Shall I ever be strong in mind or body again?" said Walter Gregory, with irritation, as he entered a crowded Broadway omnibus.

The person thus querying so despairingly with himself was a man not far from thirty years of age, but the lines of care were furrowed so deeply on his handsome face, that dismal, lowering morning, the first of October, that he seemed much older. Having wedged himself in between two burly forms that suggested thrift down town and good cheer on the avenue, he appears meagre and shrunken in contrast. He is tall and thin. His face is white and drawn, instead of being ruddy with health's rich, warm blood. There is scarcely anything remaining to remind one of the period of youth, so recently vanished; neither is there the dignity, nor the consciousness of strength, that should come with maturer years. His heavy, light-colored mustache and pallid face gave him the aspect of a ***blase*** man of the world who had exhausted himself and life at an age when wisely directed manhood should be just entering on its richest pleasures.

And such an opinion of him, with some hopeful exceptions and indications, would be correct. The expression of irritation and self- disgust still remaining on his face as the stage rumbles down town is a hopeful sign. His soul at least is not surrounded by a Chinese wall of conceit. However perverted his nature may be, it is not a shallow one, and he evidently has a painful sense of the wrongs committed against it. Though his square jaw and the curve of his lip indicate firmness, one could not look upon his contracted brow and half- despairing expression, as he sits oblivious of all surroundings, without thinking of a ship drifting helplessly and in distress. There are encouraging possibilities in the fact that from those windows of the soul, his eyes, a troubled rather than an evil spirit looks out. A close observer would see at a glance that he was not a good man, but he might also note that he was not content with being a bad one. There was little of the rigid pride and sinister hardness or the conceit often seen on the faces of men of the world who have spent years in spoiling their manhood; and the sensual phase of coarse dissipation was quite wanting.

You will find in artificial metropolitan society many men so emasculated that they are quite vain of being blase--fools that with conscious superiority smile disdainfully at those still possessing simple, wholesome tastes for things which they in their indescribable accent characterize as a "bore."

But Walter Gregory looked like one who had early found the dregs of evil life very bitter, and his face was like that of nature when smitten with untimely frosts.

He reached his office at last, and wearily sat down to the routine work at his desk. Instead of the intent and interested look with which a young and healthy man would naturally enter on his business, he showed rather a dogged resolution to work whether he felt like it or not, and with harsh disregard of his physical weakness.

The world will never cease witnessing the wrongs that men commit against each other; but perhaps if the wrongs and cruelties that people inflict on themselves could be summed up the painful aggregate would be much larger.

As Gregory sat bending over his writing, rather from weakness than from a stooping habit, his senior partner came in, and was evidently struck by the appearance of feebleness on the part of the young man. The unpleasant impression haunted him, for having looked over his letters he came out of his private office and again glanced uneasily at the colorless face, which gave evidence that only sheer force of will was spurring a failing hand and brain to their tasks.

At last Mr. Burnett came and laid his hand on his junior partner's shoulder, saying, kindly, "Come, Gregory, drop your work. You are ill. The strain upon you has been too long and severe. The worst is over now, and we are going to pull through better than I expected. Don't take the matter so bitterly to heart. I admit myself that the operation promised well at first. You were misled, and so were we all, by downright deception. That the swindle was imposed on us through you was more your misfortune than your fault, and it will make you a keener business man in the future. You have worked like a galley-slave all summer to retrieve matters, and have taken no vacation at all. You must take one now immediately, or you will break down altogether. Go off to the woods; fish, hunt, follow your fancies; and the bracing October air will make a new man of you."

"I thank you very much," Gregory began. "I suppose I do need rest. In a few days, however, I can leave better--"

"No," interrupted Mr. Burnett, with hearty emphasis; "drop everything. As soon as you finish that letter, be off. Don't show your face here again till November."

"I thank you for your interest in me," said Gregory, rising. "Indeed, I believe it would be good economy, for if I don't feel better soon I shall be of no use here or anywhere else."

"That's it," said old Mr. Burnett, kindly. "Sick and blue, they go together. Now be off to the woods, and send me some game. I won't inquire too sharply whether you brought it down with lead or silver."

Gregory soon left the office, and made his arrangements to start on his trip early the next morning. His purpose was to make a brief visit to the home of his boyhood and then to go wherever a vagrant fancy might lead.

The ancestral place was no longer in his family, though he was spared the pain of seeing it in the hands of strangers. It had been purchased a few years since by an old and very dear friend of his deceased father--a gentleman named Walton. It had so happened that Gregory had rarely met his father's friend, who had been engaged in business at the West, and of his family he knew little more than that there were two daughters--one who had married a Southern gentleman, and the other, much younger, living with her father. Gregory had been much abroad as the European agent of his house, and it was during such absence that Mr. Walton had retired from business and purchased the old Gregory homestead. The young man felt sure, how-ever, that though a comparative stranger himself, he would, for his father's sake, be a welcome visitor at the home of his childhood. At any rate he determined to test the matter, for the moment he found himself at liberty he felt a strange and an eager longing to revisit the scenes of the happiest portion of his life. He had meant to pay such a visit in the previous spring, soon after his arrival from Europe, when his elation at being made partner in the house which he so long had served as clerk reached almost the point of happiness.

Among those who had welcomed him back was a man a little older than himself, who, in his absence, had become known as a successful operator in Wall Street. They had been intimate before Gregory went abroad, and the friendship was renewed at once. Gregory prided himself on his knowledge of the world, and was not by nature inclined to trust hastily; and yet he did place implicit confidence in Mr. Hunting, regarding him as a better man than himself. Hunting was an active member of a church, and his name figured on several charities, while Gregory had almost ceased to attend any place of worship, and spent his money selfishly upon himself, or foolishly upon others, giving only as prompted by impulse. Indeed, his friend had occasionally ventured to remonstrate with him against his tendencies to dissipation, saying that a young man of his prospects should not damage them for the sake of passing gratification. Gregory felt the force of these words, for he was exceedingly ambitious, and bent upon accumulating wealth and at the same time making a brilliant figure in business circles.

In addition to the ordinary motives which would naturally lead him to desire such success he was incited by a secret one more powerful than all the others combined.

Before going abroad, when but a clerk, he had been the favored suitor of a beautiful and accomplished girl. Indeed the understanding between them almost amounted to an engagement, and he revelled in a passionate, romantic attachment at an age when the blood is hot, the heart enthusiastic, and when not a particle of worldly cynicism and adverse experience had taught him to moderate his rose-hued anticipations. She seemed the embodiment of goodness, as well as beauty and grace, for did she not repress his tendencies to be a little fast? Did she not, with more than sisterly solicitude, counsel him to shun certain florid youth whose premature blossoming indicated that they might early run to seed? and did he not, in consequence, cut Guy Bonner, the jolliest fellow he had ever known? Indeed, more than all, had she not ventured to talk religion to him, so that for a time he had regarded himself as in a very "hopeful frame of mind," and had been inclined to take a mission-class in the same school with herself? How lovely and angelic she had once appeared, stooping in elegant costume from her social height to the little ragamuffins of the street that sat gaping around her! As he gazed adoringly, while waiting to be her resort home, his young heart had swelled with the impulse to be good and noble also.

But one day she caused him to drop out of his roseate clouds. With much sweetness and resignation, and with appropriate sighs, she said that "it was her painful duty to tell him that their intimacy must cease--that she had received an offer from Mr. Grobb, and that her parents, and indeed all her friends, had urged her to accept him. She had been led to feel that they with their riper experience and knowledge of life knew what was best for her, and therefore she had yielded to their wishes and accepted the offer." She was beginning to add, in a sentimental tone, that "had she only followed the impulses of her heart"--when Gregory, at first too stunned and bewildered to speak, recovered his senses and interrupted with, "Please don't speak of your heart, Miss Bently. Why mention so small a matter? Go on with your little transaction by all means. I am a business man myself, and can readily understand your motives;" and he turned on his heel and strode from the room, leaving Miss Bently ill at ease.

The young man's first expression of having received, as it were, a staggering blow, and then his bitter satire, made an impression on her cotton-and-wool nature, and for a time her proceedings with Mr. Grobb did not wear the aspect in which they had been presented by her friends. But her little world so confidently and continually reiterated the statement that she was making a "splendid match" that her qualms vanished, and she felt that what all asserted must be true, and so entered on the gorgeous preparations as if the wedding were all and the man nothing.

It is the custom to satirize or bitterly denounce such girls, but perhaps they are rather to be pitied. They are the natural products of artificial society, wherein wealth, show, and the social eminence which is based on dress and establishment are held out as the prizes of a woman's existence. The only wonder is that so much heart and truth assert themselves among those who all their life have seen wealth practically worshipped, and worth, ungilded, generally ignored. From ultra-fashionable circles a girl is often seen developing into the noblest womanhood; while narrow, mercenary natures are often found where far better things might have been expected. If such girls as Miss Bently could only be kept in quiet obscurity, like a bale of merchandise, till wanted, it would not be so bad; but some of them are such brilliant belles and incorrigible coquettes that they are like certain Wall Street speculators who threaten to "break the street" in making their own fortunes.

Some natures can receive a fair lady's refusal with a good-natured shrug, as merely the result of a bad venture, and hope for better luck next time; but to a greater number this is impossible, especially if they are played with and deceived. Walter Gregory pre-eminently belonged to the latter class. In early life he had breathed the very atmosphere of truth, and his tendency to sincerity ever remained the best element of his character. His was one of those fine-fibred natures most susceptible to injury. Up to this time his indiscretions had only been those of foolish, thoughtless youth, while aiming at the standard of manliness and style in vogue among his city companions. High-spirited young fellows, not early braced by principle, must pass through this phase as in babyhood they cut their teeth. If there is true mettle in them, and they are not perverted by exceptionally bad influences, they outgrow the idea that to be fast and foolish is to be men as naturally as they do their roundabouts.

What a man does is often not so important as the state of the heart that prompts the act. In common parlance, Walter was as good-hearted a fellow as ever breathed. Indeed, he was really inclined to noble enthusiasms.

If Miss Bently had been what he imagined her, she might have led him swiftly and surely into true manhood; but she was only an adept at pretty seeming with him, and when Mr. Grobb offered her his vast wealth, with himself as the only incumbrance, she acted promptly and characteristically.

But perhaps it can be safely said that in no den of iniquity in the city could Walter Gregory have received such moral injury as poisoned his very soul when, in Mr. Bently's elegant and respectable parlor, the "angel" he worshipped "explained how she was situated," and from a "sense of duty" stated her purpose to yield to the wishes of her friends. Gregory had often seen Mr. Grobb, but had given him no thought, supposing him some elderly relative of the family. That this was the accepted suitor of the girl who had, with tender, meaning glances, sung for him sentimental ballads, who had sweetly talked to him of religion and mission work, seemed a monstrous perversion. Call it unjust, unreasonable, if you will, yet it was the most natural thing in the world for one possessing his sensitive, intense nature to pass into harsh, bitter cynicism, and to regard Miss Bently as a typical girl of the period.

A young man is far on the road to evil when he loses faith in woman. During the formative period of character she is, of earthly influences, the most potent in making or marring him. A kind refusal, where no false encouragement has been given, often does a man good, and leaves his faith intact; but an experience similar to that of young Gregory is like putting into a fountain that which may stain and embitter the waters of the stream in all its length.

At the early age of twenty-two he became what is usually understood by the phrase "a man of the world." Still his moral nature could not sink into the depths without many a bitter outcry against its wrongs. It was with no slight effort that he drowned the memory of his early home and its good influences. During the first two or three years he occasionally had periods of passionate remorse, and made spasmodic efforts toward better things. But they were made in human strength, and in view of the penalties of evil, rather than because he was enamored of the right. Some special temptation would soon sweep him away into the old life, and thus, because of his broken promises and repeated failures, he at last lost faith in himself also, and lacked that self-respect without which no man can cope successfully with his evil nature and an evil world.

Living in a boarding-house, with none of the restraints and purifying influences of a good home, he formed intimacies with brilliant but unscrupulous young men. The theatre became his church, and at last the code of his fast, fashionable set was that which governed his life. He avoided gross, vulgar dissipation, both because his nature revolted at it, and also on account of his purpose to permit nothing to interfere with his prospects of advancement in business. He meant to show Miss Bently that she had made a bad business speculation after all. Thus ambition became the controlling element in his character; and he might have had a worse one. Moreover, in all his moral debasement he never lost a decided tendency toward truthfulness and honesty. He would have starved rather than touch anything that did not belong to him, nor would he allow himself to deceive in matters of business, and it was upon these points that he specially prided himself.

Gregory's unusual business ability, coupled with his knowledge of French and German, led to his being sent abroad as agent of his firm. Five years of life in the materialistic and sceptical atmosphere of continental cities confirmed the evil tendencies which were only too well developed before he left his own land. He became what so many appear to be in our day, a practical materialist and atheist. Present life and surroundings, present profit and pleasure, were all in all. He ceased to recognize the existence of a soul within himself having distinct needs and interests. His thoughts centred wholly in the comfort and pleasures of the day and in that which would advance his ambitious schemes. His scepticism was not intellectual and in reference to the Bible and its teachings, but practical and in reference to humanity itself. He believed that with few exceptions men and women lived for their own profit and pleasure, and that religion and creeds were matters of custom and fashion, or an accident of birth. Only the reverence in which religion had been held in his early home kept him from sharing fully in the contempt which the gentlemen he met abroad seemed to have for it. He could not altogether despise his mother's faith, but he regarded her as a gentle enthusiast haunted by sacred traditions. The companionships which he had formed led him to believe that unless influenced by some interested motive a liberal- minded man of the world must of necessity outgrow these things. With the self-deception of his kind, he thought he was broad and liberal in his views, when in reality he had lost all distinction between truth and error, and was narrowing his mind down to things only. Jew or Gentile, Christian or Pagan, it was becoming all one to him. Men changed their creeds and religions with other fashions, but all looked after what they believed to be the main chance, and he proposed to do the same.

As time passed on, however, he began to admit to himself that it was strange that in making all things bend to his pleasure he did not secure more. He wearied of certain things. Stronger excitements were needed to spur his jaded senses. His bets, his stakes at cards grew heavier, his pleasures more gross, till a delicate organization so revolted at its wrongs and so chastised him for excess that he was deterred from self-gratification in that direction.

Some men's bodies are a "means of grace" to them. Coarse dissipation is a physical impossibility, or swift suicide in a very painful form. Young Gregory found that only in the excitements of the mind could he hope to find continued enjoyment. His ambition to accumulate wealth and become a brilliant business man most accorded with his tastes and training, and on these objects he gradually concentrated all his energies, seeking only in club-rooms and places of fashionable resort recreation from the strain of business.

He recognized that the best way to advance his own interests was to serve his employers well; and this he did so effectually that at last he was made a partner in the business, and, with a sense of something more like pleasure than he had known for a long time, returned to New York and entered upon his new duties.

As we have said, among those who warmly greeted and congratulated him, was Mr. Hunting. They gradually came to spend much time together, and business and money-getting were their favorite themes. Gregory saw that his friend was as keen on the track of fortune as himself, and that he had apparently been much more successful. Mr. Hunting intimated that after one reached the charmed inner circle Wall Street was a perfect Eldorado, and seemed to take pains to drop occasional suggestions as to how an investment shrewdly made by one with his favored point of observation often secured in a day a larger return than a year of plodding business.

These remarks were not lost on Gregory, and the wish became very strong that he might share in some of the splendid "hits" by which his friend was accumulating so rapidly.

Usually Mr. Hunting was very quiet and self-possessed, but one evening in May he came into Gregory's rooms in a manner indicating not a little excitement and elation.

"Gregory!" he exclaimed, "I am going to make my fortune."

"Make your fortune! You are as rich as Croesus now."

"The past will be as nothing. I've struck a mine rather than a vein."

"It's a pity some of your friends could not share in your luck."

"Well, a few can. This is so large, and such a good thing, that I have concluded to let a few intimates go in with me. Only all must keep very quiet about it;" and he proposed an operation that seemed certain of success as he explained it.

Gregory concluded to put into it nearly all he had independent of his investment in the firm, and also obtained permission to interest his partners, and to procure an interview between them and Mr. Hunting.

The scheme looked so very plausible that they were drawn into it also; but Mr. Burnett took Gregory aside and said: "After all, we must place a great deal of confidence in Mr. Hunting's word in this matter. Are you satisfied that we can safely do so?"

"I would stake my life on his word in this case," said Gregory, eagerly, "and I pledge all I have put in the firm on his truth."

This was the last flicker of his old enthusiasm and trust in anybody or anything, including himself. With almost the skill of genius Mr. Hunting adroitly, within the limits of the law, swindled them all, and made a vast profit out of their losses. The transaction was not generally known, but even some of the hardened gamblers of the street said "it was too bad."

But the bank-officers with whom Burnett & Co. did business knew about it, and if it had not been for their lenience and aid the firm would have failed. As it was, it required a struggle of months to regain the solid ground of safety.

At first the firm was suspicious of Gregory, and disposed to blame him very much. But when he proved to them that he had lost his private means by Hunting's treachery, and insisted on making over to them all his right and title to the property he had invested with them, they saw that he was no confederate of the swindler, but that he had suffered more than any of them.

He had, indeed. He had lost his ambition. The large sum of money that was to be the basis of the immense fortune he had hoped to amass was gone. He had greatly prided himself on his business ability, but had signalized his entrance on his new and responsible position by being overreached and swindled in a transaction that had impoverished himself and almost ruined his partners. He grew very misanthropic, and was quite as bitter against himself as against others. In his estimation people were either cloaking their evil or had not been tempted, and he felt after Hunting dropped the mask that he would never trust any one again.

It may be said, all this is very unreasonable. Yes, it is; but then people will judge the world by their own experience of it, and some natures are more easily warped by wrong than others. No logic can cope with feeling and prejudice. Because of his own misguided life and the wrong he had received from others, Walter Gregory was no more able to form a correct estimate of society than one color-blind is to judge of the tints of flowers. And yet he belonged to that class who claim pre- eminently to know the world. Because he thought he knew it so well he hated and despised it, and himself as part of it.

The months that followed his great and sudden downfall dragged their slow length along. He worked early and late, without thought of sparing himself. If he could only see what the firm had lost through him made good, he did not care what became of himself. Why should he? There was little in the present to interest him, and the future looked, in his depressed, morbid state, as monotonous and barren as the sands of a desert. Seemingly, he had exhausted life, and it had lost all zest for him.

But while his power to enjoy had gone, not so his power to suffer. His conscience was uneasy, and told him in a vague way that something was wrong. Reason, or, more correctly speaking, instinct, condemned his life as a wretched blunder. He had lived for his own enjoyment, and now, when but half through life, what was there for him to enjoy?

As in increasing weakness he dragged himself to the office on a sultry September day, the thought occurred to him that the end was nearer than he expected.

"Let it come," he said, bitterly. "Why should I live?"

The thought of his early home recurred to him with increasing frequency, and he had a growing desire to visit it before his strength failed utterly. Therefore it was with a certain melancholy pleasure that he found himself at liberty, through the kindness of his partners, to make this visit, and at the season, too, when his boyish memories of the place, like the foliage, would be most varied and vivid.

CHAPTER II
OPENING A CHESTNUT BURR

If the reader could imagine a man visiting his own grave, he might obtain some idea of Walter Gregory's feelings as he took the boat which would land him not far from his early home. And yet, so different was he from the boy who had left that home fifteen years before, that it was almost the same as if he were visiting the grave of a brother who had died in youth.

Though the day was mild, a fresh bracing wind blew from the west. Shielding himself from this on the after-deck, he half reclined, on account of his weakness, in a position from which he could see the shores and passing vessels upon the river. The swift gliding motion, the beautiful and familiar scenery, the sense of freedom from routine work, and the crisp, pure air, that seemed like a delicate wine, all combined to form a mystic lever that began to lift his heart out of the depths of despondency.

A storm had passed away, leaving not a trace. The October sun shone in undimmed splendor, and all nature appeared to rejoice in its light. The waves with their silver crests seemed chasing one another in mad glee. The sailing vessels, as they tacked to and fro across the river under the stiff western breeze, made the water foam about their blunt prows, and the white-winged gulls wheeled in graceful circles overhead. There was a sense of movement and life that was contagious. Gregory's dull eyes kindled with something like interest, and then he thought: "The storm lowered over these sunny shores yesterday. The gloom of night rested upon these waters but a few hours since. Why is it that nature can smile and be glad the moment the shadow passes and I cannot? Is there no sunlight for the soul? I seem as if entering a cave, that grows colder and darker at every step, and no gleam shines at the further end, indicating that I may pass through it and out into the light again."

Thus letting his fancy wander at will, at times half-dreaming and half-waking, he passed the hours that elapsed before the boat touched at a point in the Highlands of the Hudson, his destination. Making a better dinner than he had enjoyed for a long time, and feeling stronger than for weeks before, he started for the place that now, of all the world, had for him the greatest attraction.

There was no marked change in the foliage as yet, but only a deepening of color, like a flush on the cheek of beauty. As he was driving along the familiar road, farm-house and grove, and even tree, rock, and thicket, began to greet him as with the faces of old friends. At last he saw, nestling in a wild, picturesque valley, the quaint outline of his former home. His heart yearned toward it, and he felt that next to his mother's face no other object could be so welcome.

"Slower, please," he said to the driver.

Though his eyes were moist, and at times dim with tears, not a feature in the scene escaped him. When near the gateway he sprung out with a lightness that he would not have believed possible the day before, and said, "Come for me at five."

For a little time he stood leaning on the gate. Two children were playing on the lawn, and it almost seemed to him that the elder, a boy of about ten years, might be himself, and he a passing stranger, who had merely stopped to look at the pretty scene.

"Oh that I were a boy like that one there! Oh that I were here again as of old!" he sighed. "How unchanged it all is, and I so changed! It seems as if the past were mocking me. That must be I there playing with my little sister. Mother must be sewing in her cheery south room, and father surely is taking his after-dinner nap in the library. Can it be that they are all dead save me? and that this is but a beautiful mirage?"

He felt that he could not meet any one until he became more composed, and so passed on up the valley. Before turning away he noticed that a lady come out at the front door. The children joined her, and they started for a walk.

Looking wistfully on either side, Gregory soon came to a point where the orchard extended to the road. A well-remembered fall pippin tree hung its laden boughs over the fence, and the fruit looked so ripe and golden in the slanting rays of October sunlight that he determined to try one of the apples and see if it tasted as of old. As he climbed upon the wall a loose stone fell clattering down and rolled into the road. He did not notice this, but an old man dozing in the porch of a little house opposite did. As Gregory reached up his cane to detach from its spray a great, yellow-cheeked fellow, his hand was arrested, and he was almost startled off his perch by such a volley of oaths as shocked even his hardened ears. Turning gingerly around so as not to lose his footing, he faced this masked battery that had opened so unexpectedly upon him, and saw a white-haired old man balancing himself on one crutch and brandishing the other at him.

"Stop knockin' down that wall and fillin! the road with stuns, you--," shouted the venerable man, in tones that indicated anything but the calmness of age. "Let John Walton's apples alone, you--thief. What do you mean by robbin' in broad daylight, right under a man's nose?"

Gregory saw that he had a character to deal with, and, to divert his mind from thoughts that were growing too painful, determined to draw the old man out; so he said, "Is not taking things so openly a rather honest way of robbing?"

"Git down, I tell yer," cried the guardian of the orchard.

"Suppose 'tis, it's robbin' arter all. So now move on, and none of yer cussed impudence."

"But you call them John Walton's apples," said Gregory, eating one with provoking coolness. "What have you got to do with them? and why should you care?"

"Now look here, stranger, you're an infernal mean cuss to ask such questions. Ain't John Walton my neighbor? and a good neighbor, too? D'ye suppose a well-meanin' man like myself would stand by and see a neighbor robbed? and of all others, John Walton? Don't you know that robbin' a good man brings bad luck, you thunderin' fool?"

"But I've always had bad luck, so I needn't stop on that account," retorted Gregory, from the fence.

"I believe it, and you allers will," vociferated the old man, "and I'll tell yer why. I know from the cut of yer jib that yer've allers been eatin' forbidden fruit. If yer lived now a good square life like 'Squire Walton and me, you'd have no reason to complain of yer luck. If I could get a clip at yer with this crutch I'd give yer suthin' else to complain of. If yer had any decency yer wouldn't stand there a jibin' at a lame old man."

Gregory took off his hat with a polite bow and said: "I beg your pardon; I was under the impression that you were doing the 'cussing.' I shall come and see you soon, for somehow it does me good to have you swear at me. I only wish I had as good a friend in the world as Mr. Walton has in you." With these words he sprung from the fence on the orchard side, and made his way to the hill behind the Walton residence, leaving the old man mumbling and muttering in a very profane manner.

"Like enough it was somebody visitin' at the Walton's, and I've made a--fool of myself after all. What's worse, that poor little Miss Eulie will hear I've been swearin' agin, and there'll be another awful prayin' time. What a cussed old fool I be, to promise to quit swearin'! I know I can't. What's the good o' stoppin'? It's inside, and might as well come out. The Lord knows I don't mean no disrespect to Him. It's only one of my ways. He knows well enough that I'm a good neighbor, and what's the harm in a little cussin'?" and so the strange old man talked on to himself in the intervals between long pulls at his pipe.

By the time Gregory reached the top of the hill his strength was quite exhausted, and, panting, he sat down on the sunny side of a thicket of cedars, for the late afternoon was growing chilly. Beneath him lay the one oasis in a desert world.

With an indescribable blending of pleasure and pain, he found himself tracing with his eye every well-remembered path, and marking every familiar object.

Not a breath of air was stirring, and it would seem that Nature was seeking to impart to his perturbed spirit, full of the restless movement of city life and the inevitable disquiet of sin, something of her own calmness and peace. The only sounds he heard seemed a part of nature's silence,--the tinkle of cowbells, the slumberous monotone of water as it fell over the dam, the grating notes of a katydid, rendered hoarse by recent cool nights, in a shady ravine near by, and a black cricket chirping at the edge of the rock on which he sat-- these were all. And yet the sounds, though not heard for years, seemed as familiar as the mother's lullaby that puts a child to sleep, and a delicious sense of restfulness stole into his heart. The world in which he had so greatly sinned and suffered might be another planet, it seemed so far away. Could it be that in a few short hours he had escaped out of the hurry and grind of New York into this sheltered nook? Why had he not come before? Here was the remedy for soul and body, if any existed.

Not a person was visible on the place, and it seemed that it might thus have been awaiting him in all his absence, and that now he had only to go and take possession.

"So our home in heaven awaits us, mother used to say," he thought, "while we are such willing exiles from it. I would give all the world to believe as she did."

He found that the place so inseparably associated with his mother brought back her teachings, which he had so often tried to forget.

"I wish I might bury myself here, away from the world," he muttered, "for it has only cheated and lied to me from first to last. Everything deceived me, and turned out differently from what I expected. These loved old scenes are true and unchanged, and smile upon me now as when I was here a happy boy. Would to heaven I might never leave them again!"

He was startled out of his revery by the sharp bark of a squirrel that ran chattering and whisking its tail in great excitement from limb to limb in a clump of chestnuts near. The crackling of a twig betrayed to Gregory the cause of its alarm, for through an opening in the thicket he saw the lady who had started out for a walk with the children while he was leaning on the front gate.

Shrinking further behind the cedars he proposed to reconnoitre a little before making himself known. He observed that she was attired in a dark, close-fitting costume suitable for rambling among the hills. At first he thought that she was pretty, and then that she was not. His quick, critical eye detected that her features were not regular, that her profile was not classic. It was only the rich glow of exercise and the jaunty gypsy hat that had given the first impression of something like beauty. In her right hand, which was ungloved, she daintily held, by its short stem, a chestnut burr which the squirrel in its alarm had dropped, and now, in its own shrill vernacular, was scolding about so vociferously. She was glancing around for some means to break it open, and Gregory had scarcely time to notice her fine dark eyes, when, as if remembering the rock on which he had been sitting, she advanced toward him with a step so quick and elastic that he envied her vigor.

Further concealment was now impossible. Therefore with easy politeness he stepped forward and said: "Let me open the burr for you, Miss Walton."

She started violently at the sound of his voice, and for a moment reminded him of a frightened bird on the eve of flight.

"Pardon me for so alarming you," he hastened to say, "and also pardon a seeming stranger for addressing you informally. My name may not be unknown to you, although I am in person. It is Walter Gregory."

She had been so startled that she could not immediately recover herself, and still stood regarding him doubtfully, although with manner more assured.

"Come," said he, smiling and advancing toward her with the quiet assurance of a society man. "Let me open the burr for you, and you shall take its contents in confirmation of what I say. If I find sound chestnuts in it, let them be a token that I am not misrepresenting myself. If my test fails, then you may justly ask for better credentials."

Half smiling, and quite satisfied from his words and appearance in advance, she extended the burr toward him. But as she did so it parted from the stem, and would have fallen to the ground had he not, with his ungloved hand, caught the prickly thing. His hand was as white and soft as hers, and the sharp spines stung him sorely, yet he permitted no sign of pain to appear upon his face.

"Ah!" exclaimed Miss Walton, "I fear it hurt you."

He looked up humorously and said, "An augury is a solemn affair, and no disrespect must be allowed to nature's oracle, which in this case is a chestnut burr;" and he speedily opened it.

"There!" he said, triumphantly, "what more could you ask? Here are two solid, plump chestnuts, with only a false, empty form of shell between them. And here, like the solid nuts, are two people entitled to each other's acquaintance, with only the false formality of an introduction, like the empty shell, keeping them apart. Since no mutual friend is present to introduce us, has not Nature taken upon herself the office through this chestnut burr? But perhaps I should further Nature's efforts by giving you my card."

As Miss Walton regained composure, she soon proved to Gregory that she was not merely a shy country girl. At the close of his rather long and fanciful speech she said, genially, extending her hand: "My love for Nature is unbounded, Mr. Gregory, and the introduction you have so happily obtained from her weighs more with me than any other that you could have had. Let me welcome you to your own home, as it were. But see, your hand is bleeding, where the burr pricked you. Is this an omen, also? If our first meeting brings bloody wounds, I fear you will shun further acquaintance."

There was a spice of bitterness in Gregory's laugh, as he said: "People don't often die of such wounds. But it is a little odd that in taking your hand I should stain it with my blood. I am inclined to drop the burr after all, and base all my claims on my practical visiting card. You may come to look upon the burr as a warning, rather than an introduction, and order me off the premises."

"It was an omen of your choice," replied Miss Walton, laughing. "You have more to fear from it than I. If you will venture to stay you shall be most welcome. Indeed, it almost seems that you have a better right here than we, and your name has been so often heard that you are no stranger. I know father will be very glad to see you, for he often speaks of you, and wonders if you are like his old friend, the dearest one, I think, he ever had. How long have you been here?"

"Well, I have been wandering about the place much of the afternoon."

"I need not ask you why you did not come in at once," she said, gently. "Seeing your old home after so long an absence is like meeting some dear friend. One naturally wishes to be alone for a time. But now I hope you will go home with me."

He was surprised at her delicate appreciation of his feelings, and gave her a quick pleased look, saying: "Nature has taught you to be a good interpreter, Miss Walton. You are right. The memories of the old place were a little too much for me at first, and I did not know that those whom I met would appreciate my feelings so delicately."

The two children now appeared, running around the brow of the hill, the boy calling in great excitement: "Aunt Annie, oh! Aunt Annie, we've found a squirrel-hole. We chased him into it. Can't Susie sit by the hole and keep him in, while I go for a spade to dig him out?"

Then they saw the unlooked-for stranger, who at once rivalled the squirrel-hole in interest, and with slower steps, and curious glances, they approached.

"These are my sister's children," said Miss Walton, simply.

Gregory kindly took the boy by the hand, and kissed the little girl, who looked half-frightened and half-pleased, as a very little maiden should, while she rubbed the cheek that his mustache had tickled.

"Do you think we can get the squirrel, Aunt Annie?" again asked the boy.

"Do you think it would be right, Johnny, if you could?" she asked. "Suppose you were the squirrel in the hole, and one big monster, like Susie here, should sit by the door, and you heard another big monster say, 'Wait till I get something to tear open his house with.' How would you feel?"

"I won't keep the poor little squirrel in his hole," said sympathetic Susie.

But the boy's brow contracted, and he said, sternly: "Squirrels are nothing but robbers, and their holes are robbers' dens. They take half our nuts every year."

Miss Walton looked significantly at Gregory, and laughed, saying, "There it is, you see, man and woman."

A momentary shadow crossed his face, and he said, abruptly, "I hope Susie will be as kindly in coming years."

Miss Walton looked at him curiously as they began to descend the hill to the house. She evidently did not understand his remark, coupled with his manner.

As they approached the barn there was great excitement among the poultry. Passing round its angle, Walter saw coming toward them a quaint-looking old woman, in what appeared to be a white scalloped nightcap. She had a pan of corn in her hand, and was attended by a retinue that would have rejoiced an epicure's heart. Chickens, ducks, geese, turkeys, and Guinea fowls thronged around and after her with an intentness on the grain and a disregard of one another's rights and feelings that reminded one unpleasantly of political aspirants just after a Presidential election. Johnny made a dive for an old gobbler, and the great red-wattled bird dropped his wings and seemed inclined to show fight, but a reluctant armistice was brought about between them by the old woman screaming: "Maister Johnny, an' ye let not the fowls alone ye'll ha' na apples roast the night."

Susie clung timidly to her aunty's side as they passed through these clamorous candidates for holiday honors, and the young lady said, kindly, "You have a large family to look after, Zibbie, but I'm afraid we'll lessen it every day now."

"Indeed, an' ye will, and it goes agin the grain to wring the necks of them that I've nursed from the shell," said the old woman, rather sharply.

"It must be a great trial to your feelings," said Miss Walton, laughing; "but what would you have us do with them, Zibbie? You don't need them all for pets."

Before Zibbie could answer, an old gentleman in a low buggy drove into the large door-yard, and the children bounded toward him, screaming, "Grandpa."

A colored man took the horse, and Mr. Walton, with a briskness that one would not expect at his advanced age, came toward them.

He was a noble-looking old man, with hair and beard as white as snow, and with the stately manners of the old school. When he learned who Gregory was he greeted him with a cordiality that was so genuine as to compel the cynical man of the world to feel its truth.

Mr. Walton's eyes were turned so often and wistfully on his face that Gregory was embarrassed.

"I was looking for my friend," said the old gentleman, in a husky voice, turning hastily away to hide his feeling. "You strongly remind me of him; and yet--" But he never finished the sentence.

Gregory well understood the "and yet," and in bitterness of soul remembered that his father had been a good man, but that the impress of goodness could not rest on his face.

He had now grown very weary, and gave evidence of it.

"Mr. Gregory, you look ill," said Miss Walton, hastily.

"I am not well," he said, "and have not been for a long time. Perhaps I am going beyond my strength to-day."

In a moment they were all solicitude. The driver, who then appeared according to his instructions, was posted back to the hotel for Mr. Gregory's luggage, Mr. Walton saying, with hearty emphasis that removed every scruple, "This must be your home, sir, as long as you can remain with us, as truly as ever it was."

A little later he found himself in the "spare room," on whose state he had rarely intruded when a boy. Jeff, the colored man, had kindled a cheery wood fire on the ample hearth, and, too exhausted even to think, Gregory sank back in a great easy-chair with the blessed sense of the storm-tossed on reaching a quiet haven.

CHAPTER III
MORBID BROODING

To the millions who are suffering in mind or body there certainly come in this world moments of repose, when pain ceases; and the respite seems so delicious in contrast that it may well suggest the "rest that remaineth." Thinking of neither the past nor the future, Gregory for a little time gave himself up to the sense of present and luxurious comfort. With closed eyes and mind almost as quiet as his motionless body, he let the moments pass, feeling dimly that he would ask no better heaven than the eternal continuance of this painless, half- dreaming lethargy.

He was soon aroused, however, by a knocking at the door, and a middle- aged servant placed before him a tempting plate of Albert biscuit and a glass of home-made currant wine of indefinite age. The quaint and dainty little lunch caught his appetite as exactly as if manna had fallen adapted to his need; but it soon stimulated him out of his condition of partial non-existence. With returning consciousness of the necessity of living and acting came the strong desire to spend as much of his vacation as possible in his old home, and he determined to avail himself of Mr. Walton's invitation to the utmost limit that etiquette would permit.

His awakened mind gave but little thought to his entertainers, and he did not anticipate much pleasure from their society. He was satisfied that they were refined, cultivated people, with whom he could be as much at ease as would be possible in any companionship, but he hoped and proposed to spend the most of his time alone in wandering amid old scenes and brooding over the past. The morbid mind is ever full of unnatural contradictions, and he found a melancholy pleasure in shutting his eyes to the future and recalling the time when he had been happy and hopeful. In his egotism he found more that interested him in his past and vanished self than in the surrounding world. Evil and ill-health had so enfeebled his body, narrowed his mind, and blurred the future, that his best solace seemed a vain and sentimental recalling of the crude yet comparatively happy period of childhood.

This is sorry progress. A man must indeed have lived radically wrong when he looks backward for the best of his life. Gray-haired Mr. Walton was looking forward. Gregory's habit of self-pleasing--of acting according to his mood--was too deeply seated to permit even the thought of returning the hospitality he hoped to enjoy by a cordial effort on his part to prove himself an agreeable guest. Polite he ever would be, for he had the instincts and training of a gentleman, in society's interpretation of the word, but he had lost the power to feel a generous solicitude for the feelings and happiness of others. Indeed, he rather took a cynical pleasure in discovering defects in the character of those around him, and in learning that their seeming enjoyment of life was but hollow and partial. Conscious of being evil himself, he liked to think others were not much better, or would not be if tempted. Therefore, with a gloomy scepticism, he questioned all the seeming happiness and goodness he saw. "It is either unreal or untried," he was wont to say bitterly.

About seven o'clock, Hannah, the waitress, again appeared, saying: "Supper is ready, but the ladies beg you will not come down unless you feel able. I can bring up your tea if you wish."

Thinking first and only of self, he at once decided not to go down. He felt sufficiently rested and revived, but was in no mood for commonplace talk to comparative strangers. His cosey chair, glowing fire, and listless ease were much better than noisy children, inquisitive ladies, and the unconscious reproach of Mr. Walton's face, as he would look in vain for the lineaments of his lost friend. Therefore he said, suavely: "Please say to the ladies that I am so wearied that I should make but a dull companion, and so for their sakes, as well as my own, had better not leave my room this evening."

It is the perfection of art in selfishness to make it appear as if you were thinking only of others. This was the design of Walter's polite message. Soon a bit of tender steak, a roast potato, tea, and toast were smoking appetizingly beside him, and he congratulated himself that he had escaped the bore of company for one evening.

Notwithstanding his misanthropy and cherished desolation the supper was so inviting that he was tempted to partake of it heartily. Then incasing himself in his ample dressing-gown he placed his slippered feet on the fender before a cheery fire, lighted a choice Havana, and proceeded to be miserable after the fashion that indulged misery often affects.

Hannah quietly removed the tea-tray, and Mr. Walton came up and courteously inquired if there was anything that would add to his guest's comfort.

"After a few hours of rest and quiet I hope I shall be able to make a better return for your hospitality," Gregory rejoined, with equal politeness.

"Oh, do not feel under any obligation to exert yourself," said kind Mr. Walton. "In order to derive full benefit from your vacation, you must simply rest and follow your moods."

This view of the case suited Gregory exactly, and the prospect of a visit at his old home grew still more inviting. When he was left alone, he gave himself up wholly to the memories of the past.

At first it was with a pleasurable pain that he recalled his former life. With an imagination naturally strong he lived it all over again, from the date of his first recollections. In the curling flames and glowing coals on the hearth a panorama passed before him. He saw a joyous child, a light-hearted boy, and a sanguine youth, with the shifting and familiar scenery of well-remembered experience. Time softened the pictures, and the harsh, rough outlines which exist in every truthful portraiture of life were lost in the haze of distance. The gentle but steady light of mother love, and through her a pale, half-recognized reflection of the love of God, illumined all those years; and his father's strong, quiet affection made a background anything but dark. He had been naturally what is termed a very good boy, full of generous impulses. There had been no lack of ordinary waywardness or of the faults of youth, but they showed a tendency to yield readily to the correcting influence of love. Good impulses, however, are not principles, and may give way to stronger impulses of evil. If the influences of his early home had alone followed him, he would not now be moodily recalling the past as the exiled convict might watch the shores of his native land recede.

And then, as in his prolonged revery the fire burned low, and the ruddy coals turned to ashes, the past faded into distance, and his present life, dull and leaden, rose before him, and from regretful memories that were not wholly painful he passed to that bitterness of feeling which ever comes when hope is giving place to despair.

The fire flickered out and died, his head drooped lower and lower, while the brooding frown upon his brow darkened almost into a scowl. Outwardly he made a sad picture for a young man in the prime of life, but to Him who looks at the attitude of the soul, what but unutterable love kept him from appearing absolutely revolting?

Suddenly, like light breaking into a vault a few notes of prelude were struck upon the piano in the parlor below, and a sweet voice, softened by distance sung:

"Rock of ages, cleft for me,   let me hide myself in thee,"

How often he had heard the familiar words and music in that same home! They seemed to crown and complete all the memories of the place, but they reminded him more clearly than ever before that its most inseparable associations were holy, hopeful, and suggestive of a faith that he seemed to have lost as utterly as if it had been a gem dropped into the ocean.

He had lived in foreign lands far from his birthplace, but the purpose to return ever dwelt pleasurably in his mind. But how could he cross the gulf that yawned between him and the faith of his childhood? Was there really anything beyond that gulf save what the credulous imagination had created? Instinctively he felt that there was, for he was honest enough with himself to remember that his scepticism was the result of an evil life and the influence of an unbelieving world, rather than the outcome of patient investigation. The wish was father to the thought.

Yet sweet, unfaltering, and clear as the voice of faith ever should be, the hymn went forward in the room below, his memory supplying the well-known words that were lost from remoteness:--

"When mine eyelids close in death, When I soar to worlds unknown."

"Oh, when!" he exclaimed, bitterly. "What shall be my experience then? If I continue to fail in health as I have of late I shall know cursedly soon. That must be Miss Walton singing. Though she does not realize it, to me this is almost as cruel mockery as if an angel sang at the gates of hell."

The music ceased, and the monotone of one reading followed.

"Family prayers as of old," he muttered. "How everything conspires to- day to bring my home-life back again! and yet there is a fatal lack of something that is harder to endure than the absence of my own kindred and vanished youth. I doubt whether I can stay here long after all. Will not the mocking fable of Tantalus be repeated constantly, as I see others drinking daily at a fountain which though apparently so near is ever beyond my reach?"

Shivering with the chill of the night and the deeper chill at heart, he retired to troubled sleep.

CHAPTER IV
HOW MISS WALTON MANAGED PEOPLE

Rest, and the sunny light and bracing air of the following morning, banished much of Gregory's moodiness, and he descended the stairs proposing to dismiss painful thoughts and get what comfort and semblance of enjoyment he could out of the passing hours. Mr. Walton met him cordially--indeed with almost fatherly solicitude--and led him at once to the dining-room, where an inviting breakfast awaited them. Miss Walton also was genial, and introduced Miss Eulalia Morton, a maiden sister of her mother. Miss Eulie, as she was familiarly called, was a pale, delicate little lady, with a face sweetened rather than hardened and imbittered by time. If, as some believe, the flesh and the spirit, the soul and the body, are ever at variance, she gave the impression at first glance that the body was getting the worst of the conflict. But in truth the faintest thoughts of strife seemed to have no association with her whatever. She appeared so light and aerial that one could imagine her flying over the rough places of life, and vanishing when any one opposed her.

Miss Walton reversed all this, for she was decidedly substantial. She was of only medium height, but a fine figure made her appear taller than she was. She immediately gave the impression of power and reserve force. You felt this in her quick, elastic step, saw it in her decided though not abrupt movements, and heard it in her tone. Even the nonchalant Mr. Gregory could not ignore her in his customary polite manner, though quiet refinement and peculiar unobtrusiveness seemed her characteristics. She won attention, not because she sought it, nor on the ground of eccentricities, but because of her intense vitality. From her dark eyes a close observer might catch glimpses of a quick, active mind, an eager spirit, and--well, perhaps a passionate temper. Though chastened and subdued, she ever gave the impression of power to those who came to know her well. In certain ways, as they interpreted her, people acknowledged this force of character. Some spoke of her as very lively, others as exceedingly energetic and willing to enter on any good work. Some thought her ambitious, else why was she so prominent in church matters, and so ready to visit the sick and poor? They could explain this in but one way. And some looked knowingly at each other and said: "I wonder if she is always as smiling and sweet as when in society;" and then followed shaking of heads which intimated, "Look out for sudden gusts."

Again, as in simple morning wrapper she turned to greet Gregory, she gave him the impression of something like beauty. But his taste, rendered critical by much observation both at home and abroad, at once told him that he was mistaken.

"The expression is well enough," he thought, "but she has not a single perfect feature--not one that an artist would copy, except perhaps the eyes, and even they are not soft and Madonna-like."

He had a sybarite's eye for beauty, and an intense admiration for it. At the same time he was too intellectual to be satisfied with the mere sensuous type. And yet, when he decided that a woman was not pretty, she ceased to interest him. His exacting taste required no small degree of outward perfection crowned by ready wit and society polish. With those so endowed he had frequently amused himself in New York and Paris by a passing flirtation since the politic Miss Bently had made him a sceptic in regard to women. All his intercourse with society had confirmed his cynicism. The most beautiful and brilliant in the drawing-rooms were seldom the best. He flattered them to their faces and sneered at them in his heart. Therefore his attentions were merely of a nature to excite their vanity, stimulated by much incense from other sources. He saw this plainly manifested trait, which he contributed to develop, and despised it. He also saw that many were as eager for a good match as ever the adored Miss Bently had been, and that, while they liked his compliments, they cared not for him. Why should they? Insincere and selfish himself, why should he expect to awaken better feelings on the part of those who were anything but unsophisticated, and from knowledge of the world could gauge him at his true worth? Not even a sentimental girl would show her heart to such a man. And yet with the blind egotism of selfishness he smiled grimly at their apparent heartlessness and said, "Such is woman."

At the same time it must in justice be said that he despised men in general quite as sincerely. "Human nature is wretched stuff," had come to be the first article in his creed.

In regard to Miss Walton he concluded: "She is a goodish girl, more of a lady than the average, pious and orthodox, an excellent housekeeper, and a great comfort to her father, no doubt. She is safe from her very plainness, though confident, of course, that she could resist temptation and be a saint under all circumstances;" and he dismissed her from his mind with a sort of inward groan and protest against the necessity of making himself agreeable to her during his visit.

He did not think it worth while to disguise his face as he made these brief critical observations, and quick-witted Annie gathered something of the drift of his thoughts, as she stole a few glances at him from behind the coffee-urn. It piqued her pride a little, and she was disappointed in him, for she had hoped for a pleasant addition to their society for a time. But she was so supremely indifferent to him, and had so much to fill her thoughts and days, that his slight promise to prove an agreeable visitor caused but momentary annoyance. Yet the glimmer of a smile flitted across her face as she thought: "He may find himself slightly mistaken in me, after all. His face seems to say, 'No doubt she is a good young woman, and well enough for this slow country place, but she has no beauty, no style.' I think I can manage to disturb the even current of his vanity, if his visit is long enough, and he shall learn at least that I shall not gape admiringly at his artificial metropolitan airs."

Her manner toward Gregory remained full of kindness and grace, but she made no effort to secure his attention and engage him in conversation, as he had feared she would do. She acted as if she were accustomed to see such persons as himself at her father's breakfast-table every morning; and, though habitually wrapped up in his own personality, he soon became dimly conscious that her course toward him was not what he had expected.

Miss Eulie was all solicitude in view of his character of invalid; and the children looked at him with curious eyes and growing disapprobation. There was nothing in him to secure their instinctive friendship, and he made no effort to win their sympathies.

The morning meal began with a reverent looking to heaven for God's blessing on the gifts which were acknowledged as coming from Him; and even Gregory was compelled to admit that the brief rite did not appear like a careless signing of the cross, or a shrivelled form from which spirit and meaning had departed, but a sincere expression of loving trust and gratitude.

During the greater part of the meal, Mr. Walton dwelt on the circumstances that had led to his friendship with Gregory's father, but at last the conversation flagged a little, since the young man made so slight effort to maintain it.

Suddenly Mr. Walton turned to his daughter and said, "By the way, Annie, you have not told me where you found Mr. Gregory, for my impression is that you brought him down from the hills."

"I was about to say that I found him in a chestnut burr," replied Annie, with a twinkle in her eye. "At least I found a stranger by the cedar thicket, and he proved from a chestnut burr who he was, and his right to acquaintance, with a better logic than I supposed him capable of."

"Indeed?" asked Gregory, quickly, feeling the prick of her last words; "on what grounds were you led to estimate my logic so slightingly?"

"On merely general grounds; but you see I am open to all evidence in your favor. City life no doubt has great advantages, but it also has greater drawbacks."

"What are they?"

"I cannot think of them all now. Suffice it to say that if you had always lived in the city you could not have interpreted a chestnut burr so gracefully. Many there seem to forget Nature's lore."

"But may they not learn other things more valuable?"

Miss Walton shook her head, and said, with a laugh: "An ignorant exhorter once stated to his little schoolhouse audience that Paul was brought up at the foot of the hill Gamaliel. I almost wish he were right, for I should have had more confidence in the teachings of the hill than in those of the narrow-minded Jewish Rabbi."

"And yet you regard Paul as the very chief of the apostles."

"He became such after he was taught of Him who teaches through the hills and nature generally."

"My daughter is an enthusiast for nature," remarked Mr. Walton.

"If the people are the same as when I was here a boy, the hills have not taught the majority very much," said Gregory, with a French shrug.

"Many of them have a better wisdom than you think," answered Annie, quietly.

"In what does it consist?"

"Well, for one thing they know how to enjoy life and add to the enjoyment of others."

Gregory looked at her keenly for a moment, but saw nothing to lead him to think that she was speaking on other than general principles; but he said, a little moodily, as they rose from the table, "That certainly is a better wisdom than is usually attained in either city or country."

"It is not our custom to make company of our friends," said Mr. Walton, cordially. "We hope you will feel completely at home, and come and go as you like, and do just what you find agreeable. We dine at two, and have an early supper on account of the children. There are one or two fair saddle horses on the place, but if you do not feel strong enough to ride, Annie can drive you out, and I assure you she is at home in the management of a horse."

"Yes, indeed," echoed the little boy. "Aunt Annie can manage anything or anybody."

"That is a remarkable power," said Gregory, with an amused look and a side glance at the young girl. "How does she do it?"

"Oh, I don't know," replied the boy; "she makes them love her, and then they want to do as she says."

A momentary wrathful gleam shot from Annie's eyes at her indiscreet little champion, but with heightened color she joined in the laugh that followed.

Gregory had the ill grace to say with a sort of mocking gallantry, as he bowed himself out, "It must be delightful to be managed on such terms."

CHAPTER V
WAS IT AN ACCIDENT?

Putting on a light overcoat, for the morning air was sharp and bracing, Gregory soon found himself in the old square garden. Though its glory was decidedly on the wane, it was as yet unnipped by the frost It had a neatness and an order of its own that were quite unlike those where nature is in entire subordination to art. Indeed it looked very much as he remembered it in the past, and he welcomed its unchanged aspect. He strolled to many other remembered boyish haunts, and it seemed that the very lichens and mosses grew in the same places as of old, and that nature had stood still and awaited his return.

And yet every familiar object chided him for being so changed, and he began to find more of pain than pleasure as this contrast between what he had been and what he might have been was constantly forced upon him.

"Oh that I had never left this place!" he exclaimed, bitterly: "It would have been better to stay here and drudge as a day laborer. What has that career out in the world to which I looked forward so ardently amounted to? The present is disappointment and self-disgust, the future an indefinite region of fears and forebodings, and even the happy past is becoming a bitter mockery by reminding me of what can never be again."

Wearied and despondent, he moodily returned to the house and threw himself on a lounge in the parlor. A smouldering wood fire upon the hearth softened the air to summer temperature. The heat was grateful to his chilled, bloodless body, and gave him a luxurious sense of physical comfort, and he muttered: "I had about resolved to leave this place with its memories that are growing into torment, but I suppose it would be the same anywhere else. I am too weak and ill to face new scenes and discomfort. A little animal enjoyment and bodily respite from pain seem about all that is left to me of existence, and I think I can find these here better than elsewhere. If I am expected, however, to fall under the management of the daughter of the house on the terms blurted out by that fidgety nephew of hers, I will fly for my life. A plague on him! His restlessness makes me nervous! If I could endure a child at all, the blue-eyed little girl would make a pretty toy."

Sounds from the sitting-room behind the parlor now caught his attention, and listening he soon became aware that Miss Walton was teaching the children. "She has just the voice for a 'schoolmarm,'" he thought--"quick, clear-cut, and decided."

If he had not given way to unreasonable prejudice he might also have noted that there was nothing harsh or querulous in it.

"With her management and love of nature, she doubtless thinks herself the personification of goodness. I suppose I shall be well lectured before I get away. I had a foretaste of it this morning. 'Drawbacks of city life,' forsooth! She no doubt regards me as a result of these disadvantages. But if she should come to deem it her mission to convert or reform me, then will be lost my small remnant of peace and comfort."

But weakness and weariness soon inclined him to sleep. Miss Walton's voice sounded far away. Then it passed into his dream as that of Miss Bently chiding him affectedly for his wayward tendencies; again it was explaining that conscientious young lady's "sense of duty" in view of Mr. Grobb's offer, and even in his sleep his face darkened with pain and wrath.

Just then, school hours being over, Miss Walton came into the parlor. For a moment, as she stood by the fire, she did not notice its unconscious occupant. Then, seeing him, she was about to leave the room noiselessly, when the expression of his face arrested her steps.

If Annie Walton's eyes suggested the probability of "sudden gusts," they also at times announced a warm, kind heart, for as she looked at him now her face instantly softened to pity.

"Good he is not," she thought, "but he evidently suffers in his evil. Something is blighting his life, and what can blight a life save evil? Perhaps I had better change my proposed crusade against his vanity and cynicism to a kind, sisterly effort toward making him a better and therefore a happier man. It will soon come out in conversation that I have long been the same as engaged to another, and this will relieve me of absurd suspicions of designs upon him. If I could win a friendly confidence on his part, I'm sure I could tell him some wholesome truths, for even an enemy could scarcely look on that face without relenting."

There was nothing slow or cumbrous about Annie. These thoughts had flashed through her mind during the brief moment in which her eyes softened from surprise into sympathy as they caught the expression of Gregory's face. Then, fearing to disturb him, with silent tread she passed out to her wonted morning duties.

How seemingly accidental was that visit to the parlor! Its motive indefinite and forgotten. Apparently it was but a trivial episode of an uneventful day, involving no greater catastrophe than the momentary rousing of a sleeper who would doze again. But what day can we with certainty call uneventful? and what episode trivial? Those half- aimless, purposeless steps of Annie Walton into the quiet parlor might lead to results that would radically change the endless future of several lives.

In her womanly, pitying nature, had not God sent His angel? If a viewless "ministering spirit," as the sinful man's appointed guardian, was present, as many believe is the case with every one, how truly he must have welcomed this unselfish human companionship in his loving labor to save life; for only they who rescue from sin truly save life.

And yet the sleeper, even in his dreams, was evidently at war with himself, the world, and God. He was an example of the truth that good comes from without and not from within us. It is heaven stooping to men; heaven's messengers sent to us; truth quickened in our minds by heavenly influence, even as sunlight and rain awaken into beautiful life the seeds hidden in the soil; and, above all, impulses direct from God, that steal into our hearts as the south wind penetrates ice- bound gardens in spring.

But, alas! multitudes like Walter Gregory blind their eyes and steel their hearts against such influences. God and those allied to Him longed to bring the healing of faith and love to his wounded spirit. He scowled back his answer, and, as he then felt, would shrink with morbid sensitiveness and dislike from the kindest and most delicate presentation of the transforming truth. But the divine love is ever seeking to win our attention by messengers innumerable; now by the appalling storm, again by a summer sunset; now by an awful providence, again by a great joy; at times by stern prophets and teachers, but more often by the gentle human agencies of which Annie was the type, as with pitying face she bent over the worn and jaded man of the world and hoped and prayed that she might be able to act the part of a true sister toward him. Thorny and guarded was every avenue to his heart; and yet her feminine tact, combined with the softening and purifying influence of his old home, might gain her words acceptance, where the wisest and most eloquent would plead in vain.

After dinner he again hastened forth for a walk, his purpose being to avoid company, for he was so moody and morbid, so weak, nervous, and irritable, that the thought of meeting and decorously conversing with those whose lives and character were a continual reproach to him was intolerable. Then he had the impression that the "keen-eyed, plain- featured Miss Walton," as he characterized her in his mind, would surely commence discoursing on moral and religious subjects if he gave her a chance; and he feared that if she did, he would say or do something very rude, and confirm the bad impression that he was sure of having already made. If he could have strolled into his club, and among groups engaged with cards, papers, and city gossip, he would have felt quite at home. Ties formed at such a place are not very strong as a usual thing, and the manner of the world can isolate the members and their real life completely, even when the rooms are thronged. As Gregory grew worn and thin and his pallor increased, as he smoked and brooded more and more apart, his companions would shrug their shoulders significantly and whisper, "It looks as if Gregory would go under soon. Something's the matter with him."

At first good-natured men would say, "Come, Gregory, take a hand with us," but when he complied it was with such a listless manner that they were sorry they had asked him. At last, beyond mere passing courtesies, they had come to leave him very much alone; and in his unnatural and perverted state this was just what he most desired. His whole being had become a diseased, sensitive nerve, shrinking most from any effort toward his improvement, even as a finger pointed at a festering wound causes anticipatory agonies.

At the club he would be let alone, but these good people would "take an interest in him," and might even "talk religion," and probe with questions and surmises. If they did, he knew, from what he had already seen of them, that they would try to do it delicately and kindly, but he felt that the most considerate efforts would be like the surgical instruments of the dark ages. He needed good, decisive, heroic treatment. But who would have the courage and skill to give it? Who cared enough for him to take the trouble?

Not merely had Annie Walton looked with eyes of human pity upon his sin-marred visage that morning. The Divine personality, enthroned in the depths of her soul and permeating her life, looked commiseratingly forth also. Could demons glare from human eyes and God not smile from them?

As Annie thought much of him after her stolen glance in the morning, she longed to do that which he dreaded she would try to do--attempt his reformation. Not that she cared for him personally, or that she had grown sentimentally interested in his Byronic style of wretchedness. So far from it, her happy and healthful nature was repelled by his diseased and morbid one. She found him what girls call a "disagreeable man." But she yearned toward a sinning, suffering soul, found in any guise. It was not in her woman's heart to pass by on the other side.

CHAPTER VI
UNEXPECTED CHESTNUT BURRS

Gregory's afternoon walk was not very prolonged, for a shivering sense of discomfort soon drove him back to the house. Although the morning had been cool, the sun had shone bright and warm, but now the fore- shadowing of a storm was evident. A haze had spread over the sky, increasing in leaden hue toward the west. The chilly wind moaned fitfully through the trees, and the landscape darkened like a face shadowed by coming trouble.

Walter dreaded a storm, fearing it would shut him up with the family without escape; but at last the sun so enshrouded itself in gloom that he was compelled to return. He went to his room, for a book, hoping that when they saw him engaged they would leave him more to himself. But to his agreeable surprise he found a cheerful fire blazing on the hearth, and an ample supply of wood in a box near. The easy-chair was wheeled forward, and a plate of grapes and the latest magazine were placed invitingly on the table. Even his cynicism was not proof against this, delicate thoughtfulness, and he exclaimed, "Ah, this is better than I expected, and a hundred-fold better than I deserve. I make but poor return for their kindness. This cosey room seems to say, 'We won't force ourselves on you. You can be alone as much as you like,' for I suppose they must have noticed my disinclination for society. But they are wise after all, for I am cursed poor company for myself and worse than none at all for others."

Eating from time to time a purple grape, he so lost himself in the fresh thoughts of the magazine that the tea-bell rang ere he was aware.

"In the name of decency I must try to make myself agreeable for a little while this evening," he muttered, as he descended to the cheerful supper-room.

To their solicitude for his health and their regret that the approaching storm had driven him so early to the house, he replied, "I found in my room a better substitute for the sunlight I had lost; though as a votary of nature, Miss Walton, I suppose you will regard this assertion as rank heresy."

"Not at all, for your firelight is the result of sunlight." answered Annie, smiling.

"How is that?"

"It required many summers to ripen the wood that blazed on your hearth. Indeed, good dry wood is but concentrated sunshine put by for cold, gloomy days and chilly nights."

"That is an odd fancy. I wish there were other ways of storing up sunshine for future use."

"There are," said Miss Walton, cheerfully; and she looked up as if she would like to say more, but he instantly changed the subject in his instinctive wish to avoid the faintest approach to moralizing. Still, conversation continued brisk till Mr. Walton asked suddenly, "By the way, Mr. Gregory, have you ever met Mr. Hunting of Wall Street?"

There was no immediate answer, and they all looked inquiringly at him. To their surprise his face was darkened by the heaviest frown. After a moment he said, with peculiar emphasis, "Yes; I know him well."

A chill seemed to fall on them after that; and he, glancing up, saw that Annie looked flushed and indignant, Miss Eulie pained, and Mr. Walton very grave. Even the little boy shot vindictive glances at him. He at once surmised that Hunting was related to the family, and was oppressed with the thought that he was fast losing the welcome given him on his father's account. But in a few moments Annie rallied and made unwonted efforts to banish the general embarrassment, and with partial success, for Gregory had tact and good conversational powers if he chose to exert them. When, soon after, they adjourned to the parlor, outward serenity reigned.

On either side of the ample hearth, on which blazed a hickory fire, a table was drawn up. An easy-chair stood invitingly by each, with a little carpet bench on which to rest the feet.

"Take one of these," said Mr. Walton, cordially, "and join me with a cigar. The ladies of my household are indulgent to my small vices."

"And I will send for your magazine," said Annie, "and then you can read and chat according to your mood. You gee that we do not intend to make a stranger of you."

"For which I am very glad. You treat me far better than I deserve."

Instead of some deprecatory remark, Annie gave him a quick, half- comical look which he did not fully understand.

"There is more in her than I at first imagined," he thought.

Seated with the magazine, Gregory found himself in the enjoyment of every element of comfort. That he might be under no constraint to talk, Annie commenced speaking to her father and Miss Eulie of some neighborhood affairs, of which he knew nothing. The children and a large greyhound were dividing the rug between them. The former were chatting in low tones and roasting the first chestnuts of the season on a broad shovel that was placed on the glowing coals. The dog was sleepily watching them lest in their quick movements his tail should come to grief.

Gregory had something of an artist's eye, and he could not help glancing up from his reading occasionally, and thinking what a pretty picture the roomy parlor made.

"Annie," said Mr. Walton, after a little while, "I can't get through this article with my old eyes. Won't you finish it for me? Shall we disturb you, Mr. Gregory?"

"Not at all."

Gregory soon forgot to read himself in listening to her. Not that he heard the subject-matter with any interest, but her sweet, natural tones and simplicity arrested and retained his attention. Even the statistics and the prose of political economy seemed to fall from her lips in musical cadence, and yet there was no apparent effort and not a thought of effect. Walter mused as he listened.

"I should like to hear some quiet, genial book read in that style, though it is evident that Miss Walton is no tragedy queen."

Having finished the reading, Annie started briskly up and said, "Come, little people, your chestnuts are roasted and eaten. It's bedtime. The turkeys and squirrels will be at the nut-trees long before you to- morrow unless you scamper off at once."

"O, Aunt Annie," chimed their voices, "you must sing us the chestnut song first; you promised to."

"With your permission, Mr. Gregory, I suppose I must make my promise good," said Annie.

"I join the children in asking for the song," he replied, glad to get them out of the way on such easy conditions, though he expected a nursery ditty or a juvenile hymn from some Sabbath-school collection, wherein healthy, growing boys are made to sing, "I want to be an angel." "Moreover," he added, "I have read that one must always keep one's word to a child."

"Which is a very important truth: do you not think so?"

"Since you are using the word 'truth' so prominently, Miss Walton, I must say that I have not thought much about it. But I certainly would have you keep your word on this occasion."

"Aunt Annie always keeps her word," said Johnny, rather bluntly. By some childish instinct he divined that Gregory did not appreciate Aunt Annie sufficiently, and this added to his prejudice.

"You have a stout little champion there," Gregory remarked.

"I cannot complain of his zeal," she answered significantly, at the same time giving the boy a caress. "Mr. Gregory, this is a rude country ballad, and we are going to sing it in our accustomed way, even though it shock your city ears. Johnny and Susie, you can join in the chorus;" and she sang the following simple October glee:

> Katydid, your throat is sore,
> You can chirp this fall no more;
> Robin red-breast, summer's past,
> Did you think 'twould always last?
> Fly away to sunny climes,
> Lands of oranges and limes;
> With the squirrels we shall stay
> And put our store of nuts away.
> O the spiny chestnut burrs! O the prickly chestnut burrs!
> Harsh without, but lined with down,
> And full of chestnuts, plump and brown.
>
> Sorry are we for the flowers;
> We shall miss our summer bowers;
> Still we welcome frosty Jack,
> Stealing now from Greenland back.
> And the burrs will welcome him;
> When he knocks, they'll let him in.

> They don't know what Jack's about;
> Soon he'll turn the chestnuts out.
> O the spiny, etc.-
>
> Turkey gobbler, with your train,
> You shall scratch the leaves in vain;
> Squirrel, with your whisking tail,
> Your sharp eyes shall not avail;
> In the crisp and early dawn,
> Scampering across the lawn.
> We will beat you to the trees,
> Come you then whene'er you please.
> O the spiny, etc.--

Gregory's expression as she played a simple prelude was one of endurance, but when she began to sing the changes of his face were rapid. First he turned toward her with a look of interest, then of surprise. Miss Eulie could not help watching him, for, though she was well on in life, just such a character had never risen above her horizon. Too gentle to censure, she felt that she had much cause for regret.

At first she was pleased to see that he found the ditty far more to his taste than he had expected. But the rapid alternation from pleased surprise and enjoyment to something like a scowl of despair and almost hate she could not understand. Following his eyes she saw them resting on the boy, who was now eagerly joining in the chorus of the last verse. She was not sufficiently skilled to know that to Gregory's diseased moral nature things most simple and wholesome in themselves were most repugnant. She could not understand that the tripping little song, with its wild-wood life and movement--that the boy singing with the delight of a pure, fresh heart--told him, beyond the power of labored language, how hackneyed and blase he had become, how far and hopelessly he had drifted from the same true childhood.

And Miss Walton, turning suddenly toward him, saw the same dark expression, full of suffering and impotent revolt at his destiny, as he regarded it, and she too was puzzled.

"You do not like our foolish little song," she said.

"I envy that boy, Miss Walton," was his reply.

Then she began to understand him, and said, gently, "You have no occasion to."

"I wish you, or any one, could find the logic to prove that."

"The proof is not in logic but in nature, that is ever young. They who draw their life from nature do not fall into the only age we need dread."

"Do you not expect to grow old?"

She shook her head half humorously and said, "But these children will before I get them to bed."

He ostensibly resumed his magazine, but did not turn any leaves.

His first mental query was, "Have I rightly gauged Miss Walton? I half believe she understands me better than I do her. I estimated her as a goodish, fairly educated country girl, of the church-going sort, one that would be dreadfully shocked at finding me out, and deem it at once her mission to pluck me as a brand from the burning. I know all about the goodness of such girls. They are ignorant of the world; they have never been tempted, and they have a brood of little feminine weaknesses that of course are not paraded in public.

"And no doubt all this is true of Miss Walton, and yet, for some reason, she interests me a little this evening. She is refined, but nowhere in the world will you meet drearier monotony and barrenness than among refined people. Having no real originality, their little oddities are polished away. In Miss Walton I'm beginning to catch glimpses of vistas unexplored, though perhaps I am a fool for thinking so.

"What a peculiar voice she has! She would make a poor figure, no doubt, in an opera; and yet she might render a simple aria very well. But for songs of nature and ballads I have never heard so sympathetic a voice. It suggests a power of making music a sweet home language instead of a difficult, high art, attainable by few. Really Miss Walton is worth investigation, for no one with such a voice can be utterly commonplace. Strange as it is, I cannot ignore her. Though she makes no effort to attract my attention, I am ever conscious of her presence."

CHAPTER VII
A CONSPIRACY

When Miss Walton returned to the parlor her father said, "Annie, I am going to trespass on your patience again."

She answered with a little piquant gesture, and was soon reading in natural, easy tones, without much stumbling, what must have been Greek to her.

Gregory watched her with increasing interest, and another question than the one of finance involved in the article was rising in his mind.

"Is this real? Is this seeming goodness a fact?" It was the very essence of his perverted nature to doubt it. Now that his eyes were opened, and he closely observed Miss Walton, he saw that his prejudices against her were groundless. Although not a stylish, pretty woman, she was evidently far removed from the goodish, commonplace character that he could regard as part of the furniture of the house, useful in its place, but of no more interest than a needful piece of cabinet work. Nor did she assert herself as do those aggressive, lecturing females who deem it their mission to set everybody right within their sphere.

And yet she did assert herself; but he was compelled to admit that it was like the summer breeze or the perfume of a rose. He had resolved that very day to avoid and ignore her as far as possible, and yet, before the first evening in her presence was half over, he had left a magazine story unfinished; he was watching her, thinking and surmising about her, and listening, as she read, to what he did not care a straw about. Although she had not made the slightest effort, some influence from her had stolen upon him like a cool breeze on a sultry day, and wooed him as gently as the perfume of a flower that is sweet to all. He said to himself, "She is not pretty," and yet found pleasure in watching her red lips drop figures and financial terms as musically as a little rill murmurs over a mossy rock.

From behind his magazine he studied the group at the opposite table, but it was with the pain which a despairing swimmer, swept seaward by a resistless current, might feel in seeing the safe and happy on the shore.

Gray Mr. Walton leaned back in his chair, the embodiment of peace and placid content.

The subject to which he was listening and kindred topics had so far receded that his interest was that of a calm, philosophic observer, and Gregory thought, with a glimmer of a smile, "He is not dabbling in stocks or he could not maintain that quiet mien."

His habits of thought as a business man merely made it a pleasure to keep up with the times. In fact he was in that serene border-land between the two worlds where the questions of earth are growing vague and distant and those of the "better country" more real and engrossing, for Gregory observed, later in the evening, that he took the family Bible with more zest than he had bestowed on the motive power of the world. It was evident where his most valued treasures were stored. With a bitter sigh, Gregory thought, "I would take his gray hairs if I could have his peace and faith."

Miss Eulie, to whom he gave a passing glance, seemed even less earthly in her nature. Indeed, it appeared as if she had never more than half belonged to the material creation. Slight, ethereal, with untroubled blue eyes, and little puff curls too light to show their change to gray, she struck Gregory unpleasantly, as if she were a connecting link between gross humanity and spiritual existence, and his eyes reverted to Miss Walton, and dwelt with increasing interest on her. There at least were youth, health, and something else--what was it in the girl that had so strongly and suddenly gained his attention? At any rate there was nothing about her uncanny and spirit-like.

He did not understand her. Was it possible that a young girl, not much beyond twenty, was happy in the care of orphan children, in the quiet humdrum duties of housekeeping, and in reading stupid articles through the long, quiet evenings, with few excitements beyond church-going, rural tea-drinkings, and country walks and rides? With a grim smile he thought how soon the belles he had admired would expire under such a regimen. Could this be good acting because a guest was present? If so it was perfect, for it seemed, her daily life.

"I will watch her," he thought. "I will solve this little feminine enigma. It will divert my mind, and I've nothing else to do."

"My daughter spoils me, you see, Mr. Gregory," said Mr. Walton, starting up as Annie finished a theory that would make every one rich by the printing-press process,

"Don't plume yourself, papa," replied Annie, archly; "I shall make you do something for me to pay for all this."

With a humorous look he replied, "No matter, I have the best of the bargain, for I should have to do the 'something' anyway. But what do you think of this theory, sir?" And he explained, not knowing that Walter had been listening.

The gentlemen were soon deep in the mysteries of currency and finance, topics on which both could talk well. Annie listened with polite attention for a short time--indeed Gregory was exerting himself more for her sake than for Mr. Walton's--and she was satisfied from her father's face that his guest was interesting him; but as the subject was mainly unintelligible to her she soon turned with real zest to Miss Eulie's fancy-work, and there was an earnest whispered discussion in regard to the right number of stitches. Walter noted this and sneeringly thought, with a masculine phase of justice often seen, "That's like a woman. She drops one of the deepest and most important subjects of the day" (and he might have added, "As explained by me")-- "and gives her whole soul to a bit of thread lace;" and he soon let Mr. Walton have the discussion all his own way.

In furtherance of his purpose to draw Annie out he said, rather banteringly, "Miss Walton, I am astonished that so good a man as your father should have as an ardent friend the profane and disreputable character that I found living in the cottage opposite on the day of my arrival."

"Profane, I admit he is," she replied, "but not disreputable. Indeed, as the world goes, I think old Daddy Tuggar, as he is called in this vicinity, is a good man."

"O, Annie!" said Miss Eulie. "How can you think so? You have broader charity than I. He is breaking his poor wife's heart."

"Indeed?" said Annie, dryly; "I was not aware of it."

"I too am astonished," said Walter, in mock solemnity. "How is it that a refined and orthodox young lady, a pillar of the church, too, I gather, can regard with other than unmixed disapprobation a man who breaks the third commandment and all the rules of Lindley Murray at every breath?"

"I imagine the latter offence is the more heinous sin in your eyes, Mr. Gregory," she said, scanning his face with a quick look.

"Oh, you become aggressive. I was under the impression that I was making the attack and that you were on the defensive. But I can readily explain the opinion which you, perhaps not unjustly, impute to me. You and I judge this venerable sinner from different standpoints."

"You explain your judgment, but do not justify it," replied Annie, quietly.

"Annie, I don't see on what grounds you call Daddy Tuggar a good man," said Miss Eulie, emphatically.

"Please understand me, aunty," said Annie, earnestly. "I did not say he was a Christian man, but merely a good man as the world goes; and I know I shall shock you when I say that I have more faith in him than in his praying and Scripture-quoting wife. There, I knew I should," she added, as she saw Miss Eulie's look of pained surprise.

Mr. Walton was listening with an amused smile. He evidently understood his quaint old friend and shared Annie's opinion of him.

Gregory was growing decidedly interested, and said, "Really, Miss Walton, I must side with your aunt in this matter. I shall overwhelm you with an awful word. I think you are latitudinarian in your tendencies."

"Which Daddy Tuggar would call a new-fangled way of swearing at me," retorted Annie, with her frank laugh that was so genuinely mirthful that even Aunt Eulie joined in it.

"I half think," continued Annie, "that the churchmen in the ages of controversy did a good deal of worse swearing than our old neighbor is guilty of when they hurled at each other with such bitter zest the epithets Antinomian, Socinian, Pelagian, Calvinistic, etc."

"Those terms have an awful sound. They smite my ear with all the power that vagueness imparts, and surely must have caused stout hearts to tremble in their day," he remarked.

"We are no longer on the ground of currency and finance," said Annie, archly, "and I shall leave you to imagine that I know all about the ideas represented by the polysyllabic terms of churchmen's warfare."

He looked at her a moment in comic dismay. Really this country girl was growing too much for him in his game of banter.

"Miss Walton, I shall not dispute or question your knowledge of the Socin--cin--(you know the rest) heresy--"

"Alas!" put in Annie, quietly, "I do know all about the 'sin heresy.' I can say that honestly."

"I am somewhat inclined to doubt that," he said, quickly; then added, in sudden and mock severity, "Miss Walton, if I were a judge upon the bench I should charge that you were evading the question and befogging the case. The point at issue is, How can you regard Daddy Tuggar as a good man? As evidence against him I can affirm that I do not remember to have had such a good square cursing in my life, and I have received several."

This last expression caused Miss Eulie to open her eyes at him.

"Not for your sake, sir," said Annie, with a keen yet humorous glance at him, "who as judge on the bench have in your pocket a written verdict, I fear, but for Aunt Eulie's I will give the reasons for my estimate. I regard her in the light of an honest jury. In the first place the term you used, 'square,' applies to him. I do not think he could be tempted to do a dishonest thing; and that, as the world goes, is certainly a good point."

"And as the church goes, too," he added, cynically.

"He is a good neighbor, and considerate of the rights of others. He can feel, and is not afraid to show a sincere indignation when seeing a wrong done to another."

"I can vouch for that. I shall steal no more of your apples, Mr. Walton."

"There is not a particle of hypocrisy about him. I wish I could think the same of his wife. For some reason she always gives me the impression of insincerity. If I were as good as you are, aunty, perhaps I should not be so suspicious. One thing more, and my eulogy of Daddy--the only one he will ever receive, I fear--is over. He is capable of sincere friendship, and that is more than you can say of a great many."

"It is indeed," said Gregory, with bitter emphasis. "I should be willing to take my chances with Daddy Tuggar in this or any other world."

"You had better not," she answered, now thoroughly in earnest.

"Why so?"

"I should think memories of this place would make my meaning clear," she replied, gently.

Gregory's face darkened, and he admitted to himself that most unexpectedly she had sent an arrow home, and yet he could take no exception.

His indifference toward her had vanished now. So far from regarding her as a dull, good, country girl with a narrow horizon of little feminine and commonplace interests, he began to doubt whether he should be able to cope with her in the tilt of thought. He saw that she was quick, original, and did her own thinking, that in repartee she hit back unexpectedly, in flashes, as the lightning strikes from the clouds. He could not keep pace with her quick intuition.

Moreover, in her delicate reference to his parents' faith she had suggested an argument for Christianity that he had never been able to answer. For a little time she had caused him to forget his wretched self, but her last remark had thrown him back on his old doubts, fears, and memories. As we have said, his cynical, despondent expression returned, and he silently lowered at the fire.

Annie had too much tact to add a word. "He must be hurt--well probed indeed--before he can be well," she thought.

Country bedtime had now come, and Mr. Walton said, "Mr. Gregory, I trust you will not find our custom of family prayers distasteful."

"The absence of such a custom would seem strange to me in this place," he replied, but he did not say whether it would be agreeable or distasteful.

Annie went to the piano as if it were a habit, and after a moment chose the tender hymn--

"Come, ye disconsolate."

At first, in his morbid sensitiveness, he was inclined to resent this selection as aimed at him, but soon he was under the spell of the music and the sentiment, which he thought had never before been so exquisitely blended.

Miss Walton was not very finished or artistic in anything. She would not be regarded as a scholar, even among the girls of her own age and station, and her knowledge of classical music was limited. But she was gifted in a peculiar degree with tact, a quick perception, and the power of interpreting the language of nature and of the heart. She read and estimated character rapidly. Almost intuitively she saw people's needs and weaknesses, but so far was she from making them the ground of satire and contempt that they awakened her pity and desire to help. In other words, she was one of those Christians who in some degree catch the very essence of Christ's character, who lived and died to save. She did not think of condemning the guilty and disconsolate man that brooded at her fireside, but she did long to help him.

"I may never be able to say such words to him directly," she thought, "but I can sing them, and if he leaves our home to-morrow he shall hear the truth once more."

And she did sing with tenderness and feeling. In rendering something that required simplicity, nature, and pathos, no prima donna could surpass her, for while her voice was not powerful, and had no unusual compass, it was as sweet as that of a thrush in May.

Only deaf ears and a stony heart could have remained insensible, and Gregory was touched. A reviving breath from Paradise seemed to blow upon him and gently urge, "Arise, struggle, make one more effort, and you may yet cross the burning sands of the desert. It is not a mirage that is mocking you now."

As the last words trembled from the singer's lips he shaded his eyes with the hand on which his head was leaning, but Miss Eulie saw a tear fall with momentary glitter, and she exulted over it as his good angel might have done.

If penitent tears could be crystallized they would be the only gems of earth that angels would covet, and perhaps God's co-workers here will find those that they caused to flow on earth, set as gems in their "crown of glory that fadeth not away."

Mr. Walton, in reverential tones, read the fifty-third chapter of Isaiah, which, with greater beauty and tenderness, carried forward the thought of the hymn; and then he knelt and offered a prayer that was so simple and child-like, so free from form and cant, and so direct from the heart, that Gregory was deeply moved. The associations of his early home were now most vividly revealed and crowned by the sacred hour of family worship, the memory of which, like a reproachful face, had followed him in all his evil life.

When he arose from his knees he again shaded his face with his hand to hide his wet eyes and twitching muscles. After a few moments he bade the family an abrupt goodnight, and retired to his room.

At first they merely exchanged significant glances. Then Miss Eulie told of the tear as if it were a bit of dust from a mine that might enrich them all. For a while Annie sat thoughtfully gazing into the fire, but at last she said, "It must be plain to us that Mr. Gregory has wandered further from his old home in spirit than he has in body; but it seems equally evident that he is not happy and content. He seems suffering and out of health in soul and body. Perhaps God has sent him to us and to his childhood's home for healing. Let us, therefore, be very careful, very tender and considerate. He is naturally proud and sensitive, and is morbidly so now."

"I think he is near the Kingdom," said Miss Eulie, with a little sigh of satisfaction.

"Perhaps all are nearer than we think," said Annie, in a musing tone. "God is not far from any one of us. But it is the curse of sin to blind. He has, no doubt, been long in reaching his present unhappy condition, and he may be long in escaping from it."

"Well, the Lord reigns," said Mr. Walton, sententiously, as if that settled the question.

"Dear old father!" said Annie, smiling fondly at him, "that's your favorite saying. You have a comfortable habit of putting all perplexing questions into the Lord's hand and borrowing no further trouble. Perhaps that is the wisest way after all, only one is a long time learning it."

"I've been a long time learning it, my child," said her father. "Let us agree to carry his case often to the throne of mercy, and in His good time and way our prayers will be answered."

Thus in quaint old scriptural style they conspired for the life of their unconscious guest. This was in truth a "holy alliance." How many dark conspiracies there have been, resulting in blood, wrong, and outrage, that some unworthy brow might wear for a little time a petty, perishing crown of earth! Oh, that there were more conspiracies like that in Mr. Walton's parlor for the purpose of rendering the unworthy fit to wear the crown immortal!

CHAPTER VIII
WITCHCRAFT

Miss Eulie was doomed to disappointment, for Gregory came down late to breakfast the following morning with not a trace of his softened feelings. Indeed, because of pride, or for some reason, he chose to seem the very reverse of all she had hoped. The winter of his unbelief could not pass away so easily.

Even in January there are days of sudden relenting, when the frost's icy grasp upon nature seems to relax. Days that rightfully belong to spring drop down upon us with birds that have come before their time. But such days may end in a northeast snowstorm and the birds perish.

The simile appeared true of Gregory. As far as he took part in the table-talk he was a cold, finished man of the world, and the gloom of the early morning rested on his face. But Annie noticed that he made an indifferent breakfast and did not appear well.

After he had retired to his room to write some letters, as he said, she remarked to her father when alone with him:

"I suppose you remember Mr. Gregory's manner when you spoke of Mr. Hunting. They evidently are acquainted and not on good terms. What could have occurred between them?"

"Some quarrel resulting from business, perhaps," said Mr. Walton, musingly.

"I believe Charles has been trying to restrain Mr. Gregory in some of his fast ways," Annie continued, emphatically, "and they have had hot words. Men have so little discretion in their zeal."

"Business men are not apt to interfere with each other's foibles unless they threaten their pockets," her father replied. "It is more probable that Gregory has borrowed money of Hunting, and been compelled to pay it against his will; and yet I have no right to surmise anything of the kind."

"But Mr. Hunting is not a mere business man, father. He is bent on doing good wherever he can find opportunity. I incline to my solution. But it is clear that we must be silent in regard to him while Mr. Gregory is with us, for I never saw such bitter enmity expressed in any face. It is well that Charles is to be absent for some time, and that we have no prospect of a visit from him while our guest is here. Oh, dear! I wish Charles could come and make us a visit instead of this moody, wayward stranger."

"I can echo that wish heartily, Annie, for in the son I find little of my old friend, his father. But remember what you said last night. It may be that he was sent to us in order that we should help him become what his father was."

"I will do my best; but I do not look forward to his society with much pleasure. Still, if there should be any such result as we hope for, I should feel repaid a thousand-fold."

Gregory finished his letters and then paced restlessly up and down his room.

"That this country girl should have so moved me!" he muttered. "What does it mean? What is there about her that takes hold of my attention and awakens my interest? I wish to go downstairs now, and talk to her, and have her read to me, and am provoked with myself that I do. Yesterday at this time I wished to avoid her.

"Why should I wish to avoid her? If she amuses me, diverts my mind, beguiles my pain, or more dreary apathy, why not let her exert her power to the utmost and make herself useful? Yes, but she will try to do more than amuse. Well, suppose she does; one can coolly foil such efforts. Not so sure of that. If I were dealing with a man I could, but one must be worse than a clod to hear her sing and not feel. I suppose I made a weak fool of myself before them all last night, and they thought I was on the eve of conversion. I half wish I were, or on the eve of anything else. Any change from my present state would seem a relief. But a man cannot go into these things like an impulsive girl, even if he believes in them, which is more than I do. I seem to have fallen into a state of moral and physical imbecility, in which I can only doubt, suffer, and chafe.

"I won't avoid her. I will study and analyze her character. I doubt whether she is as good, fresh, and original as she seems. Such girls exist only in moral stories, and I've met but few even there. I will solve her mystery. Probably it is not a very deep one, and after a day or two she will become an old story and life resume its normal monotony;" and he at once descended the stairs to carry out his purpose.

The children were just coming from the sitting-room where they had their school, exclaiming, "Oh, aunty, what shall we do this awful rainy day?"

"Wait till I have given some directions to Zibbie, and I will read you a fairy story, and then you can go up into the garret until dinner- time."

"May I listen to the fairy story also?" asked Walter.

Miss Walton looked up with a smile and said, "You must be half- desperate from your imprisonment to accept of such solace. But if you can wait till I have kept my word to the children I will read something more to your taste."

"I think I should like to hear how a fairy story sounds once again after all these years."

"As Shakespeare may sound to us some time in the future," she replied, smiling.

"I can't believe we shall ever outgrow Shakespeare," he said.

"I can believe it, but cannot understand how it is possible. As yet I am only growing up to Shakespeare."

"You seem very ready to believe what you cannot understand."

"And that is woman's way, I suppose you would like to add," she answered, smiling over her shoulder, as she turned to the kitchen department. "You men have a general faith that there will be dinner at two o'clock, though you understand very little how it comes to pass, and if you are disappointed the best of your sex have not fortitude enough to wait patiently, so I must delay no longer to propitiate the kitchen divinity."

"There!" he said, "I have but crossed her steps in the hall, and she has stirred me and set my nerves tingling like an October breeze. She is a witch."

After a few minutes Miss Walton entered. Each of the children called for a story, and both clamored for their favorites.

"Johnny," said Miss Walton, "it is manly to yield to the least and weakest, especially if she be a little woman."

The boy thought a moment, and then with an amusing assumption of dignity said, "You may read Susie's story first, aunty."

"Susie, promise Johnny that his story shall be read first next time;" which Susie promptly did with a touch of the womanly grace which accompanies favors bestowed after the feminine will has triumphed.

"Now, little miniature man and woman, listen!" and their round eyes were ready for the world of wonders.

And this child of nature was at the same time showing Gregory a world as new and strange--a world that he had caught glimpses of when a boy, but since had lost hopelessly. She carried the children away into fairy-land. She suggested to him a life in which simplicity, truth, and genuine goodness might bring peace and hope to the heart.

"Well, what do you think of the fairy story?" she asked after she had finished and the children had drawn sighs of intense relief at the happy denouement, in which the ugly ogre was slain and the prince and princess were married:

"I did not hear it," he said.

"That's complimentary. But you appeared listening very closely."

"You have heard of people reading a different meaning between the lines, and I suppose one can listen to a different meaning."

"And what could you find between the lines of this fairy tale?" she asked with interest.

"It would be difficult for me to explain--something too vague and indefinite for words, I fear. But if you will read me something else I will listen to the text itself."

"Come, children, scamper off to the garret," said Annie, "and remember you are nearer heaven up there, and so must be very kind and gentle to each other."

"You will fill those youngsters' heads with beautiful superstitions."

"Superstition and faith are not so very far apart, though so unlike."

"Yes, it is hard to tell where one leaves off and the other begins."

"Is it?"

"Isn't it?"

"I don't like to contradict you, sir."

"You have contradicted me, and I suppose it is manly to yield to a lady.'"

"Not in matters of principle and honest conviction."

"Alas! if one has not very much of either!"

"It is a very great misfortune, and, I suppose I ought to add, fault."

"I have no doubt it is a misfortune, Miss Walton, but you are not reading."

"Well, make your choice."

"I leave it entirely to you."

"You don't look very well to-day. I will select something light and cheerful from Dickens."

"Excuse me, please. I am in no mood for his deliberate purpose to make one laugh."

"Then here is Irving. His style flows like a meadowbrook."

"No, he is too sentimental."

"Walter Scott, then, will form a happy medium."

"No, he wearies one with explanations and history."

"Some of Tennyson's dainty idylls will suit your fastidious taste."

"I couldn't abide his affected, stilted language to-day."

"Shakespeare, then; you regard him as perfect."

"No, he makes me think, and I do not wish to."

"Well, here are newspapers, the latest magazine, and some new novels."

"Modern rubbish--a mushroom growth. They will soon kindle kitchen fires instead of thought."

"Then I must make an expedition to the library. What shall I bring? There is Mosheim's 'Ecclesiastical Ancient History'; that has a solid, venerable sound. Or, if you prefer poetry, I will get Gray's 'Elegy.' That cannot be a literary mushroom, for he was twenty years writing it. But perhaps it is Tupper you would like. That would suit your mood exactly, Tupper's 'Proverbial Philosophy.'"

"You are growing satirical, Miss Walton. Why don't you assert plainly that I am as full of whims as a--"

"Woman, would you like to say?"

"Present company excepted. The fact is, I am two-thirds ill to-day, and the most faultless style and theme in our language would weary me. I am possessed by the evil spirits of ennui, unrest, and disgust at myself and all the world, present company always excepted. Do you know of any spell that can exorcise these demons?"

"Yes, a very simple one. Will you put yourself absolutely in my power and obey?"

"I am your slave."

Miss Walton left the room and soon returned with a large afghan. "You must take a horizontal position in order that my spell may work."

"Pshaw! you are prescribing an ordinary nap."

"I am glad to say the best things in this world are ordinary. But permit me to suggest that in view of your pledged word you have nothing to do in this matter but to obey."

"Very well;" and he threw himself on the sofa.

"The day is chilly, sir, and I must throw this afghan over you;" and she did so with a little touch of delicacy which is so grateful when one is indisposed.

Her manner both soothed and pleased him.

He was more lonely than he realized, for it had been years since he had experienced woman's gentle care and ministry; and Annie Walton had a power possessed by few to put jangling nerves at rest. Suddenly he said, "I wish I had a sister like you."

"My creed, you know," she replied, "makes all mankind kindred."

"Nonsense!" said Gregory, irritably; "deliver me from your church sisters."

"Take care!" she answered, with a warning nod, "I'm a church sister; so don't drive me away, for I am going to sing you to sleep."

"I'm half inclined to join your church that I may call you sister."

"You would be disciplined and excommunicated within a month. But hush; you must not talk."

"How would you treat me after I had been anathematized?"

"If you were as ill as you are to-day I would make you sleep. Hush; not another word. I am going to sing."

A luxurious sense of comfort stole over him, and he composed himself to listen and criticise, little imagining, though, that he would fall asleep. He saw through the window a lowering sky with leaden clouds driven wildly across it. The wind moaned and soughed around the angles of the house, and the rain beat against the glass. All without seemed emblematic of himself. But now he had a brief but blessed sense of shelter from both the storm and himself. The fire blazed cheerily on the hearth. The afghan seemed to envelop him like a genial atmosphere. Had Miss Walton bewitched it by her touch? And now she has found something to suit her, or rather him, and is singing.

"What an unusual voice she has!" he thought "Truly the spirit of David's harp, that could banish the demon from Saul, dwells in it. I wonder if she is as good and real as she seems, or whether, under the stress of temptation or the poison of flattery, she would not show herself a true daughter of Eve? I must find out, for it is about the only remaining question that interests me. If she is like the rest of us--if she is a female Hunting--then good-by to all hope. I shall not live to find anybody or anything to trust. If she is what she seems, it's barely possible that she might help me out of this horrible 'slough of despond,' if she would take the trouble. I wish that she were my sister, or that my sister had lived and had been just like her."

CHAPTER IX
MISS WALTON RECOMMENDS A HOBBY

To Gregory's surprise he waked and then admitted to himself that, contrary to his expectation and purpose, he had been asleep. His last remembered consciousness was that of sweet, low music; and how long ago was that? He looked at his watch; it was nearly two, and he must have slept several hours. He glanced around and saw that he was alone, but the fire still blazed on the hearth, and the afghan infolded him with its genial warmth as before, and it seemed that although by himself he was still cared for.

"She is a witch," he muttered. "Her spells are no jokes. But I will investigate her case like an old-time Salem inquisitor. With more than Yankee curiosity, which was at the bottom of their superstitious questionings, I will pry into her power. But she will find that she has a wary sceptic to convince. I have seen too many saints and sinners to be again deceived by fair seeming."

A broad ray of sunlight shot across the room. "By my soul! it's clearing off. Is this her work also? Has she swept away the clouds with her broomstick? And there goes the dinner-bell, too;" and he went to his room two steps at a time, as he had done when a boy.

Annie coming out of the sitting-room at that moment, smiled and said: "He must be better."

At the table she asked, "How do you find yourself now?"

"Much given to appetite." Then, turning to Mr. Walton, he said, abruptly, "Do you believe in witchcraft?"

"Well, no, sir," said Mr. Walton, a little taken aback.

"I do!" continued he, emphatically.

"When and where have you had experience of the black art?"

"This morning, and in your house, sir."

"You seem none the worse for it," said his host, smiling.

"Indeed, I have not felt so well in months. Your larder will suffer if I am practiced upon any more."

"Well, of all modern and prosaic results of witchery this exceeds," said Annie, laughing, "since only a good appetite comes of it."

"It yet remains to be seen whether this is the only result," replied Gregory. "What possessed the old Puritans to persecute the Salem witches is a mystery to me, if their experience was anything like mine."

"You must remember that the question of what was agreeable or otherwise scarcely entered into a Puritan's motives."

"I am not so sure of that," he answered, quickly. "It has ever seemed to me that the good people of other days went into persecution with a zeal that abstract right can hardly account for. People will have their excitements, and a good rousing persecution used to stir things like the burning of Chicago or a Presidential election in our day."

"Granting," said Annie, "the bigotry and cruelty of the persecutor-- and these must be mainly charged to the age--still you must admit that among them were earnest men who did from good motives what appears very wrong to us. What seemed to them evil and destructive principles were embodied in men and women, and they meant to destroy the evil through the suffering and death of these poor creatures."

"And then consider the simplicity and ease of the persecutor's method," continued Gregory, mockingly. "A man's head has become full of supposed doctrinal errors. To refute and banish these would require much study and argument on the part of the opponent. It was so much easier to take an obstinate heretic's head off than to argue with him! I think it was the simplicity of the persecutor's method that kept it in favor so long."

"But it never convinced any one," said Annie, "and the man killed merely goes into another world of the same opinion still."

"And there probably learns, poor fellow, that both were wrong, and that he had better have been content with good dinners and a quiet life, and let theology alone."

"The world would move but slowly, if all men were content with 'good dinners and a quiet life,'" said Annie, satirically. "But you have not answered my question. Could not good, earnest men have been very cruel, believing that everything depended on their uprooting some evil of their day?"

"To tell the truth, Miss Walton," he replied, a little nettled, "I have no sympathy with that style of men. To me they are very repulsive and ridiculous. They remind me of the breathless, perspiring politicians of our time, who button-hole you and assert that the world will come to an end unless John Smith is elected. To me, the desperate earnestness of people who imagine it their mission to set the world right is excessively tiresome. For one man or a thousand to proclaim that they speak for God and embody truth, and that the race should listen and obey, is the absurdity of arrogance."

"If we were to agree with you, should we not have to say that the prophets should have kept their visions to themselves, and that Luther should have remained in his cell, and Columbus have coasted alongshore and not insisted on what was to all the world an absurdity?"

"Come, Miss Walton," said Gregory, with a vexed laugh as they rose from the table, "you are a witch. I am willing to argue with flesh and blood, but I would rather hear you sing. Still, since you have swept away these clouds so I can have my ramble, I will forgive you for unhorsing me in our recent tilt."

"If you would mount some good honest hobby and ride it hard, I doubt whether any one could unhorse you," she replied in a low tone, as she accompanied him to the parlor.

"Men with hobbies are my detestation, Miss Walton."

"Nevertheless, they are the true knights-errant of our age. Of course it depends upon what kind of hobbies they ride, or whether they can manage their steeds."

"Miss Walton, your figure suggests a half-idiot, with a narrow forehead and one idea, banging back and forth on a wooden horse, but making no progress--in other words, a fussy, bustling man who can do and talk but one thing."

"Your understanding of the popular phrase is narrow and literal, and while it may have such a meaning, it can also have a very different one. Suppose that, instead of looking with languid eyes alike upon all things, a man finds some question of vital import, or a pursuit that promises good to himself and to others and that enlists his interest. He comes at last to give it his best energies and thought. The whole current of his life is setting in that direction. Of course he must ever be under the restraints of good sense and refinement. A man's life without a hobby is a weak and wavering line of battle indefinitely long. One's life with a hobby is a concentrated charge."

There was in Miss Walton's face and manner, as she uttered these words, that which caused him to regard her with involuntary admiration. Suddenly he asked, "Have you a hobby?"

Her manner changed instantly, and with an arch look she said, "If you detest a man with a hobby, what a monster a woman with one would be in your eyes!"

"I have admitted that you are a witch."

"Oh, I am a monster already, and so have no character to lose. But where is your penetration? If a man with a hobby is idiotic, narrow- browed, fussy and bustling, excessively obtrusive with his one idea, a woman must be like him with all these things exaggerated. Has it not occurred to you that I have a hobby of the most wooden and clumsy order?"

"But that was my idea of a hobby. You have spiritualized my wooden block into a Pegasus--the symbol of inspiration. Have you such a hobby?"

"I have."

"What is it?"

She went out of the room, saying smilingly over her shoulder, "You must find that out for yourself."

CHAPTER X
A PLOT AGAINST MISS WALTON

Gregory was soon off for his ramble. The storm had cleared away, leaving the air so warm and genial as to suggest spring rather than fall; but he was quite oblivious of the outer world, and familiar scenes had not the power to awaken either pleasant or painful associations. He was trying to account for the influence that Annie Walton had suddenly gained over him, but it was beyond his philosophy. This provoked him. His cool, worldly nature doubted everything and especially everybody. He believed in the inherent weakness of humanity, and that if people were exceptionally good it was because they had been exceptionally fortunate in escaping temptation. He also had a cynical pleasure in seeing such people tripping and stumbling, so that he might say in self-excusing, "We are all alike."

And yet he was compelled to admit that if Annie's goodness was seeming it was higher art than he had known before. There was also an unconscious assertion of superiority in her manner that he did not like. True, things had turned out far better than he had expected. There was no cant about her. She did not lecture him or "talk religion" in what he regarded as the stereotyped way, and he was sure she would not, even if they became better acquainted. But there is that in genuine goodness and nobility of character that always humiliates the bad and makes them feel their degradation. A real pity and sympathy for him tinged her manner, but these qualities are not agreeable to pride. And it must be admitted that she had a little self-righteous satisfaction that she was so much better than this sadly robbed and wounded man suddenly appearing at the wayside of her life. In human strength there is generally a trace of arrogance. Only divine strength and purity can say with perfect love and full allowance for all weakness and adverse influences, "Neither do I condemn thee; go, and sin no more."

Gregory had now reached a rustic bridge across a little stream that, swollen from the recent rain, came gurgling and clamoring down from the hills. Leaning upon the rail he seemed to watch the foaming water glide under his feet; but the outward vision made no impression on his mind.

At last in the consciousness of solitude he said: "She told me I must find her out. I will. I will know whether she is as free from human frailty as she seems. I have little doubt that before many days I can cause her to show all the inherent weaknesses of her sex; and I should think New York and Paris had taught me what they are. She has never been tempted. She has never been subjected to the delicate flattery of an accomplished man of the world. I am no gross libertine. I could not be in this place. I could not so wrong hospitality and the household of my father's friend. But I should like to prove to that girl her delusion, and show her that she is a weak woman like the rest; that she is a pretty painted ship that has never been in a storm, and therefore need not sail so confidently. We all start on the voyage of life as little skiffs and pleasure boats might cross the ocean. If any get safely over, it is because they were lucky enough not to meet dangerous currents or rough weather. I should like her better with her piquant ways if she were more like myself. Saints and Madonnas are well enough in pictures, but such as I would find them very uncomfortable society."

With sudden power the thought flashed upon him, "Why not let her make you as she is?" Where did the thought come from? Tell me not that the Divine Father forgets His children. He is speaking to them continually, only they will not hear. There was a brief passionate wish on the part of this bad man that she might be what she seemed and that he could become like her. As the turbulent, muddy Jordan divided that God's people might pass through, so this thought from heaven found passage through his heart, and then the current of sinful impulse and habit flowed on as before. With the stupidity of evil he was breaking the clew that God had dropped into his hand even when desperately weary of his lost state. He is wrecked and helpless on the wide ocean; a ship is coming to his rescue; and his first effort is that this vessel also may be wrecked or greatly injured in the attempt.

There is no insanity like that of a perverted heart. The adversary of souls has so many human victims doing his work that he can fold his hands in idleness. And yet according to the world's practice, and we might almost say its code, Gregory purposed nothing that would be severely condemned--nothing more than an ordinary flirtation, as common in society as idleness, love of excitement, and that power over others which ministers to vanity. He had no wish to be able to say anything worse of her than that under temptation she would be as vain and heartless a coquette as many others that he knew in what is regarded as good society. He would have cut off his right hand, as he then felt, rather than have sought to lead her into gross sin.

And yet what did Gregory purpose in regard to Annie but to take the heavenly bloom and beauty from her character? As if they can be lovely to either God or man of whom it can be said only, They commit no overt crime. What is the form of a rose without its beauty and fragrance? They who tempt to evil are the real iconoclasts. They destroy God's image.

But the supreme question of the selfish heart is, "What do I want *now?*"

Gregory wished to satisfy himself and Miss Walton that she had no grounds for claiming any special superiority over him, and he turned on his heel and went back to the house to carry out his purpose. Nature, purified and beautiful by reason of its recent baptism from heaven, had no attractions for him. Gems of moisture sparkled unseen. He was planning and scheming to turn her head with vanity, make her quiet life of ministry to others odious, and draw her into a fashionable flirtation.

Annie did not appear until the supper-bell summoned her, and then said, "Mr. Gregory, I hope you will not think it rude if father and I leave you to your books and Aunt Eulie's care this evening. It is our church prayer-meeting night, and father never likes to be absent."

"I shall miss you beyond measure. The evening will seem an age."

Something in his tone caused her to give him a quick glance, but she only said, with a smile, "You are very polite to say so, but I imagine the last magazine will be a good substitute."

"I doubt whether there is a substitute for you, Miss Walton. I am coming to believe that your absence would make that vacuum which nature so dreads. You shall see how good I will be this evening, and you shall read me everything you please, even to that 'Ancient Ecclesiastical History.' If you will only stay I will be your slave; and you shall rule me with a rod of iron or draw me with the silken cords of kindness, according to your mood."

"It is not well to have too many moods, Mr. Gregory," said Annie, quietly. "In reply to all your alluring reasons for staying at home I have only to say that I have promised father to go with him; besides, I think it is my duty to go."

"'Duty' is a harsh, troublesome word to be always quoting. It is a kind of strait-jacket which we poor moral lunatics are compelled to wear."

"'Duty' seems to me a good solid road on which one may travel safely. One never knows where the side paths lead: into the brambles or a morass like enough."

"Indeed, Miss Walton, such austerity is not becoming to your youth and beauty."

"What am I to think of your sincerity when you speak of my beauty, Mr. Gregory?"

"Beauty is a question of taste," answered Gregory, gallantly. "It is settled by no rigid rules or principles, but by the eyes of the observer."

"Oh! I understand now. My beauty this evening is the result of your bad taste."

"Calling it 'bad' does not make it so. Well, since you will not remain at home with me, will you not let me go with you to the prayer- meeting? If I'm ever to join your church, it is time I entered on the initiating mysteries."

"I think a book will do you more good in your present mood."

"What a low estimate you make of the 'means of grace'! Why, certain of your own poets have said, 'And fools who came to scoff remained to pray.'"

"The quotation does not apply to you, Mr. Gregory. For, even if you can doubt the power and truth of Christianity, the memory of your childhood will prevent you from scoffing at it."

A sudden shadow came across his face, but after a moment he said, in his old tones:

"Will you not let me go to the prayer-meeting?"

"Father will be glad to have you go with us, if you think it prudent to venture out in the night air."

"Prudence to the dogs! What is the use of living if we cannot do as we please? But will *you* be glad to have me go?"

"That depends upon your motives."

"If I should confess you wouldn't let me go," he replied with a bow. "But I will try to be as good as possible, just to reward your kindness."

The rest of the family now joined them in the supper-room, and during the meal Walter exerted himself to show how entertaining he could be if he chose. Anecdotes, incidents of travel, graphic sketches of society, and sallies of wit, made an hour pass before any one was aware.

Even the children listened with wondering eyes, and Mr. Walton and Miss Eulie were delighted with the vivacity of their guest. Annie apparently had no reason to complain of him, for his whole manner toward her during the hour was that of delicately sustained compliment. When she spoke he listened with deference, and her words usually had point and meaning. He also gave to her remarks the best interpretation of which they were capable, and by skilfully drawing her out made her surpass even herself, so that Miss Eulie said, "Why, Annie, there surely is some witchcraft about. You and Mr. Gregory are as brilliant as fireworks."

"It's all Miss Walton's work, I assure you," said Gregory. "As Pat declared, 'I'm not meself any more,' and shall surprise you, sir, by asking if I may go to the prayer-meeting. Miss Walton says I can if I will behave myself. The last time I went to the old place I made faces at the girls. I suppose that would be wrong."

"That is the sin of our age--making faces," said Annie. "Many have two, and some can make for themselves even more."

"Now that was a barbed arrow," said Gregory, looking at her keenly. "Did you let it fly at a venture?"

"Bless me!" said Mr. Walton, rising hastily, "we should have been on the road a quarter of an hour ago. You mustn't be so entertaining another prayer-meeting night, Mr. Gregory. Of course we shall be glad to have you accompany us if you feel well enough. I give you both but five minutes before joining me at the wagon."

Walter again mounted the stairs with something of his old buoyancy, and Annie followed, looking curiously after him.

It was not in human nature to be indifferent to that most skilful flattery which can be addressed to woman--the recognition of her cleverness, and the enhancing of it by adroit and suggestive questions--and yet all his manner was tinged by a certain insincere gallantry, rather than by a manly, honest respect. She vaguely felt this, though she could not distinctly point it out. He puzzled her. What did he mean, and at what was he aiming?

CHAPTER XI
A DRINKING-SONG AT A PRAYER-MEETING

Having failed in his attempt to induce Annie to remain at home, Gregory resolved that the prayer-meeting should not be one of quiet devotion. Mr. Walton made him, as an invalid, take the back seat with Annie, while he sat with the driver, and Gregory, after a faint show of resistance, gladly complied.

"It's chilly. Won't you give me half of your shawl?" he said to her.

"You may have it all," she replied, about to take it off.

"No, I'll freeze first. Do the brethren and sisters sit together?"

"No," she answered, laughing, "we have got in the queer way of dividing the room between us, and the few men who attend sit on one side and we on the other."

"Oh, it's almost a female prayer-meeting then. Do the sisters pray?"

"Mr. Gregory, you are not a stranger here that you need pretend to such ignorance. I think the meeting is conducted very much as when you were a boy."

"With this most interesting difference, that you will be there and will sing, I hope. Miss Walton, where did you learn to sing?"

"Mainly at home."

"I should think so. Your voice is as unlike that of a public singer as you are un-like the singer herself."

"It must seem very tame to you."

"It seems very different. We have an artificial-flower department in our store. There is no lack of color and form there, I assure you, but after all I would prefer your rose garden in June."

"But you would probably prefer your artificial-flower department the rest of the year," said Annie, laughing.

"Why so?"

"Our roses are annuals and are only prosaic briers after their bloom."

"Imagine them hybrid perpetuals and monthlies and you have my meaning. But your resemblance to a rose extends even to its thorns. Your words are a little sharp sometimes."

"In the thorns the resemblance begins and ends, Mr. Gregory. I assure you I am a veritable Scotch brier. But here we are at our destination. I wonder if you will see many old, remembered faces."

"I shall be content in seeing yours," he replied in a low tone, pressing her hand as he assisted her to alight.

If he could have seen the expression of her face in the darkness it would have satisfied him that she did not receive that style of compliment like many of the belles of his acquaintance, who would take the small change of flattery with the smiling complacency of a public door-keeper.

They were late. The good old pastor was absent, and one of the brethren was reading a chapter in the Bible. Gregory took a seat where he could see Annie plain-ly, and she sat with her side face toward him.

He watched her keenly, in order to see if she showed any consciousness of his presence. The only evidence in his favor was a slight flush and a firmness about the lips, as if her will was asserting itself. But soon her face had the peaceful and serious expression becoming the place and hour, and he saw that she had no thoughts for him whatever. He was determined to distract her attention, and by restlessness, by looking fixedly at her, sought her eye, but only secured the notice of some young girls who thought him "badly smitten with Miss Walton."

The long chapter having been read, a hymn was given out. The gentleman who usually led the music was also absent, and there was an ominous pause, in which the good brother's eye wandered appealingly around the room and at last rested hopefully on Annie. She did not fail him, but, with heightened color and voice that trembled slightly at first, "started the tune." It was a sweet, familiar air, and she soon had the support of other voices. One after another they joined her in widely varying degrees of melody, even as the example of a noble life will gradually secure a number of more or less successful imitators.

Gregory had seen the appeal to her with an amused, half-comical look, but her sincere and ready performance of the duty that had unexpectedly revealed itself rapidly changed the expression of his face to one of respect and admiration. Distinct, and yet blending with the others, her voice seemed both to key up and hide the little roughnesses and discords of some who perhaps had more melody in their hearts than in their tones.

Again a divine impulse, like a flower-laden breeze sweeping into a dark and grated vault at Greenwood, stirred Gregory's evil nature.

"Let her teach you the harmony of noble, unselfish living. Follow her in thought, feeling, and action, as those stammering, untuned tongues do in melody, and the blight of evil will pass from your life. Seek not to muddy and poison this clear little rill that is watering a bit of God's world. Grant that her goodness is not real, established, and thoroughly tested--that it is only a pretty surface picture. Seek not to blur that picture."

But the evil heart is like Sodom. Good angel-thoughts may come to it, but they are treated with violence and driven out. His habit of cynical doubt soon returned, and his purpose to show Miss Walton that she was a weak, vain woman after all became stronger than ever.

It seemed to have come to this, that his salvation depended on, not what Miss Walton could say or do directly in his behalf, but upon her maintenance of a character that even a sceptical world must acknowledge as inspired by heaven, and this, too, against a tempter of unusual skill and tact. She might sing with resistless pathos, and argue and plead with Paul's logic and eloquence. His nature might be stirred for a moment as a stagnant pool is agitated by the winds of heaven, and, like the pool, he would soon settle back into his old apathy. But if she could be made to show weakness, to stumble and fall, it would confirm him in his belief that goodness, if it really existed, was accidental; that those whose lives were apparently free from stain deserved no credit, because untempted; and that those who fell should be pitied rather than blamed, since they were unfortunate rather than guilty. Anything that would quiet and satisfy his conscience in its stern arraignment of his evil life would be welcome. The more he saw of Miss Walton the more he felt that she would be a fair subject upon whom to test his favorite theory. Therefore, by the time one of the brethren present had finished his homely exhortation he was wholly bent upon carrying out his plan.

But Miss Walton sat near, as innocently oblivious of this plot against her as Eve of the serpent's guile before the tempter and temptation came into fatal conjunction.

What thoughts for and against each other may dwell utterly hidden and unknown in the hearts of those so near that their hands may touch! Conspiracies to compass the death that is remediless may lurk just behind eyes that smile upon us. Of course Gregory desired no such fatal result to follow his little experiment. Few who for their own pleasure, profit, or caprice tempt others wish the evil to work on to the bitter end. They merely want a sufficient letting down of principle and virtue for the accomplishment of their purpose, and then would prefer that the downward tendency should cease or be reversed. The merchant who requires dishonorable practices of his clerk wishes him to stop at a point which, in the world's estimation, is safe. And those who, like Gregory, would take the bloom from woman's purity and holiness in thought and action, that they may enjoy a questionable flirtation, would be horrified to see that woman drop into the foul gulf of vice. With the blind egotism of selfishness, they wish merely to gratify their present inclinations, ignoring the consequences. They are like children who think it would be sport to see a little cataract falling over a Holland dike. Therefore, when the tide is in they open a small channel, but are soon aghast to find that the deep sea is overwhelming the land.

Gregory, as is usual with his kind, thought only of his own desires. When he had accomplished these Miss Walton must take care of herself. When from seeming a sweet, pure woman she had, by a little temptation, proved to be capable of becoming a vain flirt, he would go back to business and dismiss her from his thoughts with the grim chuckle, "She is like the rest of us."

And thus Annie was destined to meet her mother Eve's experience; and with the energy and promptness of evil Gregory was keenly on the alert for anything to further his purpose.

It would seem that the satanic ally in such schemes does not permit opportunity to be wanting long. The leader of the meeting again selected a hymn, but of a peculiar metre. He read only two lines, and then looked expectantly toward Annie, who could not at the moment think of a tune that would answer; and while with knit brows she was bending over her book, to her unbounded surprise she heard the hymn started by a clear, mellow tenor voice. Looking up she saw Gregory singing as gravely as a deacon. She was sufficiently a musician to know that the air did not belong to sacred music, though she had never heard it before.

In his watchfulness he had noted her hesitation, and glancing at the metre saw instantly that the measure of a drinking-song he knew well would fit the words. This fell out better than he had hoped, and with the thought, "I will jostle her out of her dignity now," he began singing without any embarrassment, though every eye was upon him. He had been out in the world long enough for that.

As Annie turned with a shocked and half-frightened expression toward him his eyes met hers with a sudden gleam of drollery which was irresistible, and he had the satisfaction of seeing her drop her head to conceal a smile. But he noticed, a moment later, that her face became grave with disapprobation.

Having sung a stanza he looked around with an injured air, as if reproaching the others for not joining in with him.

"The tune is not exactly familiar to us," said the good man leading the meeting, "but if the brother will continue singing we will soon catch the air; or perhaps the brother or some one else (with a glance at Annie) will start one better known."

Gregory deliberately turned over the leaves, and to the tune of Old Hundred started a hymn commencing:

"Unveil thy bosom, faithful tomb,　　Take this new treasure to thy trust,
And give these sacred relics room　To slumber in the silent dust."

Annie had a keen sense of the ludicrous, and the transition from what he had been singing to the funereal and most inappropriate words was almost too much for her. To her impotent anger and self-disgust she felt a hysterical desire to laugh, and only controlled herself by keeping her head down and her lips firmly pressed together during the remainder of the brief service.

Even others who did not know Gregory could not prevent a broad smile at the incongruous hymn he had chosen, but they unitedly wailed it through, for he persisted in singing it all in the most dirge-like manner. They gave him credit for doing the best he could, and supposed his unhappy choice resulted from haste and embarrassment. In the spontaneity of social meetings people become accustomed to much that is not harmonious.

Mr. Walton was puzzled. His guest was certainly appearing in an unexpected role, and he feared that all was not right.

After the meeting the brethren gathered round Gregory and thanked him for his assistance, and he shook hands with them and the elderly ladies present with the manner of one who might have been a "pillar in the temple." Many of them remembered his father and mother and supposed their mantle had fallen on him.

An ancient "mother in Israel" thanked him that he had "started a tune that they all could sing, instead of the new-fangled ones the young people are always getting up nowadays. But," said she, "I wish you could learn us that pretty one you first sang, for it took my fancy amazingly. I think I must have heard it before some-where."

Gregory gave Annie another of his suggestive glances, that sent her out hastily into the darkness, and a moment later he joined her at the carriage steps.

CHAPTER XII
FOILED IN ONE DIRECTION

Gregory lifted Miss Walton very tenderly into the carriage and took his place by her side, while her father was detained by some little matter of business.

"I am not an invalid," said Annie, rather curtly.

"Indeed you are not, Miss Walton; from your super-abundance you are even giving life to me."

"I thought from your manner you feared I was about to faint," she answered, dryly.

Mr. Walton joined them and they started homeward.

"Come, Miss Annie," said Gregory (addressing her thus for the first time); "why so distant? Was I not called a brother in the meeting? If I am a brother you are a sister. I told you I would secure this relationship."

She did not answer him.

"I think it was too bad," he continued, "that you did not second my efforts better. You would not help me sing either of the tunes I started."

"Mr. Gregory," said Annie, emphatically, "I will never go to a prayer- meeting with you again."

"What a rash resolve! But I confess that I preferred to have you stay at home with me."

"You have spoiled the whole evening for me."

"And you spoiled mine. So we are quits," he replied, laughingly.

"No, we are not. How can you turn sacred things into a jest?"

"I was possessed to see a smile light up the awful gravity of your face, and I feel amply repaid in that I succeeded. It was a delicious bit of sunshine on a cloudy day."

"And I am provoked at myself beyond measure, that I could have laughed like a silly child."

"But did you not like the first tune I sang? 'Old Hundred' was selected in deference to the wishes of the meeting."

"No, I did not like it. It was not suitable to the place and words. Though I never heard it before, its somewhat slow movement did not prevent it from smacking of something very foreign to a prayer- meeting."

"A most happy and inspired expression. Many a time I have smacked my lips when it was being sung over the best of wine."

"Was it a drinking-song, then?" she asked, quickly.

"What will you do with me if I say it was?"

"Mr. Gregory, I would not have thought this even of you."

"Even of me! That is complimentary. I now learn what a low estimate you have of me. But see how unjust you are. The musical commissaries of the church militant are ever saying, 'It's a pity the devil should have all the good music,' and so half the

Sunday-school tunes, and many sung in churches, have had a lower origin than my drinking-song. I assure you that the words are as fine as the air. Why have I not as good a right to steal a tune from the devil as the rest of them?"

"It's the motive that makes all the difference," said Annie. "But I fear that in this case the devil suffered no loss."

"I'm sure my motive was not bad. I only wished to see a bonny smile light up your face."

Before she could reply the carriage stopped at Mr. Walton's door, and with Mr. Gregory she passed into the cosey parlor. Her father did not immediately join them.

As Gregory looked at her while she took off her wraps, he thought, "By Jove! she's handsome if she is not pretty."

In fact Annie's face at that time would have attracted attention anywhere. The crisp air had given her a fine color. Her eyes glowed with suppressed excitement and anger, while the firm lines about the mouth indicated that when she spoke it would be decidedly. In spite of herself the audacity, cleverness, and wickedness of this stranger had affected her greatly. As he threw off his moodiness, as he revealed himself by word and action, she saw that he was no ordinary character, but a thorough man of the world, and with some strange caprices. The suspicion crossed her mind that he might be not only in peril himself but also a source of danger. She had determined during the ride home that even though he meant no slur upon sacred things he should carry his mocking spirit no more into them. Therefore, after a moment's thought, she turned toward him with a manner of mingled frankness and dignity, and said, "Mr. Gregory, I regret what has occurred this evening. I have a painful sense of the ludicrous, and you have taken unfair advantage of it. I am usually better and happier for going to our simple little meeting, but now I can think of the whole hour only with pain. I think I am as mirth-loving as the majority of my age, and perhaps more so. I say truly that my heart is very light and happy. But, Mr. Gregory, we look at certain things very differently from you. While I would not for a moment have you think that religion brings into my life gloom and restraint--quite the reverse--still it gives me great pain when anything connected with my faith is made a matter of jest. These things are sacred to us, and I know my father would feel deeply grieved if he understood you this evening. Do you not see? It appears to us differently from what it does to you and perhaps to the world at large. These things are to us what your mother's memory is to you. I would sooner cut off my right hand than trifle with that."

Gregory had been able to maintain his quizzical look of mischief till she named his mother; then his face changed instantly. A flush of shame crossed it, and after a moment, with an expression something like true manhood, he stepped forward and took Annie's hand, saying, "Miss Walton, I sincerely ask your pardon. I did not know--I could not believe that you felt as you do. I will give you no further reason to complain of me on this ground. I hope you will forgive me."

She at once relented, and said:

"'Who by repentance is not satisfied
Is not of heaven nor earth.'

There is an apt quotation from your favorite Shakespeare."

"You seem a delightful mixture of both, Miss Walton."

"If you were a better judge, sir, you would know that the earthly ingredient is too great. But that is in your favor, for I am sufficiently human to make allowance for human folly."

"I shall tax your charity to the utmost."

As Gregory sat in his arm-chair recalling the events of the day before retiring, he thought: "Well, my attempt has failed signally. While by her involuntary smile she showed that she was human, she has also managed this evening to prove that she is perfectly sincere in her religion, and to render it impossible for me to assail her in that direction again. As the old hymn goes, I must 'let her religious hours alone.' But how far her religion or superstition will control her action is another question. I have learned both at home and abroad that people can be very religious and very sincere in matters of faith and ceremony, and jealous of any hand stretched out to touch their sacred ark, but when through with the holy business they can live the life of very ordinary mortals. This may be true of Miss Walton. At any rate I have made a mistake in showing my hand somewhat at a prayer- meeting, for women are so tenacious on religious matters. Deference, personal attention, and compliments--these are the irresistible weapons. These inflate pride and vanity to such a degree that a miserable collapse is necessary. And yet I must be careful, for she is not like some belles I know, who have the swallow of a whale for flattery. She is too intelligent, too refined, to take compliments as large and glaring as a sunflower. Something in the way of a moss-rose bud will accomplish more. I will appear as if falling under her power; as if bewitched by her charms. Nothing pleases your plain girls more than to be thought beautiful. I shall have her head turned in a week. I am more bent than ever on teaching this little Puritan that she and I live upon the same level."

Saturday morning dawned clear and bracing, and the grass was white with hoar-frost. The children came in to breakfast with glowing cheeks and hair awry, crying excitedly in the same breath that they "had been to the chestnut trees and that Jack had opened the burrs all night."

In answer to their clamorous petitions a one-o'clock dinner was promised, and Aunt Annie was to accompany them on a nutting expedition with Jeff as pioneer to thresh and club the trees.

"Can I go too?" Gregory asked of the children.

"I suppose so," said Johnny, rather coldly; "if Aunt Annie is willing."

"You can go with me," said kind-hearted little Susie.

"Now I can go whether Aunt Annie is willing or not," said Gregory, with mock defiance at the boy.

He glanced at his aunt's face to gather how he should take this, but she settled the matter satisfactorily to him by saying, "You shall be my beau, and Mr. Gregory will be Susie's."

"Good, good!" exclaimed Susie. "I've got a beau already;" and she beamed upon Gregory in a way that made them all laugh.

"'Coming events cast their shadows before,' you perceive, Miss Walton," said he, meaningly.

"Sometimes the events themselves are but shadows," she replied, dryly.

"Now that is severe upon the beaux. How about the belles?" he asked, quickly.

"I have nothing to say against my own sex, sir."

"That is not fair. Of course I can say nothing adverse."

"If you should say what you think, I fear we should be little inclined to cry with Shylock, 'A Daniel come to judgment!'"

"You have a dreadful opinion of me, Miss Walton. I wish you would teach me how I can change it."

"You discovered so much in a chestnut burr the day you came I should not be surprised if you could find anything else there that you wish to know."

"I shall not look in burrs for chestnuts this afternoon, but for something else far more important."

Gregory spent the forenoon quietly in his own room reading, in order that he might have all the vigor possible for the ramble. And to Annie, as housekeeper, Saturday morning brought many duties.

By two o'clock the nutting expedition was organized, and with Jeff in advance, carrying a short ladder and a long limber pole, the party started for the hills. At first Johnny, oppressed with his dignity as Aunt Annie's "beau," stalked soberly at her side, and Susie also claimed Gregory according to agreement, and insisted on keeping hold of his hand.

He submitted with such grace as he could muster, for children were tiresome to him, and he wanted to talk to Miss Walton, without "little pitchers with large ears" around.

Annie smiled to herself at his half-concealed annoyance and his wooden gallantry to Susie, but she understood child life well enough to know that the present arrangement would not last very long. And she was right. They had hardly entered the shady lane leading to the trees before a chipmonk, with its shrill note of exclamation at unexpected company, started out from some leaves near and ran for its hole.

Away went Aunt Annie's beau after it, and Susie also, quite oblivious of her first possession in that line, joined in the pursuit. There was an excited consultation above the squirrel's retreat, and then Johnny took out his knife and cut a flexible rod with which to investigate the "robber's den."

Gregory at once joined Annie, saying, "Since the beau of your choice has deserted you, will you accept of another?"

"Yes, till he proves alike inconstant."

"I will see to that. A burr shall be my emblem."

"Or I do," she added, laughing.

"Now the future is beyond my power."

"Perhaps it is anyway. Johnny was bent upon being a true knight. You may see something that will be to you what the chipmonk was to him."

"And such is your opinion of man's constancy? Miss Walton, you are more of a cynic than I am."

"Indeed! Do women dwell in your fancy as fixed stars?"

"Fixed stars are all suns, are they not? I know of one with wonderful powers of attraction," said he, with a significant glance.

"Does she live in New York?" quietly asked Annie.

"You know well she does not. She is a votaress of nature, and, as I said, I shall search in every burr for the hidden clew to her favor."

"You had better look for chestnuts, sir."

"Chestnuts! Fit food for children and chipmonks. I am in quest of the only manna that ever fell from heaven. Have you read Longfellow's 'Golden Legend,' Miss Walton?"

"Yes," she replied, with a slight contraction of the brow as if the suggestion were not pleasing.

The children now came running toward them and wished to resume their old places. "No, sir," said Walter, decisively. "You deserted your lady's side and your place is filled; and Susie--

"'Thou fair, false one,'

--you renounced me for a chipmonk. My wounded heart has found solace in another."

Johnny received this charge against his gallantry with a red face and eyes that began to dilate with anger, while Susie looked at Gregory poutingly and said, "I don't like big beaux. I think chipmonks are ever so much nicer."

The laugh that followed broke the force of the storm that was brewing; and Annie, by saying, "See, children, Jeff is climbing the tree on top of the hill; I wonder who will get the first nuts," caused the wind to veer round from the threatening quarter, and away they scampered with grievances all forgotten.

"If grown-up children could only forget their troubles as easily!" sighed Gregory. "Miss Walton, you are gifted with admirable tact. Your witchery has cleared up another storm."

"They have not forgotten," said Annie, ignoring the compliment--"they have only been diverted from their trouble. Children can do by nature what we should from intelligent choice--turn away the mind from painful subjects to those that are pleasing. You don't catch me brooding over trouble when there are a thousand pleasant things to think of."

"That is easier said than done, Miss Walton. I read on your smooth brow that you have had few serious troubles, and, as you say, '*you* have a thousand pleasant things to think of.' But with others it may be very different. Some troubles have a terrible magnetism that draws the mind back to them as if by a malign spell, and there are no 'pleasant things to think of.'"

"No 'pleasant things'? Why, Mr. Gregory! The universe is very wide."

"Present company excepted," replied he gallantly. "But what do I care for the universe? As you say, it is 'very wide'--a big, uncomfortable place, in which one is afraid of getting lost."

"I am not," said Annie, gently.

"How so?"

"It's all my Father's house. I am never for a moment lost sight of. Wherever I am, I am like a little child playing outside the door while its mother, unseen, is watching it from the window."

He looked at her keenly to see if she were perfectly sincere. Her face had the expression of a child, and the thought flashed across him, "If she is so watched and guarded, how vain are my attempts!"

But he only said with a shrug, "It would be a pity to dissipate your happy superstition, Miss Walton, but after what I have seen and experienced in the world it would seem more generally true that the mother forgot her charge, left the window, and the child was run over by the butcher's cart."

"Do you think it vain confidence," said Annie, earnestly, "when I say that you could not dissipate what you term my 'superstition,' any more than you could argue me out of my belief in my good old father's love?"

CHAPTER XIII
INTERPRETING CHESTNUT BURRS

The conversation had taken a turn that Gregory wished to avoid, so he said: "Miss Walton, you regard me as wretched authority on theology, and therefore my opinions will go for nothing. Suppose we join the children on the hill, for I am most anxious to commence the search for the clew to your favor. Give me your hand, that as your attendant I may at least appear to assist you in climbing, though I suppose you justly think you could help me more than I can you."

"And if I can, why should I not?" asked Annie, kindly.

"Indeed, Miss Walton, I would crawl up first. But thanks to your reviving influences, I am not so far gone as that."

"Then you would not permit a woman to reach out a helping hand to you? Talk not against Turks and Arabs. How do Christian men regard us?"

"But you look upon me as a 'heathen.'"

"Beg your pardon, I do not."

"Miss Walton, give your honest opinion of me--just what you think."

"Will you do the same of me?"

"Oh, certainly!"

"No, do not answer in that tone. On your honor."

Gregory was now caught. If he agreed he must state his doubts of her real goodness; his low estimate of women in general which led to his purpose to tempt her. This would not only arm her against his efforts, but place him in a very unpleasant light. "I beat a retreat, Miss Walton. I am satisfied that your opinion would discourage me utterly."

"You need have no fears of that kind," she said; "although my opinion would not be flattering it would be most encouraging."

"No, Miss Walton, I am not to be caught. My every glance and word reveal my opinion of you, while yours of me amounts to what I used to hear years ago: 'You are a bad boy now, but may become a good one.' Come, give me your hand."

As she complied she gave him a quick, keen look. Her intuition told her of something hidden, and he puzzled her.

Her hand was ungloved, and he thought, "When have I clasped such a hand before? It could help a Hercules. At any rate he would like to hold it, for it is alive."

There is as much diversity of character in hands as in faces. Some are very white and shapely, and a diamond flashes prettily upon them, but having said this you have said all. Others suggest honest work and plenty of it, and for such the sensible will ever have a genuine respect. There are some hands that make you think of creatures whose blood is cold. A lady's hand in society often suggests feebleness, lack of vitality. It is a thing to touch decorously, and if feeling betray you into giving a hearty grasp and pressure, you find that you are only causing pain and reducing the member to a confused jumble of bones and sinews. There are hands that suggest fancy-work, light crochet needles, and neuralgia.

Annie's hand was not one that a sculptor would care to copy, though he would find no great fault with it; but a sculptor would certainly take pleasure in shaking hands with her--the pleasure that is the opposite of our shrinking from taking the hand of the dead. It was soft and delicate to the pressure, and yet firm. It reminded one of silk drawn over steel, and was all electric and throbbing with life. You felt that it could give you the true grasp of friendship--that it had power to do more than barely cling to something--that it could both help and sustain, yet its touch would be gentleness itself beside the couch of suffering.

When they had reached the brow of the hill he was much more exhausted than she, and sat down panting.

"Miss Walton," he asked, "do you not despise a feeble man?"

"What kind of feebleness do you mean?"

"The weakness that makes me sit pale and panting here, while you stand there glowing with life and vigor, a veritable Hebe."

"All your compliments cannot balance that imputation against me. Such weakness awakens my pity, sympathy, and wish to help."

"Ah! the emotions you would bestow on a beggar--very agreeable to a **man**. Well, what kind of feebleness do you despise?"

"I think I should despise a feeble, vacillating Hercules most of all-- a burly, assuming sort of person, who could be made a tool of, and led to do what he knew to be mean and wrong."

"You must despise a great many people then."

"No, I do not. Honestly, Mr. Gregory, I have no right to despise any one. I was only giving the reverse of my ideal man. But I assure you I share too deeply in humanity's faults to be very critical."

"I am delighted to hear, Miss Walton, that you share in our fallen humanity, for I was beginning to doubt it, and you can well understand that I should be dreadfully uncomfortable in the presence of perfection."

"If you could escape all other sources of discomfort as surely as this one, you would be most happy," replied Annie, with heightened color. "I shall ever think you are satirical when you speak in such style."

"A truce, Miss Walton; only, in mercy to my poor mortality, be as human as you can. Though you seem to suspect me of a low estimate of your sex, I much prefer women to saints and Madonnas. I am going to look for the burr."

This was adroitness itself on the part of Gregory, for, of all things, sensible Annie, conscious of faults and many struggles, did not wish to give the impression that she thought herself approaching perfection. And yet he had managed to make her sensitive on that point, and given her a strong motive to relax strict rules of duty, and act "like other people," as he would say.

Jeff's limber pole was now doing effective service. With many a soft thud upon the sward and leaves the burrs rained around, while the detached chestnuts rattled down like hail. The children were careering about this little tempest of Jeff's manufacture in a state of wild glee, dodging the random burrs, and snatching what nuts they could in safety on the outskirts of the prickly shower. At last the tree was well thrashed, and bad the appearance of a school-boy bully who, after bristling with threats and boasts for a long time, suddenly meets his master and is left in a very meek and plucked condition.

But the moment Jeff's pole ceased its sturdy strokes there was a rush for the spoils, the children awakening the echoes with their exclamations of delight as they found the ground covered with what was more precious to them than gold. Even Gregory's sluggish pulses tingled and quickened at the well-remembered scene, and he felt a little of their excitement. For the moment he determined to be a boy again, and running into the charmed circle, picked away as fast as any of them till his physical weakness painfully reminded him that his old tireless activity had passed away, perhaps forever.

He leaned against the trunk of the tree and noted with something of an artist's eye the pretty picture. The valley beneath was beginning to glow with the richest October tints, in the midst of which was his old home, that to his affection seemed like a gem set in gold, ruby, and emerald. The stream appeared white and silvery as seen through openings of the bordering trees, and in the distance the purple haze and mountains blended together, leaving it uncertain where the granite began, as in Gregory's mind fact and fancy were confusedly mingling in regard to Miss Walton.

And he soon turned from even that loved and beautiful landscape to her as an object of piquant interest, and the pleasure of analyzing and testing her character, and--well, some hidden fascination of her own, caused a faint stir of excitement at his heart, even as the October air and exercise had just tinged his pale cheeks.

But Miss Walton reminded him of a young sugar maple that he had noticed, all aflame, from his window that morning, so rich and high was her color, as, still intent upon the thickly scattered nuts, she followed the old unspent childish impulse to gather now as she had done when of Susie's age. With a half-wondering smile Gregory watched her intent expression, so like that of the other children, and thought, "Well, she is the freshest and most unhackneyed girl I have ever met for one who knows so much. It seems true, as she said, that she draws her life from nature and will never grow old. Now she is a child with those children, looking and acting like them. A moment later she will be a self-possessed young lady, with a quick, trained intellect that I can scarcely cope with. And yet in each and every character she seems so real and vital that even I, in spite of myself, feel compelled to admit her truth. Her life is like a glad, musical mountain stream, while I am a stagnant pool that she passes and leaves behind. I wonder if it is possible for one life to be awakened and quickened by another. I wonder if her vital force would be strong enough to drag another on who had almost lost the power to follow. It is said that young fresh blood can be infused directly into the veins of the old and feeble. Can the same be true of moral forces, and a glad zest and interest in life be breathed into the jaded, cloyed, ennui-cursed spirit of one who regards existence with dull eye, sluggish pulse, and heart of lead? It seems to me that if any one could have such power it would be that girl there with her intense vitality and subtle connection with nature, which, as she says, is ever young and vigorous. And yet I propose to reveal her to herself as a weak, vain creature, whose fair seeming like a pasteboard castle falls before the breath of flattery. By Jove, I half hope I shan't succeed, and yet to satisfy myself I shall carry the test to the utmost limit."

In her absorbed search for nuts, Annie had approached the trunk of the tree, and was stooping almost at Gregory's feet without noticing him. Suddenly she turned up a burr whose appearance so interested her that she stood up to examine it, and then became conscious of his intent gaze.

"There you stand," she said, "cool and superior, criticising and laughing at me as a great overgrown child."

"If you had looked more closely you would have seen anything rather than cool criticism in my face. I wish you could tell me your secret, Miss Walton. What is your hidden connection with Nature, that her strong, beautiful life flows so freely into yours?"

"You would not believe me if I told you."

"Indeed, Miss Walton, I should be inclined to believe anything you told me, you seem so real. But, pardon me, you have in your hand the very burr I have been looking vainly for. Perhaps in it I may find the coveted clew to your favor. It may winningly suggest to you my meaning, while plain, bald words would only repel. If I could only interpret Nature as you breathe her spirit I might find that the autumn leaves were like illuminated pages, and every object--even such an insignificant one as this burr--an inspired illustration. When men come to read Nature's open book, publishers may despair. *If* I wished to tell you how I would dwell in your thoughts, what poet has written anything equal to this half-open burr? It portrays our past, it gives our present relations, and suggests the future; only, like all parables, it must not be pressed too far, and too much prominence must not be given to some mere detail. These prickly outward pointing spines represent the reserve and formality which keep comparative strangers apart. But now the burr is half-open, revealing its heart of silk and down. So if one could get past the barriers which you, alike with all, turn toward an indifferent or unfriendly world, a kindliness would be found that would surround a cherished friend as these silken sides envelop this sole and favored chestnut. Again, note that the burr is half-open, indicating, I hope, the progress we have made toward such friendship. I have no true friend in the wide world that I can trust, and I would like to believe that your regard, like this burr, is opening toward me. The final suggestion that I should draw may seem selfish, and yet is it not natural? This chestnut dwells alone in the very centre of the burr. We do not like to share a supreme friendship. There are some in whose esteem we would be first."

When Gregory finished he was half-frightened at his words, for in developing his fanciful parallel in the bold style of gallantry he had learned to employ toward the belles of the ball-room, and from a certain unaccountable fascination that Annie herself had for him, he had said more than he meant.

"Good heavens!" he thought, "if she should take this for a declaration and accept me on the spot, I should then be in the worst scrape of my sorry life."

Miss Walton's manner rather puzzled him. Her heightened color and quickened breathing were alarming, while the contraction of her brow and the firmness of her lips, together with an intent look on the chestnut in the centre of the burr, rather than a languishing look at him or at nothing, were more assuring. She perplexed him still more when, as her only response to all this sentiment, she asked, "Mr. Gregory, will you lend me your penknife?"

Without a word he handed it to her, and she at the same time took the burr from his hand, and daintily plucking out the chestnut tossed the burr rather contemptuously away. "Mr. Gregory, if I understand your rather far-fetched and forced interpretation of this little 'parable of nature,' you chose to represent yourself by this great lonely chestnut occupying the space where three might have grown. On observing this emblematic nut closely I detect something that may also have a place in your 'parable';" and she pushed aside the little quirl at the small end of the nut, which partially concealed a worm-hole, and cutting through the shell showed the destroyer in the very heart of the kernel.

There was nothing far-fetched in this suggestion of nature, and he saw--and he understood that Miss Walton saw--evil enthroned in the very depths of his soul. The revelation of the hateful truth was so sudden and sharp that his face darkened with involuntary pain and anger. It seemed to him that, by the simple act of showing him the worm-infested chestnut, she had rejected anything approaching even friendship, and had also given him a good but humiliating reason why. He lost his self-possession and forgot that he deserved a stinging rebuke for his insincerity. He would have turned away in coldness and resentment. His visit might have come to an abrupt termination, had not Annie, with that delicate, womanly tact which was one of her most marked characteristics, interrupted him as he was about to say something to the effect, "Miss Walton, since you are so much holier than I, it were better that I should contaminate the air you breathe no longer."

She looked into his clouded face with an open smile, and said, "Mr. Gregory, you have been unfortunate in the choice of a burr. Now let me choose for you;" and she began looking around for one suited to her taste and purpose.

This gave him time to recover himself and to realize the folly of quarrelling or showing any special feeling in the matter. After a moment he was only desirous of some pretext for laughing it off, but how to manage it he did not know, and was inwardly cursing himself as a blundering fool, and no match for this child of nature.

Annie soon came toward him, saying, "Perhaps this burr will suggest better meanings. You see it is wide open. That means perfect frankness. There are three chestnuts here instead of one. We must be willing to share the regard of others. One of these nuts has the central place. As we come to know people well, we usually find some one occupying the supreme place in their esteem, and though we may approach closely we should not wish to usurp what belongs to another. Under Jeff's vigorous blows the burr and its contents have had a tremendous downfall, but they have not parted company. True friends should stick together in adversity. What do you think of my interpretation?"

"I think you are a witch, beyond doubt, and if you had lived a few centuries ago, you would have been sent to heaven in a chariot of fire."

"Really, Mr. Gregory, you give me a ***hot*** answer, but it is with such a smiling face that I will take no exception. Let us slowly follow Jeff and the children along the brow of the hill to the next tree. The fact is I am a little tired."

What controversy could a man have with a pretty and wearied girl? Gregory felt like a boy who had received a deserved whipping and yet was compelled and somewhat inclined to act very amiably toward the donor. But he was fast coming to the conclusion that this unassuming country girl was a difficult subject on which to perform his experiment. He was learning to have a wholesome respect for her that was slightly tinged with fear, and doubts of success in his plot against her grew stronger every moment. And yet the element of persistence was large in his character, and he could not readily give over his purpose, though his cynical confidence had vanished. He now determined to observe her closely and discover if possible her weak points. He still held to the theory that flattery was the most available weapon, though he saw he could employ it no longer in the form of fulsome and outspoken compliment. The innate refinement and truthfulness of Annie's nature revolted at broad gallantry and adulation. He believed that he must reverse the tactics he usually employed in society, but not the principles. Therefore he resolved that his flattery should be delicate, subtle, manifested in manner rather than in words. He would seem submissive; he would humbly wear the air of a conquered one. He would delicately maintain the "I-am-at- your-mercy" attitude.

These thoughts flashed through his mind as they passed along the brow of the hill, which at every turn gave them a new and beautiful landscape. But vales in Eden would not have held his attention then. To his perplexity this new acquaintance had secured his undivided interest. He felt that he ought to be angry at her and yet was not. He felt that a man who had seen as much of the world as he should be able to play with this little country girl as with a child; but he was becoming convinced that, with all his art, he was no match for her artlessness.

In the interpretation of the burr of her own choice, Annie had suggested that the central and supreme place in her heart was already occupied, and his thoughts recurred frequently to that fact with uneasiness. The slightest trace of jealousy, even as the merest twinge of pain is often precursor of serious disease, indicated the power Miss Walton might gain over one who thought himself proof against all such influence. But he tried to satisfy himself by thinking, "It is her father who occupies the first place in her affections."

Then a moment later with a mental protest at his folly, "What do I care who has the first place? It's well I do not, for she would not permit such a reprobate as I, with evil in my heart like that cursed worm in the chestnut, to have any place worth naming--unless I can introduce a little canker of evil in her heart also. I wish I could. That would bring us nearer together and upon the same level." Annie saw the landscapes. She looked away from the man by her side and for a few moments forgot him. The scenes upon which she was gazing were associated with another, and she ardently wished that that other and more favored one could exchange places with Gregory. Her eyes grew dreamy and tender as she recalled words spoken in days gone by, when, her heart thrilling with a young girl's first dream of love, she had leaned upon Charles Hunting's arm, and listened to that sweetest music of earth, all the more enchanting when broken and incoherent; and Hunting, with all his coolness and precision in Wall Street, had been excessively nervous and unhappy in his phraseology upon one occasion, and tremblingly glad to get any terms from the girl who seemed a child beside him. Annie would not permit an engagement to take place. Hunting was a distant relative. She had always liked him very much, but was not sure she loved him. She was extremely reluctant to leave her father, and was not ready for a speedy marriage; so she frankly told him that he had no rival, nor was there a prospect of any, but she would not bind him, or permit herself to be bound at that time. If they were fated for each other the way would eventually be made perfectly clear.

He was quite content, especially as Mr. Walton gave his hearty approval to the match, and he regarded the understanding as a virtual engagement. He wanted Annie to wear the significant ring, saying that it should not be regarded as binding, but she declined to do so.

Nearly two years had passed, and, while she put him off, she satisfied him that he was steadily gaining the place that he wished to possess in her affections. He was gifted with much tact and did not press his suit, but quietly acted as if the matter were really settled, and it were only a question of time. Annie had also come to feel in the same way. She did not see a very great deal of him, though he wrote regularly, and his letters were admirable. He became her ideal man and dwelt in her imagination as a demi-god. To the practical mind of this American girl his successes in the vast and complicated transactions of business were as grand as the achievements of any hero. Her father had been a merchant, and she inherited a respect for the calling. Her father also often assured her that her lover bade fair to lead in commercial circles.

"Hunting has both nerve and prudence," he was wont to say; and to impetuous Annie these qualities, combined with Christian principles, formed her very ideal man.

Her lover took great pains not to undeceive her as to his character, and indeed, with the infatuation of his class, hoped that, when he had amassed the fortune that glittered ever just before him, he could assume, in some princely mansion, the princely, knightly soul with which she had endowed him.

So he did not press matters. Indeed in his rapid accumulation of money he scarcely wished any interruption, and Annie thought all the more of him that he was not dawdling around making love half the time. There was also less danger of disenchanting her by his presence, for woman's perception is quick.

But now she inwardly contrasted her strong, masterful knight, "***sans peur et sans reproche***," as she believed, with the enfeebled, shrunken man at her side. Gregory suffered dreadfully by the comparison. The worm-eaten chestnut seemed truly emblematic, and in spite of herself her face lighted up with exultation and joy that the man of her choice was a ***man***, and not one upon whom she could not lean for even physical support.

Gregory caught her expression and said, quickly: "Your face is full of sudden gleams. Tell me what you are thinking about."

She blushed deeply in the consciousness of her thoughts, but after a moment said, "I do not believe in the confessional."

He looked at her keenly, saying, "I wish you did and that I were your father confessor."

She replied, laughing, "You are neither old nor good enough. If I were of that faith I should require one a great deal older and better than myself. But here we are at our second tree, which Jeff has just finished. I am going to be a child again and gather nuts as before. I hope you will follow suit, and not stand leaning against the tree laughing at me."

CHAPTER XIV
"A WELL-MEANIN' MAN"

The western horizon vied with the autumn foliage as at last they turned homeward. Their path led out upon the main road some distance above the house, and, laden with the spoils that would greatly diminish the squirrels' hoard for the coming winter, they sauntered along slowly, from a sense of both weariness and leisure.

They soon reached the cottage of the lame old man who had fired such a broadside of lurid words at Gregory, as he stood on the fence opposite. With a crutch under one arm and leaning on his gate, Daddy Tuggar seemed awaiting them, and secured their attention by the laconic salutation, "Evenin'!"

"Why, Daddy," exclaimed Annie, coming quickly toward him. "I am real glad to see you so spry and well. It seems to me that you are getting young again;" and she shook the old man's hand heartily.

"Now don't praise my old graveyard of a body, Miss Annie. My sperit is pert enough, but it's all buried up in this old clumsy, half-dead carcass. The worms will close their mortgage on it purty soon."

"But they haven't a mortgage on your soul," said Annie, in a low tone. "You remember what I said to you a few days ago."

"Now bless you, Miss Annie, but it takes you to put in a 'word in season.' The Lord knows I'm a well-meanin' man, but I can't seem to get much furder. I've had an awful 'fall from grace,' my wife says. I did try to stop swearin', but that chap there--"

"Oh, excuse me," interrupted Annie. "Mr. Gregory, this is our friend and neighbor Mr. Tuggar. I was under the impression that you were acquainted," she added, with a mischievous look at her companion.

"We are. I have met this gentleman before," he replied, with a wry face. "Pardon the interruption, Mr. Tuggar, and please go on with your explanation."

"Mr. Gregory, I owe you a 'pology. I'm a well-meanin' man, and if I do any one a wrong I'm willin' to own it up and do the square thing. But I meant right by you and I meant right by John Walton when I thought you was stealin' his apples. I couldn't hit yer with a stun and knock yer off the fence, as I might a dozen years ago, so I took the next hardest thing I could lay hands on. If I'd known that you was kinder one of the family my words would have been rolls of butter."

"Well, Mr. Tuggar, it has turned out very well, for *I* would rather you had fired what you did than either stones or butter."

"Now my wife would say that that speech showed you was 'totally depraved.' And this brings me back to my 'fall from grace.' Now, yer see, to please my wife some and Miss Eulie more, I was tryin' cussed hard to stop swearin'--"

"Didn't you try a little for my sake, too?" interrupted Annie.

"Lord bless you, child; I don't have to try when you're around, for I don't think swearin'. Most folks rile me, and I get a-thinkin' swearin', and then 'fore I know it busts right out. *You* could take the wickedest cuss livin' to heaven in spite of himself if you would stay right by him all the time."

"I should 'rile' you, too, if I were with you long, for I get 'riled' myself sometimes."

"Do you, now?" asked Mr. Tuggar, looking at her admiringly. "Well, I'm mighty glad to hear it."

"O Daddy! glad to hear that I do wrong?"

"Can't help it, Miss Annie. I kinder like to know you're a little bit of a sinner. 'Tain't often I meet with a sinner, and I kind o' like 'em. My wife says she's a 'great sinner,' but she means she's a great saint. 'Twouldn't do for me to tell her she's a 'sinner.' Then Miss Eulie says she's a 'great sinner,' and between you and me that's the only fib I ever caught Miss Eulie in. Good Lord! there's no more sin in Miss Eulie's heart than there is specks of dirt on the little white ruff she wears about her neck that looks like the snow we had last April around the white hyacinths. She's kind of a half-sperit anyhow. Now your goodness, Miss Annie, is another kind. Your cheeks are so red, and eyes so black, and arms so round and fat--I've seen 'em when you was over here a-beatin' up good things for the old man--that you make me think of red and pink posies. I kinder think you might be a little bit of a sinner-- just enough, you know, to make you understand how I and him there can be mighty big ones, and not be too hard on us for it."

"Mr. Tuggar, you are the man of all others to plead my cause."

"Now look here, young gentleman, you must do yer own pleadin'. It would be a 'sinful waste of time' though, as my wife would say--eh, Miss Annie? I never had no luck at pleadin' but once, and that was the worst luck of all."

Annie's face might well suggest "red posies" during the last remarks, and its expression was divided between a frown and a laugh.

"But I want you to understand," continued Daddy Tuggar, straightening himself up with dignity, and addressing Gregory, "that I'm not a mean cuss. All who know me know I'm a well-meanin' man. I try to do as I'd be done by. If I'm going through a man's field and find his bars down, so the cattle would get in the corn, I'd put 'em up--"

"Yes, Daddy, that is what you always say," interrupted Annie; "but you can't go through the fields any more and put up bars. You should try to do the duties that belong to your present state."

"But I've got the sperit to put up a man's bars, and it's all the same as if I did put 'em up," answered the old man, with some irritation. "Miss Eulie and the rest of yer is allers sayin' we must have the sperit of willingness to give up the hull world and suffer martyrdom on what looks in the picture like a big gridiron. She says we must have the sperit of them who was cold and hungry and the lions eat up and was sawn in two pieces and had an awful time generally for the sake of the Lord, and that's the way the Christians manage it nowadays. My wife gets all the money she can and keeps it, but she says she has the sperit to give up the hull world. I wish she'd give up enough of it to keep me in good terbacker. Mighty few nice bits would the old man git wasn't it for you and Miss Eulie. Then I watch the good people goin' to church. 'Mazin' few out wet Sundays. But no doubt they've all got the 'sperit' to go. They would jist as lief be sawn in two pieces 'in sperit' as not, if they can only sleep late in the mornin' and have a good dinner and save their Sunday-go-to-meetin' clothes from gettin' wet. It must be so, for the Lord gets mighty little worship out of the church on rainy Sundays. If it wasn't for you and Miss Eulie I don't know what would become of the old man and all the rest of the sick and feeble foiks around here. I ask my wife why she doesn't go to see 'em sometimes. She says she has the 'sperit to go,' but she hasn't time and strength. So I have the 'sperit' to put up a man's bars while I sit here and smoke, and what's more, Miss Annie, I did it as long as I was able."

"You did indeed, Daddy, and, though unintentionally, you have given me a good lesson. We little deserve to be mentioned with those Christians who in olden times suffered the loss of all things, and life itself."

"Lord bless you, child, I didn't mean you. Whether you've got the sperit to do a thing or not yer allers do it, and in a sweet, natteral way, as if you couldn't help it. When my wife enters on a good work it makes me think of a funeral. I'm 'mazin' glad you didn't live in old times, 'cause the lions would have got you sure 'nuff. Though, if it had to be, I would kinder liked to have been the lion:" and the old man's eyes twinkled humorously, while Gregory laughed heartily.

"Oh, Daddy Tuggar!" exclaimed Annie, "that is the most awful compliment I ever received. If you, with your spirit, were the only lion I had to deal with, I should never become a martyr. You shall have some jelly instead, and now I must go home in order to have it made before Sunday."

"Wait a moment," said Gregory. "You were about to tell us how I caused you to 'fall from grace.'"

"So I was, so I was, and I've been goin' round Robin Hood's barn ever since. Well, I'd been holdin' in on my swearin' a long time, 'cause I promised Miss Eulie I'd stop if I could. My wife said I was in quite a 'hopeful state,' while I felt all the time as if I was sort of bottled up and the cork might fly out any minute. Miss Eulie, she came and rejoiced over me that mornin', and my wife she looked so solemn (she allers does when she says she feels glad) that somehow I got nervous, and then my wife went to the store and didn't get the kind of terbacker I sent for, and I knew the cork was going to fly out. I was smokin' and in a sort of a doze, when the first thing I knowed a big stun rolled into the road, and there I saw a strange chap, as I thought, a stealin' John Walton's apples and knockin' down the fence. If they'd a been my apples I might have held in a little longer, but John Walton's--it was like a dam givin' way."

"It was, indeed," said Gregory, significantly. "It was like several."

"I knowed my wife heard me, and if she'd come right out and said, 'You've made a cussed old fool of yourself,' I think I would have felt better. I knowed she was goin' to speak about it and lament over it, and I wanted her to do it right away; but she put it off, and kept me on pins and needles for ever so long. At last she said with solemn joy, 'Thomas Tuggar, I told Miss Eulie I feared you was still in a state of natur, and, alas! I am right; but how she'll mourn, how great will be her disappointment, when she hears'; and then I fell into a 'state of natur' agin. Now, Miss Annie, if the Lord, Miss Eulie, and you all could only see I'm a well-meanin' man, and that I don't mean no disrespect to anybody; that it's only one of my old, rough ways that I learned from my father--and mother too, for that matter, I'm sorry to say--and have followed so long that it's bred in the bone, it would save a heap of worry. One must have some way of lettin' off steam. Now my wife she purses up her mouth so tight you couldn't stick a pin in it when she's riled. I often say to her, 'Do explode. Open your mouth and let it all out at once.' But she says it is not becoming for such as her ter 'explode.' But it will come out all the same, only it's like one of yer cold northeast, drizzlin', fizzlin' rain-storms. And now I've made a clean breast of it, I hope you'll kinder smooth matters over with Miss Eulie; and I hope you, sir, will just think of what I said as spoken to a stranger and not a friend of the family."

"Give me your hand, Mr. Tuggar. I hope we shall be the best of friends. I am coming over to have a smoke with you, and see if I can't fill your pipe with some tobacco that is like us both, 'in a state of natur.'"

A white-faced woman appeared at the door, and courtesying low to Miss Walton, called, "Husband, it's too late for you to be out; I fear your health will suffer."

"She's bound up in me, you see," said the old man, with a curious grimace. "Nothing but the reading of my will will ever comfort her when I die."

"Daddy, Daddy," said Annie, reproachfully, "have charity. Good-night; I will send you something nice for to-morrow."

An amused smile lingered on Gregory's face as they pursued their way homeward, now in the early twilight; but Annie's aspect was almost one of sadness. After a little he said, "Well, he is one of the oddest specimens of humanity I ever met."

She did not immediately reply, and he, looking at her, caught her expression.

"Why is your face so clouded, Miss Annie?" he asked. "You are not given to Mrs. Tuggar's style of 'solemn joy'?"

"What a perplexing mystery life is after all!" she replied, absently. "I really think poor old Daddy Tuggar speaks truly. He is a 'well- meaning' man, but he and many others remind me of one not having the slightest ear for music trying to catch a difficult harmony."

"Why is the harmony so difficult?" asked Gregory, bitterly.

"Perhaps it were better to ask, Why has humanity so disabled itself?"

"I do not think it matters much how you put the case. It amounts to the same thing. Something is required of us beyond our strength. The idea of punishing that old man for being what he is, when in the first place he inherited evil from his parents, and then was taught it by precept and example. I think he deserves more credit than blame."

"The trouble is, Mr. Gregory, evil carries its own punishment along with it every day. But I admit that we are surrounded by mystery on every side. Humanity, left to itself, is a hopeless problem. But one thing is certain: we are not responsible for questions beyond our ken. Moreover, many things that were complete mysteries to me as a child are now plain, and I ever hope to be taught something new every day. You and I at least have much to be grateful for in the fact that we neither inherited evil nor were taught it in any such degree as our poor neighbor."

"And you quietly prove, Miss Walton, by your last remark, that I am much more worthy of blame than your poor old neighbor."

"Then I said more than I meant," she answered, eagerly. "It is not for me to judge or condemn any one. The thought in my mind was how favored we have been in our parentage--our start in existence, as it were."

"But suppose one loses that vantage-ground?"

"I do not wish to suppose anything of the kind."

"But one can lose it utterly."

"I fear some can and do. But why dwell on a subject so unutterably sad and painful? You have not lost it, and, as I said before to-day, I will not dwell upon the disagreeable any more than I can help."

"Your opinion of me is poor enough already, Miss Walton, so I, too, will drop the subject."

They had now reached the house, and did ample justice to the supper awaiting them.

Between meals people can be very sentimental, morbid, and tragical. They can stare at life's deep mysteries and shudder or scoff, sigh or rejoice, according to their moral conditions. They can even grow cold with dread, as did Gregory, realizing that he had "lost his vantage- ground," his good start in the endless career. "She is steering across unknown seas to a peaceful, happy shore. I am drifting on those same mysterious waters I know not whither," he thought. But a few minutes after entering the cheerfully lighted dining-room he was giving his whole soul to muffins.

These homely and ever-recurring duties and pleasures of life have no doubt saved multitudes from madness. It would almost seem that they have also been the innocent cause of the destruction of many. There are times when the mind is almost evenly balanced between good and evil. Some powerful appeal or startling providence has aroused the sleeping spirit, or some vivifying truth has pierced the armor of indifference or prejudice, and quivered like an arrow in the soul, and the man remembers that he is a man, and not a brute that perishes. But just then the dinner-bell sounds. After the several courses, any physician can predict how the powers of that human organization must of necessity be employed the next few hours, and the partially awakened soul is like one who starts out of a doze and sleeps again. If the spiritual nature had only become sufficiently aroused to realize the situation, *life* might have been secured. Thought and feeling in some emergencies will do more than the grandest pulpit eloquence quenched by a Sunday dinner.

CHAPTER XV
MISS WALTON'S DREAM

The hickory fire burned cheerily in the parlor after tea, and all drew gladly around its welcome blaze. But even the delights of roasting chestnuts from the abundant spoils of the afternoon could not keep the heads of the children from drooping early.

Gregory was greatly fatigued, and soon went to his room also.

Sabbath morning dawned dim and uncertain, and by the time they had gathered at the breakfast-table, a northeast rain-storm had set in with a driving gale.

"I suppose you will go to church 'in sperit' this morning, as Mr. Tuggar would say," said Gregory, addressing Annie.

"If I were on the sick list I should, but I have no such excuse."

"You seriously do not mean to ride two miles in such a storm as this?"

"No, not seriously, but very cheerfully and gladly."

"I do not think it is required of you, Miss Walton. Even your Bible states, 'I will have mercy and not sacrifice.'"

"The 'sacrifice' in my case would be in staying at home. I like to be out in a storm, and have plenty of warm blood to resist its chilling effects. But even were it otherwise, what hardship is there in my wrapping myself up in a waterproof and riding a few miles to a comfortable church? I shall come back with a grand appetite and a double zest for the wood fire."

"But it is not fair on the poor horses. They have no waterproofs or wood fires."

"I think I am not indifferent to the comfort of dumb animals, and though I drive a good deal, father can tell you I am not a 'whip.' Of all shams the most transparent is this tenderness for one's self and the horses on Sunday. I am often out in stormy weather during the week, and meet plenty of people on the road. The farmers drive to the village on rainy days because they can neither plow, sow, nor reap. But on even a cloudy Sabbath, with the faintest prospect of rain, there is but one text in the Bible for them: 'A righteous man regardeth the life of his beast.' People attend parties, the opera, and places of amusement no matter how bad the night. It is a miserable pretence to say that the weather keeps the majority at home from church. It is only an excuse. I should have a great deal more respect for them if they would say frankly, 'We would rather sleep, read a novel, dawdle around *en deshabille*, and gossip.' Half the time when they say it's too stormy to venture out (oh, the heroism of our Christian age!), they should go and thank God for the rain that is providing food for them and theirs.

"And granting that our Christian duties do involve some risk and hardship, does not the Bible ever speak of life as a warfare, a struggle, an agonizing for success? Do not armies often fight and march in the rain, and dumb beasts share their exposure? There is more at stake in this battle. In ancient times God commanded the bloody sacrifice of innumerable animals for the sake of moral and religious effect. Moral and religious effect is worth just as much now. Nothing can excuse wanton cruelty; but the soldier who spurs his horse against the enemy, and the sentinel who keeps his out in a winter storm, are not cruel. But many farmers about here will over-work and underfeed all the week, and on Sunday talk about being 'merciful to their beasts.' There won't be over twenty-five out to-day, and the Christian heroes, the sturdy yeomanry of the church, will be dozing and grumbling in chimney-corners. The languid half-heartedness of the church discourages me more than all the evil in the world."

Miss Walton stated her views in a quiet undertone of indignation, and not so much in answer to Gregory as in protest against a style of action utterly repugnant to her earnest, whole-souled nature. As he saw the young girl's face light up with the will and purpose to be loyal to a noble cause, his own aimless, self-pleasing life seemed petty and contemptible indeed, and again he had that painful sense of humiliation which Miss Walton unwittingly caused him; but, as was often his way, he laughed the matter off by saying, "There is no need of my going to-day, for I have had my sermon, and a better one than you will hear. Still, such is the effect of your homily that I am inclined to ask you to take me with you."

Annie's manner changed instantly, and she smilingly answered, "You will find an arm-chair before a blazing fire in your room upstairs, and an arm-chair before a blazing fire in the parlor, and you can vacillate between them at your pleasure."

"As a vacillating man should, perhaps you might add."

"I add nothing of the kind."

"Will you never let me go to church with you again?"

"Certainly, after what you said, any pleasant day."

"Why can't I have the privilege of being a martyr as well as yourself?"

"I am not a martyr. I would far rather go out to-day than stay at home."

"It will be very lonely without you."

"Oh, you are the martyr then, after all. I hope you will have sufficient fortitude to endure, and doze comfortably during the two hours of my absence."

"Now you are satirical on Sunday, Miss Walton. Let that burden your conscience. I'm going to ask your father if I may go."

"Of course you will act at your pleasure," said Mr. Walton, "but I think, in your present state of health, Annie has suggested the wiser and safer thing to do."

"I should probably be ill on your hands if I went, so I submit; but I wish you to take note, Miss Walton, that I have the 'sperit to go.'"

The arm-chairs were cosey and comfortable, and the hickory wood turned, as is its wont, into glowing and fragrant coals, but the house grew chill and empty the moment that Annie left. Though Mr. Walton and Miss Eulie accompanied her, their absence was rather welcome, but he felt sure that Annie could have beguiled the heavy-footed hours.

"She has some unexplained power of making me forget my miserable self," he muttered.

And yet, left to himself, he had now nothing to do but think, and a fearful time he had of it, lowering at the fire, in the arm-chair, from which he scarcely stirred.

"I have lost my vantage-ground," he groaned--"lost it utterly. I am not even a 'well-meaning man.' I purpose evil against this freshest, purest spirit I have ever known since in this house I looked into my mother's eyes. I am worse than the wild Arab of the desert. I have eaten salt with them; I have partaken of their generous hospitality, given so cordially for the sake of one that is dead, and in return have wounded their most sacred feelings, and now propose to prove the daughter a creature that I can go away and despise. Instead of being glad that there is one in the world noble and good, even though by accident--instead of noting with pleasure that every sweet flower has not become a weed--I wish to drag her down to my own wretched level, or else I would have her exhibit sufficient weakness to show that she would go as far as she was tempted to go. A decent devil could hardly wish her worse. I would like to see her show the same spirit that animates Miss Belle St. Glair of New York, or Mrs. Grobb, my former adored Miss Bently--creatures that I despise as I do myself, and what more could I say? If I could only cause her to show some of their characteristics the reproach of her life would pass away, and I should be confirmed in my belief that humanity's unutterable degradation is its misfortune, and the blame should rest elsewhere than on us. How absurd to blame water for running down hill! Give man or woman half a chance, that is, before habits are fixed, and they plunge faster down the inclined moral plane. And the plague of it is, this seeming axiom does not satisfy me. What business has my conscience, with a lash of scorpion stings, to punish me this and every day that I permit myself to think? Did I not try for years to be better? Did I not resist the infernal gravitation? and yet I am falling still. I never did anything so mean and low before as I am doing now. If it is my nature to do evil, why should I not do it without compunction? And as I look downward--there is no looking forward for me--there seems no evil thing that I could not do if so inclined. Here in this home of my childhood, this sacred atmosphere that my mother breathed, I would besmirch the character of one who as yet is pure and good, with a nature like a white hyacinth in spring. I see the vileness of the act, I loathe it, and yet it fascinates me, and I have no power to resist. Why should a stern, condemning voice declare in recesses of my soul, 'You could and should resist'? For years I have been daily yielding to temptation, and conscience as often pronounces sentence against me. When will the hateful farce cease? Multitudes appear to sin without thought or remorse. Why cannot I? It's my mother's doings, I suppose. A plague upon the early memories of this place. Will they keep me upon the rack forever?"

He rose, strode up and down the parlor, and clenched his hands in passionate protest against himself, his destiny, and the God who made him.

A chillness, resulting partly from dread and partly from the wild storm raging without, caused him to heap up the hearth with wood. It speedily leaped into flame, and, covering his face with his hands, he sat cowering before it. A vain but frequent thought recurred to him with double power.

"Oh that I could cease to exist, and lose this miserable consciousness! Oh that, like this wood, I could be aflame with intense, passionate life, and then lose identity, memory, and everything that makes *me*, and pass into other forms. Nay, more, if I had my wish, I would become nothing here and now."

The crackling of flames and the rush of wind and rain against the windows had caused the sound of wheels, and a light step in the room, to be unheard.

He was aroused by Miss Walton, who asked, "Mr. Gregory, are you ill?"

He raised his woe-begone face to hers, and said, almost irritably, "Yes--no--or at least I am as well as I ever expect to be, and perhaps better." Then with a sudden impulse he asked, "Does annihilation seem such a dreadful thing to you?"

"What! the losing of an eternity of keen enjoyment? Could anything be more dreadful! Really, Mr. Gregory, brooding here alone has not been good for you. Why do you not think of pleasant things?"

"For the same reason that a man with a raging toothache does not have pleasant sensations," he answered, with a grim smile.

"I admit the force of your reply, though I do not think the case exactly parallel. The mind is not as helpless as the body. Still, I believe it is true that when the body is suffering the mind is apt to become the prey of all sorts of morbid fancies, and you do look really ill. I wish I could give you some of my rampant health and spirits to- day. Facing the October storm has done me good every way, and I am ravenous for dinner."

He looked at her enviously as she stood before him, with her waterproof, still covered with rain-drops, partially thrown back and revealing the outline of a form which, though not stout, was suggestive of health and strength. She seemed, with her warm, high color, like a hardy flower covered with spray. Instead of shrinking feebly and delicately from the harsher moods of nature, and coming in pinched and shivering, she had felt the blood in her veins and all the wheels of life quickened by the gale.

"Miss Walton," he said, with a glimmer of a smile, "do you know that you are very different from most young ladies? You and nature evidently have some deep secrets between you. I half believe you never will grow old, but are one of the perennials. I am glad you have come home, for you seem to bring a little of yesterday's sunshine into the dreary house."

As they returned to the parlor after dinner, Gregory remarked, "Miss Walton, what can you do to interest me this afternoon, for I am devoured with ennui?"

She turned upon him rather quickly and said, "A young man like you has no business to be 'devoured with ennui.' Why not engage in some pursuit, or take up some subject that will interest you and stir your pulse?"

With a touch of his old mock gallantry he bowed and said, "In you I see just the subject, and am delighted to think I'm going to have you all to myself this rainy afternoon."

With a half-vexed laugh and somewhat heightened color she answered, "I imagine you won't have me all to yourself long."

She had hardly spoken the words before the children bounded in, exclaiming, "Now, Aunt Annie, for our stories."

"You see, Mr. Gregory, here are previous and counter-claims already."

"I wish I knew of some way of successfully disputing them."

"It would be difficult to find. Well, come, little people, we will go into the sitting-room and not disturb Mr. Gregory."

"Now, I protest against that," he said. "You might at least let me be one of the children."

"But the trouble is, you won't be one, but will sit by criticising and laughing at our infantile talk."

"Now you do me wrong. I will be as good as I can, and if you knew how long and dreary the day has been you would not refuse."

She looked at him keenly for a moment, and then said, a little doubtfully, "Well, I will try for once. Run and get your favorite Sunday books, children."

When they were alone he asked, "How can you permit these youngsters to be such a burden?"

"They are not a burden," she answered.

"But a nurse could take care of them and keep them quiet."

"If their father and mother were living they would not think 'keeping them quiet' all their duty toward them, nor do I, to whom they were left as a sacred trust."

"That awful word 'duty' rules you, Miss Walton, with a rod of iron."

"Do I seem like a harshly driven slave?" she asked, smilingly.

"No, and I cannot understand you."

"That is because your philosophy of life is wrong. You still belong to that old school who would have it that sun, moon, and stars revolve around the earth. But here are the books, and if you are to be one of the children you must do as I bid you--be still and listen."

It was strange to Gregory how content he was to obey. He was surprised at his interest in the old Bible stories told in childish language, and as Annie stopped to explain a point or answer a question, he found himself listening as did the eager little boy sitting on the floor at her feet. The hackneyed man of the world could not understand how the true, simple language of nature, like the little brown blossoms of lichens, has a beauty of its own.

At the same time he had a growing consciousness that perhaps there was something in the reader also which mainly held his interest. It was pleasant to listen to the low, musical voice. It was pleasant to see the red lips drop the words so easily yet so distinctly, and chief of all was the consciousness of a vitalized presence that made the room seem full when she was in it, and empty when she was absent, though all others remained.

He truly shared the children's regret when at last she said, "Now I am tired, and must go upstairs and rest awhile before supper, after which we will have some music. You can go into the sitting-room and look at the pictures till the tea-bell rings. Mr. Gregory, will my excuse to the children answer for you also?"

"I suppose it must, though I have no pictures to look at."

She suddenly appeared to change her mind, and said, briskly, "Come, sir, what you need is work for others. I have read to you, and you ought to be willing to read to me. If you please, I will rest in the arm-chair here instead of in my room."

"I will take your medicine," he said, eagerly, "without a wry face, though an indifferent reader, while I think you are a remarkably good one; and let me tell you it is one of the rarest accomplishments we find. You shall also choose the book."

"What unaccountable amiableness!" she replied, laughing. "I fear I shall reward you by going to sleep."

"Very well, anything so I am not left alone again. I am wretched company for myself."

"Oh, it is not for my sake you are so good, after all!"

"You think me a selfish wretch, Miss Walton."

"I think you are like myself, capable of much improvement. But I wish to rest, and you must not talk, but read. There is the 'Schonberg- Cotta Family.' I have been over it two or three times, so if I lose the thread of the story it does not matter."

He wheeled the arm-chair up to the fire for her, and for a while she listened with interest; but at last her lids drooped and soon closed, and her regular breathing showed that she was sleeping. His voice sank in lower and lower monotone lest his sudden stopping should awaken her, then he laid down his book and read a different story in the pure young face turned toward him.

"It is not beautiful," he thought, "but it is a real, good face. I should not be attracted toward it in a thronged and brilliant drawing- room. I might not notice it on Fifth Avenue, but if I were ill and in deep trouble, it is just such a face as I should like to see bending over me. Am I not ill and in deep trouble? I have lost my health and lost my manhood. What worse disasters this side death can I experience? Be careful, Walter Gregory, you may be breaking the one clew that can lead you out of the labyrinth. You may be seeking to palsy the one hand that can help you. Mother believed in a special Providence. Is it her suggestion that now flashes in my mind that God in mercy has brought me to this place of sacred memories, and given me the companionship of this good woman, that the bitter waters of my life may be sweetened? I do not know from whom else it can come.

"And yet the infernal fascination of evil! I cannot--I will not give up my purpose toward her. Vain dreams! Miss Walton or an angel of light could not reclaim me. My impetus downward is too great.

"Oh, the rest and peace of that face! Physical rest and a quiet, happy spirit dwell in every line. She sleeps there like a child, little dreaming that a demon is watching her. But she says that she is guarded. Perhaps she is. A strong viewless one with a flaming sword may stand between her and me.

"Weak fool! Enough of this. I shall carry out my experiment fully, and when I have succeeded or failed, I can come to some conclusion on matters now in doubt.

"I should like to kiss those red parted lips. I wonder what she would do if I did?" Annie's brow darkened into a frown. Suddenly she started up and looked at him, but seemed satisfied from his distance and motionless aspect.

"What is the matter?" he asked.

"Oh, nothing. I had a dream," she said, with a slight flush.

"Please tell it," he said, though he feared her answer.

"You will not like it. Besides, it's too absurd."

"You pique my curiosity. Tell it by all means."

"Well, then, you mustn't be angry; and remember, I have no faith in sleeping vagaries. I dreamed that you were transformed into a large tiger, and came stealthily to bite me."

He was startled as he recalled his thought at the moment of her awaking, but had the presence of mind to say, "Let me interpret the dream."

"Well."

"You know, I suppose, that dreams go by contraries. Suppose a true friend wished to steal a kiss in your unconsciousness."

"True friends do not steal from us," she replied, laughing. "I don't know whether it was safe to let you read me to sleep?"

"It's not wrong to be tempted, is it? One can't help that. As Mr. Tuggar says, I might have the 'sperit to do it,' and yet remain quietly in my chair, as I have."

"You make an admission in your explanation. Well, it was queer," she added, absently.

Gregory thought so too, and was annoyed at her unexpected clairvoyant powers. But he said, as if a little piqued, "If you think me a tiger you had better not sleep within my reach, or you may find your face sadly mutilated on awaking."

"Nonsense," she said. "Mr. Gregory, you are a gentleman. We are talking like foolish children."

The tea-bell now rang, and Gregory obeyed its summons in a very perplexed state. His manner was rather absent during the meal, but Annie seemed to take pains to be kind and reassuring. The day, so far from being a restraint, appeared one of habitual cheerfulness, which even the dreary storm without could not dampen.

"We shall have a grand sing to-night with the assistance of your voice, I hope, Mr. Gregory," said Mr. Walton, as they all adjourned to the parlor.

"I do not sing by note," he replied. "When I can I will join you, though I much prefer listening to Miss Walton."

"Miss Walton prefers nothing of the kind, and we shall sing only what you know," she said, with a smiling glance at him over her shoulder, as she was making selections from the music-stand.

Soon they were all standing round the piano, save Mr. Walton, who sat near in his arm-chair, his face the picture of placid enjoyment as he looked on the little group so dear to him. They began with the children's favorites from the Sabbath-school books, the little boy dutifully finding the place for his grandfather. Many of them were the same that Gregory had sung long years before, standing in the same place, a child like Johnny, and the vivid memories thus recalled made his voice a little husky occasionally. Annie once gave him a quick look of sympathy, not curious but appreciative.

"She seems to know what is passing in my soul," he thought; "I never knew a woman with such intuitions."

The combined result of their voices was true home music, in which were blended the tones of childhood and age. Annie, with her sweet soprano, led, and gave time and key to them all, very much as by the force and loveliness of her character she influenced the daily harmony of their lives. The children, with their imitative faculty, seemed to gather from her lips how to follow with fair correctness, and they chirped through the tunes like two intelligent robins. Miss Eulie sang a sweet though rather faint alto that was like a low minor key in a happy life. Mr. Walton's melody was rather that of the heart, for his voice was returning to the weakness of childhood, and his ear was scarcely quick enough for the rapid changes of the air, and yet, unless "grandpa" joined with them, all felt that the circle was incomplete.

Gregory was a foreign element in the little group, almost a stranger to its personnel, and more estranged from the sacred meanings and feeling of the hour; yet such was the power of example, so strong were the sweet home-spells of this Christian family, that to his surprise he found himself entering with zest into a scene that on the Sabbath before he would have regarded as an unmitigated bore. The thought flashed across him, "How some of my club acquaintances would laugh to see me standing between two children singing Sabbath-school hymns!"

It was also a sad truth that he could go away from all present influences to spend the next Sabbath at his club in the ordinary style.

When the children's hour had passed and they had been tucked away to peaceful spring-time dreams, though a storm, the precursor of winter, raged without, Annie returned to the parlor and said, "Now, Mr. Gregory, we can have some singing more to your taste."

"I have been one of the children to-day," he replied, "so you must let me off with them from any further singing myself."

"If you insist on playing the children's role you must go to bed. I have some grand old hymns that I've been wishing to try with you."

"Indeed, Miss Walton, I am but half a man. At the risk of your contempt I must say in frankness that my whole physical nature yearns for my arm-chair. But please do not call my weakness laziness. If you will sing to me just what you please, according to your mood, I for one will be grateful."

"Even a dragon could not resist such an appeal," said Annie, laughing. She sat down to her piano and soon partially forgot her audience, in an old Sabbath evening habit, well known to natural musicians, of expressing her deeper and more sacred feelings in words and notes that harmonized with them. Gregory sat and listened as the young girl unwittingly revealed a new element in her nature.

In her every-day life she appeared to him full of force and power, practical and resolute. To one of his sporting tastes she suggested a mettled steed whose high spirit was kept in check by thorough training. Her conversation was piquant, at times a little brusque, and utterly devoid of sentimentality. But now her choice of poetic thought and her tones revealed a wealth of womanly tenderness, and he was compelled to feel that her religion was not legal and cold, a system of duties, beliefs, and restraints, but something that seemed to stir the depths of her soul with mystic longings, and overflow her heart with love. She was not adoring the Creator, nor paying homage to a king; but, as the perfume rises from a flower, so her voice and manner seemed the natural expression of a true, strong affection for God Himself, not afar off, but known as a near and dear friend. In her sweet tones there was not the faintest suggestion of the effect or style that a professional singer would aim at. She thought no more of these than would a thrush swaying on its spray in the twilight of a June evening. As unaffectedly as the bird she sang according to the inward promptings of a nature purified and made lovely by the grace of God.

No one not utterly given over to evil could have listened unmoved, still less Gregory, with his sensitive, beauty-loving, though perverted nature. The spirit of

David's harp again breathed its divine peace on his sin-disquieted soul. The words of old Daddy Tuggar flashed across him, and he muttered:

"Yes, she could take even me to heaven, 'if she stayed right by me.'"

When finally, with heartfelt sincerity, she sang the following simple words to an air that seemed a part of them, he envied her from the depths of his soul, and felt that he would readily barter away any earthly possession and life itself for a like faith:

> Nearer, nearer, ever nearer,
>   Come I gladly unto Thee;
> And the days are growing brighter
>   With Thy presence nearer me.
>
> Though a pilgrim, not a stranger;
>   This Thy land, and I Thine own;
> At Thy side, thus free from danger,
>   Find I paths with flowers strown.
>
> Voices varied, nature speaking,
>   Call to me on every side;
> Friends and kindred give their greeting,
>   In Thy sunshine I abide.
>
> Though my way were flinty, thorny,
>   Were I sure it led to Thee,
> Could I pass one day forlornly,
>   Home and rest so near to me?

Then she brought the old family Bible, indicating that after that hour she was in no mood for commonplace conversation. In the hush that followed, the good old man reverently read a favorite passage, which seemed not to consist of cold, printed words, but to be a part of a loving letter sent by the Divine Father to His absent children.

As such it was received by all save Gregory. He sat among them as a stranger and an alien, cut off by his own acts from those ties which make one household of earth and heaven. But such was the influence of the evening upon him that he realized as never before his loss and loneliness. He longed intensely to share in their feelings, and to appropriate the words of love and promise that Mr. Walton read.

The prayer that followed was so tender, so full of heart-felt interest in his guest, that Gregory's feelings were deeply touched. He arose from his knees, and again shaded his face to hide the traces of his emotion.

When at last he looked up, Mr. Walton was quietly reading, and the ladies had retired. He rose and bade Mr. Walton good-night with a strong but silent grasp of the hand.

The thought flashed across him as he went to his room, that after this evening and the grasp as of friendship he had just given the father, he could not in the faintest degree meditate evil against the daughter. But so conscious was he of moral weakness, so self- distrustful in view of many broken resolutions, that he dared resolve on nothing. He at last fell into a troubled sleep with the vain, regretful thought, "Oh that I had not lost my vantage-ground! Oh that I could live my life over again!"

CHAPTER XVI
AN ACCIDENT IN THE MOUNTAINS

In view of her recent stormy mood, Nature seemed full of regretful relentings on Monday, and, as if to make amends for her harshness, assumed something of a summer softness. The sun had not the glaring brightness that dazzles, and the atmosphere, purified by the recent rain, revealed through its crystal depths objects with unusual distinctness.

"It is a splendid day for a mountain ramble," said Annie, with vivacity, at the breakfast-table.

"Why don't you take old Dolly and the mountain wagon, and show Mr. Gregory some of our fine views this afternoon?" asked Mr. Walton.

"Nothing would please me more," said his daughter, cordially; "that is, if Mr.

Gregory feels equal to the fatigue."

"I'd be at my last gasp if I refused such an offer," said Gregory, eagerly. "It would do me good, for I feel much stronger than when I first came, and Miss Walton's society is the best tonic I know of."

"Very well," said she, laughing. "You shall take me this afternoon as a continuation of the tonic treatment under which you say you are improving."

"To carry on the medical figure," he replied, "I fear that I am to you the embodiment of the depletive system."

"From my feelings this bright morning you have very little effect. I prescribe for you a quiet forenoon, as our mountain roads will give you an awful jolting. You, if not your medicine, will be well shaken to-day."

"You are my medicine, as I understand it, so I shall take it according to the old orthodox couplet."

"No, the mountain is your medicine, and I anticipate no earthquakes."

"It is settled then," said Mr. Walton, smiling, "that you adopt Mahomet's compromise and go to the mountain. I will tell Jeff to fit you out in suitable style."

Gregory, in excellent spirits, retired to his room for a quiet morning. The prospect for the afternoon pleased him greatly, and a long tete-a-tete with Annie among the grand and beautiful solitudes of nature had for him an attraction that he could scarcely understand.

"She is just the one for a companion on such an expedition," he said to himself. "She seems a part of the scenes we shall look upon. The free, strong mountain spirit breathes in her every word and act. Old Greek mythology would certainly make her a nymph of the hills."

After dinner they started, Gregory's interest centring mainly in his companion, but Annie regarding him as a mere accessory to a sort of half-holiday in her busy life, and expecting more enjoyment from the scenery and the exhilarating air than from his best efforts to entertain her. And yet in this respect she was agreeably disappointed. Gregory was in a mood that he scarcely understood himself. If Annie had been somewhat vain and shallow, though possessing many other good traits, with the practiced skill of a society man he would have made the most of these weaknesses, amused himself with a piquant flirtation, and soon have been ready for his departure for New York with a contemptuous French shrug at the whole affair.

But her weaknesses did not lie in that direction. Her naturally truthful and earnest nature, deepened and strengthened by Christian principle, from the first had foiled his unworthy purposes, and disturbed his contemptuous cynicism. Then as he was compelled to believe in her reality, her truth and nobleness, all that was in his own nature responsive to these traits began to assert itself. Even while he clung to it and felt that he had no power to escape it, the evil of his life grew more hateful to him, and he condemned himself with increasing bitterness. When good influences are felt in a man's soul, evil seems to become specially active. The kingdom of darkness disputes every inch of its ill-gotten power. Winter passes away in March storms. It is the still cold of indifference that is nearest akin to death.

The visit to his old home, and the influence of Annie Walton, were creating March weather in Walter Gregory's soul. There were a few genial moods like gleams of early spring sunshine. There were sudden relentings and passionate longings for better life, as at times gentle, frost-relaxing showers soften the flinty ground. There were fierce spiritual conflicts, wild questionings, doubts, fears, and forebodings, and sometimes despair, as in this gusty month nature often seems resolving itself back to primeval chaos. But too often his mood was that of cold hard scepticism, the frost of midwinter. The impetus of his evil life would evidently be long in spending itself.

And yet the quiet influence of the hallowed Sabbath evening, and Annie Walton's hymns of faith and love, could not readily be lost. The father's prayer still echoed in his soul, and even to him it seemed that the heavens could not be deaf to such entreaty. These things affected him as no direct appeals possibly could. They were like the gentle but irresistible south wind.

He was now simply drifting. He had not definitely abandoned his purpose of tempting Annie, nor did he consciously thrust it from him. Quite convinced that she was what she seemed, and doubting greatly whether during his brief visit there would be time to affect her mind seriously by any evil influences he could bring to bear, and won unwittingly by her pure spirit to better things himself, he let the new and unexpected influence have full play.

He was like a man who finds himself in the current above Niagara, and gives up in despair, allowing his boat to glide onward to the fatal plunge. A breeze springs up and blows against the current. He spreads a sail and finds his downward progress checked. If the wind increases and blows steadily, he may stem the rushing tide and reach smooth, safe waters.

A faint glimmering of hope began to dawn in his heart. An unexpected gale from heaven, blowing against the current of evil, made it seem possible that he too might gain the still waters of a peaceful faith. But the hope dwelt in his mind more as a passing thought, a possibility, than an expectation.

In his wavering state the turn of the scales would depend mainly upon the mood of his companion. If she had been trifling and inclined to flirt, full of frivolous nonsense, bent upon having a good time in the frequent acceptation of the phrase, little recking the consequences of words or acts, as is often the case with girls in the main good- hearted and well-meaning, Gregory would have fallen in with such a mood and pushed it to the extreme.

But Annie was simply herself, bright and exhilarating as the October sunshine, but as pure and strong. She was ready for jest and repartee. She showed almost a childish delight in every odd and pretty thing that met her eye, but never for a moment permitted her companion to lose respect for her.

Her cheeks were like the crimson maple-leaves which overhung them. Her eyes were like the dark sparkle of the little brook as it emerged from the causeway over which they drove. Her brown hair, tossed by the wind, escaped somewhat from its restraints and enhanced the whiteness of her neck, and the thought occurred to Gregory more than once, "If she is not pretty, I never saw a face more pleasant to look at."

The wish to gain her esteem and friendship grew stronger every moment, and he exerted himself to the utmost to please her. Abandoning utterly his gallantry, his morbid cynicism, he came out into the honest sunlight of truth, where Annie's mind dwelt, and directed the conversation to subjects concerning which, as an educated and travelled man, he could speak frankly and intelligently. Annie had strong social tastes and the fondness for companionship natural to the young, and she was surprised to find how he stimulated and interested her mind, and how much they had in common. He appeared to understand her immediately, and to lead her thoughts to new and exciting flights.

It was their purpose to cross a spur of the main mountain range. After a long and toilsome climb, stopping to give Dolly many a breathing spell, they at last reached the brow of the wooded height, and turned to look at the autumn landscape glimmering in the bright October sunshine. It is impossible by either pen or brush to give a true picture of wide reaches of broken and beautiful country, as seen from some of the more favored points of outlook among the Highlands on the Hudson. The loveliness of a pretty bit of scenery or of a landscape may be enhanced by art, but the impressive grandeur of nature, when the feature of vast and varied expanse predominates, cannot be adequately expressed. The mind itself is oppressed by the extensiveness of the scene, and tends to select some definite object, as a village, hamlet, or tree-embowered farmhouse, on which to dwell. These accord more with the finite nature of the beholder. Spires and curling wreaths of smoke suggested to Annie and Gregory many a simple altar and quiet hearth, around which gathered the homely, contented life, spiritual and domestic, of those who occupied their own little niche in the great world, and were all unburdened with thought or care for the indefinite regions that stretched away beyond their narrow circle of daily acquaintance. Only God can give to the whole of His creation the all-seeing gaze that we bestow upon some familiar scene. His glance around the globe is like that of a mother around her nursery, with her little children grouped at her feet.

The laden orchards, with men climbing long ladders, and boys in the topmost branches looking in the distance like huge squirrels, were pleasant objects to the mountain ramblers. Huskers could be discerned in the nearer cornfields, and the great yellow ears glistened momentarily in the light, as they were tossed into golden heaps. There was no hum of industry as from a manufacturing village, or roar of turbulent life as from a city, but only the quiet evidence to the eye of a life kindred to that which nature so silently and beautifully elaborates.

"How insignificant we are!" said Gregory, gloomily; "how the great world goes right on without us! It is the same when one dies and leaves it, as we left it by climbing this mountain. In the main we are unknown and uncared for, and even to those who know us it is soon the same as if we had never been."

"But the world cannot go on without God. Though forgotten, He never forgets! His friends need never have the sense of being lost or lonely--any more than a child travelling with his father in a foreign land among indifferent strangers. God does not look at us, His creatures, as we do at the foliage of these forests, seeing only the general effect. He sees each one as directly as I now look at you."

"I wish I could believe He looked as kindly."

"I wish you could, Mr. Gregory. It is sad to me that people can't believe what is so true. The fondest look your mother ever gave you was cold compared with the yearning, loving face God turns toward every one of us, even as we go away from Him."

He looked at her earnestly for a moment and saw that sincerity was written on her face. He shook his head sadly, and then said, rather abruptly, "Those lengthening shadows remind us that we must be on our way"; and then their thoughts dwelt on lighter subjects as they ascended another lofty mountain terrace, and paused again to scan the wider prospect that made the sense of daily life in the valleys below as remote as the world seems to the hermit in his devotional seclusion. Then they began to descend the sloping plateau which inclined toward the brow of the hill overlooking the region of the Walton residence.

After one or two hours of broken but very agreeable conversation Annie suddenly sighed deeply.

"Now, Miss Walton," said Gregory, "that sigh came from the depths. What hidden sorrow could have caused it?"

With a slight flush and laugh, she said, "It was caused by a mere passing thought, like that cloud there sailing over the mountain slope."

"Your simile is so pretty that I should like to know the thought."

"I hardly know whether to tell it to you. It might have the same effect as if that cloud should expand and cover the sky."

"Might not the telling also have the same effect as if the cloud were dissipated altogether?"

She looked at him quickly and said, "How apt your answer is! Yes, it might if you would be sensible. I do not know you so very well yet. Are you not a little ready to take offence?"

"You do not look as if about to say anything I should resent very deeply. But I promise that the cloud shall vanish."

"I am not so sure about that. The cloud represents my thought; and yet I hope it may eventually vanish utterly. The thought occurred to me after the pleasant hours of this afternoon what congenial friends we *might* be."

"And that caused you to sigh so deeply?"

"I laid emphasis on the word *might*."

"And why should you, Miss Annie? Why need you?" he asked, eagerly.

"You have shown a great deal of tact and consideration this afternoon, Mr. Gregory, in choosing topics on which we could agree, or about which it is as nice to differ a little. I wish it were the same in regard to those things that make up one's life, as it were;" and she looked at him closely to see how he would take this.

After a moment he said, a little bitterly, "In order to be your friend, must one look at everything through the same colored glass that you employ?"

"Oh, no," she replied, earnestly; "it is not fair to say that. But you seem almost hostile to all that I love best and think most of, and my sigh was rather an earnest and oft-recurring wish that it were otherwise."

Again he was silent for a short time, then said, with sudden vehemence, "And I also wish it were otherwise"; adding more quietly, "but it is not, Miss Walton. You know me too well, even if I wished to deceive you. And yet I would give a great deal for such a friendship as you could bestow. Why can you not give it as it is? The Founder of your faith was a friend of publicans and sinners."

"He was indeed their friend, and has been ever since," she answered. "But was it not natural that He found more that was attractive and congenial in that little group of disciples who were learning to know and believe in Him?"

"I understand you, Miss Walton. I was unfortunate in my illustration, and you have turned it against me. You can be my friend, as the missionary is the friend of the heathen."

"You go to extremes, Mr. Gregory, and are hardly fair. I am not a missionary, nor are you a heathen. I make my meaning clear when I echo your thought of a moment ago, and wish that just such a friendship might exist between us as that between your father and mine."

"I am what I am," he said, with genuine sadness.

"I wish you had my faith in the possibilities of the future," she replied, turning brightly toward him.

But he shook his head, saying, "I have about lost all faith in everything as far as I am concerned. Still I feel that if any one could do me any good, you might, but I fear it is a hopeless task." Then he changed the subject in such a way as to show that it was painful, and that he preferred it should be dropped.

After all, the cloud had overcast the sky. The inevitable separation between those guided by divine principles and those controlled by earthly influences began to dawn upon him. He caught a glimpse of the "great gulf," that is ever "fixed" between the good and evil in their deepest consciousness. The "loneliness of guilt" chilled and oppressed him, even with the cheery, sympathetic companion at his side. But he hid his feelings under a forced gayety, in which Annie joined somewhat, though it gave her a vague shiver of pain. She felt they had been **en rapport** for a little while, but now a change had come, even as the damp and chill of approaching night were taking the place of genial sunshine.

Suddenly she said, as they were riding along on the comparatively level plateau among thick copse-wood and overshadowing trees that already created a premature twilight, "It is strange we do not come out on the brow of the mountain overlooking our home. This road does not seem familiar either, though it is two or three years since I have been over it, and then Jeff drove. I thought I knew the way well. Can it be possible we have taken the wrong turning?"

"I ought to be familiar with these roads, Miss Walton, but I am sorry to say I too am confused. I hunted over these hills to some extent when a boy, but did not pay much heed to the roads, as I took my own courses through the woods."

"I think I must be right," said Annie, after a little time; "the brow of the hill must be near;" and they hastened the old horse along as fast as possible under the circumstances. But the road continually grew rougher and gave evidence of very little travel, and the evening deepened rapidly. At last they resolved to turn round at the first place that would permit of it, but this was not readily found, there being only a single wheel-track, which now stretched away before them like a narrow cut between banks of foliage, that looked solid in the increasing darkness; the road also was full of rocks, loose stones, and deep ruts, over which the wagon jolted painfully. With a less sure-footed horse than Dolly they would soon have come to grief. Gregory was becoming greatly fatigued, though he strove to hide it, and both were filled with genuine uneasiness at the prospect before them. To make matters seemingly desperate, as they were descending a little hill a fore-wheel caught between two stones and was wrenched sharply off. Quick, agile Annie sprang as she felt the wagon giving, but Walter was thrown out among the brushwood by the roadside. Though scratched and bruised, he was not seriously hurt, and as quickly as possible came to the assistance of his companion. He found her standing by Dolly's head, holding and soothing the startled beast. Apparently she was unhurt. They looked searchingly at the dusky forest, their broken vehicle, and then at each other. Words were unnecessary to explain the awkwardness of their situation.

CHAPTER XVII
"PROMISE OR DIE"

While they were thus standing irresolute after the accident, suddenly a light glimmered upon them. It appeared to come from a house standing a little off from the road. "Shall I leave you here and go for assistance?" asked Walter.

"I think I would rather go with you. Dolly will stand, and I do not wish to be left alone."

They soon found a grassy path leading to a small house, from which the light shone but faintly through closely curtained windows. They met no one, nor were their footsteps heard till they knocked at the door. A gruff voice said, "Come in," and a huge bull-dog started up from near the fire with a savage growl.

They entered. A middle-aged man with his coat off sat at work with his back toward them. He rose hastily and stared at them with a strangely blended look of consternation and anger.

"Call off your dog," said Gregory, sharply.

"Down, Bull," said the man, harshly, and the dog slunk growling into a corner, but with a watchful, ugly gleam in his eyes.

The man's expression was quite as sinister and threatening.

"Who are you, and what do you want?" he asked, sternly.

"We want help," said Gregory, with a quickened and apprehensive glance around, which at once revealed to him why their visit was so unwelcome. The man had been counterfeiting money, and the evidences of his guilt were only too apparent. "We have lost our way, and our wagon is broken. I hope you have sufficient humanity to act the part of a neighbor."

"Humanity to the devil!" said the man, brutally, "I am neighbor to no one. You have come here to pry into what is none of your business."

"We have not," said Gregory, eagerly. "You will find our broken wagon in the road but a little way from here."

The man's eye was cold, hard, and now had a snake-like glitter as he looked at them askance with a gloomy scowl. He seemed thinking over the situation in which he found himself.

Gregory, in his weak, exhausted state, and shaken somewhat by his fall, was nervous and apprehensive. Annie, though pale, stood firmly and quietly by.

Slowly and hesitatingly, as if deliberating as to the best course, the man reached up to the shelf and took down a revolver, saying, with an evil-boding look at them, "If I thought you had come as detectives, you would have no chance to use your knowledge. You, sir, I do not know, but I think this lady is Squire Walton's daughter. As it is, you must both solemnly promise me before God that you will never reveal what you have seen here. Otherwise I have but one method of self- protection," and he cocked his pistol. "Let me tell you," he added, in a blood-curdling tone, "you are not the first ones I have silenced. And mark this--if you go away and break this promise, I have confederates who will take vengeance on you and yours."

"No need of any further threats," said Gregory, with a shrug. "I promise. As you say, it is none of my business how much of the 'queer' you make."

Though naturally not a coward, Gregory, in his habit of self-pleasing and of shunning all sources of annoyance, would not have gone out of his way under any circumstances to bring a criminal to justice, and the thought of risking anything in this case did not occur to him. Why should they peril their lives for the good of the commonwealth? If he had been alone and escaped without further trouble, he would have thought of the matter afterward as of a crime recorded in the morning paper, with which he had no concern, except perhaps to scrutinize more sharply the currency he received.

But with conscientious Annie it was very different. Her father was a magistrate of the right kind, who sincerely sought to do justice and protect the people in their rights. From almost daily conversation her mind had been impressed with the sacredness of the law. When she was inclined to induce her father to give a lighter sentence than he believed right he had explained how the well-being and indeed the very existence of society depended upon the righteous enforcement of the law, and how true mercy lay in such enforcement. She had been made to feel that the responsibility for good order and morals rested on every one, and that to conceal a known crime was to share deeply in the guilt. She also was not skilled in that casuistry which would enable her to promise anything with mental reservations. The shock of their savage and threatening reception had been severe, but she was not at all inclined to be hysterical; and though her heart seemed to stand still with a chill of dread which deepened every moment as she realized what would be exacted of her, she seemed more self-possessed than Gregory. Indeed, in the sudden and awful emergencies of life, woman's fortitude is often superior to man's, and Annie's faith was no decorous and conventional profession for Sabbath uses, but a constant and living reality. She was like the maidens of martyr days, who tremblingly but unhesitatingly died for conscience' sake. While there was no wavering of purpose, there was an agony of fear and sorrow, as, after the momentary confusion of mind caused by the suddenness of the occurrence, the terrible nature of the ordeal before her became evident.

Through her father she had heard a vague rumor of this man before. Though he lived so secluded and was so reticent, his somewhat mysterious movements had awakened suspicion. But his fierce dog and his own manner had kept all obtrusive curiosity at a distance. Now she saw her father's worst fears and surmises realized.

But the counterfeiter at first gave all his attention to her companion, thinking that he would have little trouble with a timid girl; and after Gregory's ready promise, looked searchingly at him for a moment, and then said, with a coarse, scornful laugh, "No fear of you. You will keep your skin whole. You are a city chap, and know enough of me and my tribe to be sure I can strike you there as well as here. I can trust to your fears, and don't wish to shed blood when it is unnecessary. And now this girl must make the same promise. Her father is a magistrate, and I intend to have no posse of men up here after me to-morrow."

"I can make no such promise," said Annie, in a low tone.

"What?" exclaimed the man, harshly, and a savage growl from the dog made a kindred echo to his tone.

Deathly pale, but with firm bearing, Annie said, "I cannot promise to shield crime by silence. I should be a partaker in your guilty secrets."

"Oh, for God's sake, promise!" cried Gregory, in an agony of fear, but in justice it must be said that it was more for her than for himself.

"For God's sake I cannot promise."

The man stepped menacingly toward her, and the great dog also advanced unchecked out of his corner.

"Young woman," he hissed in her ear, "you must promise or die. I have sworn never to go to prison again if I wade knee-deep in blood."

There came a rush of tears to Annie's eyes. Her bosom heaved convulsively a moment, and then she said, in a tone of agony, "It is dreadful to die in such a way, but I cannot make the promise you ask. It would burden my conscience and blight my life. I will trust to God's mercy and do right. But think twice before you shed my innocent blood."

Gregory covered his face with his hands and groaned aloud.

The man hesitated. He had evidently hoped by his threats to frighten her into compliance, and her unexpected refusal, while it half frenzied him with fear and anger, made his course difficult to determine upon. He was not quite hardened enough to slay the defenceless girl as she stood so bravely before him, and the killing of her would also involve the putting of Gregory out of the way, making a double murder that would be hard to conceal. He looked at the dog, and the thought occurred that by turning them out of doors and leaving them to the brute's tender mercies their silence might be effectually secured.

It is hard to say what he would have done, left to his own fears and evil passions; but a moment after Annie had spoken, the doors opened and a woman entered with a pail of water, which she had just brought from a spring at some little distance from the house.

"What does this mean?" she asked, with a quick, startled glance around.

"It means mischief to all concerned," said the man, sullenly.

"This is Miss Walton," said the woman, advancing.

"Yes," exclaimed Annie, and she rushed forward and sobbed out, "save me from your husband; he threatened to take my life."

"'My husband!'" said the woman, with intense bitterness, turning toward the man. "Do you hear that, Vight? Quiet your fears, young lady. Do you remember the sick, weary woman that you found one hot day last summer by the roadside? I was faint, and it seemed to me that I was dying. I often wish to, but when it comes to the point and I look over into the black gulf, I'm afraid--"

"But, woman--" interrupted the man, harshly.

"Be still," she said, imperiously waving her hand.

"Don't rouse a devil you can't control." Then turning to Annie, she continued, "I was afraid then; I was in an agony of terror. I was so weak that I could scarcely do more than look appealingly to you and stretch out my hands. Most ladies would have said, 'She's drunk,' and passed contemptuously on. But you got out of your wagon and took my cold hand. I whispered, 'I'm sick; for God's sake help me.' And you believed me and said, 'I will help you, for God's sake and your own.' Then you went to the carriage, and got some cordial which you said was for another sick person, and gave me some; and when I revived, you half carried me and half lifted me into your nice covered little wagon, that kept the burning sun off my head, and you took me miles out of your way to a little house which I falsely told you was my home. I heard that you afterward came to see me. You spoke kindly. When I could speak I said that I was not fit for you to touch, and you answered that Jesus Christ was glad to help touch any human creature, and that you were not better than He! Then you told me a little about Him, but I was too sick to listen much. God knows I've got down about as low as any woman can. I dare not pray for myself, but since that day I've prayed for you. And mark what I say, Vight," she added, her sad, weird manner changing to sudden fierceness, "not a hair of this lady's head shall be hurt."

"But these two will go and blab on us," said the man, angrily. "At least the girl will. She won't promise to keep her secret. I have no fears for the man; I can keep him quiet."

"Why won't you promise?" asked the woman, gently, but with surprise.

"Because I cannot," said Annie, earnestly, though her voice was still broken by sobs. "When we hide crime, we take part in it."

"And would you rather die than do what you thought wrong?"

"It were better," said Annie.

"Oh that I had had such a spirit in the fatal past!" groaned the woman.

"But won't you protect me still?" exclaimed Annie, seizing her hand. "It would kill my poor old father too, if I should die. I cannot burden my soul with your secrets, but save me--oh, save me, from so dreadful a death!"

"I have said it, Miss Walton. Not a hair of your head shall be hurt."

"What do you advise then, madam?" asked the man, satirically. "Shall we invite Mr. Walton and the sheriff up to-morrow to take a look at the room as it now stands?"

"I advise nothing," said the woman, harshly. "I only say, in a way you understand, not a hair of this girl's head shall be hurt."

"Thank God, oh, thank God," murmured Annie, with a feeling of confidence and inexpressible relief, for there was that in the woman's bearing and tone which gave evidence of unusual power over her associate in crime.

Then Annie added, still clinging to a hand unsanctified by the significant plain ring, "I hope you will keep my companion safe from harm also."

During the scene between Annie and her strange protector, who was evidently a sad wreck of a beautiful and gifted woman, Gregory had sunk into a chair through weakness and shame, and covered his face with his hands.

The woman turned toward him with instinctive antipathy, and asked, "How is it, sir, you have left a young girl to meet this danger alone?"

Gregory's white, drawn face turned scarlet as he answered, "Because I am like you and this man here, and not like Miss Walton, who is an angel of truth and goodness."

"'Like *us*,' indeed!" said she, disdainfully. "I don't know that you have proved us *cowards* yet. And could you be bad and mean enough to see this brave maiden slain before your eyes, and go away in silence to save your own miserable self?"

"For aught I know I could," answered he, savagely. "I would like to see what mean, horrible, loathsome thing, this hateful, hated thing I call myself could not do."

Gregory showed, in a way fearful to witness, what intense hostility and loathing a spirit naturally noble can feel toward itself when action and conscience are at war.

"Ah," said the woman, bitterly, "now you speak a language I know well. Why should I fear the judgment-day?" she added, with a gloomy light in her eyes, as if communing with herself. "Nothing worse can be said of me than I will say now. But," she sneered, turning sharply to Gregory, "I do not think I have fallen so low as you."

"Probably not," he replied, with a grim laugh, and a significant shrug which he had learned abroad. "I will not dispute my bad pre-eminence. Come, Vight, or whatever your name is," he continued, rising, "make up your mind quickly what you are going to do. I am a weak man, morally and physically. If you intend to shoot me, or let your dog make a meal of me, let us have it over as soon as possible. Since Miss Walton is safe, I am as well prepared now as I ever shall be."

"I entreat you," pleaded Annie, still clinging to the woman, "don't let any harm come to him."

"What is the use of touching him?" said the man, gruffly. Then turning to Gregory he asked, "Do you still promise not to use your knowledge against me? You might do me more harm in New York than here."

"I have promised once, and that is enough," said Gregory, irritably. "I keep my word for good or evil, though you can't know that, and are fools for trusting me."

"I'll trust neither of you," said the man, with an oath. "Here, Dencie, I must talk with you alone. I'm willing to do anything that's reasonable, but I'm not going to prison again alive, mark" that (with a still more fearful imprecation). "Don't leave this room or I won't answer for the consequences," he said, sternly to Gregory and Annie, at the same time looking significantly at the dog.

Then he and the woman went into the back room, and there was an earnest and somewhat angry consultation.

Gregory sat down and leaned his head on the table in a manner that showed he had passed beyond despondency and fear into despairing indifference as to what became of him. He felt that henceforth he must be simply odious to Miss Walton, that she would only tolerate his presence as long as it was necessary, veiling her contempt by more politeness. In his shame and weakness he would almost rather die than meet her true, honest eyes again.

Annie had the courage of principle and firm resolve, rather than that which is natural and physical. The thought of sudden and violent death appalled her. If her impulsive nature were excited, like that of a soldier in battle, she could forget danger. If in her bed at home she were wasting with disease, she would soon submit to the Divine will with childlike trust. But her whole being shrunk inexpressibly from violent and unnatural death. Never before did life seem so sweet. Never before was there so much to live for. She could have been a martyr in any age and in any horrible form for conscience' sake, but she would have met her fate tremblingly, shrinkingly, and with intense longings for life. And yet with all this instinctive dread, her trust in God and His promises would not fail. But instead of standing calmly erect on her faith, and confronting destiny, it was her nature, in such terrible emergencies, to cling in loving and utter dependence, and obey.

She therefore in no respect shared Gregory's indifference, but was keenly alive to the situation.

At first, with her hand upon her heart to still its wild throbbings, she listened intently, and tried to catch the drift of the fateful conference within. This being vain, her eyes wandered hurriedly around the room. Standing thus, she unconsciously completed a strange picture in that incongruous place, with her dejected companion on one side, and the great dog, eying her savagely, on the other. Gregory's despairing attitude impressed her deeply. In a sudden rash of pity she felt that he was not as cowardly as he had seemed. A woman with difficulty forgives this sin. His harsh condemnation and evident detestation of himself impelled her generous nature instinctively to take the part of his weak and wronged spirit. She had early been taught to pity rather than to condemn those whom evil is destroying. In all his depravity he did not repel her, for, though proud, he had no petty, shallow vanity; and the evident fact that he suffered so deeply disarmed her.

Moreover, companionship in trouble which she felt was partly her fault, drew her toward him, and, stepping to his side, she laid her hand on his shoulder and said, gently, "Cheer up, my friend; I understand you better than you do yourself. God will bring us safely through."

He shrunk from her hand, and said, drearily, "With better reason than younder woman I can say, 'I am not fit for you to touch.' As for God, He has nothing to do with me."

She answered, kindly, "I do not think that either of those things is true. But, Mr. Gregory, what will they do with us? They will not dare--"

She was interrupted by the entrance of the strangely assorted couple into whose crime-stained hands they had so unexpectedly fallen. Both felt that but little trust could be placed in such perverted and passion-swept natures--that they would be guided by their fears, impulses, and interests. Annie's main hope was in the hold she had on the woman's sympathies; but the latter, as she entered, wore a sullen and disappointed look, as if she had not been given her own way. Annie at once stepped to her side and again took her hand, as if she were her best hope of safety. It was evident that her confidence and unshrinking touch affected the poor creature deeply, and her hand closed over Annie's in a way that was reassuring.

"I suppose you would scarcely like to trust yourselves to me or my dog," said the man, with a grim laugh. "What's more, I've no time to bother with you. Since my companion here feels she owes you something, Miss Walton, she can now repay you a hundred-fold. But follow her directions closely, as you value your lives;" and he left the house with the dog. Soon after, they heard in the forest what seemed the note of the whippoorwill repeated three times, but it was so near and importunate that Annie was startled, and the woman's manner indicated that she was not listening to a bird. After a few moments she said, gloomily: "Miss Walton, I promised you should receive no harm, and I will keep my word. I hoped I could send you directly home to-night, but that's impossible. I can do much with Vight, but not everything. He has sworn never to go to prison again alive, and none of our lives would be worth much if they stood in the way of his escape. We meant to leave this region before many months, for troublesome stories are getting around, and now we must go at once. I will take you to a place of safety, from which you can return home to-morrow. Come."

"But father will be wild with anxiety," cried Annie, wringing her hands.

"It is the best I can do," said the woman, sadly. "Come, we have no time to lose."

She put on a woollen hood, and taking a long, slender staff, led the way out into the darkness.

They felt that there was nothing to do but follow, which they did in silence. They did not go back toward their broken wagon, but continued down the wheel-track whereon their accident had occurred. Suddenly the woman left this, taking a path through the woods, and after proceeding with difficulty some distance, stopped, and lighted a small lantern she had carried under her shawl. Even with the aid of this their progress was painful and precarious in the steeply descending rocky path, which had so many intricate windings that both Annie and Gregory felt that they were indeed being led into a ***terra incognita***. Annie was consumed with anxiety as to the issue of their strange adventure, but believed confidence in her guide to be the wisest course. Gregory was too weary and indifferent to care for himself, and stumbled on mechanically.

At last he said, sullenly, "Madam, I can go no further. I may as well die here as anywhere."

"You **must** go," she said, sharply; "for my sake and Miss Walton's, if not for your own. Besides, it's not much further. What I do to-night must be done rightly."

"Well, then, while there is breath left, Miss Walton shall have the benefit of it."

"May we not rest a few minutes?" asked Annie. "I too am very tired."

"Yes, before long at the place where you must pass the night."

The path soon came out in another wheel-track, which seemed to lead down a deep ravine. Descending this a little way, they reached an opening in which was the dusky outline of a small house.

"Here we part," said their guide, taking Annie's hand, while Gregory sank exhausted on a rock near. "The old woman and her son who live in that house will give you shelter, and to-morrow you must find your best way home. This seems poor return for your kindness, but it's in keeping with my miserable life, which is as dark and wild as the unknown flinty path we came. After all, things have turned out far better than they might have done. Vight was expecting some one, and so had the dog within doors. He would have torn you to pieces had he been without as usual."

"Lead this life no longer. Stay with us, and I will help you to better things," said Annie, earnestly.

The look of intense longing on the woman's face as the light of the flickering lantern fell on it would haunt Annie to her dying day.

"Oh that I might!" she groaned. "Oh that I might! A more fearful bondage never cursed a human soul!"

"And why can you not?" pleaded Annie, putting her hand on the trembling woman's shoulder. "You have seen better days. You were meant for a good and noble life. You can't sin unfeelingly. Then why sin at all? Break these chains, and by and by peace in this life and heaven in the life to come will reward you."

The woman sat down by the roadside, and for a moment her whole frame seemed convulsed with sobs. At last she said, brokenly, "You plead as my good angel did before it left me--but it's no use--it's too late. I have indeed seen better days, pure, happy days; and so has he. We once stood high in the respect of all. But he fell, and I fell in ways I can't explain. You cannot understand, that as love binds with silken cords, so crime may bind with iron chains. No more--say no more. You only torment me," she broke in, harshly, as Annie was about to speak again. "You cannot understand. How could you? We love, hate, and fear each other at the same time, and death only can part us. But that may soon--that may soon;" and she clenched her hands with a dark look.

"But enough of this. I have too much to do to tire myself this way. You must go to that house; I cannot. Old Mrs. Tompkins and her son will give you shelter. I don't wish them to get into trouble. There will be a close investigation into all this. I know what your father's disposition is. And now farewell. The only good thing about me is, I shall still pray for you, the only one who has ever treated me like a woman since--since--since I fell into hell," she said in a low, hoarse tone, and printing a passionate kiss on Annie's hand, she blew out her light, and vanished in the darkness.

It seemed to swallow her up, and become a type of the mystery and fate that enshrouded the forlorn creature. Beyond the bare fact that she took the train the following morning with the man she called "Vight," Annie never heard of her again. Still there was hope for the wretched wanderer. However dark and hidden her paths, the eyes of a merciful God ever followed her, and to that God Annie prayed often in her behalf.

NOTE--This chapter has some historic basis. The man called "Vight" is not altogether an imaginary character, for a desperate and successful counterfeiter dwelt for a time among the mountains on the Hudson, plying his nefarious trade. It is said that he took life more than once to escape detection.

CHAPTER XVIII
IN THE DEPTHS

After the departure of their strange guide, who had befriended them as best she could, Gregory at once went to the house and knocked. There was a movement within, and a quavering voice asked, "Who's there?"

"Friends who have lost their way, and need shelter."

"I don't know about lettin' strangers in this time o' night," answered the voice.

"There are only two of us," said Annie. "Perhaps you know who Miss Walton is. I entreat you to let us in."

"Miss Walton, Miss Walton, sartin, I know who she is. But I can't believe she's here."

"Our wagon broke down this afternoon, and we have lost our way," explained Gregory.

Again there was a stir inside, and soon a glimmer of light. After a few moments the door was opened slightly, and a woman's voice asked, apprehensively, "Be you sure it's Miss Walton?"

"Yes," said Annie, "you need have no fears. Hold the light, and see for your-self."

This the woman did, and, apparently satisfied, gave them admittance at once.

She seemed quite aged, and a few gray locks straggled out from under her dingy cap, which suggested anything but a halo around her wrinkled, withered face. A ragged calico wrapper incased her tall, gaunt form, and altogether she did not make a promising hostess.

Before she could ask her unexpected guests any further questions, the cry of a whippoorwill was again heard three times. She listened with a startled, frightened manner. The sounds were repeated, and she seemed satisfied:

"Isn't it rather late in the season for whippoorwills?" asked Annie, uneasily, for this bird's note, now heard again, seemed like a signal.

"I dunno nothin' about whippoorwills," said the woman, stolidly. "The pesky bird kind o' started me at first. Don't like to hear 'em round. They bring bad luck. I can't do much for you, Miss Walton, in this poor place. But such as 'tis you're welcome to stay. My son has been off haulin' wood; guess he won't be back now afore to-morrow."

"When do you think he will come?" asked Annie, anxiously.

"Well, not much afore night, I guess."

"What will my poor father do?" moaned Annie. "He will be out all night look-ing for us."

"Sure now, will he though?" said the woman, showing some traces of anxiety herself. "Well, miss, you'll have to stay till my son gits back, for it's a long way round through the valley to your house."

There was nothing to do but wait patiently till morning. The woman showed Gregory up into a loft over the one room of the house, saying, "Here's where my son sleeps. It's the best I can do, though I s'pose you ain't used to such beds."

He threw his exhausted form on the wretched couch, and soon found respite in troubled sleep.

Annie dozed away the night in a creaky old rocking-chair, the nearest approach to a thing of comfort that the hovel contained. The old woman had evidently been so "started" that she needed the sedative of a short clay pipe, highly colored indeed, still a connoisseur in meerschaums would scarcely covet it. This she would remove from her mouth now and then, as she crouched on a low stool in the chimney-corner, to shake her head ominously. Perhaps she knew more about whippoorwills than she admitted. At last it seemed that the fumes, which half strangled Annie, had their wonted effect, and she hobbled to her bed and was soon giving discordant evidence of her peace. Annie then noiselessly opened a window, that she too might breathe.

When Gregory waked next morning, it was broad day. He felt so stiff and ill he could scarcely move, and with difficulty made his way to the room below. The old woman was at the stove, frying some sputtering pork, and its rank odor was most repulsive to the fastidious habitue of metropolitan clubs.

"Where is Miss Walton?" he asked, in quick alarm.

"Only gone to the spring after water," replied the woman, shortly. "Why didn't you git up and git it for her?"

"I would if I had known," he muttered, and he escaped from the intolerable air of the room to the door, where he met Annie, fresh and rosy from her morning walk and her toilet at the brook that brawled down the ravine.

"Mr. Gregory, you are certainly ill," she exclaimed. "I am so sorry it has all happened!"

He looked at her wonderingly, and then said, "You appear as if nothing had happened. I am ill, Miss Walton, and I wish I were dead. You can not feel toward me half the contempt I have for myself."

"Now, honestly, Mr. Gregory, I have no contempt for you at all."

He turned away and shook his head dejectedly.

"But I mean what I say," she continued, earnestly.

"Then it is your goodness, and not my desert."

"As I told you last night, so again I sincerely say, I think I understand you better than you do yourself."

"You are mistaken," he answered, with gloomy emphasis. "Your intuitions are quick, I admit. I have never known your equal in that respect. But there are some things I am glad to think you never can understand. You can never know what a proud man suffers when he has utterly lost hope and self-respect. Though I acted so mean a part myself, I can still appreciate your nobleness, courage, and fidelity to conscience. I thought such heroism belonged only to the past."

"Mr. Gregory, I wish I could make you understand me," said Annie, with real distress in her tone. "I am not brave; I was more afraid than you. Indeed, I was in an agony of fear. I refused that man's demand because I was compelled to. If you looked at things as I do, you would have done the same."

"Please say no more, Miss Walton," said he, his face distorted by an expression of intense self-loathing. "Do not try to palliate my course. I would much rather you would call my cowardly selfishness and lack of principle by their right names. The best thing I can do for the world is to get out of it, and from present feelings, this 'good- riddance' will soon occur. Will you excuse me if I sit down?" and he sank upon the door-step in utter weakness.

Annie had placed her pail of water on the door-step and forgotten it in her wish to cheer and help this bitterly wounded spirit.

"Mr. Gregory," she said, earnestly, "you are indeed ill in body and mind, and you take a wrong and morbid view of everything. My heart aches to show you how complete and perfect a remedy there is for all this. It almost seems as if you were dying from thirst with that brook yonder running--"

"There is no remedy for me," interrupted he, almost harshly. Then he added in a weary tone, pressing his hand on his throbbing brow, "Forgive me, Miss Walton; you see what I am. Please waste no more thought on me."

"If yer want any breakfast to-day, yer better bring that water," called the old woman from within.

Annie gave him a troubled, anxious look, and then silently carried in the pail.

"Have you any tea?" she asked, not liking the odor of the coffee.

"Mighty little," was the short answer.

"Please let me have some, and I will send you a pound of our best in its place," said Annie.

"I hain't such a fool as to lose that bargain," and the old woman hobbled with alacrity to a cupboard; but to Annie's dismay the hidden treasure had been hoarded too near the even more prized tobacco, and seemed redolent of the rank odor of some unsavory preparation of that remarkable weed which is conjured into so many and such diverse forms. But she brewed a little as best she could before eating any breakfast herself, and brought it to Gregory as he still sat on the step, leaning against the door-post.

"Please swallow this as medicine," she said.

"Indeed, Miss Walton, I cannot," he replied.

"Please do," she urged, "as a favor to me. I made it myself; and I can't eat any breakfast till I have seen you take this."

He at once complied, though with a wry face.

"There," said she, with a touch of playfulness, "I have seldom received a stronger compliment. After this compliance I think I could venture to ask anything of you."

"The tea is like myself," he answered. "You brought to it skilled hands and pure spring water, and yet, from the nature of the thing itself, it was a villanous compound. Please don't ask me to take any more. Perhaps you have heard an old saying, 'Like dislikes like.'"

She determined that he should not yield to this morbid despondency, but had too much tact to argue with him; therefore she said, kindly, "We never did agree very well, Mr. Gregory, and don't now. But before many hours I hope I can give you a cup of tea and something with it more to your taste. I must admit that I am ready even for this dreadful breakfast, that threatens to destroy my powers of digestion in one fatal hour. You see what a poor subject I am for romance;" and she smilingly turned away to a meal that gave her a glimpse of how the "other half of the world lives."

Before she had finished, the sound of wheels and horses' hoofs coming rapidly up the glen brought her to the door, and with joy she recognized a near neighbor of her father's, a sturdy, kind-hearted farmer, who had joined in the search for the missing ones the moment he learned, in the dawn of that morning, that they had not returned.

He gave a glad shout as he saw Annie's form in the doorway, and to her his broad, honest face was like that of an angel. All are beautiful to those they help.

"Your father is in a dreadful state, Miss Annie," said Farmer Jones; "but I told him if he would only stay at home and wait, I, and a few other neighbors, would soon find you. He was up at the foot of the mountain ever since twelve o'clock last night. Then he came home to see if you hadn't returned some other way. I'm usually out as soon as it's light, so I hailed him as he passed and asked what on earth he was up for at that time of day. He told me his trouble, so I hitched up my light wagon and got to your house as soon as he did. When he found you hadn't come yet, he was for starting right for the mountains, but I saw he wasn't fit, so I says, 'Mr. Walton, you'll just miss 'em. They've taken a wrong road, or the wagon has broken down, but they'll be home before ten o'clock. Now send Jeff up the road you expected them on. I'll send Mr. Harris, who lives just beyond me, out on the road they took first. My horse is fast, and I'll go round up this valley, and in this way we'll soon scour every road;' and so with much coaxing I got him to promise to stay till I returned. So jump in quick, and I'll have you home in little over an hour."

"But we can't leave Mr. Gregory here. Let him go first. He is ill, and needs attention immediately."

"Miss Walton, please return at once to your father," said Gregory, quickly. "It is your duty. I can wait."

"No, Mr. Gregory, it would not be right to leave you here, feeling as you do. As soon as father knows I am safe his mind will be at rest. I am perfectly well, and you have no idea how ill you look."

"Miss Walton," said Gregory, in a tone that was almost harsh in its decisiveness, "I will not return now."

"I am real sorry," said Mr. Jones, "that my wagon is not larger, but I took the best thing that I had for fast driving over rough roads. Come, Miss Walton, your friend has settled it, and if he is sick he had better come more slowly in an easier carriage."

After cordially thanking the old woman for such rude hospitality as she had bestowed, and renewing her promise to send ample recompense, she turned with gentle courtesy to Gregory and assured him that he would not have long to wait.

He gave her a quick, searching look, and said, "Miss Walton, I do not understand how you can speak to me in this way. But go at once. Do not keep your father in suspense any longer."

"I hope we shall find you better when we come for you," she said, kindly.

"It were better if you found me dead," he said, in sudden harshness, but it was toward himself, not her.

So she understood it, and waving her hand encouragingly, was rapidly driven away.

As they rode along she related to Mr. Jones the events already known to the reader, but carefully shielded Gregory from blame. She also satisfied her companion's evident curiosity about the young man by stating so frankly all it was proper for him to know that he had no suspicion of anything concealed. She explained his last and unusual expression by dwelling with truth on the fact that Gregory appeared seriously ill and was deeply depressed in spirits.

Mr. Walton received his daughter with a joy beyond words. She was the idol of his heart--the one object on earth that almost rivalled his "treasures in heaven." His mind had dwelt in agonized suspense on a thousand possibilities of evil during the prolonged hours of her absence, and now that he clasped her again, and was assured of her safety, he lifted his eyes heavenward with overflowing gratitude in his heart.

But Annie's success in keeping up before him was brief. The strain had been a little too severe. She soon gave way to nervous prostration and headache, and was compelled to retire to her room instead of returning for Gregory as she had intended. But he was promptly sent for, Miss Eulie going in her place, and taking every appliance possible for his comfort.

She found him in Mrs. Tompkins's hovel, sitting in the creaky arm- chair that Annie had occupied the night before, and enduring with a white, grim face the increasing suffering of his illness. He seemed to have reached the depths of despair, and, believing the end near, determined to meet it with more than Indian stoicism.

Many, in their suicidal blindness and remorse, pass sentence upon themselves, and weakly deliver their souls into the keeping of that inexorable jailer, Despair, forgetting the possibilities--nay, certainties--of good that ever dwell in God. If man had no better friend than himself, his prospects would be sombre indeed. Many a one has condemned himself and sunk into the apathy of death, but He who came to seek and to save the lost has lifted him with the arms of forgiving love, and helped him back to the safety and happiness of the fold. Satan only, ***never the Saviour***, bids the sinner despair. But poor Gregory was taking advice from his enemy and not from his Friend. During the long hours of pain and almost mortal weakness of that dreary morning, he acknowledged himself vanquished--utterly defeated in the battle of life. As old monkish legends teach, the devil might have carried him off bodily and he would not have resisted. In his prostrated nature, but one element of strength was apparent--a perverted pride that rose like a shattered, blackened shaft, the one prominent relic of seemingly utter ruin.

At first he coldly declined the cordial and nourishment Miss Eulie brought, and said, with a quietness that did not comport with the meaning of his words, that she had better leave him to himself, for he would not make trouble for any one much longer.

Miss Eulie was shocked, finding in these words and in his general appearance proof that he was more seriously ill than she had anticipated.

He was indeed; but his malady was rather that of a morbid mind depressing an enfeebled body than actual disease. But mental distress could speedily kill a man like Gregory.

Miss Eulie soon brought him to terms by saying, "Mr. Gregory, you see I am alone. Mr. Walton was too exhausted to accompany me, and Annie did not send any of the neighbors, as she thought the presence of strangers would be irksome to you."

"She said she would come herself, but she has had time to think and judge me rightly," muttered he, interrupting her.

"No, Mr. Gregory," Miss Eulie hastened to say; "you do her wrong. She was too ill to come, as she intended and wished to do, and so with many anxious charges sent me in her place. I am but a woman, and dependent on your courtesy. I cannot compel you to go with me. But I am sure you will not wrong my brother's hospitality, and make Miss Walton's passing indisposition serious, by refusing to come with me. If you did she would rise from her sick bed and come herself."

Gregory at once rose and said, "I can make no excuse for myself. I seem fated to do and say the worst things possible under the circumstances."

"You are ill," said Miss Eulie, kindly, as if that explained everything.

Declining aid, he tottered to the carriage, into which Jeff, with some curious surmises, helped him.

Miss Eulie made good Annie's promises to Mrs. Tompkins fourfold, and left the shrivelled dame with a large supply of one of the elements of her heaven--tea, and with the means of purchasing the other--tobacco, besides more substantial additions to the old woman's meagre larder.

Gregory was averse to conversation during the long, slow ride. The jolting, even of the easy cushioned carriage, was exceedingly painful, and by the time they reached home he was quite exhausted. Leaning on Mr. Walton's arm he at once went to his room, and at their urgent entreaties forced himself to take a little of the dainty supper that was forthcoming. But their kindly solicitude was courteously but coldly repelled. Acting reluctantly upon his plainly manifested wish, they soon left him to himself, as after his first eager inquiry concerning Miss Walton it seemed a source of pain to him to see or speak to any one.

At first his arm-chair and the cheery wood-fire formed a pale reflection of something like comfort, but every bone in his body ached from the recent cold he had taken. He had just fever enough to increase the distortion of the images of his morbid and excited mind. Hour after hour he sat with grim white face and fixed stare, scourging himself with the triple scorpion-whip of remorse, vain regret, and self-disgust. But an old and terrible enemy was stealing on him to change the nature of his torment--neuralgic headache; and before morning he was walking the floor in agony, a sad type, while the world slept and nature rested, of that large class, all whose relations, physical and moral, are a jangling discord.

CHAPTER XIX
MISS WALTON MADE OF DIFFERENT
CLAY FROM OTHERS

Simple remedies and prolonged rest were sufficient to restore Annie after the serious shock and strain she had sustained. She rose even earlier than usual, and hastily dressed that she might resume her wonted place as mistress of her father's household. In view of her recent peril and the remediless loss he might have suffered, she was doubly grateful for the privilege of ministering to his wants and filling his declining years with cheer and comfort.

She had not been awake long before Gregory's irregular steps in the adjoining room aroused her attention and caused anxious surmises. But she was inclined to think that his restlessness resulted from mental distress rather than physical. Still she did not pity him less, but rather more. Though so young, she knew that the "wounded spirit" often inflicts the keener agony. Her strong womanly nature was deeply moved in his behalf. As we have seen, it was her disposition to be helpful and sustaining, rather than clinging and dependent. She had a heart "at leisure from itself, to soothe and sympathize." From the depths of her soul she pitied Gregory and wished to help him out of a state which the psalmist with quaint force describes as "a horrible pit and the miry clay."

She was a very practical reformer, and determined that a dainty breakfast should minister to the outer man before she sought to apply a subtler balm to the inner. Trusting not even to Zibbie's established skill, she prepared with her own hands some inviting delicacies, and soon that which might have tempted the most exacting of epicures was ready.

Mr. Walton shared the delight of the children at seeing Annie bustling round again as the good genius of their home, and Miss Eulie's little sighs of content were as frequent as the ripples on the shore. Miss Eulie could sigh and wipe a tear from the corner of her eye in the most cheerful and hope-inspiring way, for somehow her face shone with an inward radiance, and, even in the midst of sorrow and when wet with tears, reminded one of a lantern on a stormy night, which, covered with rain-drops, still gives light and comfort.

Breakfast was ready, but Gregory did not appear. Hannah, the waitress, was sent to his room, and in response to her quiet knock he said, sharply, "Well?"

"Breakfast is waiting."

"I do not wish any," was the answer, in a tone that seemed resentful, but was only an expression of the intolerable pain he was suffering. Hannah came down with a scared look and said she "guessed something was amiss with Mr. Gregory."

Annie looked significantly at her father, who immediately ascended to his guest's door.

"Mr. Gregory, may I come in?" he asked.

"Do not trouble yourself. I shall be better soon," was the response.

The door was unlocked, and Mr. Walton entered, and saw at once that a gentle but strong will must control the sufferer for his own good. Mental and nervous excitement had driven him close to the line where reason and his own will wavered in their decisions, and his irregular, tottering steps became the type of the whole man. His eyes were wild and bloodshot. A ghastly pallor gave his haggard face the look of death. A damp dullness pervaded the heavy air of the room, which in his unrest he had greatly disordered. The fire had died out, and he had not even tried to kindle it again. His broodings had been so deep and painful during the earlier part of the night that he had been oblivious of his surroundings, and then physical anguish became so sharp that all small elements of discomfort were unnoted.

With fatherly solicitude Mr. Waiton stepped up to his guest, who stood staring at him as if he were an intruder, and taking his cold hand, said, "Mr. Gregory, you must come with me."

"Where?"

"To the sitting-room, where we can take care of you and relieve you. Come, I'm your physician for the time being, and doctors must be obeyed."

Gregory had not undressed the night before, and, wrapped in his rich dressing-gown and with dishevelled hair, he mechanically followed his host to the room below and was placed on the lounge.

"Annie has prepared you a nice little breakfast. Won't you let me bring it to you?" said Mr. Waiton, cheerily.

"No," said Gregory, abruptly, and pressing his hands upon his throbbing temples, "the very thought of eating is horrible. Please leave me. Indeed I cannot endure even your kindly presence."

Mr. Walton looked perplexed and scarcely knew what to do, but after a moment said, "Really, Mr. Gregory, you are very ill. I think I had better send for our physician at once."

"I insist that you do not," said his guest, starting up. "What could a stupid country doctor do for me, with his owl-like examination of my tongue and clammy fingering of my pulse, but drive me mad? I must be alone."

"Father," said Annie, in a firm and quiet voice, "I will be both nurse and physician to Mr. Gregory this morning. If I fail, you may send for a doctor."

Unperceived she had entered, and from Gregory's manner and words understood his condition.

"Miss Waiton," said Gregory, hastily, "I give you warning. I am not even the poor weak self you have known before, and I beg you leave me till this nervous headache passes off, if it ever does. I can't control myself at such times, and this is the worst attack I ever had. I am low enough in your esteem. Do not add to my pain by being present now at the time of my greatest weakness."

"Mr. Gregory," she replied, "you may speak and act your worst, but you shall not escape me this morning. It's woman's place to remove pain, not fly from it. So you must submit with the best grace you can. If after I have done all in my power you prefer the doctor and another nurse, I will give way, but now you have no choice."

Gregory fell back on the sofa with a groan and a muttered oath. At a sign from his daughter, Mr. Walton reluctantly and doubtfully passed through the open door into the parlor, where he was joined by Miss Eulie.

Annie quietly stepped to the hearth and stirred the fire to a cheerful blaze. She then went to the parlor and brought the afghan, and without so much as saying, "by your leave," spread it over his chilled form.

Gregory felt himself helpless, but there was something soothing in this assertion of her strong will, and like a sick child he was better the moment he ceased to chafe and struggle.

She left the room a few moments, and even between the surges of pain he was curious as to what she would do next. He soon learned with a thrill of hope that he was to experience the magnetism of her touch, and to know the power of the hand that had seemed alive in his grasp on the day of their chestnutting expedition. Annie returned with a quaint little bottle of German cologne, and, taking a seat quietly by his side, began bathing his aching temples.

"You treat me like a child," he said, petulantly.

"I hope for a while you will be content to act like one," she replied.

"I may, like a very bad one."

"No matter," she said, with a laugh that was the very antidote of morbidness; "I am accustomed to manage children."

But in a very brief time he had no disposition to shrink from her touch or presence. Her hand upon his brow seemed to communicate her own strong, restful life; his temples throbbed less and less violently. Silent and wondering he lay very still, conscious that by some subtle power she was exorcising the demons of pain. His hurried breathing became regular; his hands unclinched; his form, which had been tense and rigid, relaxed into a position of comfort. He felt that he was under some beneficent spell, and for an hour scarcely moved lest he should break it and his torment return. Annie was equally silent, but with a smile saw the effects of her ministry. At last she looked into his face, and said, with an arch smile, "Shall I send for Doctor Bludgeon and Sairy Gamp to take my place?"

He was very weak and unstrung, and while a tremulous smile hovered about his mouth, his eyes so moistened that he turned toward the wall. After a moment he said, "Miss Walton, I am not worthy of your kindness."

"Nor are you unworthy. But kindness is not a matter of business--so much for so much."

"Why do you waste your time on me?"

"That is a childish question. What a monster I should be if I heedlessly left you to suffer! The farmers' wives around would mob me."

"I am very grateful for the relief you are giving me, even though mere humanity is the motive."

"Mere humanity is not my motive. You are our guest, the son of my father's dearest friend, and for your own sake I am deeply interested in you."

"Miss Walton, I know in the depths of your soul you are disgusted with me.

You seek to apply those words to my spirit as you do cologne to my head."

"I beg your pardon. It is not the cologne only that relieves your headache."

"I know that well. It is your touch, which seems magical."

"Well then, you should know from my touch that I am not sitting here telling fibs. If I should bathe your head with a wooden hand, wouldn't you know it?"

"What an odd simile! I cannot understand you." "It is not necessary that you should, but do not wrong me by doubting me again."

"I have done nothing but wrong you, Miss Walton."

"I'm not conscious of it, so you needn't worry, and I assure you I find it a pleasure to do you good."

"Miss Walton, you are the essence of goodness."

"Oh, no, no; why say of a creature what is only true of God? Mr. Gregory, you are very extravagant in your language."

A scowl darkened his face, and he said, moodily, "God seems to me the essence of cruelty."

"'Seems, seems!' An hour since I seemed a torment, and you were driving me away."

"Yes, but you soon proved yourself a kind, helpful, pitiful friend. I once thought my cheek would flame with anger even if I were dying, should I be regarded as an object of pity. But you, better than any one, know that I am one."

"I, better than any one, know that you are not, in the sense you mean."

"Come, Miss Walton, you cannot be sincere now. Do you think I can ever forget the miserable scene of Monday evening, when you placed yourself beside the martyrs and I sank down among the cowards of any age? I reached the bottom of the only perdition I believe in. I have lost my self-respect."

"Which I trust God will help you regain by showing you the only sure and safe ground on which self-respect can be maintained. Much that is called self-respect is nothing but pride. But, Mr. Gregory, injustice to one's self is as wrong as injustice to another. Answer me honestly this question. Did you act that evening only from fear--because you have it not in you to face danger? or did you promise secrecy because you felt the man's crime was none of your business, and supposed I would take the same view?"

Gregory started up and looked at her with a face all aglow with honest, grateful feeling, and said, "God knows the latter is the truth."

"And I know it too. I knew it then."

"But the world could never be made to see it in that light."

"Now pride speaks. Self-respect does not depend upon the opinion of the world. The world has nothing to do with the matter. You certainly do not expect I am going to misrepresent you before it."

He bent a look upon her such as she had never sustained before. It was the look of a man who had discovered something divine and precious beyond words. It was a feeling such as might thrill one who was struggling in darkness, and, as he supposed, sinking in the deep sea, but whose feet touched something which seemed to sustain him. The thought, "I can trust her--she is true," came to him at that time with such a blessed power to inspire hope and give relief that for a moment he could not speak. Then he began, "Miss Walton, I cannot find words--"

"Do not find them," she interrupted, laughingly. "See, your temples are beginning to throb again, and I am a sorry nurse, a true disciple of Mrs. Gamp, to let you excite yourself. Lie down, sir, at once, and let your thoughts dwell the next half-hour on your breakfast. You have much reason for regret that the dainty little tidbits that I first prepared are spoiled by this time. I doubt whether I can do so well again."

"I do not wish any breakfast. Please do not leave me yet."

"It makes no difference what you wish. The idea of an orthodox physician consulting the wishes of his patient! My practical skill sees your need of breakfast."

"Have you had any yourself?" he asked, again starting up, and looking searchingly at her.

"Well, I have had a cup of coffee," she replied, coloring a little.

"What a brute I am!" he groaned.

"In that charge upon yourself you strongly assert the possession of an animal nature, and therefore of course the need of a breakfast."

"May I be choked by the first mouthful if I touch anything before I know you have had your own."

"What an awful abjuration! How can you swear so before a lady, Mr. Gregory?"

"No, it is a solemn vow."

"Then I must take my breakfast with you, for with your disposition to doubt I don't see how you can 'know' anything about it otherwise."

"That is better than I hoped. I will eat anything you bring on those conditions, if it does choke me--and I know it will."

"A fine compliment to my cooking," she retorted and laughingly left the room.

Gregory could not believe himself the haggard wretch that Mr. Walton had found two hours since. Then he was ready to welcome death as a deliverer. Insane man! As if death ever delivered any from evil but the good! But so potent had been the sweet wine of Annie's ministry that his chilled and benumbed heart was beginning to glow with a faint warmth of hope and comfort. Morbidness could no more exist in her presence than shadows on the sunny side of trees. With her full knowledge of the immediate cause of his suffering, and with her unusual tact, she had applied balm to body and spirit at the same time. The sharp, cutting agony in his head had been charmed away. The paroxysm had passed, and the dull ache that remained seemed nothing in comparison--merely the heavy swell of the departed storm.

He forgot himself, the source of all his trouble, in thinking about Miss Walton. The plain girl, as he had at first regarded her, with a weak, untried character that he had expected to topple over by the breath of a little flattery, now seemed divinely beautiful and strong. She reminded him of the graceful, symmetrical elm, which, though bending to the tempest, is rarely broken or uprooted.

He hardly hoped that she would give him credit for the real state of his mind which had led to his ready promise of secrecy. To the counterfeiter's wretched companion he had seemed the weakest and meanest of cowards, and if the story were generally known he would appear in the same light to the world. To his intensely proud nature this would be intolerable. And why should it not be known? If Miss Walton chose to regard his choice as one of cowardice, how could he prove, even to her, that it was not?

Moreover, his low estimate of human nature led him to believe that even Annie would use him as a dark background for her heroism; and he well knew that when such a story is once started, society's strongest tendency is to exaggerate man's pusillanimity and woman's courage. He shuddered as he saw himself growing blacker and meaner in every fireside and street corner narration of the strange tale, till at last his infamy should pass into one of the traditions of the place. A man like Gregory could not long have endured such a prospect. He would have died, either by every physical power speedily giving way under mental anguish, or by his own hand; or, if he had lived, reason would have dropped its sceptre and become the sport of wild thoughts and fancies.

Little wonder that Annie appeared an angel of light when she stood between him and such a future. The ugliest hag would have been glorified and loved in the same position. But when she did this with her own peculiar grace and tact, as a matter of justice, his gratitude and admiration knew no bounds. He was in a fair way to become an idolater and worship the country girl he had once sneered at, as no pictured Madonna was ever revered even in superstitious Italy. Besides placing him under personal obligation, she had, by tests certain and terrible, proved herself true and strong in a world that he believed to be, in the main, utterly false at heart. It is one of our most natural instincts to trust and lean upon something, and Annie Walton seemed one whose friendship he could value above life.

He did not even then realize, in his glad sense of relief, that in escaping the charge of cowardice he fell upon the other horn of the dilemma, namely, lack of principle--that the best explanation of his conduct admitted that he was indifferent to right and wrong, and even to the most serious crime against society, so long as he was not personally and immediately injured. He had acted on the selfish creed that a man is a fool who puts himself to serious trouble to serve the public. The fact that he did not even dream that Annie would make the noble stand she did proves how far selfishness can take a man out of his true course when he throws overboard compass and chart and lets himself drift.

But in the world's code (which was his) cowardice is the one deadly sin. His lack of anything like Christian principle was a familiar fact to him, and did not hurt him among those with whom he associated.

Even Annie, woman-like, could more readily forgive all his faults than a display of that weakness which is most despised in a man. But she too was sufficiently familiar with the world not to be repelled or shocked by a life which, compared with all true, noble standards, was sadly lacking. And yet she was the very last one to be dazzled by a fast, brilliant man of the world. She had been too well educated for that, and had been early taught to distinguish between solid worth and mere tinsel. Her native powers of observation were strong, and her father, and mother also before she died, had given her opportunities for exercising them. Instead of mere assertions as to what was right and wrong and general lecturing on the subject, they had aimed to show her right and wrong embodied in human lives. They made her feel that God wanted her to do right for the same reason that they did, because He loved her. First in Bible narrative told in bedtime stories, then in history and biography, and finally in the experience of those around them, she had been shown the happy contrast of good, God- pleasing life with that which is selfish and wicked. So thorough and practical had been the teaching in this respect, and so impressed was she by the lesson, that she would as soon have planted in her flower- bed the seeds of tender annuals on the eve of autumn frosts, and expected bloom in chill December, as to enter upon a course that God frowns upon, and look for happiness. Her father often said, "A human being opposing God's will is like a ship beating against wind and tide to certain wreck."

An evil life appeared therefore to her a moral madness, under the malign influence of which people were like the mentally deranged who with strange perversity hate their best friends and cunningly watch for chances of self-destruction. While on one hand she shrunk from them with something of the repulsion which many feel toward the unsound in mind, on the other she cherished the deepest pity for them. Knowing how full a remedy ever exists in Him whose word and touch removed humanity's most desperate ills, it was her constant wish and effort to lead as many as possible to this Divine Friend. If she had been like many sincere but selfish religionists, she would have said of Gregory, "He is not congenial. We have nothing in common," and, wrapped in her own spiritual pleasures and pursuits, would have shunned, ignored, and forgotten him. But she chiefly saw his pressing need of help, and said to herself, "If I would be like my Master, I must help him."

Gregory at first had looked upon himself as immeasurably superior to the plain country girl. He little imagined that she at the same time had a profound pity for him, and that this fact would become his best chance for life. She had not forgotten the merciful conspiracy entered into the second evening after his arrival, but was earnestly seeking to carry out its purposes. In order to do this, she was anxious to gain his good-will and confidence, and now saw with gratitude that their adventure on the mountain, that had threatened to end in death, might be the beginning of a new and happy life. She exulted over the hold she had gained upon him, not as the selfish gloat over one within their power, whom they can use for personal ends--not as the coquette smiles when another human victim is laid upon the altar of her vanity, but as the angels of heaven rejoice when there is even a chance of one sinner's repentance.

And yet Annie had no intention of "talking religion" to him in any formal way, save as the subject came up naturally; but she hoped to live it, and suggest it to him in such an attractive form that he would desire it for his own sake.

But her chief hope was in the fact that she prayed for him; and she no more expected to be unheard and unanswered than that her kind father would listen with a stony face to some earnest request of hers.

But Annie was not one to go solemnly to work to compass an event that would cause joy in heaven. She would ask one to be a Christian as she would invite a captive to leave his dungeon, or tell the sick how to be well. She saw that morbid gloom had become almost a disease with Gregory, and she proposed to cure him with sunshine.

And sunshine embodied she seemed to him as she returned, her face glowing with exercise and close acquaintance with the kitchen-range. In each hand she carried a dish, while Hannah followed with a tray on which smoked the most appetizing of breakfasts.

"Your rash vow," she said, "has caused you long waiting. I'm none of your ethereal heroines, but have a craving for solids served in quantity and variety. And while I could have soon got your breakfast it was no bagatelle to get mine."

How fresh and bright she looked saying all this! and he ejaculated, "Deliver me from the ghastly creatures you call 'ethereal heroines.'"

"Indeed, sir," she retorted, "if you can't deliver yourself from them you shall have no help from me. But let us at once enter upon the solemnities, and as you have a spark of gallantry, see to it that you pay my cookery proper compliment."

"Your 'cookery,' forsooth!" said he, with something of her own light tone. "That I should find Miss Walton stealing Zibbie's laurels!"

"Chuckle when you find her doing it. Hannah, who prepared this breakfast?"

"Yourself, miss," answered the woman, with an admiring grin.

"That will do, Hannah; we will wait upon ourselves. Shame on you, sir! You are no connoisseur, since you cannot tell a lady's work from a kitchen-maid's. Moreover, you have shown that wretched doubting disposition again."

Now that they were alone, Gregory said, earnestly, "I shall never doubt you again."

"I hope you never will doubt that I wish to do you good, Mr. Gregory," she replied, passing him a cup of tea.

"You have done me more good in a few brief hours than I ever hoped to receive. Miss Walton, how can I repay you?"

"By being a better friend to yourself. Commence by eating this."

He did not find it very difficult to comply. After a little time he said, "But my conscience condemns me for caring too much for myself." "And no doubt your conscience is right. The idea of being a friend to yourself and going against your conscience!"

"Then I have ever been my own worst enemy."

"I can believe that, and so you'll continue to be if you don't take another piece of toast."

"And yet there has always seemed a fatal necessity for me to do wrong and go wrong. Miss Walton, you are made of different clay from me and most people that I know. It is your nature to be good and noble."

"Nonsense!" said Annie, with a positive frown. "Different clay indeed! I imagine you do wrong for the same reason that I do, because you wish to; and you fail in doing right because you have nothing but your weak human will to keep you up."

"And what keeps you up, pray?"

"Can you even suppose that I or any one can be a Christian without Christ?"

He gave one of his incredulous shrugs.

"Now what may that mean?" she asked.

"Pardon me if I say that I think yours is a pretty and harmless superstition. This world is one of inexorable law and necessity down to the minutest thing. A weed is always a weed. A rose is always a rose. It's my misfortune to be a weed. It's your good fortune to be a rose."

Annie looked as if she might become a briery one at that moment, for this direct style of compliment, though honest, was not agreeable. Conscious of many struggles with evil, it was even painful, for it did her injustice in two aspects of the case. So she said, dryly, "What an automaton you make me out to be!"

"How so?" "If I merely do right as the rose grows, I deserve no credit. I'm but little better than a machine."

"Not at all. I compared you to something that has a beautiful life of its own. But I would willingly be a machine, and a very angular, uncouth one too, if some outside power would only work me right and to some purpose."

"Such talk seems to me idle, Mr. Gregory. I know that I have to try very hard to do right, and I often fail. I do not believe that our very existence begins in a lie, as it were, for from earliest years conscience tells us that we needn't do wrong and ought not to. Honestly now, isn't this true of your conscience?"

"But my reason concludes otherwise, and reason is above conscience-- above everything, and one must abide by its decisions."

For a moment Annie did not know how to answer. She was not versed in theology and metaphysics, but she knew he was wrong. Therefore she covered her confusion by quietly pouring him out another cup of tea, and then said, "Even my slight knowledge of the past has taught me how many absurd and monstrous things can be done and said in the name of reason. Religion is a matter of revelation and experience. But it is not contrary to reason, certainly not to mine. If your reason should conclude that this tea is not hot, what difference would that make to me? My religion is a matter of fact, of vivid consciousness."

"Of course it is. It's your life, your nature, just as in my nature there is nothing akin to it. That is why I say you are made of different clay from myself; and I am very glad of it," he added with an air of pleasantry which she saw veiled genuine earnestness, "for I wish you the best of everything now and always."

Annie felt that she could not argue him out of his folly; and while she was annoyed, she could not be angry with him for expressions that were not meant as flattery, but were rather the strong language of his gratitude. "Time will cure him of his delusions," she thought, and she said, lightly, "Mr. Gregory, from certain knowledge of myself which you cannot have I disclaim all your absurd ideas in regard to the new- fangled clay of my composition. I know very well that I am ordinary flesh and blood, a fact that you will soon find out for yourself. As your physician, I pronounce that such wild fancies and extravagant language prove that you are out of your head, and that you need quieting sleep. I am going to read you the dullest book in the library as a sedative."

"No, please, sing rather."

"What! after such a breakfast! Do you suppose that I would ruin the reputation of my voice in one fell moment? Now what kind of clay led to this remark? Do as your doctor says. Recline on the lounge. Close your eyes. Here is a treatise on the Nebular Hypothesis that looks unintelligible enough for our purpose."

"Nebular Hypothesis! Another heavenly experience such as you are ever giving me."

"Come, Mr. Gregory, punning is a very bad symptom. You must go to sleep at once." And soon her mellow voice was finding its way into a labyrinth of hard scientific terms, as a mountain brook might murmur among the stones. After a little time she asked of Gregory, whose eyes remained wide open, "How does it sound?"

"Like the multiplication table set to music."

"Why don't you go to sleep?"

"I'm trying to solve a little nebular hypothesis of my own. I was computing how many million belles such as I know, and how many ages, would be required to condense them into a woman like yourself."

Annie shut the book with a slam, and with an abrupt, half-vexed "good- by," left the room. For a brief time Gregory lay repenting of his disastrous levity, and then slept.

CHAPTER XX
MISS WALTON MADE OF ORDINARY CLAY

When Gregory awoke, the sun had sunk behind the mountains that he could not even look toward now without a shudder, and the landscape, as seen from the window, was growing obscure in the early dusk of an autumn evening. But had the window opened on a vista in Paradise he would not have looked without, for the one object of all the world most attractive to him was present. Annie sat near the hearth with some light crochet-work in her hands. She had evidently been out for a walk, for she was drying her feet on the fender. How trim and cunning they looked, peeping from under the white edge of her skirt, and what a pretty picture she made sitting there in the firelight! The outline of her figure surely did not suggest the "ethereal heroine," but rather the presiding genius in a happy home, in which the element of comfort abounded. She looked as if she would be a sweet-tempered, helpful companion, in the every-day cares and duties of a busy life:

"A creature not too bright or good   For human nature's daily food."

"How dark and lustrous her eyes are in the firelight!" Gregory thought. "It seems as if another and more genial fire were burning in them. What can she be thinking of, that such happy, dreamy smiles are flitting across her face? If I had such a hearth as that, and such a good angel beside it to receive me after the day's work was over, I believe I could become at least a man, if not a Christian;" and he sighed so deeply that Annie looked hastily up, and encountered his wistful gaze.

"What a profound remark you just made!" she said. "What could have led to it?"

"You."

"I do not think that I am an object to sigh over. I'm perfectly well, I thank you, and have had my dinner."

"You have no idea what a pretty picture you made."

"Yes, in this poor light, and your disordered imagination. But did you sigh on that account?"

"No, but because to me it is only a picture--one that shall have the chief place in the gallery of my memory. In a few days I shall be in my cheerless bachelor apartments, with nothing but a dusty register in the place of this home-like hearth."

"Come, Mr. Gregory, you are growing sentimental. I will go and see if supper is ready."

"Please stay, and I will talk of the multiplication table."

"No, that led to the 'Nebular Hypothesis.' You had better prepare for supper;" and she vanished.

"It's my fate," he said, rising, "to drive away every good and pleasant thing."

He went to the fire and stood where she had sat, and again thought was busy.

"She seems so real and substantial, and yet so intangible! Her defensive armor is perfect, and I cannot get near or touch her unless she permits it. The sincerest compliment glances off. Out of her kindness she helps me and does me good. She bewitches and sways me by her spells, but I might as well seek to imprison a spirit of the air as to gain any hold upon her. I wonder whom or what she was thinking of, that such dreamy, tender smiles should flit across her face."

How his face would have darkened with wrath and hate, if he had known that his detestation, Hunting, had inspired them!

The tea-bell reminded him how time was passing, and he went to his room with an elastic step that one would suppose impossible after seeing him in the morning. But, as is usual with nervous organizations, he sank or rallied rapidly in accordance with circumstances. When he appeared at the table, Mr. Walton could hardly believe his eyes.

"It is again the result of Miss Walton's witchcraft," explained Gregory. "The moment I felt her hand upon my brow, there came a sense of relief. In Italy they would make a saint of her, and bring out the sick for her to touch."

"And so soon lose their saint by some contagious disease," said Annie, laughing.

"I fear, sir, I was very rude to you this morning, but in truth I was beside myself with pain."

"Annie has a wonderful power of magnetism; I don't know what else to call it," said Miss Eulie. "She can drive away one of my headaches quicker than all other remedies combined."

"You are making out," said Annie, "that my proper calling is that of a nurse. If you don't change the subject, I'll leave you all to take care of yourselves, and go down to Bellevue."

"If you do," laughed Gregory, "I'll break every bone in my body, and be carried into your ward as a homeless stranger."

The supper-hour passed away in light and cheerful conversation. As if by common consent, the scenes on the mountain were not mentioned in the presence of the children, and they evidently had had their curiosity satisfied on the subject.

Annie seemed tired and languid after supper and Miss Eulie volunteered to see the children safely to their rest. Mr. Walton insisted that Annie should take his easy-chair, and Gregory placed a footstool at her feet, and together they "made a baby of her," she said. The old gentleman then took his seat, and seemed to find unbounded content in gazing on his beloved daughter. Their guest appeared restless and began to pace the room. Suddenly he asked Mr. Walton, "Have you heard anything of the fugitives?"

"Not a word beyond the fact that they bought tickets for New York and took the train. I have telegraphed to the City Police Department, and forwarded the description of their persons which Annie gave me. Their dwelling has been examined by a competent person, but evidently he is an old and experienced criminal and knows how to cover up his tracks. I think it extremely providential that they did nothing worse than send you over on the other side of the mountain in order to clear a way for escape. Such desperate people often believe only in the silence of death. They might have caused that dog to tear you to pieces and have appeared blameless themselves. If caught, only your testimony could convict them, though I suspect Mrs. Tompkins and her son. Young Tompkins brought them with their luggage to the depot. He says the man called 'Vight' met him returning from the delivery of a load of wood, and engaged his services. As he often does teaming for people in those back districts his story is plausible; and he swears he knew nothing against the man. But he is a bad drinking fellow, and just the one to become an accomplice in any rascality. I fear they will all escape us, and yet I am profoundly grateful that matters are no worse."

While Mr. Walton was talking, Gregory was looking intently at Annie. She was conscious of his scrutiny, and her color rose under it, but she continued to gaze steadily at the fire.

"And I am going to increase that gratitude a hundred-fold, sir," he said, earnestly.

Annie looked up at him with a startled, deprecatory air. "No, Miss Walton," he said, answering her look, "I will not be silent. While it is due to your generosity that the world does not hear of your heroism as the story would naturally be told, it is your father's right that he should hear it, and know the priceless jewel that he has in his daughter. I know that appearances will be against me. If you can take her view of the matter, sir, I shall be glad, otherwise I cannot help it;" and he related the events as they had actually occurred, softening or palliating his course in not the slightest degree.

Mr. Walton turned ashen pale as he thus for the first time learned the desperate nature of his daughter's peril. Then rising with a sudden impulse of pride and affection he clasped her in his arms.

Gregory was about to leave the room, when Mr. Walton's voice detained him. "Do not go, sir. You will pardon a father's weakness."

"Father, I give you my word and honor," cried Annie, eagerly, "that Mr. Gregory did not act the part of a coward. He scarcely does himself justice in his story. He did not realize the principle involved, and saw in the promise he gave the readiest way out of an awkward and dangerous predicament. He did not think the man's crime was any of our business--"

"There is no need of pleading Mr. Gregory's cause so earnestly, my dear," interrupted her father. "I think I understand his course fully, and share your view of it. I am too well accustomed to the taking of evidence not to detect the ring of truth."

"I cannot tell you, sir, what a relief it is to me that you and Miss Walton can judge thus correctly of my action. This morning and yesterday I believed that you and all the world would regard me as the meanest of cowards, and the bitterness of death was in the thought."

"No, sir," said Mr. Walton, kindly but gravely; "your course did not result from cowardice. But permit an old man and your father's friend to say that it did result from the lack of high moral principle. Its want in this case might have been fatal, for the world, as you feared, would scarcely do you justice. Let it be a lesson to you, my dear young friend, that only the course which is strictly right is safe, even as far as this world is concerned."

Gregory's face flushed deeply, but he bowed his head in humility at the rebuke.

"At the same time," continued Mr. Walton, "it was manly in you to state the case frankly to me as you have done; for you knew that you might shield yourself behind Annie's silence."

"It was simply your right to know it," said Gregory, in a low tone.

After a few moments of musing silence, Annie said, earnestly, "I do so pity that poor woman!"

"I imagine she is little better than her companion," said Mr. Walton.

"Indeed she is, father," said Annie, eagerly. "I cannot tell you how I feel for her, and I know from her manner and words that her guilty life is a crushing burden. It must be a terrible thing to a woman capable of good (as she is), and wishing to live a true life, to be irrevocably bound to a man utterly bad."

"She is not so bound to him," said her father; "can she not leave him?"

"Ah! there comes in a mystery," she replied, and the subject dropped. Soon after, they separated for the night.

But Gregory had much food for painful thought. After the experience of that day his chief desire was to stand well in Miss Walton's esteem. And yet how did he stand--how could he stand, being what he was? He was not conscious of love for her as yet. He would have been satisfied if she had said, "I will be your friend in the truest sense of the word." He had no small vanity, and understood her kindness. She was trying to do good to him as she would to any one else. She was sorry for him as for the wretched woman who also found an evil life bitter, but she could never think of him as a dear, congenial, trusted friend. Even her father, in her presence, had rebuked his lack of principle, asserting that his nature was like the vile weed; and this had been proved every day of his visit. If she should come to know of his purpose and effort to tempt her into the display of petty weakness and lack of principle herself, would she not regard him as "utterly bad," and shrink with loathing even from the bonds of friendship?

He was learning the lesson that wrong sooner or later will bring its own punishment, and that the little experiment upon which he had entered as a relief from ennui might become the impassable gulf between him and happiness; for he knew that, if their relations ever verged toward mutual confidence, she would ask questions that would render lies his only escape. He could not sink to that resort. It was late before he found in sleep refuge from painful thoughts.

The next day he was much alone. The news of their adventure having got abroad, many because of their sincere regard for Annie, and not a few out of curiosity, called to talk the matter over. After meeting one or two of these parties, and witnessing the modesty and grace with which Annie satisfied and foiled their curiosity at the same time, he was glad to escape further company in a long and solitary ramble. The air was mild, so that he could take rest in sunny nooks, and thus he spent most of the day by himself. His conscience was awakened, and the more pure and beautiful Annie's character grew in his estimation, the more dastardly his attempt upon it seemed. Never before had his evil life appeared so hideous and hateful.

And yet his remorse had nothing in it of true penitence. It was rather a bitter, impotent revolt at what he regarded as cruel necessity. Now that he had been forced to abandon his theory that people are good as they are untempted, he adopted another, which, if it left him in a miserable predicament, exonerated him from blame. He had stated it to Annie when he said, "You are made of different clay from other people." He tried hard to believe this, and partially succeeded. "It is her nature to be good, and mine to be evil," he often said to himself that long and lonely day. "I have had a fatal gravitation toward evil ever since I can remember."

But this was not true. Indeed, it could be proved out of his own memory that he had had as many good and noble impulses as the majority, and that circumstances had not been more adverse to him than to numerous others. He was dimly conscious of these facts, though he tried to shut his eyes to them.

A man finally gets justice at the bar of his own conscience, but it is extorted gradually, reluctantly, with much befogging of the case.

Still this theory would not help him much with Annie Walton, for he knew that she would never entertain it a moment.

Thus he wandered for hours amid old scenes and boyish haunts, utterly oblivious of them, brooding more and more darkly and despondingly over his miserable lot. He tried to throw off the burden of depressing thought by asking, in sudden fierceness, "Well, what is Annie Walton to me? I have only known her a short time, and having lived thus long, can live the rest of my days--probably few--without her."

But it was of no use. His heart would not echo the words, but in its very depths a voice clear and distinct seemed to say, "I want to be with her--to be near her. With her, the hours are winged; away, they are leaden-footed. She awakens hope, she makes it appear possible to be a man."

He remembered her hand upon his aching brow, and groaned aloud in view of the gulf that his own life had placed between them.

"'Neither can they pass to us,'" he said, unconsciously repeating the words of Scripture. "With her nature what I know it to be, she cannot in any way ally it to mine."

As the shadows of evening deepened he sauntered wearily and despondingly to the house. There were still guests in the parlor, and he passed up to his room. For the first time he found it chilly and fireless. It had evidently been forgotten, and he felt himself neglected; and it seemed that he could drop out of existence unnoted and uncared for. In what had been his own home, the place where for so many years he had experienced the most thoughtful tenderness, there came over him a sense of loneliness and desolation such as he had never before known or believed possible. He felt himself orphaned of heaven and earth, of God and man.

But a process had commenced in Annie's mind that would have surprised him much. Unconsciously as yet even to herself, she was disproving his "superior clay" theory. Though carefully trained, and though for years she had prayerfully sought to do right, still she was a true daughter of Eve, and was often betrayed by human weakness. She had not the small, habitual vanity of some pretty women, who take admiration and flattery as their due, and miss it as they do their meals. Still there were pride and vanity in her composition, and the causes that would naturally develop them were now actively at work. She considered herself plain and unattractive personally, and so she was to the careless glance of a stranger, but she speedily became beautiful, or, what was better, fascinating, to those who learned to know her well. All are apt to learn their strong points rather than their weak ones, and Annie had no little confidence in her power to win the attention and then the respect and regard of those whose eyes turned away indifferently after the first perception of her lack of beauty. She did not use this power like a coquette, but still she exulted in it, and was pleased to employ it where she could innocently. She was amused by Gregory's sublime indifference at first, and thought she could soon change that condition of his mind. She did not know that she was successful beyond her expectation or wishes.

But while she rejected and was not affected by the fulsome flattery with which he at first plied her, detecting in it the ring of insincerity, she had noted, with not a little self-gratulation, how speedily she had made him conscious of her existence and developed a growing interest. She knew nothing of his deliberate plot against her, or of its motive. Therefore his manner had often puzzled her, but she explained everything by saying, "He has lived too long in Paris."

Still it is justice to her to say that while, from the natural love of power existing in every breast, she had her own little complacencies, and often times of positive pride and self-glorification, yet she struggled against such tendencies, and in the main she earnestly sought to use for their own good the influence she gained over others.

But of late there had been enough to turn a stronger head than hers. Gregory's homage and admiration were now sincere, and she knew it, and it was no trifling thing to win such unbounded esteem from a man who had seen so much of the world and was so critical. "He may be bad himself, but he well knows what is good and noble," was a thought that often recurred to her. Then, in a moment of sudden and terrible peril, she had been able to master her strong natural timidity, and be true to conscience, and while she thanked God sincerely, she also was more and more inclined to take a great deal of credit to herself. Gregory's words kept repeating themselves, "You are made of different clay from others." While she knew that this was not true as he meant it, still the tempter whispered, "You are naturally superior, and you have so schooled yourself that you are better than many others." Her father's intense look of pride and pleasure when he first learned of her fortitude, and his strong words of thankfulness, she took as incense to herself. Then came a flock of eager, curious, sympathizing people, who continued to feed her aroused pride by making her out a sort of heroine. Chief of all she was complacent in the consciousness of so generously shielding Gregory when, if she had told the whole story, she, in contrast with him, would appear to far greater advantage.

Altogether, her opinion of Annie Walton was rising with dangerous rapidity; and the feeling grew strong within her that, having coped successfully with such temptations, she had little to fear from the future. And this feeling of overweening self-confidence and self- satisfaction was beginning to tinge her manner. Not that she would ever show it offensively, for she was too much of a lady for that. But at the supper-table that evening she gave evident signs of elation and excitement. She talked more than usual, and was often very positive in matters where Gregory knew her to be wrong; and she was also a little dictatorial. At the same time the excitement made her conversation more brilliant and pointed, and as Gregory skilfully drew her out, he was surprised at the force and freshness of her mind.

And yet there was something that jarred unpleasantly, a lack of the sincere simplicity and self-forgetfulness which were her usual characteristics. He had never known her to use the pronoun "I" with such distinctness and emphasis before. Still all this would not have seemed strange to him in another, but it did in her.

She did not notice the cloud upon his brow, or that he spoke only in order to lead her to talk. She was too much preoccupied with herself for her customary quick sympathy with the moods of others. She made no inquiries as to how he had spent the day, and seemingly had forgotten him as completely as he had been absorbed in her. He saw with a deeper regret than he could understand that, except when he awakened her pity by suffering, or entertained her by his conversation as any stranger might, he apparently had no hold upon her thoughts.

After supper, in answer to the children's demand for stories, she said almost petulantly that she was "too tired," and permitted Aunt Eulie to take them with sorrowful faces away to bed earlier than usual.

"I need a little rest and quiet," she said.

Gregory was eager for further conversation in order that he might obtain some idea how mercy would tinge her judgment of him if she should ever come to know the worst, but she suddenly seemed disinclined to talk, or give him any attention at all.

Taking the arm-chair he usually occupied, and leaving the other for her father, she leaned back luxuriously and gazed dreamily into the fire. Mr. Walton politely offered Gregory his. Then Annie, suddenly, as if awakening, rose and said, "Excuse me," and was about to vacate her seat.

But Gregory insisted upon her keeping it, saying, "You need it more than I, after the unusual fatigues of the day. I am no longer an invalid. Even the ache in my bones from my cold has quite disappeared."

She readily yielded to his wish, and again appeared to see something in the fire that quite absorbed her. After receiving a few courteous monosyllables he apparently busied himself with a magazine.

Suddenly she said to her father, "Are you sure the steamer is due to- day?"

He replied with a nod and a smile that Gregory did not understand, and he imagined that she also gave him a quick look of vexed perplexity.

She did, for by that steamer she expected her lover, Mr. Hunting, who had been abroad on a brief business visit, and she hoped that in a day or two he would make his appearance. Conscious of the bitter enmity that Gregory for some unknown reason cherished toward him, she dreaded their meeting. As Gregory watched her furtively, her brow contracted into a positive frown. The following thoughts were the cause: "It will be exceedingly stiff and awkward to have two guests in the house who are scarcely on speaking terms, and unless I can make something like peace, it will be unendurable. Moreover, I don't want any strangers around, much less this one, while Charles is here."

Thus in the secret of her soul Annie's hospitality gave out utterly, and in spirit she had incontinently turned an unwelcome guest out of doors. Now that she had really won a vantage-ground that could be used effectively, all her Christian and kindly purposes were forgotten in the self-absorption that had suddenly mastered her.

The evening was a painful one to Gregory. His sense of loneliness was deepened, and nowhere is such a feeling stronger than at a fireside where one feels that he has no right. Mr. Walton was occupied that evening with some business papers. He had not a thought of discourtesy toward his guest. Indeed, in the perfection of hospitality, he had adopted Gregory so completely into his household that he felt that he could treat him as one of the family. And yet Mr. Walton was also secretly uneasy at the prospect of entertaining hostile guests, and, with his knowledge of the world, was not sure that peace between them could be made in an hour.

The disposition of those around us often creates an atmosphere, nothing tangible but something felt; and the impression on Gregory's mind, that he belonged not to this household, but to the outside world--that the circle of their lives did not embrace him, and that his visit might soon come to an end without much regret on their part --was not without cause. And yet they would have consciously failed in no duty of hospitality had he stayed for weeks.

But never before had Gregory so felt his isolation. He had but few relatives, and they were not congenial. His life abroad, and neglect, had made them comparative strangers. But here, in the home of his childhood, the dearest spot of earth, were those who might become equally loved with it. In a dim, obscure way the impression was growing upon him that his best chance for life and happiness still centred in the place where he had once known true life and happiness. Annie Walton seemed to him the embodiment of life. She was governed and sustained by a principle which he could not understand, and which from his soul he was beginning to covet.

His good father and mother had been like old Mr. Walton. Their voyage of life was nearly over as he remembered them, and they were entering the quiet, placid waters of the harbor. Whether they had reached their haven of rest through storm and temptation, he did not know, but felt that they never could have had his unfortunate experience or been threatened with utter wreck. They belonged to his happier yet vanished past, which could never return.

But Annie unexpectedly awakened hope for the present and future. This eager-eyed, joyous girl, looking forward with almost a child's delight to the life he dreaded--this patient woman already taking up the cares and burdens of her lot with cheerful acceptance--this strong, high- principled maiden, facing and mastering temptation in the spirit of the olden time--this daughter of nature was full of inspiration. Never had he found her society a weariness. On the contrary she had stirred his slow, feeble pulse, and revived his jaded mind, from the first. Her pure, fresh thought and feeling had been like a breath from an oasis to one perishing in the desert. But chiefly had her kindness, delicacy, and generosity, when in his moral and physical weakness he had been completely at her mercy, won his deepest gratitude. Also he felt that in all his after life he could never even think of her touch upon his aching temples without an answering thrill of his whole nature that appeared to have an innate sympathy with hers.

And yet the exasperating mystery of it all! While she was becoming the one source of life and hope for him, while his very soul cried out for her friendship and sisterly regard (as he would then have said), she seemed, in her preoccupation, unconscious of his existence, and he instinctively felt that she would bid him "goodby" on the following day, perhaps, with a sense of relief, and the current of her life flow on as smoothly and brightly as if he had never caused a passing agitation.

With gnawing remorse he inwardly cursed his evil life and unworthy character, for these he believed formed the hopeless gulf that separated them.

"It is the same," he said, in his exaggerating way, "as if a puddle should mirror the star just above it, and, becoming enamored, should wish it to fall and be quenched in its foul depths."

But he did himself great wrong; for in the fact that Annie so attracted him he proved that he possessed large capabilities of good.

He could not bear to see her sitting there so quietly forgetful of him, and so made several vain attempts during the evening to draw her into conversation. Finding her disinclined to talk, he at last ventured to ask her to sing. With something like coldness she replied, "Really, Mr. Gregory, I am not in the mood for it this evening; besides, I am greatly fatigued."

What a careless, indifferent shrug he usually gave when fair ladies denied his requests! Now, for some unaccountable reason, he flushed deeply and a sharp pain came into his heart. But he only said, "Pardon me, Miss Walton, for not seeing this myself. But you know that I am selfishness embodied, and your former good-nature leads me to presume."

Annie gave him a hurried smile, as she answered, "Another time I will try to keep up my character better"; and then she was absorbed again in a picture among the hickory coals.

Like many who live in the country and are much alone, she was given to fits of abstraction and long reveries. She had no idea how the time was passing, and meant to exert herself before the evening was over for the benefit of her father and guest. But her lively imagination could not endure interruption till it had completed some scenes connected with him she hoped so soon to see. Moreover, as we have said, the tendency to self-absorption had been developing rapidly.

After the last rebuff, Gregory was very quiet, and soon rose and excused himself, saying that he had taken longer walks than usual and needed rest.

Annie awakened, as if out of a dream, with a pang of self-reproach, and said, "I have been a wretched hostess this evening. I hope you will forgive me. The fact is, I've been talked out to-day."

"And I had not the wit to entertain and interest you, so I need forgiveness more. Good-night."

Mr. Walton looked up from his business papers and smiled genially over his spectacles and then was as absorbed as before.

Annie sat down with a vague sense of discontent. With their guest, her dreams also had gone, and she became conscious that she had treated him with almost rude neglect, and that he had borne it in a spirit different from that which he usually showed. But she petulantly said to herself, "I can't always be exerting myself for him as if he were a sick child."

But conscience replied, "You have so much to make you happy, and he so little! You are on the eve of a great joy, and you might have given him one more pleasant evening."

But she met these accusations with a harshness all unlike herself. "It's his own fault that he is not happy. He had no business to spoil his life."

"Yes," retorted conscience, "but you have promised and purposed to help him find the true life, and now you wish him out of the way, and have lost one of your best opportunities and perhaps your last; for he will not stay after Hunting comes;" and, self-condemned, she felt that she had spent a very selfish and profitless evening.

For some reason she did not feel like staying to prayers with her father and Miss Eulie, who now came in, but, printing a hasty kiss on Mr. Walton's cheek, said, "Good-night. I'm tired, and going to bed." Even in her own room there was a malign influence at work that made her devotion formal and brief, and she went to sleep, "out of sorts."

CHAPTER XXI
PASSION AND PENITENCE

The cloud on her brow had not disappeared on the ensuing morning when she came down to breakfast. Unless the causes are removed, the bad moods of one day are apt to follow us into the next.

Annie was now entering upon one of those periods when, in accordance with a common expression, "everything goes wrong," and the world develops a sudden perverseness that distracts and irritates even the patient.

The butcher had neglected to fill the order for breakfast, and Jeff, also under the baleful spell, had killed an ancient hen instead of a spring chicken, to supply the sudden need.

"Couldn't cotch nothin' else," he answered stolidly to Annie's sharp reprimand, so sharp that Gregory, who was walking toward the barn, was surprised.

Zibbie was fuming in the broadest Scotch, and had spoiled her coffee, and altogether it was a sorry breakfast to which they sat down that morning; and Annie's worried, vexed looks did not make it more inviting. Gregory tried to appear unconscious, and directed his conversation chiefly to Mr. Walton and Miss Eulie.

"Annie," said her father, humorously, "it seems to me that this fowl must have reminiscences of the ark."

But she could not take a jest then, and pettishly answered that "if he kept such a stupid man as Jeff, he could not expect anything else."

Annie was Jeff's best friend, and had interceded for him in some of his serious scrapes, but her mood now was like a gusty day that gives discomfort to all.

After a few moments she said, suddenly, "O father, I forgot to tell you. I invited the Camdens here to dinner to-day."

His face clouded instantly, and he looked exceedingly annoyed.

"I am very sorry to hear it," he said.

"Why so?" asked Annie, with an accent that Gregory had never heard her use toward her father.

"Because I shall have to be absent, for one reason. I meant to tell you about it last evening, but you seemed so occupied with your own thoughts, and disappeared at last so suddenly, that I did not get a chance. But there is no help for it. I have very important business that will take me out to Woodville, and you know it requires a good long day to go and come."

"It will never do in the world for you to be away," cried Annie.

"Can't help it, my dear; it's business that must be attended to."

"But, father," she urged, "the Camdens are new people, and said to be very wealthy. We ought to show them some attention. They were so cordial yesterday, and spoke so handsomely of you, expressing a wish to meet you and be social, that I felt that I could not do otherwise than invite them. For reasons you understand it may not be convenient to see them very soon after to-day."

The old gentleman seemed to share his daughter's vexation, but from a different cause, and after a moment said, "You are right; they are 'new people' in more senses than one, and appear to me to be assuming a great deal more than good taste dictates in view of the past. As mistress of my home I wish you to feel that you have the right to invite any one you please, within certain limits. The Camdens are people that I would do any kindness to and readily help if they were in trouble, but I do not wish to meet them socially."

Tears of shame and anger glistened in Annie's eyes as she said, "I'm sure you know very well that I wish to entertain no vulgar, pushing people. I knew nothing of their 'past.' They seemed pleasant when they called. They were said to have the means to be liberal if they wished, and I thought they would be an acquisition to our neighborhood, and that we might interest them in our church and other things."

"In my view," replied Mr. Walton, a little hotly, "the church and every good cause would be better off without their money, for, in plain English, it was acquired in a way that you and I regard as dishonorable. I'm very sorry they've come to spend it in our neighborhood. The fact may not be generally known here, but it soon will be. I consider such people the greatest demoralizers of the age, flaunting their ill-gotten wealth in the faces of the honest, and causing the young to think that if they only get money, no matter how, society will receive them all the same. I am annoyed beyond measure that we should seem to give them any countenance whatever. Moreover, it is necessary that I go to Woodville."

"O dear!" exclaimed Annie, in a tone of real distress, "what shall I do? If I had only known all this before!" Then, turning with sudden irritation to her father, she asked, "Why did you not tell me about them?"

"Because you never asked, and I saw no occasion to. I do not like to speak evil of my neighbors, even if it be true. I did not know of your call upon them till after it occurred, and then remarked, if you will remember, that they were people that I did not admire."

"Yes," she exclaimed, in a tone of strong self-disgust, "I do remember your saying so, though I had no idea you meant anything like what you now state. The wretched mystery of it all is, why could I not have remembered it yesterday?"

"Well, my dear," replied the father, with the glimmer of a smile, "you were a bit preoccupied yesterday; though I don't wonder at that."

"I see it all now," cried Annie, impetuously. "But it was with myself I was preoccupied, and therefore I made a fool of myself. I was rude to you last night also, Mr. Gregory, so taken up was I with my own wonderful being."

"Indeed, Miss Walton, I thought you were thinking of another," said he, with a keen glance, and she blushed so deeply that he feared she was; but he added, quickly, "You once told me that it was as wrong to judge one's self harshly as another. I assure you that I've no complaints to make, but rather feel gratitude for your kindness. As to this other matter, it seems to me that in your ignorance of these people you have acted very naturally."

"I'm sorry I did not tell you more about them," said her father. "I did intend to, but somehow it escaped me."

"Well," said Annie, with a long breath, "I am fairly in the scrape. I've invited them, and the question now is, what shall we do?"

The old merchant, with his intense repugnance to anything like commercial dishonesty, was deeply perturbed. The idea of entertaining at his board as guest a man with whom he would not have a business transaction was exceedingly disagreeable. Leaving the unsatisfactory breakfast half-finished, he rose and paced the room in his perplexity. At last he spoke, as much to himself as to his daughter. "It shall never be said that John Walton was deficient in hospitality. They have been invited by one who had the right, so let them come, and be treated as guests ever are at our house. This much is due to ourselves. But after to-day let our relations be as slight as possible. Mr. Gregory, you are under no obligation to meet such people, and need not appear unless you wish."

"With your permission I will be present, sir, and help Miss Walton entertain them. Indeed, I can claim such slight superiority to these Camdens or any one else that I have no scruples."

"How is that?" asked Mr. Walton, with a grave, questioning look. "I trust you do not uphold the theory that seems to prevail in some commercial circles, that any mode by which a man can get money and escape State prison is right?"

"I imagine I am the last one in the world to uphold such a 'theory,'" replied Gregory, quickly, with one of his expressive shrugs, "inasmuch as I am a poor man to-day because this theory has been put in practice against me. No, Mr. Walton," he continued, with the dignity of truth, "it is but justice to myself to say that my mercantile life has been as pure as your own, and that is the highest encomium that I could pass upon it. At the same time it has been evident to you from the first day I came under your roof that I am not the good man that you loved in my father."

The old gentleman sighed deeply. He was too straightforward to utter some trite, smooth remark, such as a man of the world might make. Regarding Gregory kindly, he said, almost as if it were a prayer, "May his mantle fall on you. You have many traits and ways that remind me strongly of him, and you have it in you to become like him."

Gregory shook his head in deep dejection, and said in a low tone, "No, never."

"You know not the power of God," said Mr. Walton, gravely. "At any rate, thank Him that He has kept you from the riches of those who I am sorry to find must be our guests to-day."

The children now came in from their early visit to the chestnut-trees, and the subject was dropped. Mr. Walton left the room, and Gregory also excused himself. Miss Eulie had taken no part in the discussion. It was not in her nature to do so. She sat beaming with sympathy on both Annie and her brother-in-law, and purposing to do all she could to help both out of the dilemma. She felt sorry for them, and sorry for the Camdens and Gregory, and indeed everybody in this troubled world; but such were her pure thoughts and spiritual life that she was generally on the wing, so far above earthly things that they had little power to depress her.

The burden of the day fell upon Annie, and a heavy one she found it. Her lack of peace within was reflected upon her face, and in her satellites that she usually managed with such quiet grace. Zibbie was in one of her very worst tantrums, and when she heard that there was to be company to dinner, seemed in danger of flying into fragments. The thistle, the emblem of her land, was a meek and downy flower compared with this ancient dame. When she took up or laid down any utensil, it was in a way that bade fair to reduce the kitchen to chaos before night. Jeff had "got his back up" also about the hen, and was as stupid and sullen as only Jeff knew how to be; and even quiet Hannah was almost driven to frenzy by Zibbie reproaching her for being everything under heaven that she knew she was not. In her usual state of mind Annie could have partly allayed the storm, and poured oil on the troubled waters, but now disquietude sat on her own brow, and she gave her orders in the sharp, decisive tone that compels reluctant obedience.

The day was raw and uncomfortable, and Gregory resolved to make his easy-chair by the parlor fire the point from which he would watch the development of this domestic drama. He had no vulgar, prying curiosity, but an absorbing interest in the chief actor; and was compelled to admit that the being whom he had come to regard as faultless was growing human faster than he liked.

This impression was confirmed when the children came tearing through the main hall past the parlor to the dining-room opposite, which they entered, leaving the door open. Annie was there preparing the dessert. Country house-keepers can rarely leave these matters to rural cooks, and Zibbie could be trusted to sweeten nothing that day.

With exclamations of delight the children clamored to help, or "muss" a little in their own way, a privilege often given them at such times. But Annie sent them out-of-doors again with a tone and manner that caused them to tip-toe back past the parlor with a scared look on their faces, and the dining-room door was shut with a bang.

Gregory was puzzled. Here was one who had foiled his most adroit temptations, and resisted wrong in a way that was simply heroic, first showing something very like vanity and selfishness, and then temper and passion on what seemed but slight provocation. He did not realize, as many do not, that the petty vexations of life will often sting into the most humiliating displays of weakness one who has the courage and strength to be a martyr. Generals who were as calm and grand in battle as Mont Blanc in a storm have been known to fume like small beer, in camp, at very slight annoyances.

Annie's spirit was naturally quick and imperious, brooking opposition from no one. She was also fond of approbation. She rated Gregory's hollow French gallantry at its true worth, but his subsequent sincere respect and admiration, after their mountain adventure, had unconsciously elated her, especially as she felt that she had earned them well.

Thus, when he had not intended it, and had given over as hopeless his purpose to tempt her, and dropped it in self-loathing that he should ever have entertained it, he had by his honest gratitude and esteem awakened the dormant vanity which was more sensitive to tributes to her character than to mere personal compliments. The attention she had received the day before had developed this self-complacency still more, and the nice balance of her moral life had been disturbed.

It seems that the tempter watches for every vantage. At any rate, as she expressed it, "everything went wrong" that day. One weakness, one wrong, prepares the way for another as surely as when one soldier of Diabolus gets within the city he will open the gates to others; and Annie's temper, that she had so long and prayerfully schooled, was the weak point inevitably assailed. She was found with her armor off. She had closed the preceding day and entered on the present with the form and not the reality of prayer. Therefore it was Annie Walton alone who was coping with temptation. She felt that all was wrong without and within. She felt that she ought to go to God at once in acknowledgment and penitence, and regain her peace; but pride and passion were aroused. She was hurried and worried, full of impotent revolt at herself and everything. She was in no mood for the dreaded self- examination that she knew must come. She was like a little wayward child, that, while it loves its parents, yet grieves and wrongs them by lack of obedience and simple trust, and having wronged them, partly from pride and partly from fear, does not humbly seek reconciliation.

The obnoxious guests came, and the dinner followed. Mr. Walton was the embodiment of stately courtesy, but it was a courtesy due to John Walton rather than to them, and it somewhat awed and depressed the Camdens. Zibbie had done her best to spoil the dinner, and, in spite of Annie, had succeeded tolerably well. Only the dessert, which Annie had made, did credit to her housekeeping. Hannah waited on them as if she were assisting at their obsequies. Altogether it was a rather heavy affair, though Gregory honestly did his best to entertain, and talked on generalities and life abroad, which the Camdens were glad to hear about, so incessantly that he scarcely had time to eat. But he was abundantly rewarded by a grateful look from Annie.

As for herself, she could not converse connectedly or well. She was trammelled by her feeling toward the guests; she was so vexed with herself, mortified at the dinner, and angry with Zibbie, whom she mentally vowed to discharge at once, that she felt more like crying than talking graceful nonsense; for the Camdens soon proved themselves equal only to chit-chat. She sat at her end of the table, red, flurried, and nervous, as different as possible from the refined, elegant hostess that she could be.

Gregory was also much interested in observing how one so truthful would act under the circumstances, and he saw that she was sorely puzzled continually by her efforts to be both polite and honest.

The Camdens were puzzled also, and severely criticised their entertainers, mentally concluding and afterward asserting, with countless variations, that Miss Walton was wonderfully overrated--that she was a poor housekeeper, and, they should judge, but little accustomed to good society.

"I never saw a girl so flustered," Mrs. Camden would remark, complacently. "Perhaps our city style rather oppressed her; and as for Mr. Walton, he put on so much dignity that he leaned over backward. They evidently don't belong to our set."

That was just the trouble, and Mrs. Camden was right and wrong at the same time.

Their early departure was satisfactory to both parties. Mr. Walton drew a long breath of immeasurable relief, and then called briskly to Jeff, who was coming up from the garden, "Harness Dolly to my buggy."

"Why, father, where are you going?" exclaimed Annie.

"To Woodville."

"Now, father--" began Annie, laying hold of his arm.

"Not a word, my dear; I must go."

"But it will be late in the night before you can get back. The day is cold and raw, and it looks as if it would rain."

"I can't help it. It's something I can't put off. Hurry, Jeff, and get ready to go with me."

"O dear!" cried Annie; "this is the worst of all. Let me go for you-- please do."

"I'm not a child," said the old gentleman, irritably. "Since I could not go this morning, I must go now. Please don't worry me. It's public business that I have no right to delay, and I promised that it should be attended to today;" and with a hasty "good-by" he took his overcoat and started.

Annie was almost beside herself with vexation and self-reproach, and her feelings must find vent somewhere. Gregory prudently retired to his room.

"There's Zibbie," she thought; "I'll teach her one lesson;" and she went to the kitchen and discharged the old servant on the spot.

Zibbie was in such a reckless state of passion that she didn't care if the world came to an end. The only comfort Annie got in this direction was a volley of impudence.

"I hod discharged mesel' afore ye spoke," said the irate dame. "An' ye think I'm gang to broil an ould hen for a spring chicken in peace and quietness, ye're a' wrong. An' then to send that dour nagur a speerin' roun' among my fowl that I've raised from babies--I'll na ston it. I'll gang, I'll gang, but ye'll greet after the ould 'ooman for a' o' that."

Annie then retreated to the sitting-room, where Miss Eulie was placidly mending Susie's torn apron, and poured into her ears the story of her troubles.

"To be sure--to be sure," Aunt Eulie would answer, soothingly; "but then, Annie dear, it all won't make any difference a hundred years from now."

This only irritated Annie more, and at the same time impressed her with her own folly in being so disturbed by comparative trifles.

Gregory found his room chill and comfortless, therefore he put on his overcoat, and started for a walk, full of surprise and painful musings. As he was descending the stairs, Johnny came running in, crying in a tone of real distress, "Oh, Aunt Annie, Aunt Annie, I'm so sorry, so very sorry--"

Annie came running out of the sitting-room, exclaiming sharply, "What on earth is the matter now? Hasn't there been trouble enough for one day?"

"I'm so sorry," sobbed the little boy, "but I got a letter at the post-office, and I--I--lost it coming across the lots, and I--I--can't find it."

This was too much. This was the ardently-looked-for letter that had glimmered like a star of hope and promise of better things throughout this miserable day, and Annie lost all control of herself. Rushing upon the child, she cried, "You naughty, careless boy! I'll give you one lesson"; and she shook him so violently that Gregory's indignation got the better of him, and he said, in a low, deep tone, "Miss Walton, the child says he is 'very, very sorry.' He has not meant to do wrong."

Annie started back as if she were committing sacrilege, and covered her face with her hands. Her back was toward Gregory, but he could see the hot blood mantling her very neck. She stood there for a moment, trembling like a leaf, and he, repenting of his hasty words, was about to apologize, when she suddenly caught the boy in her arms, and sped past him up the stairs to her own room.

To his dying day he would never forget the expression of her face.

It cannot be described. It was the look of a noble spirit, deeply wounded, profoundly penitent. Her intense feeling touched him, and the rough October winds brushed a tear from his own eyes more than once before he returned.

CHAPTER XXII
NOT A HEROINE, BUT A WOMAN

The cold, cynical man of the world was in a maze. He was deeply and painfully surprised at Miss Walton, and scarcely less so at himself. How could he account for the tumult at his heart? When he first saw that outburst of passion against a trembling, pleading child, he felt that he wished to leave the house then and forever. The next moment, when he saw Annie's face as she convulsively clasped the boy to her breast, and with supernatural strength fled to the refuge of her room, he was not only instantly disarmed of anger, but touched and melted as he had never been before.

Feeling is sometimes so intense that it is like the lightning, and burns its way instantly to the consciousness of others. Words of condemnation would have died on the lips of the sternest judge had he seen Annie's face. It would have shown him that the harshest things that he could utter were already anticipated in unmeasured self- upbraidings.

From anger and disgust Gregory passed to the profoundest pity. The children's unbounded affection for Annie proved that she was usually kind and patient toward them. A little thought convinced him that the act he saw was a sudden outburst of passion for which the exasperating events of the day had been a preparation. Her face showed as no language could how sincere and deep would be her repentance. He had not gone very far into the early twilight of a grove before he was conscious of a strong and secret exultation.

"She is not made of different clay from others," he said. "She cannot condemn me so utterly now; and, in view of what I have seen, she cannot loftily deny the kinship of human weakness.

"What a nature she has, with its subterranean fires! She is none of your cool, calculating creatures, who cipher out from day to day what is policy to do. She will act rightly till there is an irrepressible irruption, and then, beware. And yet these ebullitions enrich her life as the lava flow does the sides of Vesuvius. I shall be greatly disappointed if she is not ten times more kind, sympathetic, and self- forgetful than she was before; and as for that boy, she will keep him in the tallest clover for weeks to come, to make up for this.

"How piquant she is! I do not fear her quick, flame-like spirit when it is combined with so much conscience and principle. Indeed, I like her passion. It warms my cold, heavy heart. I wish she had shaken me, who deserved it, instead of the child, and if any makings-up like that in yonder room could follow, I would like to be shaken every day in the week. It would make a new man of me."

In the excitement of his feelings, he had gone further than he had intended, and the dusk was deepening fast when he reached the house on his return. He felt not a little uneasy as to his reception after the rebuke he had given, but counted much on Annie's just and generous disposition. He entered quietly at a side door and passed through the dining-room into the hall. The lamp in the parlor was un-lighted, but the bright wood fire shed a soft, uncertain radiance throughout the room. A few notes of prelude were struck on the piano, and he knew that Miss Walton was there. Stepping silently forward opposite the open door, he stood in the dark hall watching her as she sung the following words:

"My Father, once again Thy wayward child
  In sorrow, shame, and weakness comes to Thee,
Confessing all my sin, my passion wild,
  My selfishness and petty vanity.

"O Jesus, gentle Saviour, at Thy feet
  I fall, where often I have knelt before;
Thou wilt not spurn, nor charge me with deceit,
  Because old faults have mastered me once more.

"Thou knowest that I would be kind and true,
  And that I hate the sins that pierced Thy side;
Thou seest that I often sadly view
  The wrong that in my heart will still abide.

"But Thou didst come such erring ones to save,
  And weakness wins Thy strong and tender love;
So not in vain I now forgiveness crave,
  And cling to hopes long stored with Thee above.

"And yet I plead that Thou would'st surely keep
  My weak and human heart in coming days;
Though now in penitence I justly weep,

O fill my future life with grateful praise."

As in tremulous, melting tones she sung this simple prayer with tears glistening in her eyes, Gregory was again conscious of the strong, answering emotion which the presence of deep feeling in those bound to us by some close tie of sympathy often excites. But far more than mere feeling moved him now. Her words and manner vivified an old truth familiar from infancy, but never realized or intelligently believed-- the power of prayer to secure practical help from God.

How often men have lived and died poor just above mines of untold wealth! Gaunt famine has been the inmate of households while there were buried treasures under the hearthstone. So multitudes in their spiritual life are weak, despairing, perishing, when by the simple divinely appointed means of prayer they might fill their lives with strength and fulness. How long men suffered and died with diseases that seemed incurable, before they discovered in some common object a potent remedy that relieved pain and restored health!

As is the case with many brought up in Christian homes, with no one thing was Gregory more familiar than prayer. For many years he had said prayers daily, and yet he had seldom in all his life prayed, and of late years had come to be a practical infidel in regard to this subject. People who only say prayers, and expect slight, or no results from them, or are content year after year to see no results--who lack simple, honest, practical faith in God's word, such as they have in that of their physician or banker--who only feel that they ought to pray, and that in some vague, mystical manner it may do them good, are very apt to end as sceptics in regard to its efficacy and value. Or they may become superstitious, and continue to say prayers as the poor Indian mutters his incantation to keep off the witches. God hears prayer when His children cry to Him--when His faithful friends speak to Him straight and true from their hearts; and such know well that they are answered.

As Gregory looked at and listened to Annie Walton, he could no more believe that she was expressing a little aimless religious emotion, just as she would sing a sentimental ballad, than he could think that she was only showing purposeless filial affection if she were hanging on her father's arm and pleading for something vital to her happiness. The thought flashed across him, "Here may be the secret of her power to do right--the help she gets from a source above and beyond herself. Here may be the key to both her strength and weakness. Here glimmers light even for me."

Annie was about to sing again, but the interest which she had awakened was so strong that he could not endure delay. Anxiety as to his personal reception was forgotten, and he stepped forward and interrupted her with a question.

"Miss Walton, do you honestly believe that?"

"Believe what?" said she, hastily, quite startled.

"What I gathered from the hymn you sung--that your prayer is really heard and answered?"

"Why, certainly I believe it," said Annie, in a shocked and pained tone. "Do you think me capable of mockery in such things? And yet," she added, sadly, "perhaps after to-day you think me capable of anything."

"Now you do both yourself and me wrong," Gregory eagerly replied. "I do believe you are sincerely trying to obey your conscience. Did I not see your look of sorrow as you passed me on the stairs?--when shall I forget it! Remember words that must have been inspired, which you once quoted to me--

"'Who by repentance is not satisfied
Is not of heaven nor earth,'

and pardon me when I tell you that I have been listening the last few moments out in the hall. Your tones and manner would melt the heart of an infidel, and they have made me wish that I were not so unbelieving. Forgive me for even putting such thoughts in your mind--I feel it is wicked and selfish in me to do it--but how do you know that your prayer, though so direct and sincere, was not sound lost in space?"

"Because it has been answered," she replied, eagerly. "Peace came even as I spoke the words. Because whenever I really pray to God he answers me."

They now stood on opposite sides of the hearth, with the glowing fire between them. In its light Annie's wet eyes glistened, but she had forgotten herself in her sincere and newly awakened interest in him whom she had secretly hoped and purposed before to lead to better things. It had formed no small part of her keen self-reproach that she had forgotten that purpose, and wished him out of the way, just as she was beginning to gain a decided influence over him for good. After what he had witnessed that afternoon she felt that he would never listen to her again.

He would not had he detected the slightest tinge of acting or insincerity on her part, but her penitence had been as real as her passion.

She was glad and grateful indeed when he approached her again in the spirit he now manifested.

As she stood there in the firelight, self-forgetful, conscious only of her wish to say some words that would be like light to him, her large, humid eyes turned up to his face, she made a picture that his mother would like to see.

He leaned against the mantel and looked dejectedly into the fire. After a moment he said, sadly, "I envy you, Miss Walton. I wish I could believe in a personal God who thought about us and cared for us --that is, each one of us. Of course I believe in a Supreme Being--a great First Cause; but He hides Himself behind the stars; He is lost to me in His vast universe. I think my prayers once had an effect on my own mind, and so did me some good. But that's past, and now I might as well pray to gravitation as to anything else."

Then, turning to her, he caught her wistful, interested look--an expression which said plainly, "I want to help you," and it touched him. He continued, feelingly, "Perhaps you are not conscious of it, but you now look as if you cared whether I was good or bad, was sad or happy, lived or died. If I could only see that God cared in something the same way! He no doubt intends to do what is best for the race in the long run, but that may involve my destruction. I dread His terrible, inexorable laws."

"Alas!" said Annie, tears welling up into her eyes, "I am not wise enough to argue out these matters and demonstrate the truth. I suppose it can be done by those who know how."

"I doubt it," said he, shaking his head decisively.

"Well, I can tell you only what I feel and know."

"That is better than argument--that is what I would like. You are not a weak, sentimental woman, full of mysticism and fancies, and I should have much confidence in what you know and feel."

"Do not say that I am not a weak woman; I have shown you otherwise. Be sincere with me, for I am with you. Well, it seems to me that this question of prayer is simply one of fact. We know that God answers prayer, not only because He said He would, but because He does. From my own experience I am as certain of it as of my existence. I think that many who sneer or doubt in regard to prayer are very unfair. I ask you, is it scientific for men to say, 'Nothing is true save what we have seen and know ourselves?' How that would limit one's knowledge. If some facts are discovered in Europe and established by a few proper witnesses, we believe them here. Now in every age multitudes have said that it was a fact that God heard and answered their prayers. What right has any one to ignore these truths any more than any other truths of human experience? I ask my earthly father for something. The next day I find it on my dressing-table. Is it a delusion to believe that he heard and granted my request? When I ask my Heavenly Father for outward things, He sometimes gives them, and sometimes He does not, as He sees is best for me, just as my parents did when I was a little child. And I have already seen that He has often been kinder in refusing. But when I ask for that which will meet my deeper and spiritual needs I seldom ask in vain. If you should ask me how I know it, I in return ask how you know that you are ill, or well, that you are glad or sad, or tired, or anything about yourself that depends on your own inner consciousness? If I should say unjust, insulting things to you now, how would you know you were angry? If I should say, Mr. Gregory, you are mocking me; what I am now saying has no interest for you; you don't hear me, you don't understand me, you are thinking of something else, what kind of proof to the contrary could you offer? Suppose that I should say I want mathematical proof that you do feel an interest, or physical proof--something that I can measure, weigh, or see--should I be reasonable? Do I make it clear to you why I say I know this?"

"Clearer than it was ever made to me before. I cannot help seeing that you are sincere and sure about it. But pardon me--I've got in such an inveterate habit of doubting--are not good Catholics just as sure about the Virgin and the saints hearing and answering them? and do not pagans feel the same way about their deities?"

"Now, Mr. Gregory," said Annie, with a little indignant reproach in her tone, "do you think it just and reasonable to compare my faith, or that of any intelligent Christian, with the gross superstitions you name? Christianity is not embraced only by the ignorant and weak- minded: multitudes of the best and ripest scholars in the world are honest believers."

"Indeed, Miss Walton, I did not mean you to draw any such inference as that," replied he, hastily and in some confusion.

"I do not see how any other can be drawn," she continued; "and I know from what I have read and heard that unbelievers usually seek to give that impression. But it's not a fair one. The absurdities of paganism, monkish legends, and even the plausible errors of the Romish Church, will not endure the light of intelligent education; but the more I know the more I see the beauty and perfection of the Christian religion and the reasonableness of prayer, and so it is with far stronger and wiser heads than mine. Your father and mine were never men to be imposed upon, nor to believe anything just because they were told to do so when children."

"Really, Miss Walton, you said you couldn't argue about this matter. I think you can, like a lawyer."

"If you mean that I am using a lawyer's proverbial sleight of hand, I'm sorry."

"I don't mean that at all, but that you put your facts in such a way that it's hard to meet them."

"I only try to use common-sense. It's about the only sense I have. But I was in hopes you did not want to meet what I say adversely, but would like to believe."

"I would, Miss Walton, honestly I would; but wishes go little way against stubborn doubt. This one now rises: How is it that scientific men are so apt to become infidel in regard to the Bible and its teachings, and especially prayer?"

"I'm sure I hardly know," she answered, with a sigh; "but I will tell you what I think. I don't believe the majority of them know much about either the Bible or prayer. With my little smattering of geology I should think it very presuming to give an opinion contrary to that held by the best authorities in that science; and I think it very presuming in those who rarely look into a Bible and never pray, to tell those who read and pray daily that they don't know what they do know. Then again, scientific people often apply gross material tests to matters of faith and religious experience. The thing is absurd. Suppose a man should seek to investigate light with a pair of scales that could not weigh anything less than a pound. There is a spiritual and moral world as truly as a physical, and spiritual facts are just as good to build on as any other; and I should think they ought to be better, because the spirit is the noblest part of us. A man who sees only one side of a mountain has no right to declare that the other is just like it. Then again your scientific oracles are always contradicting one another, and upsetting one another's theories. Science to-day laughs at the absurdities believed by the learned a hundred years ago; and so will much that is now called science, and because of which men doubt the Bible, be laughed at in the future. But my belief is the same substantially as that of Paul, St. Augustine, Luther, and the best people of my own age; and Luther, who did more for the world than any other mere man, said that to 'pray well was to work well.'"

When Annie was under mental excitement, she was a rapid, fluent talker, and this was especially her condition this evening. As she looked earnestly at Gregory while she spoke, her dark eyes glowing with feeling and intelligence and lighting her whole face, he was impressed more than he could have been by the labored arguments of a cool, logical scholar. Her intense earnestness put a soul into the body of her words. He was affected more than he wished her to know, more than was agreeable to his pride. What she had said seemed so perfectly true and real to her that for the time she made it true to him; and yet to admit that his long-standing doubts could not endure so slight an assault as this, was to show that they had a very flimsy basis. Moreover, he knew that when, left to himself, he should think it all over, new questions would rise that could not be answered, and new doubts return. Therefore he could not receive now what he might be disposed to doubt to-morrow. He was a trifle bewildered, and wanted time to think. He was as much interested in Miss Walton as in what she was saying, and when her words proved that she was a thoughtful woman, and could be the intelligent companion of any man, the distracting fear grew stronger that when she came to know him well, she would coldly stand aloof. The very thought was unendurable. In all the world, only in the direction of Annie Walton seemed there any light for him. So to gain time he instinctively sought to give a less serious turn to the conversation, by saying, "Come, Miss Walton, this is the best preaching I've ever heard. It seems to me quite unusual to find a young lady so interested and well versed in these matters. You must have given a good deal of thought and reading to the subject."

Annie looked disappointed. She had hoped for a better result from her earnest words than a compliment and a little curiosity as to herself. But she met him in his own apparent mood, and said, "Now see how easily imposed upon your sceptical people are! I could palm myself off, like Portia, as a Daniel come to judgment, and by a little discreet silence gain a blue halo as a woman of deep research and profound reading. Just the contrary is true. I am not a very great reader on any subject, and certainly not on theology and kindred topics. The fact is I am largely indebted to my father. He is interested in the subjects and takes pains to explain much to me that would require study; and since mother died he has come to talk to me very much as he did to her. But it seems to me that all I have said is very simple and plain, and you surely know that my motive was not to air the little instruction I have received."

Gregory's policy forsook him as he saw her expression of disappointment; and as he looked at her flushed and to him now lovely face, acting upon a sudden impulse he asked, "Won't you please tell me your motive?"

His manner and tone convinced her in a moment that he was more moved and interested than she had thought, and answering with a like impulse on her part, she said, frankly, "Mr. Gregory, pardon me for saying it, but from the very first day of your visit it seemed clear to me that you were not living and feeling as those who once made this your home could wish, and the thought was impressed upon me, impressed strongly, that perhaps God had sent you in your feeble health and sadness (for you evidently were depressed in mind also), to this place of old and holy memories, that you might learn something better than this world's philosophy. I have hoped and prayed that I might be able to help you. But when to-day," she continued, turning away her head to hide the rising tears, "I showed such miserable weakness, I felt that you would never listen to me again on such subjects, and would doubt more than ever their reality, and it made me very unhappy. I feel grateful that you have listened to me so patiently. I hope you won't let my weakness hurt my cause. Now you see what a frank, guileless conspirator I am," she added, trying to smile at him through her tears.

While she spoke Gregory bent upon her a look that tried to search her soul. But the suspicious man of the world could not doubt her perfect sincerity. Her looks and words disclosed her thought as a crystal stream reveals a white pebble over which it flows. He stepped forward and took her hand with a pressure that caused it pain for hours after, but he trusted himself to say only, "You are my good angel, Miss Walton. Now I understand your influence over me," and then abruptly left the room.

But he did not understand her influence. A man seldom does when he first meets the woman whose words, glances, and presence have the subtle power to fill his thoughts, quicken his pulse, stir his soul, and awaken his whole nature into new life. He usually passes through a luminous haze of congeniality, friendship, Platonic affinity, or even brotherly regard, till something suddenly clears up the mist and he finds, like the first man, lonely in Eden, that there is but one woman for him in all the world.

Gregory was in the midst of the cloud, but it seemed very bright around him as he paced his room excitedly.

CHAPTER XXIII
GREGORY'S FINAL CONCLUSION
IN REGARD TO MISS WALTON

Annie Walton was now no longer an enigma to Gregory. He had changed his views several times in regard to her. First, she was a commonplace, useful member of the community, in a small way, and part of the furniture of a well-ordered country-house--plain furniture too, he had said to himself. But one evening in her company had convinced him that such a Miss Walton was a fiction of his own mind, and he who had come to regard average society girls as a weariness beyond endurance was interested in her immediately.

Then her truth and unselfishness, and the strong religious element in her character, had been a constant rebuke to him, but he had soothed himself with the theory that she differed from others only in being untempted. He then had resolved to amuse himself, ease his conscience, and feed his old grudge against her sex, by teaching the little saint that she was only a weak, vain creature. Yet she had sustained not only his temptations, but another ordeal, so searching and terrible that it transformed her into a heroine, a being of superior clay to that of ordinary mortals. "It's her nature to be good, mine to be bad," he had said; "I'm a weed, she is a flower." But Annie herself had rudely dispelled this illusion.

Now he saw her to be a woman who might, did she yield to the evil within her and without, show all the vanity, weakness, and folly generally, of which he had at first believed her capable, but who, by prayer and effort, daily achieved victories over herself. In addition, she had manifested the most beautiful and God-like trait that can ennoble human character--the desire to save and sweeten others' lives. To have been lectured and talked to on the subject of religion in any conventional way by one outside of his sympathies would have been as repulsive as useless, but Annie had the tact to make her effort appear like angelic ministry.

There is that about every truly refined woman with a large loving heart which is irresistible. The two qualities combined give a winning grace that is an "open sesame" everywhere. The trouble is that culture and polish are too often the sheen of an icicle.

He believed he saw just her attitude toward him. It reminded him of Miss Bently's efforts in his behalf, but with the contrast that existed between Miss Bently and Annie. He now wondered that he could have been interested in such a vain, shallow creature as Mrs. Grobb had proved herself, and he excused himself on the ground that he had idealized her into something that she was not. All that Annie said and did had the solidity of truth, and not the hollowness of affectation. And yet there was one thing that troubled him. While her effort to help him out of his morbid, unhappy state was so sincere, she showed no special personal interest in himself, such as he had in her. If he should now go away, she would place him merely in the outer circle of her friends or acquaintance, and make good the old saying, "Out of sight, out of mind." But already the conviction was growing strong that it would be long before she would be out of his mind. Though he had plenty of pride, as we have seen, he was not conceited, and from long familiarity with society could readily detect the difference between the regard she would feel for a man personally attractive and the interest of aroused sympathies which she might have in any one, and which her faith and nature led her to have in every one. Of course he was not satisfied with the latter, and it was becoming one of his dearest hopes to awaken a personal feeling, though of just what kind he had not yet even defined to himself.

When the tea-bell rang, much later than usual on account of the chaos of the day, he was glad to go down. Her society was far pleasanter than his own, and future events might make everything clearer.

His supposition in regard to Johnny was correct. As he descended the stairs, the boy came out of the sitting-room, holding Annie tightly by the hand and beaming upon her like the sun after a shower, and when he found by his plate a huge apple that had been roasted specially for him, his cup of happiness was full and he was ready for another shaking. If the apple once caused discord it here confirmed peace.

The supper was as inviting as the dinner had been forbidding, indicating a change of policy in the kitchen cabinet. In fact, after Zibbie cooled off, she found that she was not ready for "the world to come to an end" (or its equivalent, her leaving the Waltons after so many years of service and kindness). She had not yet reached the point of abject apology, though she knew she would go down on her old rheumatic knees rather than leave her ark of refuge and go out into the turbulent waters of the world; still she made propitiating overtures in the brownest of buttered toast, and a chicken salad that might have been served as ambrosia on Mount Olympus. Zibbie was a guileless strategist, for in the success of the supper she proved how great had been her malign ingenuity and deliberation in spoiling the dinner. She could never claim that it was accidental. Hannah no longer waited as if it were a funeral occasion, and the domestic skies were fast brightening up, except in one quarter: Mr. Walton's chair was vacant, and Gregory noticed that Annie often looked wistfully and sadly toward it.

With the sensitiveness of one who habitually hid his deeper feeling from the world, Gregory tried to act as if his last conversation with Annie had been upon the weather; and as might be expected of refined people, no allusion was made to the unpleasant features of the day. Neither then nor afterward was a word adverse to the Camdens spoken. They had been guests, and that was enough for the Waltons' nice sense of courtesy. Only Susie, with a little sigh of relief, gave expression to the general feeling by saying, "Somehow I feel kind of light to- night. I felt dreadfully heavy this morning."

Annie, with a smile on her lips and something like a tear in her eye, noticed the child's remark by adding, "I think we should all feel light if grandpa were only here."

After supper she sung to the children and told them a bedtime story, and then with a kiss of peace sent them off to their dream-wanderings.

During Annie's absence from the parlor, Gregory remained in his room. He was in no mood to talk with any one else. Even Miss Eulie's gentle patter of words would fall with a sting of pain.

When Annie came down to the parlor she said, "Now, Mr. Gregory, I will sing as much as you wish, to make up for last evening. Indeed I must do something to get through the hours till father's return, for I feel so anxious and self-reproachful about him."

"And so make happiness for others out of your pain," said he. "Why don't you complain and fret all the evening and make it uncomfortable generally?"

"I have done enough of that for one day. What will you have?"

An impulse prompted him to say "You," but he only said, "Your own choice," and walked softly up and down the room while she sung, now a ballad, now a hymn, and again a simple air from an opera, but nothing light or gay.

He was taking a dangerous course for his own peace. As we have seen, Annie's voice was not one to win special admiration. It was not brilliant and highly cultivated, and had no very great compass. She could not produce any of the remarkable effects of the trained vocalist. But it was exceedingly sweet in the low, minor notes. It was sympathetic, and so colored by the sentiment of the words that she made a beautiful language of song. It was a voice that stole into the heart, and kept vibrating there long hours after, like an Aeolian harp just breathed upon by a dying zephyr.

As was often the case, she forgot her auditor, and began to reveal herself in this mode of expression so natural to her, and to sing as she did long evenings when alone. At times her tones would be tremulous with pathos and feeling, and again strong and hopeful. Then, as if remembering the great joy that soon would be hers in welcoming back her absent lover, it grew as tender and alluring as a thrush's call to its mate.

> "O'er the land and o'er the sea
> Swiftly fly my thoughts to thee;
> Haste thee and come back to me:
> I'm waiting.
>
> "Thou away, how sad my song!

When alone, the days are long;
Soon thou'lt know how glad and strong
My welcome.

"Haste thee, then, o'er sea and land:
Quickly join our loving band,
Waiting here to clasp thy hand
In greeting."

"Indeed, Miss Walton," said Gregory, leaning upon the piano, "that would bring me from the antipodes."

She did not like his tone and manner, and also became conscious that in her choice of a ballad she had expressed thoughts that were not for him; so she tried to turn the matter lightly off by saying, "Where you probably were in your thoughts. What have you been thinking about all this long time while I have fallen into the old habit of talking to myself over the piano?"

"You, I might say; but I should add, in truth, what you have said to me this evening."

"I hope only the latter."

"Chiefly, I've been enjoying your singing. You have a very peculiar voice. You don't 'execute' or 'render' anything, any more than a bird does. I believe they have been your music teachers."

"Crows abound in our woods," she answered, laughing.

"So do robins and thrushes."

Her face suddenly had an absent look as if she did not hear him. It was turned from the light, or the rich color that was mantling it would have puzzled him, and might have inspired hope. With some abruptness and yet hesitation, such as is often noted when a delicate subject is broached, she said, "Mr. Gregory, I wish I could make peace between you and Mr. Hunting. I think you are not friendly."

As she looked to see the effect of her remark the light shone on his face, and she was again deeply pained to see how instantly it darkened. For a moment he did not reply; then in a cold, constrained voice, he said, "He is a friend of the family, I suppose."

"Yes," she replied, eagerly.

"I too would like to be regarded as a friend, and especially to you; so I ask it as a great personal favor that you will not mention that gentleman's name again during the brief remnant of my visit."

"Do you mean any imputation against him?" she asked, hotly.

Policy whispered, "Don't offend her. Hunting may be a near relation;" so he said, quietly, "Gentlemen may have difficulties concerning which they do not like to speak. I have made no imputation against him whatever, but I entreat you to grant my request."

Annie was not satisfied, but sat still with knit brows. At that moment she heard her father's step and ran joyfully to meet him. He had come home chilled from a long ride in the raw wind, and she spent the rest of the evening in remorseful ministrations to his comfort. As she flitted around him, served his tea and toast, and petted him generally, Gregory felt that he would ride for a night after the "Wild Huntsman" to be so treated.

He also rightly felt that Annie's manner was a little cool toward him. It was not in her frank, passionate nature to feel and act the same toward one who had just expressed such bitter hostility toward her lover. But the more he thought of it the more determined he was that there should be no alienation between them on account of Hunting.

"Curse him!" he muttered, "he has cost me too much already."

He had the impression that Hunting was a relative of the family. That he was the accepted lover of the pure and true girl that he himself was unconsciously learning to love was too monstrous a thought to be entertained. Still Annie's words and manner caused him some sharp pangs of jealousy, till he cast the very idea away in scorn as unworthy of both himself and her.

"Evil as my life has been, it is white compared with his," he said to himself.

In accordance with his purpose to keep the vantage-ground already gained, he was geniality itself, and so entertained Miss Eulie and Mr. Walton that Annie soon relented and smiled upon him as kindly as ever. She was in too humbled and softened a mood that evening to be resentful, except under great provocation, and she was really very grateful to Gregory for his readiness to overlook her weakness and give her credit for trying to do right. Indeed, his sincere admiration and outspoken desire for her esteem inclined her toward him, for was she not a woman?

"After all," she thought, "he has said nothing against Charles. They have had a quarrel, and he no doubt is the one to blame. He is naturally very proud and resentful, and would be all the more so in that degree that he was wrong himself. If I can help him become a Christian, making peace will be an easy affair; so I will not lose the hold that I have gained upon him. When Charles comes he will tell me all about it, and I will make him treat Gregory in such a way that enmity cannot last."

How omnipotent girls imagine themselves to be with those who swear they will do anything under heaven to please them, but who usually go on in the old ways!

It was late when the family separated for the night, but later far when Gregory retired. The conclusion of his long revery was that in Annie Walton existed his only chance of life and happiness. She seemed to possess the power to wake up all the man left in him, and if there were any help in God, she only could show him how to find it.

Thus his worldly wisdom had taught him, as many others had been taught, to lean on a human arm for his main support and chief hope, while possibly in the uncertain future some help from heaven might be obtained. He was like a sickly plant in the shade saying to itself, "Yonder ray of sunlight would give me new life," while it has no thought of the sun from which the ray came. He truly wished to become a good man for his own sake as well as Annie's, for he had sufficient experience in the ills of evil; but he did not know that a loving God does not make our only chance dependent on the uncertain action and imperfect wisdom of even the best of earthly friends. The One who began His effort of saving man by dying for him will not afterward neglect the work, or commit it wholly to weak human hands.

The next morning, being that of Saturday, brought Annie many duties, and these, with callers, so occupied her time that Gregory saw but little of her. The shadow between them seemed to have passed away, and she treated him with the utmost kindness. But there was a new shadow on her face that he could not understand, and after breakfast he said to her as they were passing to the parlor, "Miss Walton, you seem out of spirits. I hope nothing painful has happened."

"Jeff found my lost letter this morning," she said, "and I have been deservedly punished anew, for it brought me unpleasant tidings;" and she hastily left the room, as if not wishing to speak further on the matter.

It had indeed inflicted a heavy disappointment, for it was from Hunting, stating that business would detain him some days longer in Europe. But she had accepted it with resignation, and felt that it was but a light penalty for all her folly of the two preceding days.

Gregory was not a little curious about it, for he was interested now in everything connected with her; but as she did not speak of it again, good taste required that he should not. An uncomfortable thought of Hunting as the possible writer crossed his mind, but he drove it from him with something like rage.

As Gregory sat brooding by his fire, waiting till the sun should grow higher before starting for a walk, Jeff came up with an armful of wood, and seemed bubbling over with something. He, too, had suffered sorely in the storm he had helped to raise the preceding day, and had tremblingly eaten such dinner as the irate Zibbie had tossed on the table for him, as a man might lunch in the vicinity of a bombshell. He seemed to relieve himself by saying, with his characteristic grin, as he replenished the fire, "It was dreadful 'pestuous yesterday, but de winds is gone down. I'se glad dat ole hen is done for, but she hatch a heap ob trouble on her las' day."

Jeff belonged to that large school of modern philosophers who explain the evils of the day on very superficial grounds. The human heart is all right. It's only "dat ole hen" or unfavorable circumstances of some kind, that do the mischief.

CHAPTER XXIV
"THE WORM-INFESTED CHESTNUT"
--GREGORY TELLS THE WORST

In his solitary ramble, Gregory again thought long and deeply over the situation. The impression was growing strong that the supreme hour of his life, which would decide his destiny for good or evil, was fast approaching. For years previously he had given up the struggle against the latter, and had sunk deep in moral apathy, making greater effort to doubt everything concerning God than to believe. Then he had lost even his earthly ambition, and become mere driftwood on the tide of time. But a sweet, true woman was doing a work for him like that of Elsie for Prince Henry in the Golden Legend. A consciousness of power to take up his burden again and be a man among men was coming back, and old Daddy Tuggar's words were growing into a hope-inspiring prophecy: "She could take the wickedest man livin' to heaven, if she'd stay right by him."

And yet his self-distrust was painfully and dangerously great, and he feared that when Annie came to know the worst about him, and how he had plotted against her, she would shrink from him. If she despaired of him he would despair of himself. He was certain that he could not win even an intimate congenial acquaintance, much less a more tender regard, unless he became a true, good man, worthy of her confidence. He could not become such by commencing in deception--by hiding the past, and trying to appear what he was not. For in the first place she would certainly find him out and despise him, and in the second place his own nature now revolted at anything false in his relations with her. After long anxious thought, he concluded that the only safe, as well as the only honorable, course was perfect frankness. If he began wrong, the end would be disastrous. He was no longer subject to school-boy impulses, but was a mature and thoughtful man, and had trained himself in business to look far and keenly into the consequences of present action. He saw in this Walton blood an intense antipathy to deceit. His own nature was averse to it also, and his experience with Hunting had made it doubly hateful. His pride revolted at it, for his lack of hypocrisy had been the one ground of self- respect that remained in him. If in his folly and wickedness he had blotted out the possibility of a happy future, he must endure the terrible truth as he could. To try to steal into heaven, earthly or celestial, by the back door of specious seeming, only to be discovered in his true character and cast out with greater ignominy, was a course as revolting as foolish. Annie knew him to be a man of the world, with sceptical tendencies, but to her guileless nature and inexperience this might not mean anything very bad. In the secret of his own soul, however, he had to meet these terrible questions:

"Can God receive and pardon a willing unbeliever, a man who has sinned against the clearest light, a gambler, a libertine, an embodiment of selfishness? Can it be that Annie Walton will ever receive even friendship from one so stained, knowing the additional fact that I plotted against her and sought for my own sense-less gratification to prove that she was a weak, vain woman, who would be no better than myself if tempted in like manner? It is true that I never betrayed innocence or wronged a man out of a dollar. It is true that in the code of the world I have done nothing to lose my character as a gentleman, and even my design upon Miss Walton would pass as a harmless flirtation in society; but the code of the world has no force in her pure mind, and the license it permits is an insult to the law of God. And now it is not with the world, but with her and Heaven that I have to deal. Things at which society shrugs its shoulders indifferently are to them crimes, and black ones too. I might as well seek her love with a felon's indictment hanging over me as to seek it hiding my past life. When she came to find me out she would feel that I had wronged her unutterably, and confidence, the only basis of lasting esteem, would be gone.

"Deep in my heart I have never doubted my mother's faith. When I imagined I did I was self-deceived. Everything here confirms it, and Miss Walton more than all. I will consult the divine oracle. She shall be the fair vestal, the gentle priestess. She lives near to heaven, and knows its mind. If her kind and womanly nature shrinks from me, if she coldly draws her skirts aside that I pollute them not even with a touch--if she by word or even manner proves that she sees an impassable gulf between us--then she need waste no breath in homilies over repentance and in saying that God can receive those whom man cannot. I'll not even listen, but go back to the city and meet my fate. If imperfect human creatures cannot forgive each other--if I have gone so far beyond the mercy of a tender-hearted woman--then I need look for nothing from a just and holy God. It's mockery for good people, with horror and disgust slightly veiled upon their faces, to tell poor wretches that God will receive them and love them, while they would no more take them into their confidence and esteem than they would a pestilence. It's like people saying to one in the last stage of consumption, 'I hope you will be better soon.' They don't hope or expect any such thing. The Bible is said to teach that a man can sin away his day of grace. I had about believed that I had sinned away mine. This genuine, honest Christian girl has made me think differently. She has inspired the strong hope that she could lead me to become a good man--even a Christian. She shall either fulfil that hope or show it to be false."

Such was the outline of his thoughts that long day, during which hope and fear balanced an even scale. But the evening shadows found fear predominating. His awakened conscience and his recent contact with true moral standards revealed him to himself in darker and still darker shadow. At times he was almost ready to despair, to bid his entertainers a courteous farewell on Monday, and go back to the city as he came, with the additional wretchedness of having seen the heaven he could not enter.

But when he came down to supper, Annie smiled so sweetly and looked so gentle and kind, that he thought, "She does not seem one to push a wretch over a precipice. That warm little hand that charmed away my headache so gently cannot write Dante's inscription over my 'Inferno,' and bid me enter it as 'my own place'; and yet I dread her sense of justice."

In his anxiety and perturbation of mind he was unusually grave and silent during the meal and evening. Annie exulted secretly over him.

"He is thinking in earnest now. His old apathy and trifling manner are gone."

He was indeed thinking in terrible earnest. Her effort had awakened no schoolgirl interest and penitence that she could soothe and reward by quoting a few sweet promises, but had aroused a spirit like that which came down from the hills of Gadara, and which no man could bind.

Men and women in good society may be very polished and refined, and yet their souls in God's sight and their own be shameful, "naked," wearing no robe of righteousness, bound by no laws of purity and right, and "always, night and day, crying and cutting" themselves in the unrest of remorse. Sad and yet true it was that the demon- possessed man, the terror of the Gadarenes, was but too true a type of the gentlemanly and elegant Walter Gregory, as he sat that night in a torment of dread and hope at the peaceful fireside of a Christian family. If his fears were realized--if Annie turned from him when he revealed his true self to her--there seemed to him every probability that evil evermore would be his master. While she was innocently hoping and praying that her words and influence might lead him to read his Bible, go to church, and eventually find his way into the "green pastures beside the still waters," it seemed that within a few hours she would either avert or complete that most awful of tragedies--the loss of a soul.

He accompanied them to church the following morning, and his manner was grave even to solemnity. Little wonder. In a certain sense, in view of his resolution, the Judgment Day had come to him.

With heavy, contracted brows he listened to a sermon anything but reassuring. The good old minister inclined to a legal and doctrinal gospel, and to-day his subject was the perfection and searching character of the divine law. He showed how God could make no terms with sin--that he hated it with a terrible and vindictive hatred, because in all respects it was opposite and antagonistic to His nature--because it defiled, degraded, and destroyed. He traced all human wretchedness to this poisonous root, and Gregory trembled and his face grew dark with despair as he realized how it was inwoven with every fibre of his heart. Then in simple but strong language the silver-haired old man, who seemed a type of the ancient prophets, portrayed the great white throne of God's justice, snowy, too dazzling for human eyes, and the conscience-stricken man shrunk and cowered.

He turned to Annie to see how this train of thought, so terrific to him, affected her. Not a trace of fear was upon her face, but only serene, reverent awe. He glanced at Mr. Walton, but the old magistrate sat in his place, calm and dignified, evidently approving the action of the greater Judge. Miss Eulie's face, as seen between himself and the light of the window, appeared spirit-like.

"Thus they will look on the Judgment Day," thought Gregory, "while I tremble even at its picture. O the vital difference between guilt and innocence, between faith and unbelief!"

If the venerable clergyman had been talking personally to Gregory or any sinful creature, he would not have concluded his subject where he did. He would have shown how between the throne of justice and the sinner there stood an Advocate, an Intercessor, a Saviour. But having logically developed his text, he finished his discourse. Perhaps on the following Sabbath he might present the mercy of God with equal clearness. But the sermon of the day, standing alone and confirming the threatenings of an accusing conscience, depressed Gregory greatly. It did not anger him, as such truth usually did. He was too weak and despairing. He now felt the hopelessness and folly of opposition. The idea of getting into a passion with fate! Only weak natures fume at the inevitable. There is a certain dignity in silent, passive despair.

Annie's voice singing the closing hymn beside him sounded like an angel's voice across the "great gulf." Almost mechanically he walked down the aisle out into the sunny noon of a warm October day. Birds were twittering around the porch. Fall insects filled the air with their cheery chirpings. The bay of a dog, the shrill crowing of a cock, came softened across the fields from a neighboring farm. Cow- bells tinkled faintly in the distance, and two children were seen romping on a hillside, flitting here and there like butterflies. The trees were in gala dress of crimson and gold, and even the mountains veiled their stern grandeur in a purple haze, through which the sun's rays shimmered with genial but not oppressive warmth.

The people lingered around the door, shaking hands and greeting one another with the plain but cordial courtesy of the country. Gregory heard one russet-apple-faced man say that "Betsy was better," and an old colored woman, with a visage like that apple in black and mottled decay, said in cheerful tones that "little Sampson was gittin' right peart." A great raw-boned farmer asked a half-grown boy, "How's yer mare?" and the boy replied that the animal was better also. All seemed better that bright day, and from a group near came the expression, "Crops were good this year." While the wealthier and more cultured members of the congregation had kindly nods and smiles for all, they naturally drew together, and there seemed a little flutter of excitement over the renewal of the sewing society that had been discontinued during the summer.

Gregory stood apart from all this, with the heavy contraction still upon his brow, and asked himself, "What have these simple, cheery, commonplace people, with their petty earth-born cares and interests, to do with that 'great white throne' of which we have just heard? and where in this soft, dreamy landscape, so suggestive of peace, rest, and everyday life, lurks any hint of the 'wrath of a just and holy God'?"

And then the old pastor, who a little before had seemed a prototype of John, the stern reformer from the wilderness, came out smiling and benignant, greeting his flock as a father might his children. The very hand that had been raised in denunciation, and in threatening a doom that would appall the heart of courage itself, was given to Gregory in a warm and cordial grasp. The man he had trembled before now seemed the personification of sweet-tempered human kindness. The contrast was so sharp that it seemed to Gregory that either what he saw or what he had heard must be an utter delusion.

As they were driving home, he suddenly broke the moody silence by asking Miss Walton, "How do you reconcile the scene at the church door, so matter-of-fact, cheery, and earthly, with the terrible pictures suggested by the sermon? If such things are before us, it seems to me that bright, sunny days like these are mockery."

She looked at him wistfully. The sermon had not been what she would have wished, but she trusted it would do him good by cutting away every hope based on anything in himself or in vague general ideas of God's indiscriminate mercy. She answered gently, "The contrast was indeed great, now I think of it, and yet each scene was matter-of-fact to me in the sense of being real. Besides, that one which our pastor described was a court of justice. I shall have an Advocate there who will clear me. As for 'bright days,' I believe they are just what God means His people to have always."

"Yes," said he, gloomily, "that is your side of the question."

"It may be yours also," she replied, in a low tone.

He shook his head and looked away to hide his pain.

After a short time he again said, "Do you not think that the view of God which your minister gave is very depressing to the average man? Is not His law too perfect for imperfect humanity?"

"Not at all," she answered, eagerly; but before she could say more, Mr. Walton, unaware of the subject occupying them, turned from the front seat and introduced another topic.

After dinner, Gregory went to his room, which he restlessly paced.

"Even her creed, her faith, as well as her purity and truth, raises a wall as high as heaven between us," he exclaimed, bitterly. "She has only to see me as God sees, to shrink away appalled, disgusted. Well, she shall," he muttered, grinding his teeth; "I shall not add the worst torment of all to my perdition by deceiving her."

As he came down stairs, Annie had just finished reading to the children, and he said, "Miss Walton, will your ideas of Sabbath- keeping prevent you from taking a stroll in the garden with me?"

"Not at all," she replied, smiling. "A garden is a good place to keep Sunday in."

He walked silently at her side across the lawn down a shady walk. Annie hoped much from this interview, and sent a swift, earnest prayer to Heaven that she might speak wisely. She feared that his dejection would pass into discouragement and despair. She saw that he was much depressed, and judged correctly that it was because he had seen only one side of a great truth. She hoped to cheer and inspire him with the other side. Moreover, her religion was very simple. It was only becoming God's friend, instead of remaining indifferent or hostile. To her, no matter what the burden, it was simply leading the heavy-laden to the strong Divine Friend as people were brought to Him of old, and establishing the personal relations of love, faith, and following.

But she did not realize the desperate nature or the complications of Gregory's moral infirmity. Still she was a safe adviser, for she did not propose to cure him herself. She wished to rally and cheer him, to inspire hope, and to turn his eyes from sin to the Saviour, so she said, "Mr. Gregory, why do you look as if marching to execution?"

"Perhaps because I feel as if I were," he said.

Just then a variegated leaf parted from a spray overhanging the path somewhat in advance of them, and fluttered to their feet.

"Poor little leaf!" said Gregory, picking it up, "your bright colors will soon be lost. Death has come to you too. Why must this wretched thought of death be thrust on one at every turn? Nature is full of it. Things only live, apparently, for the sake of dying. Just as this leaf becomes most beautiful it drops. What a miserable world this is, with death making havoc everywhere! Then your theology exaggerates the evil a thousand-fold. If a man must die, let him die and cease to be. But your minister spoke to-day of a living death, in which one only exists to suffer. What a misfortune to have existed!"

As Gregory gloomily uttered these bitter words, they stood looking at the leaf that had suggested them. Annie's face brightened with a sudden thought. She turned, and after a few rapid steps sprung lightly up and caught the twig from which the leaf had fallen. Then turning to her companion, who regarded with surprise and admiration the agile grace of the act, she said, "Mr. Gregory, you need lessons in logic. If the leaf you hold is your theme, as you gave me reason to believe, you don't stick to it, and you draw from it conclusions that don't follow the premise. Another thing, it is not right to develop a subject without regard to its connection. Now from just this place," she continued, pointing with her finger, "the leaf dropped. What do you see? What was its connection?"

"Why, a little branch full of other leaves. These would soon have dropped off and died also, if you had not hastened their fate."

"That's a superficial view, like the one you just took of this 'miserable world,' as you call it. I think it is a very good world--a much better one than we deserve. And now look closely and justly at your theme's connection, and tell me what you see. Look just here;" and her finger rested on the little green spot where the stem of the leaf had joined the spray.

"I see a very small bud," he said, intelligence of her meaning dawning in his face.

"Which will develop next spring into other leaves and perhaps into a new branch. All summer long your leaf has rustled and fluttered joyously over the certainty that a richer and fuller life would come after it, a life that it was providing for through the sunny days and dewy nights. There is no death here, only change for the better. And so with everything that has bloomed and flourished in this garden during the past season, provision has been made for new and more abundant life. All these bright but falling leaves and fading flowers are merely Nature's robes, ornaments that she is throwing carelessly aside as she withdraws for a little time from her regal state. Wait till she appears again next spring, as young, fresh, and beautiful as when, like Eve, she saw her first bright morning. Come and see her upon her throne next June. Nature full of death! Why, Mr. Gregory, she speaks of nothing but life to those who understand her language."

"O that you would teach it to me!" he said, with a deeper meaning than she detected.

"Again," she continued, "our theology does not represent death as making havoc anywhere. It is sin that makes the havoc, and death is only one of its consequences. And even this enemy God compels to work for the good of His friends. Do not think," she continued, coming a step nearer in her earnestness, "that I make such allusions to pain you, but only in my sincere wish to help you, and illustrate my meaning by something you know so well. Did death make havoc in your mother's case? Was it not rather a sombre-liveried janitor that opened for her the gates of heaven?"

He was deeply touched, and turned away his face. After a moment he continued his walk, that they might get further away from the house and the danger of interruption.

He suddenly startled Annie by saying, in a tone of harsh and intense bitterness, "Her death made 'havoc' for me. If she had lived I might have been a good man instead of the wretch I am. If death as janitor opens the gates of heaven, your religion teaches that it also opens the gates of hell. How can I love a God who shuts up the sinful in an inferno--in dungeons of many and varied tortures, and racks them forever? Can I, just to escape all this, pretend that I love Him, when in truth I fear and dread Him unspeakably? No, I'll never be a hypocrite."

Tears glistened in Annie's eyes as he turned to look at her.

"You pity me," he said, more gently. "Your God does not. If He wanted to be loved He should never have revealed a hell."

"Should He not in mercy, if it really existed? And does it not exist? Will merely a beautiful place make heaven for anybody? Mr. Gregory, look around this lovely autumn evening. See the crimson glory of those clouds yonder in the west. See that brightness shading off into paler and more exquisite tints. Look, how those many-hued leaves reflect the glowing sky. The air is as sweet and balmy as that of Eden could have been. The landscape is beautiful in itself, and especially attractive to you. To our human eyes it hardly seems as if heaven could be more perfect than this. And yet, standing in the one spot of all the earth most beautiful to you, Mr. Gregory, pardon me for saying it, your face expresses nothing but pain. There is not a trace of happiness in it. You were not happy when you came here. I saw that the first day. All the pleasant surroundings of your own home have not made you happy. Have they given you even peace and quiet? Place does not make heaven, but something we carry in our own bosoms," she concluded, leaving him to supply the rest of her thought.

His face was white with fear, and there was terror in his tone as he turned and said to her, in a low voice, "Miss Walton, that is what I have been coming to see and dread, of late, and as you put the thoughts into words I see that it is true. I carry perdition in my own heart. When I am alone my imaginings frighten me; and when with others, impulses arise to do the devil's own work."

"But it is the nature of God to save from all this. I am so sorry that you do not understand Him better."

"He saves some," said Gregory, gloomily.

"But many will not let Him save them," urged Annie.

"I should be only too glad to have Him save me, but whether He will or not is the point at issue, and my hope is very faint. Everything to- day, but you, seems to confirm my fate. Miss Walton, won't you take that little rustic seat there by the brook? I wish to tell you something that will probably settle this question."

Annie wonderingly complied. This was an experience she had never had before. She was rapidly realizing the difference between being the spiritual guide of the girls in her Bible-class and being the adviser of this strong-minded yet greatly perverted man. But she turned to him a face full of sympathy and encouragement.

For a moment it seemed he did not know how to begin, and he paced restlessly up and down before her. Then he said, "Miss Walton, you remember that worm-infested chestnut through which you gave me such a just lesson?"

"Please do not speak of my foolish words at that time," she replied, eagerly.

"Pardon me, they were not foolish. They, with the illustration of my own choice, revealed me to myself as nothing had ever done before. Had it not been for your graceful tact, I should have made a fool of myself by being angry. If you had known what I deserved then you would not have let me off so easily. But it's true. That lonely, selfish chestnut, with a worm in its kernel, was a good emblem of myself. Evil is throned in my heart supreme and malignant. I suppose it's through my own fault, but be that as it may, it's there, my master. I groan over and curse the fact, but I do evil and think evil continually, and I fear I always shall.

"No, listen to me to the end," he continued, as she was about to speak.

"When on that strange mountain expedition, you made the remark, 'What congenial friends we might be!' Those words have echoed in my heart ever since, like the refrain of a home-song to a captive. I would give more than I can express for your friendship--for the privilege of seeing you and speaking to you frankly on these subjects occasionally, for you and you only have inspired a faint hope that I might become a better man. You are making Christianity seem a reality and not a fashion. Though possessing human weakness, you triumph over it, and you say it is through prayer to God. I find it impossible not to believe everything you say, for whatever your faults are you are truth itself. Through your influence the thought has come that God might also hear and help me, but I have the fear and almost the belief that I have placed myself beyond His mercy. At any rate I have almost lost hope in anything I can do by myself. I was in moral despair when I came here, and might as well have been dead, but you have led me to a willingness to make one more struggle, and a great one, if I can see in it any chance of success. I fear I am deceiving myself, but when with you, though you are immeasurably better than I, hope steals into my heart, that before was paralyzed by despair. When you come to know me as I know myself, I fear that you will shrink in just horror away, and that I shall see reflected in your face the verdict of heaven. But you shall know the worst--the very worst. I can never use deceit with you. If afterward you ever take my stained hand again--"

He did not finish the sentence, but heaved a great sigh, as if of longing and hope that words could not utter.

It was the old truth illustrated, that God must become human to gain humanity. Abstract truth could not save this lost and guilty man, but the wanderer hoped that in this sweet human life he had found the clew back to the divine life.

Annie trembled at the responsibility that now suddenly burdened her as she saw this trembling spirit clinging to her as the one frail barrier between himself and the gulf of utter despair. She nerved herself, by prayer and the exertion of all her will, to be equal to the emergency.

And yet it was a fearful ordeal that she was called to go through as the remorseful and deeply agitated man, his face flushed with shame, now with impassioned, more often with despairing gesture and accent, poured out the story of his past life, and laid bare his evil heart, while he paced up and down the little walk before her.

The transaction with Hunting he purposely passed over, speaking of it merely as a business misfortune that had robbed him even of earthly ambition. She saw a few sin-stained pages of that dreadful book of human guilt which God must look at every day.

Gregory did not spare himself, and palliated nothing, softening and brightening no harsh and dark lines. On the contrary, he was stern and blunt, and it was strange indeed to hear him charging himself before a pure, innocent young girl, whose good opinion was life to him, with what she regarded as crimes. When he at last came to speak of his designs against herself, of how he had purposed to take the bloom and beauty from her character that he might laugh at goodness as a dream and pretence, and despise her as he did himself, his eye flashed angrily, and he grew vindictive as if denouncing an object of his hate. He could not even look at her during the last of his confession, but turned away his face, fearing to see Annie's expression of aversion and disgust.

It was with a paling cheek and growing dread that she looked into that dark and fearful place, a perverted human heart, and her every breath was a prayer that God would enable her to see and act as Christ would were some poor creature revealing to Him his desperate need.

Gregory suddenly paused in his low but passionate flow of words, and put his hand to his head as if the pain were insupportable. In fact, his anguish and the intense feeling of the day had again brought on one of his old nervous headaches. Thus far he had scarcely noticed it, but now the sharp, quivering pangs proved how a wronged physical nature could retaliate; how much more the higher and more delicate moral nature!

After the paroxysm had passed, he continued, in the hard, weary tone of utter dejection (for he had dreaded even to look at Annie, and her silence confirmed his worst fears), "Well, Miss Walton, you now know the worst. On this peaceful Sabbath evening you have seen more of perdition than you ever will again. You cannot even speak to me, and I dare not look at your face. The expression of horror and disgust which I know must be there would blast me and haunt me forever. It would be worse than death, for I did have a faint hope--"

He was interrupted by an audible sob, and turning, saw Annie with her face buried in her hands, weeping as if her heart would break. He was puzzled for a moment, and then, in the despairing condition of his mind interpreted her wrongly. Standing near her with clenched hands, he said, in the same hard tones which seemed to have passed beyond the expression of feeling, "I'm a brute and worse. I have been wounding you as with blows by my vile story. I have been dragging your pure thoughts through the mire of my wretched life."

Annie tried to speak, but apparently could not for excess of emotion.

"Why could I not have gone away and died by myself, like some unclean beast?" he muttered. Then, in a tone which she never forgot, and with the manner of one who was indeed leaving hope and life behind him, he said, "Farewell, Miss Walton; you will be better after I am gone."

She sprung up, and laying restraining hands upon his arm, sobbed, "No--no.

Why don't you--you--understand me? My heart's--breaking for you--wait till I can speak."

He placed her gently on the seat again. A great light was coming into his eyes, and he stood bending toward her as if existence depended on her next words. Could it be that her swelling throat and sobs meant sympathy for him?

She soon controlled herself, and looking up at him, with a light in her eyes that shone through her tears as sun-rays through the rain, said, "Forgive me. I never realized before that so much sin and suffering could exist in one unhappy life. I do pity you, as God does far more. I will help you as He will."

Gregory knelt at her feet, and kissed her hand with the fervor of a captive who had just received life and liberty.

"See, I do not shrink from you," she continued. "My Master would not. Why should I? He came to save just such, and just such we all would be but for His grace and shielding. I'm so--sorry for you."

He turned hastily away for a moment to hide his feelings, and said, slowly, "I cannot trust myself--I cannot trust God yet; but I trust you, and I believe you have saved a soul from death."

He stood looking toward the glowing west, and, for the first time in years, hoped that his life might close in brightness.

"Mr. Gregory," said Annie, in a voice so changed that he started and turned toward her hardly knowing what to expect. She stood beside him, no longer a tender, compassionate woman grieving for him, as if his sin were only misfortune, but her face was almost stern in its purity and earnestness. "Mr. Gregory, the mercy which God shows, and which I faintly reflect, is for *you* in sharp distinction from your sin. Do not for a moment think that I can look with any lenience or indulgence on all the horrible evil you have laid before me. Do not think I can excuse or pass lightly over it as something of little consequence. I hate your sin as I hate my own. I can honestly feel and frankly show the sympathy I have manifested, only in view of your penitence, and your sincere purpose, with God's help, to root out the evil of your life. This I am daily trying to do, and this you must do in the one and only way in which there is any use in trying. It is only with this clear understanding that I can give you my hand in the friendship of mutual helpfulness, and in the confidence of respect."

He reverently took her hand and said, "Your conditions are just, Miss Walton, and I accept your friendship as offered with a gratitude beyond words. I can never use deceit where you are concerned, even in thought. But please do not expect too much of me. I have formed the habit of doubting. It may be very long before I have your simple, beautiful faith. I will do just the best I can! It seems that if you will trust me, help me, pray for me, I can succeed. If I am mistaken, I will carry my wretchedness where the sight of it will not pain you. If I ever do reach your Christian life, I will lavish a wealth of gratitude upon you that cannot be expressed. Indeed, I will in any case, for you have done all that I could hope and more."

"I will do all you ask," she said, heartily, giving at the same time his hand a strong pressure with her warm, throbbing palm, that sent a subtle current of hope and strength into his heart. Her face softened into an expression of almost sisterly affection, and with a gleam of her old mirthfulness she continued, "Take counsel of practical common- sense, Mr. Gregory. Why talk so doubtfully of success, seeking it as you purpose to? What right have you even to imagine that God will bestow upon you the great distinction of making you the first one of the race He refused to hear and answer? Be humble and believe that He will treat you like other people."

He stopped in their slow walk toward the house and said, with glad animation, "Miss Walton, do you know you have done more to strengthen me in that little speech than by a long and labored argument?"

And so they passed in out of the purple twilight, Annie's heart thrilling with something of the joy of heaven, and Gregory feeling as if the dawn were coming after Egyptian night.

As they left the garden a dusky face peered out of some thick shrubbery and looked cautiously around. Then Jeff appeared and attributed to the scene just described a very different meaning from its real significance.

CHAPTER XXV
THE OLD HOME IN DANGER
--GREGORY RETRIEVES HIMSELF

Gregory made desperate efforts to keep up at the supper-table, but could not prevent slight evidences of physical pain, which Annie silently noticed. After tea he hoped to escape to his room, for he could not endure to show even his physical weakness so soon again. On the contrary, he was longing intensely for an opportunity to manifest a little strength of some kind. After his recent interview he felt that he could even bear one of his nervous headaches alone. But as he was about to excuse himself, Annie interrupted, saying, "Now, Mr. Gregory, that is not according to agreement. Do you suppose I cannot see that you are half beside yourself with one of your old headaches? Was I such a poor physician the last time that you seek to escape me now? Come back to the parlor. I will not go out to church this evening, but devote myself to you."

"Miss Walton," he replied, in a low tone, "when can I make any return for all your kindness? I must seem weakness itself in every respect, and I dread to appear to you always in that light."

"Your pride needs bringing down, sir; see how towering it is. Here you would go off by yourself, and endure a useless martyrdom all night perhaps, when by a few simple remedies I can relieve you, or at least help you forget the pain. I have not the slightest objection to your being a martyr, but I want some good to come out of it."
"But I shall spoil your evening."

"Certainly you will, if I think of you groaning up there by yourself, while I am singing, perhaps:

"'I love to steal awhile away From every cumbering care!'"
"Then I'm a cumbering care!"

"Whether you are or not, I'm not going to steal away from you to- night. Come, do as I bid you."

He was only too glad to submit to her delicious tyranny. She wheeled the lounge up to the fire, and placed her chair beside it, while the rest of the family, seeing that he had his old malady, went to the sitting-room.

"I have great pride in my nursing powers," she continued, in her cheery way. "Now, if I were a man, I'd certainly be a doctor."

"Thank Heaven you are not!" he said, with a devout earnestness that quite startled her.

"What? A doctor?" she asked, quickly.

"Yes--no; I mean a man, and doctor too."

"I see no reason why you should show such bitter opposition to my being a man or a doctor either. Why should you?"

"O--well--I think you are just right as a woman. You make me believe in the doctrine of election, for it seems to me that you were destined from all eternity to be just what you are."

"What a strange, unfathomable doctrine that is!" said Annie, softly and musingly.

"It's nothing but mystery all around us," he replied, wearily and dejectedly.

"No, not 'all around us,'" she answered, quickly. "It's clear when we look up. Faith builds a safe bridge to God, and to Him there are no mysteries."

Her touch upon his brow thrilled him, and her presence was both exhilarating and restful.

At last she said, "I am sorry you have these dreadful headaches so often."

"I shall never be again."

"Why so?"

"Because they have led to this evening. It has been so many long, miserable years since I experienced anything like this."

"Ah, I see, you have been very lonely. You have had no one to care for you, and that I believe has been the cause of half your trouble--evil, I mean. Indeed, they are about the same thing. Don't you see? The world is too large a place for a home. You need a nook in it, with some one there to look after you and for you to think about."

He looked at her searchingly, and then turned away his face in pain. She could not utter such words in that placid style, were she not utterly devoid of the feeling that was filling his soul with an ecstasy of hope and fear.

"Do not think that even many of our sex are like Miss Bently. You will see and choose more wisely hereafter, and find that, in exchanging that wretched club-life for a cosey home of your own, you take a good step in all respects."

"Would to Heaven that I had met such a girl as you at first!" he ventured to say. "How different then all might have been!"

"There is no use in dwelling on the past," she replied, innocently. "You are now pledged to make the future right."

"God helping me, I will. I will use every means in my power," he said, in a tone of deep earnestness; and, as principal part of the means, determined to take her advice, but with reference to herself. After a few moments he said, "Miss Walton, as I promised to be perfectly frank with you, I want to ask an explanation of something that I do not understand, and which has been almost a heavenly surprise to me. I was nearly certain before this afternoon that when you came to know what a stained, evil man I am--"

"Was," interrupted Annie.

"No, what I am. Character is not made in a moment. As yet, I only hope and purpose to do better. I can hardly understand why you do not shrink from me in disgust. It seemed that both your faith and your nature would lead you to do this. I thought it possible that out of your kindness you might try to stand at a safe distance and give me some good advice across the gulf. But that which I feared would drive you from me forever has only brought you nearer. Again I say, it has been a heavenly surprise."

"You use the word 'heavenly' with more appropriateness than you think," she replied, gravely. "All such surprises are heavenly in their origin, and my course is but a faint reflection of Heaven's disposition toward you, and was prompted by the duty I owe to God as well as to you. Self-righteousness would have led me in Pharisaic pride to say, 'Stand aside, I am holier than thou.' But you have only to read the life of the perfect One to know that in so doing I should not have been like Him. He laid His rescuing hands on both the physical and the moral leper--"

"As you have upon me," said Gregory, with a look of such intense gratitude that she was embarrassed.

"I deserve no great credit, for it was only right that I should do the utmost in my power to help you. How else could I be a Christian in any real sense? But there is nothing strange about it. Christianity is not like false religions, that require unnatural and useless sacrifices. If I were a true physician, and found you suffering from a terrible and contagious disease, while I feared and loathed the disease, I might have the deepest sympathy for you and do my best to cure you. I do loathe the sin you confessed, inexpressibly. See how near it came to destroying you. While God hates the sin, He ever loves the sinful."

"I hope you will always be divine in that respect," he could not forbear saying, with rising color.

But her thoughts were so intent on what was uppermost in her heart that she did not notice his covert meaning, and said, innocently, "I will give you honest friendship so long as you honestly try to redeem the pledges of to-day."

"Then I have your friendship for life, be it long or short," said he, decisively.

With more lightness in her tone she continued, "And I too will ask a question that has a bearing on a little theory of my own. Supposing I had shrunk from you, and tried to give some good advice from a safe distance, what would you have done?"

"Left for New York to-morrow, and gone straight to the devil as one of his own imps," he replied, without a moment's hesitation.

She sighed deeply, and said, "I fear you would--that is, if left to yourself. And the worst of it is, it seems to me that this is the way the Church is trying to save the world. Suppose a doctor should address his patients through a speaking-trumpet and hand them his remedies on the end of a very long rod. Death would laugh at his efforts. People can be saved only as Christ saved them. We must go where they are, lay our hands upon them, and look sympathy and hope right into their eyes. If Christ's followers would only do this, how many more might be rescued who now seem hopelessly given over to evil!"

"Those who won't do it," said Gregory, bitterly, "are in no sense His true followers, but are merely the 'hangers on' of His army, seeking to get out of it all they can for self. Every general knows that the 'camp-followers' are the bane of an army."

"Come, Mr. Gregory," said she, gently, "we are not the general, and therefore not the judge. After this I shall expect to see you in the regular ranks, ready to give and take blows."

They now joined Mr. Walton and Miss Eulie in the sitting-room, and Gregory professed to feel, and indeed was, much better, and after a little music they separated for the night. Although still suffering, Gregory sat by his fire a long time, forgetful of pain.

High, blustering winds prevailed all the following day, but they only made the quiet and cosiness of Mr. Walton's fireside more delightful. Gregory did not care to go out if he went alone. He wished to be where he could see Annie as often as possible, for every word and smile from her in the intervals of her duties was precious. He did honestly mean to become a good man if it were possible, but he saw in her the only hopeful means. He did not pretend to either faith in God or love for Him as yet, but only felt a glow of gratitude, a warming of his heart toward Him in view of His great mercy in sending to his aid such a ministering spirit as Annie had proved. He took it as an omen that God meant kindly by him, and through this human hand might save at last.

And he clung to this hand as the drowning do to anything that keeps them from sinking into dark and unknown depths. He saw in Annie Walton earthly happiness certainly, and his best prospect of heaven. What wonder then that his heart lay at her feet in entire consecration? Apart from the peculiar fascination that she herself had for him, he had motives for loving her that actuate but few. If she had saved him from physical death it would have been a little thing in comparison, but he shuddered to think of the precipice from which she had drawn him back.

He was cautious in revealing himself to her. The presence of others was a restraint, and he plainly saw that she had no such regard for him as he felt for her. But he hoped with intense fervor--yes, he even prayed to that God whom he had so long slighted--that in time she might return his love. To-day he would close his eyes on the past and future. She, the sunshine of his soul, was near, and he was content to bask in her smiles.

Annie had given her father and aunt to understand that their conspiracy promised to result in success, and they treated him with marked but delicate kindness. The day passed in music, reading, and conversation, and it was to Gregory the happiest he remembered--one of the sweet May days that, by some happy blunder of nature, occasionally bless us in March--and he made the very most of it. Its close found Annie Walton enthroned in his heart.

As for Annie, he perplexed her a little, but she explained everything peculiar in his words and manner on the ground of his gratitude only, and the glow of his newly awakened moral nature. If she had been an experienced belle, she might have understood his symptoms better, but she was one of the last in the world to imagine people falling in love with her. Never having received much admiration from strangers, with no long list of victims, and believing from her own experience that love was a gradual growth resulting from long knowledge and intimacy with its object, she could not dream that this critical man, who had seen the beauties of two continents, would in a few days be carried away by her plain face. Nor was he by her face, but by herself.

Men of mind are rarely captivated by a face merely, however beautiful, but by what it represents, or what they imagine it does. Woe be to the beauty who has no better capital than her face! With it she can allure some one into marrying her; but if he marries for an intelligent companion, he is likely to prove the most disappointed and indifferent of husbands on discovering the fraud. The world will never get over its old belief that the fair face is the index of graces slightly veiled, and ready to be revealed when the right to know is gained. In nursery rhymes, fairy tales, and the average novel, the beautiful heroine is also lovely, and so in spite of adverse experience the world will ever expect wisdom and truth from red lips, till they say too much--till the red lips themselves prove the contrary. Then come the anger and disgust which men ever visit upon those who deceive and disappoint them. Beauty is a dainty and exquisite vestibule to a temple; but when a worshipper is beguiled into entering, only to find a stony, misshapen idol and a dingy shrine, this does not conduce to future devotion.

Annie's face would not arrest passers-by, and so she had not been spoiled by too much homage, which is not good for man or woman. But after passing the plain, simple portico of externals into the inner temple of her sweet and truthful life, the heart once hers would worship with undying faith and love.

Gregory had come to interest her deeply, not only on the ground of his need, but because she saw in him great capabilities for good. In all his evil, his downright honesty and lack of conceit inspired a kind of respect. She also saw that this excessively fastidious man had learned to admire and esteem her greatly. It was not in her woman's nature to be indifferent to this fact. She felt that if he could be redeemed from his evil he might become a congenial and valuable friend indeed, and if she could be the means of rescuing the son of her father's friend it would ever be one of her happiest memories. But with her heart already occupied by a noble ideal of Hunting, the possibility of anything more than friendship never entered her mind. The very fact that her affections were so engaged made her blind to manifestations on the part of Gregory which might otherwise have awakened suspicion. Still the confidential relations growing up between them made her wish that she might reveal to him her virtual engagement to Hunting; and she would have done so, had he not resented the slightest allusion in that direction. It now seemed probable that Hunting would return before Gregory took his departure, and if so, she felt that she could immediately reconcile them. She came to the conclusion that her best course was to wait till she could bring them together, and so make the reconciliation certain by her own presence and influence; for now, in her increasing regard for Gregory, she was determined that they all should be on good terms, so that in the city home to which she looked forward the man she was trying to lead to true life might be a frequent and welcome visitor.

But it is a difficult thing to keep such friendships Platonic in their nature under any circumstances, and in view of Gregory's feelings, Annie's pretty dreams of the future would be but baseless visions.

Monday evening brought one of those genial domestic experiences that make home more satisfying in its pleasures than all the excitements of the world. Mr. Walton had a slight cold, and Annie was nursing and petting him, while contributing to the general enjoyment by reading the daily paper and singing some new ballads which she had just obtained from New York. Her father's indisposition was so slight that it merely called for those little attentions which are pleasant for affection to bestow and receive. The wind howled dismally without, only to enhance the sense of peace and comfort within, and at the usual hour all retired to rest, without even the passing thought that anything might disturb them before they should meet again at the cheerful breakfast-table.

Some time during the night Gregory seemed to hear three distinct peals of thunder, wrathful and threatening, and then a voice like that of Annie Walton calling him to escape a great danger. But it seemed that he was paralyzed, and strove in vain to move hand or foot. Again and louder pealed the thunder, and more urgent came the call of the warning voice. By a desperate effort he sprung with a bound upon the floor, and then realized that what seemed thunder in the exaggeration of his dream was loud knocking at his door. Annie's voice again called, "Mr. Gregory, awake, dress. There is a fire. There may be danger."

He assured her that he would be out in a few moments, and had only to open a shutter to obtain plenty of light, though he could not see whence it came. In five minutes he hastened downstairs and found Mr. Walton just issuing from his room; and all went out on the front piazza. Gregory then saw that a large factory some distance up the stream was burning, and that the fire was under such headway that nothing could save the building. The wind had increased during the night and fanned the flames into terrific fury. The building was old and dry, inviting destruction in every part.

For a while they gazed with that fearful awe which this terrible element, when no longer servant, but master, always inspires. Susie had not been well during the night, and in waiting on her, Annie had discovered the disaster.

A warning cough from Mr. Walton revealed to Annie the danger of staying out in the raw winds; but from the windows everything was apparent, and silently they watched the rapid progress of the flames. The fire had caught in the lower part of the building, and was advancing up from floor to floor with its horrid illumination at the windows.

"Do you think I can do any good by going there?" asked Gregory.

"Not at all," said Mr. Walton. "The whole of the New York Fire Department could not save it now; and from the sounds I hear, there will soon be throngs of people there. Indeed, I am anxious about my own place. When that shingle roof begins to burn there is no telling how far the wind will carry the cinders."

Annie looked at her father in quick alarm, then drew Miss Eulie aside, and they immediately went upstairs.

With a more painful interest, Gregory now watched the scene. The tall ladders which had first been raised against the building were withdrawn. They were useless for the whole interior seemed ablaze. Great tongues of fire began leaping from the windows, mocking every effort. The rapid steps of those hastening to the scene resounded along the road, and the startling cry of "Fire! Fire!" was heard up and down the valley till all merged in the shouts and cries around the burning building.

Mingling with the deeper, hoarser tones of men were the shrill voices of women, showing that they too had been drawn to witness a destruction that meant to them loss of bread. The foliage near was red as blood in the dreadful glare, and the neighboring pines tossed their tasselled boughs like dark plumes at a torch-light funeral. With a sudden roar a pyramid of flame shot up through the roof, and was echoed by a despairing cry from those whose vocation now indeed was gone. A moment later a fiery storm of flakes and burning shingles filled the sky.

To the great joy of our friends the wind was from such a quarter as to carry this destructive tempest past them into the woodland back of the house, which happily had been rendered damp by recent rains.

But a cinder frequently sailed by unpleasantly near, reminding one of scattering shots in a battle. A slight change of wind would be their destruction, and a single stray fire-brand would endanger them.

Just as they began to breathe somewhat freely, hoping that danger was past, a sudden side-eddy of the gale scattered a shower of sparks and burning shingles over the house and out-buildings. Mr. Walton immediately rushed forth, and, with a little whistle which he usually carried, gave a shrill summons for Jeff, who lived in a cottage near. But Jeff was off to the fire, and so did not appear. Gregory and Annie also hastened out, and the former ran to the barn and out-buildings first, as from their nature they were most inflammable. To his and Mr. Walton's joy, no traces of fire were seen. One or two smoking brands lay in the door-yard, where they could cause no injury. But a cry of alarm from Annie, who had stayed nearer the house, brought Mr. Walton and Gregory to her side instantly. Pointing to the roof of their house, she said, in tones of strong excitement, "See there--oh, see there!"

A burning piece of wood had caught on the highest part near the ridge, and was smoking and smouldering in a way that, with the strong wind fanning it, would surely cause destruction if it were not dislodged.

"Oh, what shall we do?" she cried, wringing her hands. "Can a ladder reach it?"

"The roof is too steep, even if it did," said Mr. Walton.

"Where is the ladder?" cried Gregory.

"By the carriage-house. But I fear it is useless."

"Will you help me bring it, sir?"

They instantly brought the longest ladder on the place, but saw that though it might touch the eaves, it would not reach the ridge. The roof was so steep that one could not keep footing on it; and when they took time to look and consider, both gentlemen admitted that an effort in that direction would fail, and probably at the cost of life.

"Is there no scuttle by which to get out on the roof?" asked Gregory.

"No. Quick, Annie, get out what you can, for we shall soon be homeless."

"Wait," said Gregory. "Is there no way to reach the roof?"

"None that we can use. A light and daring climber might possibly reach the ridge by the lighting-rod, after leaving the ladder."

"Where is it?" cried Gregory, eager to do something to make impossible even the thought that he was cowardly; for the memory of his course in the counterfeiter's den rankled deeply.

"No," cried both Mr. Walton and Annie, laying their hands on him. "Your life is worth more than the house."

"My life is my own," he answered. "I *will* make an effort to save the old place. Quick, help me. Here, girls" (to Zibbie and Hannah, who now stood beside them in dismay), "take hold of that end of the ladder and carry it out there. Now push it up while I hold its foot. There, that's it. I will do it. You cannot hinder, but only help. Miss Walton, get me a rope. Hurry, while I prepare to climb."

With the help of the stout women, whose strength was doubled by their fears and excitement, he placed the ladder against the lightning-rod and siding of the house just under the ridge. His tones were determined and authoritative.

He was now acting as Annie would if she were a man, and she admired and respected him as never before. In two or three moments she and her father returned with a line, but again expostulated.

"Mr. Gregory, the risk is too great."

"You can't prevent it," said he, firmly. "I absolve you from all responsibility. I take the risk in spite of you. Make haste--see how it's burning. There, that will do. Stand back."

Even as he spoke he was climbing.

"Now that's generous," said Annie; "but if you are injured, I shall never forgive myself."

He turned, and for a second smiled down upon her.

The strength of his new-born love made him glad to endanger even life in her service, and the thought, "I can at last win a little respect, as well as sympathy," nerved him to double his ordinary powers. Like most country boys, he had been a bold, active climber, and his knowledge and former skill made the attempted feat possible. The main question was whether in his feeble state his strength would hold out. But the strong excitement of the moment would serve him in place of muscle. He had thrown off his coat and boots, and, with a small rope fastened about his waist, he swiftly ascended to the top of the ladder. But there were three or four feet that he must overhand up the lightning-rod in order to reach the ridge. It was large and twisted, and gave him a good hold, but he had to take the risk of its being strong enough in its fastening to sustain his weight. Fortunately it was, and he unhesitatingly commenced the perilous effort. He made good progress till he was within a foot of the ridge. Then his strength began to fail, and plainly to those below he wavered.

With white face, clasped hands, and lips moving in prayer, Annie watched him. Her heart almost stood still with dread; and when toward the last he slowly and still more slowly overhanded upward, plainly indicating that his strength was ebbing, she cried, in an agony of fear, "Come back, oh come back! What is all here to your life?" A second before it seemed to him that he must fail, that he might suddenly fall at her feet a crushed and lifeless mass; but her voice revived him, and the passionate thought came with inspiring power, "I can do more to win her love now than by years of effort"; and he made a desperate struggle, gained the ridge, and crawled out upon it, panting for a moment, and powerless to do more than cling for support.

The burning cinder was now but little in advance of him, and he saw that there was not a second to lose. It had charred and blackened the roof where it had caught, and, fanned by the wind, was a live, glowing coal. The shingles under it were smoking--yes, smouldering. Had it not been for their dampness and mossy age, they would have been blazing. In a few moments nothing could have saved the house.

As soon as he got his breath, he crept along the ridge within reach of the fiery flake. There seemed no place where he could lay hold of it without burning himself.

It would not do to simply detach it, as it might catch further down the steep roof where it could not be reached. Above all, there was not a moment to spare. He did not hesitate, but with sufficient presence of mind to use his left instead of his right hand, he seized the fatal brand and hurled it, a fiery meteor, clear of the house. It hurt him cruelly, and for a moment he felt sick and faint; but a round of applause from those below (for now Miss Eulie and the children were out, looking trem- blingly on), and Annie's cry of joy and encouragement, again gave him strength.

But as he looked closely at the spot where the cinder had laid, his fears were realized. It had ignited the roof. A little water would extinguish it now, but in a few moments, under the wild wind that was blowing, all would be ablaze.

He crawled to the end of the ridge and shouted, "Tie a light pail of water to the cord--not much at a time, or I can't draw it up."

Annie darted to the house for a lighter pail than Hannah had brought, and to Gregory's joy he found that he had strength enough to lift it, though with his burned band it was agony to do so. But with the now good prospect of finishing his work successfully, his spirits rose. He grew more familiar and confident in his dan- gerous position. He did not look down from his giddy height, and permitted himself to think of nothing but his task. Indeed, in his strong excitement, he felt that it would not be a bitter thing to die thus serving the woman he loved; and in his false philosophy he hoped this brave act might atone for the wrong of the past.

It is the nature of noble, generous deeds to exalt a man's soul so that he can fearlessly face death, when in calm moments he would shrink back appalled. In the excitement of the hour, and under the inspiration of his strong human love, Gregory was not afraid to die, though life seemed, with its new possibilities, sweeter than ever before. He knew that his strength was failing fast, that reaction would soon set in, and that he would be helpless, and his great hope was that he could save the house first.

He determined therefore not to waste a drop of water, and to make this one pail answer if possible. He therefore poured it slowly out, and let it run over the burning part. The continued hissing and smoke proved that the fire had penetrated deeper than he thought. The last drop was gone, and still the place smoked. A little more was absolutely necessary.

"Will my strength hold out?" he asked himself, in almost an agony of doubt.

Crawling back to the end of the ridge, he once more lowered the pail.

"Fill it again," he cried.

"Can you stand it?" Mr. Walton asked.

"I must, or all is useless," was his answer.

Again, but more slowly and painfully, he pulled the water up.

Annie wrung her hands in anguish as she saw in the red glare of the still burning factory how pale and exhausted he was.

But he once more managed to reach the point above the still smouldering spot, and caused the water to trickle down upon it. By the time he had half emptied the pail the smoke ceased.

After a moment it again faintly exuded, but another little stream of water quenched the fire utterly. But for five minutes he watched the place to make sure that there was not a lingering spark, and then let the rest of the water flow over the place to saturate it completely.

He was now certain that the house was saved. But he was satisfied from his sensations that he had but little time in which to save himself. Reaction was fast setting in.

He untied the rope from his waist, and let pail and all roll clattering down the roof. This noise was echoed by a cry of alarm from those below, who feared for a moment that he was falling. They all had the sickening dread which is felt when we look at one in great peril, and yet can do nothing to help.

At first Gregory thought that he would lie down upon the ridge and cling to it, thus gaining strength by a little rest. But he soon found that this would not answer. His overtaxed frame was becoming nerveless, and his only hope was to escape at once. In trembling weakness he crawled back to the edge and looked over. Annie stepped forward to the foot of the ladder and extended her hands as if to catch him.

"Stand back," he cried; "if I fall, I shall kill you."

"I will not stand back," she answered. "You shall not take all the risk."

But her father, who still kept his presence of mind in the terrible excitement of the moment, forced her away, and saved her from the danger of this useless sacrifice. As soon as she could do nothing, her fortitude vanished, and she covered her face with her hands and wept bitterly.

The chief point of difficulty in Gregory's weak state was to get off the ridge upon the lightning-rod without losing his hold and falling at once. If he could turn the edge and begin to descend in safety, his strength might hold out till he reached the ladder and so the ground. But he realized the moment of supreme peril, and hesitated.

Then, with something like a prayer to God and with a wistful look at Annie, he resolutely swung himself over. His hands held the weight of his body, and he commenced the descent. Annie's glad cry once more encouraged him. He gained the ladder and descended till not far from the ground.

Suddenly everything turned black before his eyes, and he fell.

CHAPTER XXVI
CHANGES IN GREGORY

When Gregory became conscious, he was lying on the ground, with his head in Miss Eulie's lap, and Annie was bending over him with a small flask. She again gave him a teaspoonful of brandy, and after a moment he lifted himself up, and, passing his hand across his brow, looked around.

"You are not hurt. Oh, please say you are not hurt!" she exclaimed, taking his hand.

He looked at her a moment, and then it all came back to him, and he smiled and said, "Not much, I think; and if I am it does not signify. You've helped me on my feet once or twice before. Now see if you can again;" and he attempted to rise.

As Daddy Tuggar had intimated, there was plenty of muscle in Annie's round arms, and she almost lifted him up, but he stood unsteadily. Mr. Walton gave him his arm, and in a few moments he was on the sofa in the sitting-room, where a fire was soon kindled. Zibbie was told to make coffee, and to provide something more substantial.

They were all profuse in expressions of gratitude, in praises of his heroism, but he waived the whole matter off by saying, "Think of me as well as you can, for Heaven knows I have need to retrieve my character. But please do not speak as if I had done more than I ought. For a young man to stand idly by, and see the home of his childhood, the place where he had received unbounded hospitality, destroyed, would be simply base. If I had not been reduced by months of ill health, the thing would not have been difficult at all. But you, Miss Walton, displayed the real heroism in the case, when you stood beneath with your arms out to catch me. I took a risk, but you took the certainty of destruction if I had fallen. Still," he added, with a humorous look as if in jest, though he was only too sincere, "the prospect was so inviting that I should have liked to fall a little way."

"And so you did," cried innocent Johnny, eagerly. "You fell ever so far, and Aunt Annie caught you."

"What!" exclaimed Gregory, rising. "Is this true? And are you not hurt?"

"That's the way with children," said Annie, with heightened color and a reproachful look at the boy, who in the excitement of the hour was permitted to stay up for an hour or more; "they let everything all out. No, I'm not hurt a bit. You didn't fall very far. I'm so thankful that your strength did not give out till you almost reached the ground. O dear! I shudder to think what might have happened. Do you know that I thought, with a thrill of superstitious dread, of your chestnut-burr omen, when you stained my hand with your blood. If you had fallen--if--" and she put her hand over her eyes to hide the dreadful vision her imagination presented. "If anything had happened," she continued, "my hands would have been stained, in that they had not held you back."

"What a tender, innocent conscience you have!" he replied, looking fondly at her. "I confess I'd rather be here listening to you than somewhere else."

She gave him a troubled, startled look. To her that "somewhere else" had a sad and terrible meaning. She sat near him, and could not help saying in a low, earnest tone, "How could you, how could you take such a risk without--" She did not finish the sentence, which was plain enough in its meaning, however.

On the impulse of the moment, Gregory was about to reply indiscreetly --in a way that would have revealed more of his feelings toward her than he knew would be wise at that time. But just then Hannah came in with the lunch, and the attention of the others, who had been talking eagerly on the other side of the room, was directed toward them. He checked some rash words as they rose to his lips, and Annie, suspecting nothing of the wealth of love that he was already lavishing upon her, rose with alacrity, glad to serve one who had just served her so well. The generous coffee and the dainty lunch, combined with feelings to which he had long been a stranger, revived Gregory greatly, and he sprang up and walked the room, declaring that with the exception of his burned hand, which had been carefully dressed, he felt better than he had for a long time.

"I'm so thankful!" said Annie, with glistening eyes.

"We all have cause for thankfulness," said Mr. Walton, with fervor. "Our kind Father in heaven has dealt with us all in tender mercy. Home, and more precious life, have been spared. Before we again seek a little rest, let us remember all His goodness;" and he led them in a simple, fervent prayer, the effect of which was heightened by Mr. Walton saying, after he rose from his knees, "Annie, we must see that none of our poor neighbors lack for anything, now that their employment has so suddenly been taken away."

That is acceptable devotion to God which leads to practical, active charity toward men, and the most unbelieving are won by such a religion.

Annie noticed with some anxiety that her father's voice was very hoarse, and that he put his hand upon his chest several times, and she expressed the fear that the exposure would greatly add to his cold. He treated the matter lightly, and would do nothing more that evening than take some simple remedies.

When Gregory bade them good-night, Annie followed him to the foot of the stairs, and giving his hand one of her warm grasps, said, "Mr. Gregory, I can't help feeling that your mother knows what you have done to-night."

Tears started to his eyes. He did not trust himself to reply, but, with a strong answering pressure, hastened to his room, happier than he had been in all his past.

It was late the next morning when they assembled at the breakfast- table, and they noted with pain that Mr. Walton did not appear at all well, though he made a great effort to keep up. He was very hoarse, and complained of a tightness in his chest.

"Now, father," said Annie, "you must stay in the house, and let me nurse you."

"I am very willing to submit," he replied, "and hope I shall need no other physician." But he was feverish all day. His indisposition did not yield to ordinary remedies. Still, beyond a little natural solicitude, no anxiety was felt.

Gregory was a different man. Even his sincere human love for so worthy an object had lifted him out of the miserable depths into which he had been sinking. It had filled his heart with pure longings, and made him capable of noble deeds.

As a general thing a woman inspires love in accordance with her own character. Of course we recognize the fact that there are men with natures so coarse that they are little better than animals. These men may have a passing passion for any pretty woman; but the holy word Love should not be used in such connection. But of men--of those possessing true manhood, even in humblest station--the above assertion I think will be found true. The woman who gains the boundless power which the undivided homage of an honest heart confers will develop in it, and quicken into life, traits and feelings corresponding to her own. If the great men of the world have generally had good mothers, so as a parallel fact will it be found that the strong, useful, successful men--men who sustain themselves, and more than fulfil the promise of their youth--have been supplemented and continually inspired to better things by the ennobling companionship of true women.

Good breeding, the ordinary restraints of self-respect, and fear of the world's adverse opinion, greatly reduce the outward diversities of society. Well-bred men and women act and appear very much alike in the public eye. But there is an inner life, a real character, upon which happiness here and heaven hereafter depend, which results largely from that tie and intimacy which is closest of all. A shallow, frivolous girl, having faith in little else than her pretty face and the dressmaker's art, may unfortunately inspire a good, talented man, who imagines her to possess all that the poets have portrayed in woman, with a true and strong affection, but she will disappoint and dwarf him, and be a millstone about his neck. She will cease to be his companion. She may be thankful if, in his heart, he does not learn to despise her, though a man can scarcely do this and be guiltless toward the mother of his children.

What must be the daily influence on a man who sees in his closest friend, to whom he is joined for life, a passion for the public gaze, a boundless faith in eternals, a complete devotion to the artificial enhancing of ordinary and vanishing charms, combined with a contemptuous neglect of the graces of mind and heart? These alone can keep the love which outward appearance in part may have won at first. Mere dress and beauty are very well to skirmish with during the first approaches; but if a woman wishes to hold the conquered province of a man's heart, and receive from it rich revenues of love and honor, she must possess some queenly traits akin to divine royalty, otherwise she only overruns the heart she might have ruled, and leaves it a blighted waste.

As we have seen, Annie's actual character rebuked and humiliated the evil-minded Gregory from the first. He could not rest in her presence. To relieve himself from self-condemnation, he must prove her goodness a sham or an accident--mere chance exemption from temptation. Her safety and happy influence did not depend upon good resolutions, wise policy, and careful instruction, but upon her real possession of a character which had been formed long before, and which met and foiled him at every point. Lacking this, though a well-meaning, good girl in the main, she would have been a plaything in the hands of such a man. Her absolute truth and crystal purity of principle incased her in heaven's armor, and neither he nor any other evil-disposed person could harm her. She would not listen to the first insidious suggestion of the tempter. Thus the man who expected to go away despising now honored, reverenced, loved her, and through her strong but gentle ministry had turned his back on evil, and was struggling to escape its degrading bondage.

Gregory was right in thinking that such a woman as Annie could help him to an extent hard to estimate, but fatally wrong in looking to her alone. The kind Father who regards the well-being of His children for eternity rather than for the moments of time, must effectually cure him of this error.

But those two days were memorable ones to him. The cold and stormy weather shut them all in the house, and that meant to him Annie's society. He was seldom alone with her; he noted with pain that her manner was too frank and kindly, too free from all consciousness, to indicate anything more than the friendship she had promised; but, not knowing how her heart was preoccupied, he hoped that the awakening of deeper feeling was only a question of time. His present peace and rest were so blessed, her presence was so satisfying, and his progress in her favor so apparent as he revealed his better nature, that he was content to call his love friendship until he saw her friendship turning into love.

Had not Annie expected Hunting every day she would have told Gregory all about her relation with him, but now she determined that she would bring them together under the same roof, and not let them separate till she had banished every trace of their difficulty. A partial reconciliation might result in future coolness and estrangement. This she would regard as a misfortune, even if it had no unfavorable influence on Gregory, for he now proved himself the best of company. Indeed, they seemed to have a remarkable gift for entertaining each other.

While Wednesday did not find Mr. Walton seriously ill to all appearance, he was still far from being well. He employed himself with his papers and seemed to enjoy Gregory's conversation greatly.

"He now grows very like his father, and reminds me constantly of him," he said more than once to Annie.

Mr. Walton's indisposition was evidently not trivial. There was a soreness about the lungs that made it painful for him to talk much, and he had a severe, racking cough. They were all solicitude in his behalf. The family physician had been called, and it was hoped that a few days of care would remove this cold.

As he sat in his comfortable arm-chair by the fire he would smilingly say he was having such a good time and so much petting that he did not intend to get well very soon.

Though Gregory's burn was painful, and both hands were bruised and cut from climbing, he did not regret the suffering, since it also secured from Annie some of the attention she would otherwise have given her father.

Wednesday afternoon was pleasant, and Gregory went out for a walk. He did not return till rather late, and, coming down to supper, found by his plate a letter which clouded his face instantly.

Annie was radiant, for the same mail had brought her one from Hunting, stating that he might be expected any day now. As she saw Gregory's face darken, she said, "I fear your letter has brought you unpleasant news."

"It has," he replied. "Mr. Burnett, the senior partner, is quite ill, and it is necessary that I return immediately."

"I'm so sorry," she exclaimed, with such hearty emphasis that he looked at her earnestly and said, "Are you really?"

"You shouldn't ask such a question," she answered, reproachfully.

"Why, Miss Walton, I've made a very long visit."

"So much has happened that it does seem a long time since you came. But I wish it were to be longer. We shall miss you exceedingly. Besides," she added, with rising color, "I have a special reason for wishing you to stay a little longer."

His color rose instantly also. She puzzled him, while he perplexed her.

"I hope Mr. Gregory's visit has taught him," said Mr. Walton, kindly, "that he has not lost his former home through our residence here, and that he can run up to the old place whenever he finds opportunity."

"I can say sincerely," he responded, "that I have enjoyed the perfection of hospitality;" adding, in a low tone and with a quick, remorseful look at Annie, "though little deserving it."

"You have richly repaid us," said Mr. Walton, heartily. "It would have been very hard for me at my years to have to seek a new home. I have become wedded to this old place with my feelings and fancies, and the aged, you know, dislike change. I wish to make only one more, then rest will be complete."

"Now, father," said Annie, with glistening eyes, "you must not talk in that way. You know well that we cannot spare you even to go to heaven."

"Well, my child," answered he, fondly. "I am content to leave that in our best Friend's hands. But I cannot say," he added, with a touch of humor, "that it's a heavy cross to stay here with you."

"Would that such a cross were imposed upon me!" echoed Gregory, with sudden devoutness. "Miss Walton, did not my business imperatively demand my presence, I would break anything save my neck, in order to be an invalid on your hands."

"Come," cried Annie, half-vexed; "a truce to this style of remark. I think it's verging toward the sentimental, and I'm painfully matter- of-fact. Father, you must not think of going to heaven yet, and I don't like to hear you talk about it. Mr. Gregory can break his little finger, if he likes, so we may keep him longer. But do let us all be sensible, and not think of anything sad till it comes. Why should we? Mr. Gregory surely can find time to run up and see us, if he wishes, and I think he will."

Before he could reply, an anxious remark from little Susie enabled them to leave the table in the midst of one of those laughs that banish all embarrassment.

"But we'll be burned up if Mr. Gregory goes away."

CHAPTER XXVII
PLEADING FOR LIFE AND LOVE

Knowing that it was to be Gregory's last day with them, Annie determined it should be full of pleasant memories. She sung with him, and did anything he asked. Her heart overflowed toward him in a genial and almost sisterly regard, but his most careful analysis could find no trace even of the inception of warmer feelings. She evidently had a strong and growing liking for him, but nothing more, and she clearly felt the great interest in his effort to become a man of Christian principles. This fact gave him his main hope. Her passion to save seemed so strong that he trusted she might be approached even thus early upon that side.

He felt that he must speak--must get some definite hope for the future before he went away. It seemed to him that he could fairly bring his great need as a motive to bear upon her. Her whole course encouraged him to do this, for she had responded to every such appeal. Still with fear and trembling he admitted that he was about to ask for more now than ever before.

But he felt that he must speak. He had no hope that he could ever be more than his wretched self without her. He would ask nothing definite--only encouragement that if he could make himself worthy of her she would give him a chance to win her love. In her almost sisterly frankness it seemed that the idea of loving him had never occurred to her, and would not after he had gone. The thought of leaving her heart all disengaged, for some other to come and make a stronger impression, was torture. He never could be satisfied with the closest friendship, therefore he must plainly seek a dearer tie, even though for a time their frank, pleasant relations should be disturbed. He resolved to take no denial, but to give fair warning, before it was too late, that he was laying siege to her heart. He dreaded that attitude of mind upon her part which enables a woman to say to some men, "I could be your sister, but never your wife."

So he said before they separated for the night, "Miss Walton, I'm going to snatch a few hours from the hurry and grind of business, and shall not return to town till to-morrow afternoon. Won't you take one more ramble with me in the morning?"

"With pleasure," she replied, promptly. "I will devote myself to you to-morrow, and leave you without excuse for not coming again."

He flushed with pleasure at her reply, but said, quickly, "By the way that reminds me. Won't you tell me what your 'special reason' was for wishing me to stay a little longer?"

It was her turn to blush now, which she did in a way that puzzled him. She answered, hesitatingly, "Well, I think I'll tell you to-morrow."

"Good-night," said Mr. Walton, feelingly retaining Gregory's hand when he came to his chair. "We are coming to treat you almost as one of the family. Indeed it seems hard to treat you in any other way now, especially in your old home, now doubly yours since you have saved it from destruction. Every day you remind me more of my dear old friend. For some reason he has seemed very near me of late. If it should be my lot to see your sainted parents before you do, as it probably will, I believe it will be in my power to add even to their heavenly joys by telling them of your present prospects. Good-night, and may the blessing of your father's and mother's God rest upon you."

Tears sprung into the young man's eyes, and with a strong responsive pressure of Mr. Walton's hand, he hastened to his room, to hide what was not weakness.

That was the last time he saw his father's friend.

Annie's eyes glistened as she looked after him, and throwing her arms around her father's neck, she whispered, "God did send him here I now truly believe. We have not conspired and prayed in vain."

Mr. Walton fondly stroked his daughter's brown hair, and said, "You are right, Annie; he will be a gem in your crown of rejoicing. You have acted very wisely, very womanly, as your mother would, in this matter. He was a bad man when he first came here, and if I had not known you so well, I should not have trusted you with him as I have. Be as faithful through life, and you may lead many more out of darkness."

"Dear father," said Annie, tenderly, "this whole day, with Charles's good letter, and crowned with these precious words from you, seem like a benediction. May we have many more such."

"May God's will be done," said the riper Christian, with eyes turned homeward.

Thus in hope, peace, and gladness the day ended for all.

"Ye know not what shall be on the morrow."

To Gregory's unfeigned sorrow Mr. Walton was not well enough to appear at the breakfast-table the following morning. Annie was flitting in and out with a grave and troubled face. But by ten o'clock he seemed better and fell asleep. Leaving Miss Eulie watching beside him, she came and said, "Now, Mr. Gregory, I can keep my promise in part, and take a short walk with you. You can well understand why I cannot be away long."

"Please do not feel that you must go," he said. "However great the disappointment, I could not ask you to leave your father if he needs you."

"You may rest assured that nothing would tempt me from father if he needed me. But I think the worst is now over. He is sleeping quietly. I can trust aunty even better than myself. Besides, I want to go. I need the fresh air, and I wish to see more of you before you leave us."

He cordially thanked her and said, "I shall wait for you on the piazza."

They went down across the lawn through the garden. The sun was shining brightly, though occasionally obscured by clouds.

"How beautiful everything is," said Annie, "even now, when the leaves are half off the trees and falling fast! At any season, the moment I get out of doors I feel new life and hope."

"What nature does for you, Miss Annie, you seem to do for others. I feel 'new life and hope' the moment I am with you."

She looked at him quickly, for she did not quite like his tone and manner. But she only said, "You must believe, as I do, in a power behind nature."

"But even you believe He works through human agencies."

"Yes, up to a certain point."

"But who can say where that point is in any experience? Miss Walton," he continued, in grave earnestness, stopping and pointing to the rustic seat where, on the previous Sabbath, he had revealed to her his evil life, "that place is sacred to me. No hallowed spot of earth to which pilgrimages are made can compare with it. You know that in some places in Europe they raise a rude cross by the roadside where a man has been murdered. Should there not be a monument where one was given life?"

As they resumed their walk, he said in a low, meaning tone, "Do you remember old Daddy Tuggar's words--'You could take the wickedest man living straight to heaven if you'd stay right by him?'"

"But he was wrong," she replied.

"Pardon me if I differ with you, and agree with him. Miss Walton, I've been in your society scarcely three weeks. You know what I was when I came. I make no great claims now, but surely if tendencies, wishes, purposes count for anything, I am very different. How can you argue me out of the consciousness that I owe it all to you?"

"You will one day understand," she answered, earnestly, "that God has helped us both, and how futile my efforts would have been without such help. But, Mr. Gregory," she continued, looking frankly into his flushed face (for she was beginning to suspect now something of his drift, and instinctively sought to ward off words which might disturb their pleasant relations), "I do not intend to give you up from this day forth. As our quaint old friend suggests, I do mean to stand right by you as far as circumstances will allow me. I recognize how isolated and lonely you are, and I feel almost a *sister*'s interest in you."

"You emphasize the word 'sister.' I suppose I ought to be more than satisfied. Believe me I am very grateful that you can so speak. But suppose the frankness I promised compels me to say that it does not, and never can satisfy?"

"Then I shall think you very unreasonable. You have no right to ask more than one has the power to give," she answered, with a look and manner that were full of pain. "But surely, Mr. Gregory, we do not understand each other."

"But I want you to understand me," he exclaimed, earnestly. "If you had the vanity and worldly experience of most women, you would have known before this that I love you."

Tears rushed into Annie's eyes, and for a few moments she walked on in utter silence. This was so different an ending from what she had expected! She felt that she must be very careful or she would undo all she had attempted. She now dreaded utter failure, utter estrangement, and how to avoid these was her chief thought.

They had reached the cedar thicket near which they had first met, and she sat down upon the rock where she had found Gregory. Her whole aim was to end this unfortunate matter so that they might still continue friends. And yet the task seemed wellnigh impossible, for if he felt as he said, how could she tell him about Hunting without increasing alienation? But her impression was strong that he was acting under an exaggerated sense of her services and under a mistaken belief that she was essential to him. Therefore she tried at first to turn the matter off lightly by saying, "Mr. Gregory, you are the most grateful man I ever heard of. You need not think you must reward my slight services by marrying me."

"Now you greatly wrong me," he answered. "Did I not say I loved you? How deeply and truly you can never know. I cannot reward you. I did not dream of such a thing. My best hope was that some time in the future, when by long and patient effort I had become truly a man, you might learn to think of me in the way I wish."

"Mr. Gregory," said she, in a voice full of trouble, "has my manner or words led you to hope this? If so, I can never forgive myself."

"You have no cause for self-reproaches," he said, earnestly. "Though my suit should ever prove hopeless, in the depths of my heart I will acquit you of all blame. You have been what you promised--a true friend, nothing more. But please understand me. I ask nothing now, I am not worthy. Perhaps I never shall be. If so, I will not bind you to me with even a gossamer thread. I have too deep a respect for you. But I am so self-distrustful! I know my weakness better than you can. Still I am confident that if *you* could 'reward' me, and give the hope that you would crown the victory with yourself, I could do anything. In loving me, you would save me."

"Pardon me, but you are all wrong. I'm only an oar, but you look upon me as the lifeboat itself. In that you persist in looking to me, a weak, sinful creature, instead of to Him who alone 'taketh away the sin of the world,' you discourage me utterly."

"I will look to Him, but I want you to lead me to Him, and keep me at His side."

"I can do that just as well by being your friend."

"I can never think so. I shall go away from this place utterly disheartened unless you give me some hope, no matter how faint, that I shall not have to struggle alone."

She sprung up quickly, for he incensed her, while at the same time she pitied him. She could not understand how he had so soon learned to love her "deeply and truly." It rather appeared true that he had formed the mistaken opinion that she was essential to his success, and that he was bent upon bolstering himself up in his weakness, and sought to place her as a barrier between him and his old evil life; and she felt that he might need some wholesome truth rather than tender sympathy. At any rate her womanly nature took offence at his apparent motive, as she understood it--a motive that appeared more selfish and unworthy every moment. He was asking what he had no right to expect of any one. But she would not misunderstand him, and therefore said with a grave, searching look, "Only then as I give you the hope you ask for, will you make the effort you have promised to make?"

"Only then can I make it," he replied, in some confusion. "Can effort of any kind be asked of one utterly disabled?"

Sudden fire leaped into her dark eyes, but she said, with dignity, "Mr. Gregory, you disappoint me greatly. You assume a weakness--a disability--which does not and cannot exist under the circumstances. You made me a promise, but now impose a new condition which I did not dream of at the time, and which I cannot accept. You are asking more than you have a right to ask. However imperfect my efforts have been in your behalf, they were at least sincere and unselfish, and I was beginning to have a warm regard for you as a friend. I tell you frankly that I am most anxious that we should remain friends as before. If so, this kind of folly must cease now and forever. I have no right to listen to such words at all, and would not but for your sake, and in the hope of removing from your mind a very mistaken and unworthy idea. You are entirely wrong in thinking that your future depends solely upon me. It cannot--it ought not. It rests between you and God, and you cannot shift the responsibility. I am willing to do all you can ask of a sister, but no more. Do you think I have no needs, no weakness, myself? In a husband I want a man I can lean upon as well as help. I wish to marry one with a higher moral character than mine, to whom I can look up. There is the widest difference in the world between giving help, and even sincere affection to those who win it, and giving one's self away. Simple justice requires that my happiness and feelings be considered also. It is selfish in you to ask of me this useless sacrifice of myself."

Annie's quick, passionate nature was getting the better of her. It seemed in a certain sense disloyalty to Hunting to have listened thus long to Gregory. Moreover, not believing in nor understanding the latter's love for her, she was indignant that he should seek to employ her as a sort of stepping-stone into heaven. She would despise the man who sought her merely to advance his earthly interests, and she was growing honestly angry at Gregory, who, it seemed, wanted her only as a guide and staff in his pilgrimage--justly angry, too, if she were right.

Gregory became very pale as her words quivered in his heart like arrows, but in the consciousness of a true and unselfish love, he looked at her unfalteringly to the last, and said, "In justice to myself I might again urge that you misunderstand me. I asked for nothing now, only a hope for the future based on what I possibly might become. But, as you say, I now know I asked too much--more than I had a right to. You can never look up to me, and with a sadness you will never understand, I admit myself answered finally. But there is one imputation in your words that I cannot rest under. I solemnly assert before God, and in the name of my mother, that my love for you is as strong, pure, and unselfish as can exist in my half-wrecked nature."

"Oh dear!" exclaimed Annie, in a tone of mingled vexation and distress, "why has it all turned out so miserably? I'm so sorry, so very sorry; but in kindness I must show you how hopeless it all is. I am the same as engaged to another."

Gregory started violently. His despairing words had been not quite despairing. But now a chill like death settled about his heart. He was well satisfied that she was one who would be true as steel to all such ties, and that no man who had learned to know her would ever prove inconstant. But, with a white face and firmly compressed lips, he still listened quietly.

"I came out this morning hoping to tell you a little secret as I might confide in a brother, and I trusted that your friendship for me would prove strong enough to enable me to make you his friend also. I wanted you to stay a little longer, that you might meet him, and that I might reconcile you, and prepare the way for pleasant companionship in the future. I am expecting Charles Hunting now every--

"What is the matter? What do you mean by that look of horror? What have you against him, that you should show such deep hostility before, and now stare at me in almost terror?"

But he only staggered against a tree for support.

"Speak," cried she, passionately seizing his arm. "I will not endure the innuendo of your look and manner."

"I will speak," he answered, in sudden vehemence. "I've lost too much by him. Charles Hunting is--"

But he stopped, clinched his hands, and seemed to make a desperate effort at self-control. She heard him mutter as he turned away a few steps, "Stop! stop! All that is left you now is a little self-respect. Keep that--keep that."

Annie misunderstood him, and thought he referred to some slander that he had hesitated to utter against his enemy even in his anger and jealousy. With flashing eyes she said, "Let me complete the sentence for you. Charles Hunting is a Christian gentleman. You may well think twice before you speak one word against him in my presence."

"Did I say one word against him?" he asked, eagerly.

"No, but you looked much more than words can express."

"I could not help that. Your revelation was sudden, Miss Walton."

"How could it be otherwise?" she asked, indignantly. "The first evening of your arrival, when his name was mentioned, your face grew as black as night. When I again sought to speak to you of him, you adjured me never to mention his name. You taxed my forbearance severely at that time. But I hoped you would become so changed that such enmity would be impossible."

"I see it all now," he groaned--"the miserable fatality of it all. I must shut off the one way of escape, and then go forward. By my own act, I must destroy my one chance. If I had only known this in time. And yet it's through my own act that I did not know. Your God is certainly one of justice. I'm punished now for all the past. But it seems a trifle cruel to show one heaven and then shut the door in one's face. If I had only known!"

"There," exclaimed Annie, in the deepest distress; "because of this little thing you fall back into your old scepticism."

"This 'little thing' is death to me," he said, in a hard, bitter tone. "Oh no, I'm not at all sceptical. The 'argument from design,' the nature of the result, are both too clear. I'm simply being dealt with according to law. Though perfectly sincere, you were entirely too lenient that Sunday evening when I told you what I was. My conscience was right after all. I only wish that I had fallen from yonder roof the other night. I might then have made my exit decently."

"Mr. Gregory, you shock me," she said, almost sternly. "You have no right to insult my faith in a merciful God by such words, and your believing Him cruel and vindictive on this one bit of your experience is the sheerest egotism. It is the essence of selfishness to think everything wrong when one does not have one's own way."

He only bowed his answer, then stepped out to the point of the hill, and took a long, lingering look at the valley and his old home, sighed deeply, turned, and said to her, quietly, "Perhaps it is time for you to return to your father."

CHAPTER XXVIII
WHAT A LOVER COULD DO

Without a word they descended the hill. Gregory was very pale, and this, with a certain firmness about his mouth, was the only indication of feeling on his part. Otherwise, he was the same finished man of the world that he had appeared when he came. Annie's face grew more and more troubled with every glance at him.

"He is hardening into stone," she thought; and she was already reproaching herself for speaking so harshly. "I might have known," she thought, "that his rash, bitter words were only incoherent cries of pain and disappointment."

He perplexed her still more by saying at the foot of the hill, in his old light tone, "See, Miss Walton, our 'well-meaning friend' has not been here to put up the bars, and we can take the shorter way through the orchard. I would like to see them picking apples once more. By the way, you must say good-by for me to your old neighbor, and tell him that out of respect for his first honest greeting, I'm going to fill his pipe for the winter."

But Annie's heart was too full to answer.

"How familiar these mossy-trunked trees are!" he continued, determined that there should be no awkward pauses, no traces to the eyes of others of what had occurred. "How often I've picked apples from this one and that one--indeed from all! Good-by, old friends."

"Do you never expect to come back to these 'old friends,' and others that would be friends again?" she asked, in low, trembling tones. "Mr. Gregory, you are cruel. You are saying good-by as if it were a very ordinary matter."

He did not trust himself to look at her, but he said, firmly, "Miss Walton, in a few moments we shall be under the eyes of others, and perhaps I shall never have another chance to speak to you alone. Let me say a few plain, honest words before I go. I am not ashamed of my love for you, nor to have it known. I am glad there was man enough in me to love such a woman as you are. You are not one of those society belles who wish to boast of their conquests. I wish merely to leave in a manner that will save you all embarrassing questions and surmises, and enable you to go back to your father as if nothing had happened. The best I can do is to maintain the outward semblance of a gentleman with which I came. In regard to Charles Hunting--please listen patiently--I know that you will not believe any statement of mine. It is your nature to trust implicitly those you love. But since I have had time to think, even the little conscience I possess will not permit me to go away in silence in regard to him. Do not think my words inspired by jealousy. I have given you up. You are as unattainable by me as heaven. But that man is not worthy of you. Think well before you--"

"You are right," she interrupted, hotly. "I will not believe anything against him whom I have known and loved for years. If sincere, you are mistaken. But I entreat you, for my own sake as well as yours, never speak a word against him again. Because, if you do, it will be hard for me to forgive you. If you place the slightest value on my good opinion and continued regard, you will not throw them away so uselessly. I do feel--I ever wish to feel--a deep and friendly interest in you, therefore speak for yourself, and I will listen with honest sympathy. Give me hope, if possible, that you will think better of all this folly--that you will visit your old home and those who wish to be your true friends--that you will give me a chance to make you better acquainted with one whom you now greatly wrong. Please give me something better than this parting promises to end in."

He merely bowed and said, "I supposed it would be so. It is like you. As for myself--I do not know what my future will be, save that it will be full of pain. Rest assured of one thing, however. I can never be a common, vulgar sinner again, after having loved you. That would be sacrilege. Your memory will blend with that of my mother, and shine like a distant star in my long night. But you have no right to ask me to come here any more. Though you do not believe in my love, it is a reality nevertheless, and I cannot inflict upon myself the unbearable pain of seeing you, yet hedged about with that which must ever keep me at a distance. With my feelings, even my poor sense of honor forbids my seeking your presence. Can I visit you feigning friendship, while my heart is consuming with love? Come, Miss Walton, we shall have our real leave taking here, and our formal one at the house. I don't think gratitude will ever fade out of my heart for all you have tried to do for me, wherever I am. Even the 'selfish' Walter Gregory can honestly wish you happiness unalloyed. And you will have it, too, in spite of-- well, in spite of everything, for your happiness is from within, not without. Give me your hand, and say good-by under the old mossy trees."

Annie burst into tears and said, "I can't say good-by and have you leave us so unhappy--so unbelieving. Mr. Gregory, will you never trust in God?"

"I fear not--not after what I know to-day. He seems wronging you who are so true to Him, as well as me. You see I am honest with you, as I said I would be. Can you take the hand of such as I?"

She did take it in both of hers, and said, with passionate earnestness, "O that I could save you from yourself by main force!"

He was deeply moved, but after a moment said, gently, "That is like your warm heart. But you cannot. Good-by, Annie Walton. Go on in your brave, noble life to the end, and then heaven will be the better for your coming."

"Will you forgive my harsh words?"

"They were more true than harsh. They were forgiven when spoken."

"Mr. Gregory," she cried, "I will not say farewell as you say it. I have prayed for you, and so has your mother. I will still pray for you unceasingly. You cannot prevent it, and I will not doubt God's promise to hear."

"I cannot share your faith. I am saying good-by in the saddest sense."

He stooped and kissed her hand, and then said, firmly, "The end has come. We really part here. I leave you as I came."

With eyes downcast and blinded with tears she accompanied him out of the deep shade to the further side of the orchard nearest the house. Jeff was on a tall ladder that leaned against a heavily laden tree, and was just about to descend.

"That's right," cried Gregory; "come down with your basket and give me a taste of those apples. They look the same as when I used to pick them sixteen years ago."

Jeff obeyed with alacrity. Gregory accompanied him a few steps, and dropped a banknote into the basket, saying, "That's for the jolly wood-fires you made for me," and then turned quickly toward Annie to escape the profuse thanks impending.

He had turned none too soon. The apple-boughs, relieved of the weight of the fruit and Jeff's solid person, threw out the heavy ladder that had been placed too nearly in a perpendicular position at first. It had trembled and wavered a moment, but was now inclining over the very spot where Annie was standing.

"Miss Walton!" he cried, with a look of horror; rushed toward her, and stood with head bent down between her and the falling ladder.

She heard a rushing sound, and then with a heavy thud the ladder struck him, glanced to one side, grazing her shoulder, and fell to the ground.

He lay motionless beneath it.

For a moment she gazed vacantly at him, too stunned to think or speak.

But Jeff ran and lifted the ladder off Gregory, exclaiming, "Lor' bless him, Miss Annie, he jus' done save your life."

She knelt at his side and took his hand, but it seemed that of the dead. She moaned, "The omen's true. His blood is on me now--his blood is on me now. He died for my sake, and I called him selfish."

She took his head into her lap, and put her hand over his heart.

She thought she felt a faint pulsation.

In a moment all trace of weakness vanished, and her face became resolute and strong.

"Jeff," she said, in clear-cut, decided tones, "go to the house, tell Hannah and Zibbie to come here; tell Hannah to bring brandy and a strong double blanket. Not a word of this to my father. Go, quick."

Jeff ran as he had done once before when the bloodhounds were after him, saying under his breath all the way, "Lor' bless him! He save Miss Annie's life; he orter have her sure 'nuff."

Annie was left alone with the unconscious man. She pushed his hair from his damp brow, and, bending down, impressed a remorseful kiss upon it.

"God forgive me that I called you selfish," she murmured. "Where is your spirit wandering that I cannot call it back? O live, live; I can never be happy if you die. Can this be the end? God keep my faith from failing."

Again she put her hand over his heart, whose love she could doubt no more.

Did it beat? or was it only the excited throbbing of her own hand?

Jeff now returned, and, with white, scared faces, the women soon followed. Annie tried to give Gregory brandy, but he did not seem to swallow it. They then lifted him on the blanket and carried him to the house, and up the back stairway to his room, so that Mr. Walton might not know.

"Now, Jeff," whispered Annie, "harness the fastest horse to the buggy, and bring the doctor--mind, bring him. Don't tell him to come. Hannah, tell Miss Eulie to come here--quietly now. Zibbie, bring hot water."

Again she poured a teaspoonful of brandy into his mouth, and this time he seemed to swallow it. She bathed his face and hands with spirits, while her every breath was a prayer.

Miss Eulie did not want a long explanation. Annie's hurried words, "A ladder fell on him," satisfied her, and she set to work, and more effectively with her riper experience. She took off his collar and opened his shirt at the throat, and soon, with a look of joy, to Annie, said, "His heart beats distinctly."

Again they gave him brandy, and this time he made a manifest effort to swallow it.

With eyes aglow with excitement and hope they re-doubled their exertions, Hannah and Zibbie helping, and at last they were rewarded by seeing their patient make a faint movement.

Now with every breath Annie silently sent the words heavenward, "O God, I thank thee."

She bent over him, and said, in a low, thrilling tone, "Mr. Gregory." A happy smile came out upon his face, but this was the only response.

"Do you think he is conscious?" she whispered to her aunt.

"I hardly know. Let me give him a little more stimulant."

After receiving it he suddenly opened his eyes and looked fearfully around. Then he tried to rise, but fell back, and asked, faintly, "Where is Miss Walton? Is she safe? I heard her voice."

"You did. I'm here. Don't you know me?"

"Are you really here unhurt?"

"Yes, yes," she answered, eagerly; "thanks to you."

Again he closed his eyes with a strange and quiet smile.

"Can't you see me?" she asked.

"There seems a blur before my eyes. It does not signify. I know your voice, so true and kind."

"Why can't he see?" she asked, drawing her aunt aside.

"I don't know. What I fear most are internal injuries. Did the ladder strike his head?"

"O merciful Heaven!" said Annie, again in an agony of fear. "I don't know. Oh, if he should die--if he should die--" and she wrung her hands with terror at the thought.

The doctor now stepped lightly in. Jeff had told him enough to excite the gravest apprehensions. He made a few inquiries and felt Gregory's pulse.

"It's very feeble," he said. "More brandy."

Then he added, "I must make such examination as I can now without disturbing him much. Miss Morton, you and Jeff stay and help me."

Annie went down to her father with a greater anxiety as to the result of the examination than if the danger had been her own.

She found her father awake, and wondering at the sounds in the room above.

"Annie," he said, feebly, "what is going on in Mr. Gregory's room?"

As she looked at him, she saw that he was not better, as she hoped, but that his face had a shrunken look, betokening the rapid failing of the vital forces. The poor girl felt that trouble was coming like an avalanche, and in spite of herself she sat down, and, burying her face in her father's bosom, sobbed aloud. But she soon realized the injury she might do him in thus giving way, and by a great effort controlled herself so as to tell him the softened outlines of the accident. But the ashen hue deepened on the old man's face, as he said, fervently, "God bless him! God bless him! He has saved my darling's life. What should I have done in these last days without you?"

"But, father, don't you think he will get well?" she asked, eagerly.

"I hope so. I pray so, my child. But I know the ladder, and it is a heavy one. This is time for faith in God. We cannot see a hand's- breadth in the darkness before us. He has been very merciful to us thus far, very merciful, and no doubt has some wise, good purpose in these trials and dangers. Just cling to Him, my child, and all will be well."

"O father, how you comfort me! We must leave everything in His hands. But, father, you feel better, do you not?"

"Yes, much better; not much pain now; and yet for some reason I feel that I shall soon be where pain never comes. How otherwise can I explain my almost mortal weakness?"

Annie again hid her tearful eyes on the bedside. Her father placed his hand upon her bowed head and continued, "It won't break your heart, my little girl, will it, to have your father go to heaven?"

But she could not answer him.

At last the doctor came down, and said, "His injuries are certainly serious, and may be more so than I can yet discover. The ladder grazed his head, inflicting some injury, and struck him on the shoulder, which is much bruised, and the collar-bone is badly broken. The whole system has received a tremendous shock, but I hope that with good care he will pull through. But he must be kept very quiet in mind and body. And so must you, sir. Now you know all, and have nothing to suspect. It's often injurious kindness to half hide something from the sick."

"Well, doctor, do your very best by him, as if he were my own son. You know what a debt of gratitude we owe him. Spare no expense. If he needs anything, let it be sent for. If I were only up and around; but the Lord wills it otherwise."

Annie followed the physician out and said, "You have told us the very worst then?"

"Yes, Miss Walton, the very worst. Unless there are injuries that I cannot now detect I think he will get better. I will send a young man whom I can trust to take care of him. Best assured I will do all that is possible, for I feel very grateful to this stranger for saving my much-esteemed little friend. I suppose you know we all think a great deal of you in our neighborhood, and I shudder to think how near we came to a general mourning. You see he was nearer the base of the ladder than you, Jeff says. The ladder therefore would have struck you with greater force, and you would not have had a ghost of a chance. You ought to be very grateful, eh, Miss Annie?" he added, with a little sly fun in his face.

But she shook her head sadly, and only said with deep feeling, "I am very, very grateful." Then she added, quickly, "What about father?"

The doctor's face changed instantly and became grave.

"I don't quite understand his case. He was threatened with pneumonia; but there seems no acute disease now, and yet he appears to be failing. The excitement and exposure of the other night were too much for him. You must make him take all the nourishment possible. Medicine is of no use."

Agitated by conflicting fears and hopes Annie went to the kitchen to make something that might tempt her father's appetite.

Blessed are the petty and distracting cares of the household, the homely duties of the sick-room. They divert the mind and break the force of the impending blow. If, when illness and death invade a house, the fearing and sorrowing ones had naught to do but sit down and watch the remorseless approach of the destroyer, they might go mad.

When Annie stole noiselessly back to Gregory's room he was sleeping, though his breathing seemed difficult.

What a poor mockery the dinner hour was! Even the children were oppressed by the general gloom and talked in whispers. But before it was over there came a bright ray of light to Annie in the form of a telegram from Hunting, saying that he had arrived in New York safely, and would be at the village on the 5 P.M. train.

"O I am so glad!" cried Annie; "never was he so needed before."

And yet there was a remorseful twinge at her heart as she thought of Gregory. But she felt sure of reconciliation now, for would not Hunting overwhelm her preserver with gratitude, and forgive everything in the past?

She said to Jeff, "Have Dolly and the low buggy ready for me at half- past four."

Her father seemed peculiarly glad when he heard that his relative, the man he hoped would soon be his son, was coming.

"It's all turning out for the best," he said, softly.

The hour soon came, for it was already late, and Annie slipped away, leaving both her father and Gregory sleeping. To her great joy Hunting stepped down from the train and was quickly seated by her side. As they drove away in the dusk he could not forbear a rapturous kiss and embrace which she did not resist.

"O Charles, I'm so glad you've come--so very glad!" she exclaimed almost breathlessly; "and I've so much to tell you that I hardly know where to begin. How good God is to send you to me now, just when I need you most!"

"So you find that you can't do without me altogether? That's grand news. How I've longed for this hour! If I'd had my own way I would have exploded the boilers in my haste to reach port to see you again. It was real good of you to come, and not send for me. Come Annie, celebrate my return by the promise that you will soon make a home for me. I am happy to say that I can now give you the means of making it a princely one."

"I haven't the time nor the heart to think about that now, Charles. Father is very ill. I'm exceedingly anxious about him."

"Indeed!" said Hunting, "that is bad news;" and yet his grief was not very deep, for he thought, "If she is left alone she will come to me at once."

"What is more," cried Annie, a little hurt at the quiet manner in which he received her tidings, "suppose, instead of meeting me strong and well, you had found me a crushed and lifeless corpse to-night?"

"Annie," he said, "what do you mean?"

"I mean that this would have been true but for one with whom I am sorry you are on bad terms. Walter Gregory is at our house."

He gave a great start at the mention of this name, and even in the deep twilight his face seemed very white.

"I don't understand," he almost gasped.

"I knew you would be deeply affected," said the unsuspicious Annie. "He stood between me and death to-day, and it may cost him his own life. He was severely injured--how badly we can hardly tell yet;" and she rapidly related all that had occurred. "And now, Charles," she concluded, "no matter what he may have done, or how deeply he may have wronged you, I'm sure you'll do everything in your power to effect a complete reconciliation, and cement a lasting friendship. If possible, you must become his untiring nurse. How much you owe him!"

She noticed that he was trembling. After a moment he asked, hesitatingly, "Has he--how long has he been here, did you say?"

"About three weeks. You know our place was his old home, and his father was a very dear friend of my father."

"If I knew it I had forgotten it," he answered, with a chill of fear growing deeper every moment. "Did he--has he said anything about our difficulties?"

"Nothing definite," said she, a little wonderingly at Hunting's manner. "Father happened to mention your name the first evening of his arrival, and the bitter enmity that came out upon his face quite startled me. You know well that I wouldn't hear a word against you. He once commenced saying something to your prejudice, but I stopped him and said I would neither listen to nor believe him--that he did not know you, and was entirely mistaken in his judgment. It was evident to us that Mr. Gregory was not a good man. Indeed, he made no pretence of being one; but he has changed since, as yon can well understand, or he couldn't have sacrificed himself as he has to-day. I told father that I thought the cause of your trouble arose from your trying to restrain him in some of his fast ways, but he thought it resulted from business relations."

"You were both right," said Hunting, slowly, as if he were feeling his way along. "He was inclined to be very dissipated, and I used to remonstrate with him; but the immediate cause was a business difficulty. He would have kept me out of a great deal of money if he could."

His words were literally true, but they gave an utterly false impression. Annie was satisfied, however. It seemed a natural explanation, and she trusted Hunting implicitly. Indeed, with her nature, love could scarcely exist without trust.

"That's all past now," said Annie, eagerly. "You surely will not let it weigh with you a moment. Indeed, Charles, I shall expect you to do everything in your power to make that man your friend."

"O, certainly, I could not act otherwise," he said, rather absently. He was scheming with desperate earnestness to meet and avert the impending dangers. Annie's frank and cordial reception showed him that so far as she was concerned he was as yet safe. But he knew her well enough to feel sure that if she detected falsehood in him his case would be nearly hopeless. He recognized that he was walking on a mine that at any moment might be sprung. With his whole soul he loved Annie Walton, and it would be worse than death to lose her. The thought of her had made every gross temptation fall harmless at his feet, and even his insatiate love of wealth had been mingled with the dearer hope that it would eventually minister to her happiness. But he had lived so long in the atmosphere of Wall Street that his ideas of commercial integrity had become exceedingly blurred. When a questionable course opened by which he could make money, he could not resist the temptation. He tried to satisfy himself that business required such action, and called his sharp practice by the fine names of skill, sagacity. But when on his visits to Annie, which, of late, during the worst of his transactions, had been frequent rather than prolonged, he had had a growing sense of humiliation and fear. He saw that she could never be made to look upon his affair with Burnett & Co. as he regarded it, and that her father was the soul of commercial honor. Though Mr. Walton's fortune was moderate, not a penny had come to him stained. After these visits Hunting would go back to the city, resolved to quit everything illegitimate and become in his business and other relations just what he seemed to them. But some glittering temptation would assail him. He would make one more adroit shuffle of the cards, and then, from being hollow, would become morally and religiously sound at once.

During his voyage home, there was time for thought. A severe gale, while lashing the sea into threatening waves, had also disturbed his guilty conscience. He had amassed sufficient to satisfy even his greed of gold for the present, and his calculating soul hinted that it was time to begin to put away a little stock in heaven as well as on earth. He resolved that he would withdraw from the whirlpool of Wall Street speculation and engage in only legitimate operations. Moreover, he began to long for the refuge and more quiet joys of home, and he felt, as did poor Gregory, that Annie of all women could do most to make him happy here and fit him for the future life. Therefore he had returned with the purpose of pressing his suit for a speedy marriage as strongly as a safe policy would permit.

The bright October day of his arrival in New York seemed emblematic of his hopes and prospects, and now again the deepening night, the rising wind, and the wildly hurrying clouds but mirrored back himself.

His safest and wisest course would have been to make an honest confession to Annie of the wrong he had done Gregory. As his mind recovered from its first confusion this thought occurred to him. But he had already given her the impression that he had received the wrong, or rather that it had been attempted against him. Moreover, by any truthful confession he would stand convicted of deceiving and swindling Burnett & Co. He justly feared that Annie would break with him the moment she learned this. So like all schemers, he temporized, and left his course open to be decided by circumstances rather than principle.

His first course was to learn of Annie all that he could concerning Gregory and his visit, so that he might act in view of the fullest knowledge possible. She told him frankly what had occurred, so far as time permitted during their ride home. But of Gregory's love she did not speak, and was perplexed as to her proper course. Loyalty to her lover seemed to require that he should know all, and yet she was sure that Gregory would not wish her to speak of it, and she owed so much to him that she felt she could not do what was contrary to his wishes. But Hunting well surmised that, whether Annie knew it or not, Gregory could not have been in her society three weeks and go away an indifferent stranger.

"Jeff can give me more light," he thought.

Conscious of deceit himself, he distrusted every one, even crystal- souled Annie.

CHAPTER XXIX
DEEPENING SHADOWS

Mr. Walton received Hunting in a fatherly way. Indeed, he looked upon the young man as a son, and the thought of leaving Annie to his protection was an un- speakable comfort.

Altogether Hunting was reassured by his reception, which proved that his re- lations were as yet undisturbed. But in the depths of his soul he trembled at the presence of Gregory in the house; and when Miss Eulie came down and said, after an affectionate greeting, that Gregory was in something like a stupor, he was even base enough to wish that he might never come out of it.

At the word "stupor," Annie's face grew pale. She had a growing dissatisfaction with Hunting's manner in regard to Gregory, and felt that he did not feel or show the interest or gratitude that he ought; but there was nothing tangible with which she could tax him.

The doctor, who came early in the evening, reassured her, and said that the state of partial consciousness was not necessarily a dangerous symptom, as it might be the result of a severe shock. The young man he brought was installed as nurse under Miss Eulie's charge, and Annie said that Mr. Hunting would also take his turn as watcher.

Then she, Mr. Hunting, and her father had a long talk over what had happened in his absence, Mr. Walton dwelling most feelingly on what he regarded as the providential character of the visit from the son of his old friend.

"If he never leaves our house alive, I have a strong assurance that he will join his father in the better home. Indeed, I may soon be there with them."

"Please don't talk so, father," pleaded Annie.

"Well, my child, perhaps it's best I should, and prepare your minds for what may be near. It's a great consolation to see Charles again, and he will help you bear whatever is God's will."

"You can trust her to me," said Hunting, fervently. "I have ample means to gratify her most extravagant wish, and my love will shelter her and think for her even as yours would. But I trust you will soon share our home with us."

"I expect to, my children, but it will be our eternal home."

Annie strove bravely to keep her tears back, for her father's sake, but they would come.

"Annie," said Hunting, "won't you please let your father put this ring on your engagement finger?" and he gave Mr. Walton a magnificent solitaire diamond.

Mr. Walton took his daughter's hand, and looked earnestly into her tearful, blushing face.

"Annie," he said, in a grave, sweet tone, "I hope for your sake that I may be wrong, but I have a presentiment that my pilgrimage is nearly ended. You have made its last stage very happy. A good daughter makes a good wife, Mr. Hunting; and, Annie, dear, I shall tell your mother that you supplied her place, as far as a daughter could. It will add greatly to my peace if I can leave you and my sister, and the dear little ones, under the care of one so competent to protect and provide for you all. Mr. Hunting, do you feel that you can take them to your home and heart, with my daughter?"

"Certainly," said Hunting. "I had no other thought; and Annie's will shall be supreme in her future home."

"But, after all, the chief question is, Does this ring join your hearts? I'm sure I'm right in thinking so, Annie?"

"Yes," she said, in a low tone.

Slowly, with his feeble, trembling hands he put the flashing gem on Annie's finger, and then placed her hand in Hunting's, and, looking solemnly to heaven, said, "May God bless this betrothal as your father blesses it."

Hunting stooped and kissed her hand and then her lips. With mingled truth and policy, he said, "This ceremony is more solemn and binding to me than the one yet to come at the altar."

Annie was happy in her engagement. It was what she expected, and had been consummated in a way that seemed peculiarly sweet and sacred; and yet her thoughts, with a remorseful tinge, would keep recurring to the man who even then might be dying for her sake.

After they had sat a little while in silence, which is often the best expression of deep feeling, she suddenly said, with an involuntary sigh, "Poor Mr. Gregory! I'm so sorry for him!"

Thus Hunting knew where her thoughts were, and instantly the purpose formed itself in his mind to induce her through her father to consent to an immediate marriage. He saw more plainly than Annie the great change in her father, and based his hope on the fact that the parent might naturally wish to give his child a legal protector before he passed away.

Mr. Walton now showed such signs of weariness that they left him in Miss Eulie's care, who seemed to flit like a ministering spirit between the two patients.

After the great excitement of the day, Annie, too, was very weary, and soon the household sought such rest as was possible with two of its inmates apparently very near the boundaries that separate the known world from the unknown. Glimmering all night long, like signals of distress at sea, the faint lights of the watchers reminded late passers-by of the perilous nature of earthly voyaging.

Annie had gone with Miss Eulie to take a parting look at Gregory. She bent over him and said, "Mr. Gregory," but his spirit seemed to have sunk into such far depths that even her voice could not summon him.

"Oh, if he should die now!" she moaned, shudderingly, and on the night of her engagement sobbed herself to sleep.

The next morning saw little change in the patients, save that Mr. Walton was evidently weaker. Miss Eulie said that Gregory had roused up during the night and seemed perfectly conscious. He had inquired after Mr. Walton and Annie, but toward morning had fallen into his old lethargy.

After breakfast Annie took Hunting up to see him, but was pained at the darkening of her lover's face as he looked at the prostrate and unconscious man. She could not understand it. He seemed to have no wish to remain. She felt almost indignant, and yet what could she say more than she had said? Gregory's condition, and the cause, should naturally plead for him beyond all words.

Annie spent most of the day with her father, and purposed watching with him that night. The doctor came and reported more favorably of Gregory, but said that everything depended upon his being quiet. Annie purposed that Hunting should commence the duties of watcher as soon as possible. Therefore she told her aunt to tell Gregory, as soon as she thought it would answer, that Hunting had arrived. In the afternoon, Gregory seemed to come out of his lethargy more decidedly than he had before, and took some nourishment with marked relish. Then he lay quietly looking at the fire.

"Do you feel better now?" Miss Eulie asked, gently.

"I'm sure I don't know," he answered, wearily. "I have a numb, strange feeling."

"Would you like to see Miss Walton?"

"No, not now; I am satisfied to know she is well."

"She wished me to tell you that Mr. Hunting had arrived."

He turned away his face with a deep scowl, but said nothing.

After some time she came to his side and said, "Is there anything you would like?"

"Nothing," he replied, gently. "I appreciate your great kindness."

Miss Eulie sighed and left the room, feeling dimly that there were internal injuries after all, but such as were beyond the doctor's skill.

Annie echoed her sigh when she heard how he received Miss Eulie's information. She determined to prepare and take him his supper.

When she noiselessly entered, he was again looking fixedly at the fire. But she had not advanced far into the room before he recognized her step and looked up quickly.

"See," she said, cheerily, coming to his side, "I've prepared and brought you this supper with my own hands, and shall expect in return that you compliment it highly. Now, isn't it a good supper?" she asked, holding it before him.

But his eyes fastened on the glittering and significant ring, whose meaning he too well understood. With an expression of intense pain he turned his face to the wall without a word.

"Mr. Gregory," pleaded Annie, "I never thought you would turn away from me."

"Not from you, not from you," he said, in a low tone, "but I'm very weak, and the light of that diamond is too strong for me yet."

"Forgive me," she said, in a tone of deep reproach; "I did not think."

"No, forgive me. Please leave me now, and remember in charity how weak I am."

She put the tray down and hastened from the room. He ate no supper that night, neither did she. Hunting watched her gloomily, with both fear and jealousy at heart. The latter, however, was groundless, for Annie's feeling was only that of profound sorrow for something she could not help. But lack of strongly manifested interest and sympathy for Gregory injured him in her estimation; for woman-like she unconsciously took the side of the one he wronged. She could understand Gregory's enmity, but it seemed to her that Hunting should be full of generous enthusiasm for one who was suffering so much in her behalf.

"Men are so strange!" she said, half-vexedly. "They fall in love without the slightest provocation, and hate each other forever, when a woman would have sharp words and be over with it. They never do what you would naturally expect."

During the day Hunting had found time to see Jeff alone, but had found him inclined to be sullen and uncommunicative. Jeff had changed sides, and was now an ardent adherent of Gregory's, who had given him five dollars without imposing any conditions; and then, what was of far greater import, had saved the house and Annie's life, and, according to Jeff's simple views of equity, he ought to have both. And yet a certain rude element of honesty made him feel that he had made a bargain with Hunting, and that he must fulfil his part and then they would be quits. But he was not disposed to do it with a very good grace. So when Hunting said, "Well, Jeff, I suppose you've seen a good deal since I was last here."

"Yes, I've seen a mighty lot," said Jeff, sententiously.

"Well, Jeff, you remember our agreement. What did you see? Only the truth now."

"Sartin, sah, only de truf. I'se belong to de Walton family, and yous doesn't get nothin' but de truf from dem."

"All right, Jeff; I'm glad your employers have so good an influence on you. Well?"

"I'se seen Misser Gregory on de roof," said Jeff, drawing on his imagination, as he had only heard about that event through Zibbie's highly colored story, "where some other folks wouldn't dar go, and now I'se see dat house dar, which I wouldn't see dar, wasn't it for Misser Gregory."

"Well, well," said Hunting, impatiently, "I've heard all about that. What else?"

"I'se seen Miss Annie roun' all day bloomin' and sweet as a rose, and I'se seen how she might have been a crushed white lily," Jeff continued, solemnly, with a rhetorical wave of the hand.

There existed in Jeff the raw material of a colored preacher, only it was very crude and undeveloped. But upon any important occasion he always grew rhetorical and figurative in his language.

"Come, come, Jeff, tell me something new."

"Well," said Jeff, "since I'se promised to tell you, and since I'se spent de ten dollars, and hasn't got it to give you back again, I'se seen Misser Gregory las' Sunday evenin', a kneelin' afore Miss Annie as if he was a sayin' his prayers to her, and I shouldn't wonder if she heard 'em (with a chuckle); anyhow she wasn't lofty and scornful, and Misser Gregory he's looked kinder glorified ever since; afore that he looked glum, and Miss Annie, she's been kinder bendin' toward him since dat evenin', like a rosebud wid de dew on it."

Hunting's face darkened with suppressed anger and jealousy. After a moment he said, "Is that all?"

"Dat's all."

"Well, Jeff, here's ten dollars more, and look sharper than ever now."

"'Scuse me, Misser Hunting. We'se squar' now. I'se done what I agreed, and now I'se gwine out ob de business."

"Has Gregory engaged your services?" asked Hunting, quickly.

"No, sah, he hab not. I reckon Misser Gregory tink he doesn't need any help."

"Why won't you do as I wish, then?"

"Well, Mr. Hunting, it kinder makes me feel bad here," said Jeff, rubbing his hand indefinitely over several physical organs. "I don't jes' believe Miss Annie would like it, and after seein' Mr. Gregory under dat pesky ladder, I couldn't do nothin' dat he wouldn't like. If it hadn't been for him I'd sorter felt as if I'd killed Miss Annie by leavin' dat doggoned ladder so straight up, and I nebber could hab gone out in de dark agin all my life."

"Why, you old black fool," said Hunting, irritably, "don't you know I'm going to marry Miss Annie? You'd better keep on the right side of me."

"Which is de right side?" Jeff could not forbear saying, with a suppressed chuckle.

"Come, sir, no impudence. You won't serve me any more then?"

"Oh yes, Misser Hunting. I'se black yer boots, make de fire, harness de hoss, do anything dat won't hurt in here," with a gesture that seemed to indicate the pit of his stomach. "Anything more, please 'scuse me."

"You will not speak of what has passed between us?"

"I'se given my word," said Jeff, drawing himself up, "de word ob one dat belongs to de Waltons."

Hunting turned on his heel and strode away. Annie had given one aspect to the scene on that Sabbath evening, and Jeff had innocently given another. Hunting was not loyal enough even to such a woman as Annie to believe her implicitly. But it is the curse of conscious deceit to breed suspicion. Only the true can have absolute faith in the truth of others. Moreover, Hunting, in his hidden selfishness and worldliness could not understand Annie's ardent effort to save a fellow-creature from sin. Skilled in the subtle impulses of the heart, he believed that Annie, unconsciously even to herself, was drifting toward the man he hated all the more because he had wronged him, while the danger of his presence made him almost vindictive. Yet he realized the necessity of disguising his feelings, for if Annie discovered them he might well dread the consequence. But the idea of watching alone with Gregory was revolting. It suggested dark thoughts which he tried to put from him in horror, for he was far from being a hardened villain. He was only a man who had gradually formed the habit of acting from expedience and self-interest, instead of principle. Such a rule of life often places us where expedience and self-interest require deeds that are black indeed.

But he was saved from the ordeal of spending hours alone with a man who even in his helplessness might injure him beyond remedy, for on the following morning Annie again sought Gregory's room bent on securing reconciliation at once. She felt that she could endure this estrangement no longer.

The young man employed as watcher was out at the time.

Gregory was gazing at the fire with the same look of listless apathy. A deep flush overspread his deathly pale face as she came and sat down beside him, but he did not turn from her.

"Mr. Gregory," she said, very gently, "it seems that I can do nothing but receive favors from you, and I've come now to ask a great one."

He suspected something concerning Hunting, and his face darkened forbiddingly. Though Annie noted this, she would not be denied.

"Do you think," she said, earnestly, "that, after your sacrifice for me, I can ever cease to be your friend in the truest and strongest sense?"

"Miss Walton," he said, calmly, "I've made no sacrifice for you. The thought of that episode in the orchard is my one comfort while lying here, and will be through what is left of life. But please do not speak of it, for it will become a pain to me if I see the obligation is a burden to you."

"It is not," she said, eagerly. "I'm glad to owe my life to you. But do you think I can go on my way and forget you?"

"It's the very best you can do, Miss Walton."

"But I tell you it's impossible. Thank God, it's not my nature to do it!"

He turned toward her with a wistful, searching look.

"We must carry out our old agreement," continued Annie. "We must be close and lasting friends. You should not blame me for an attachment formed years ago."

"I do not blame you."

"Then you should not punish me so severely. You first make your friendship needful to me, and then you deny it."

"I am *your* friend, and more."

"How can we enjoy a frank and happy friendship through coming years, after-- after--you feel differently from what you do now, when you will not even hear the name of him who will one day be my second self?"

Again his face darkened; but she continued rapidly, "Mr. Hunting is deeply grateful to you, and would like to express his feelings in person. He wishes to bury the past--"

"He will, with me, soon," interrupted Gregory, gloomily.

"No; please do not speak in that way," she pleaded. "He wishes to make what little return he can, and offers to watch with you night and day."

He turned upon her almost fiercely, and said, "Are you too in league with my evil destiny, in that you continually persecute me with that man? Miss Walton, I half doubt whether you know what love means, or you would not make such a proposition. Let me at least die quietly. With the memory of the past and the knowledge of the present, his presence in my room would be death by torture. Pardon me, but let us end this matter once for all. We have both been unfortunate, you in inspiring a love that you cannot return; I in permitting my heart to go from me, beyond recall, before learning that my passion would be hopeless. I do not see that either of us has been to blame, you certainly not in the slightest degree. But, however vain, my love is an actual fact, and I cannot act as if it were not. As well might a man with a mortal wound smile and say it's but a scratch. I cannot change my mind merely in view of expedience and invest such feelings in another way. The fact of my love is now a past disaster, and I must bear the consequences with such fortitude as I can. But what you ask would drive me mad. If I should live, possibly in the future I might meet you often without the torturing regret I now feel. But to make a smiling member of Charles Hunting's friendly circle would require on my part the baldest hypocrisy; and I can't do it, and won't try. If that man comes into my room, I will crawl out if I can."

He was trembling with excitement, his face flushed and feverish, and his eyes unnaturally bright.

"And you banish me too," said Annie, hurt and alarmed at the same time.

"Yes, yes; forgive me for saying so. Yes; till I'm stronger. See how I've spoken to you. I've no self-control."

She was most reluctant to go, and stood a moment, hesitating. Timidly she ventured to quote the line:

"Earth has no sorrows that Heaven cannot cure."

"That's a comforting fact for those who are going there," he said, coldly.

With a sudden burst of passionate grief she stooped and kissed his hand, then fled to her own room, and cried as if her heart would break. It seemed as if he were lost to her and heaven, and yet he was capable of being so noble and good!

Miss Eulie entered Gregory's room soon after, and was alarmed at his feverish and excited appearance. She decided that Annie's visits must cease for the present. However, she took no apparent notice of his disturbed condition, but immediately gave a remedy to ward off fever, and a strong opiate, which, with the reaction and his weakness, caused him to sink back into something like his old lethargy.

Hunting had spent the morning with Mr. Walton, preparing his mind for the plan of immediate marriage. He found the failing man not averse to the project, as his love ought to secure to Annie every help and solace possible.

After Annie had removed from her face, to the best of her ability, every trace of her emotion, she came down and took her place at her father's side, intending to leave it only when compelled to. Hunting knew of her mission to Gregory, and looked at her inquiringly, but she sadly shook her head. He tried to look hurt, but only succeeded in looking angry. He soon controlled himself, however, though he noted with deep uneasiness Annie's sad face and red eyes. Mr. Walton fortunately was dozing and needed no explanation.

That night he was much worse, and had some very serious symptoms. Annie did not leave his side. But toward morning he rallied and fell into a quiet sleep. Then she took a little rest.

The next day she was told that there was a gentleman in the parlor who wished to see her. The stranger proved to be one of Gregory's partners, Mr. Seymour, who courteously said, "I should have been here before, but the senior partner, Mr. Burnett, is unable to attend to business at present, and I came away the first moment I could leave. I felt sure also that everything would be done that could be. I hope the injury is not so serious as was first supposed."

"You may rest assured that we have tried to do everything," said Annie, gravely, "but Mr. Gregory is in a very precarious condition. You would like to see him, I suppose."

"If I can with safety to him."

"I think a brief interview may do him good. He needs rallying."

At that moment Hunting, not knowing who was present, entered. Both gentleman started, but Mr. Seymour gave no sign of recognition, nor did Hunting, though he could not at first hide a certain degree of nervous agitation. Annie presented him. Mr. Seymour bowed stiffly, and said, rather curtly, "We have met before," and then gave him no further attention, but continuing to address Annie, said, "I well understand that Mr. Gregory needs rallying. That has been just his need for the last few months, during which time his health has been steadily failing. I was in hopes he would come back--" and then he stopped, quite puzzled for a moment by the sudden change in Annie's manner, which had become freezingly cold toward him, while there was a look of honest indignation upon her face.

"Excuse me, sir," she said, briefly. "I will send you my aunt, who will attend to your wishes;" and she left Mr. Seymour standing in the middle of the room, both confused and annoyed; but he at once surmised that it was on account of his manner toward Hunting, who sat down with a paper at the further side of the room, as if he were alone.

But when, a moment later, Miss Eulie entered with her placid, unruffled face, Mr. Seymour could not be otherwise than perfectly polite, and after a few words, followed her to Gregory's room.

Annie at once came to Hunting and asked, "Why did that man act so?"

"Why, don't you see?" answered he, hastily. "Mr. Seymour is Mr. Gregory's partner. They all have the same reason for feeling hostile toward me, though perhaps Gregory has special reasons," he added, with a searching look.

Annie blushed deeply at this allusion, but said with emphasis, "No man shall treat you in that way in my presence and still receive courtesy from me."

But his jealous spirit had noticed her quick blush more than her generous resentment of the insult she supposed offered him. Therefore he said, "Mr. Gregory would treat me worse if he got a chance."

"But his case is different from any one's else," she said, with another quick flush.

"Evidently so in your estimation."

Then for the first time she noted his jealousy, and it hurt her sorely. She took a step nearer and looked very gravely into his face for a moment without speaking, and then said, with that calmness which is more effective than passion, "Charles, take care. I'm one that will be trusted. Though it seems a light matter to you that he has saved my life, at perhaps the cost of his own, it does not to me."

The cool and usually cautious man had for once lost his poise, and he said, with sudden irritation, "I hear that and nothing else. What else could he have done? If you had stayed at your father's side you would have been safe. He took you out to walk, and any man would have risked his life to bring you back safely."

He now saw in Annie a spirit he could never control as he managed people in Wall Street, for, with a sudden flash in her eyes, she said, hotly, "I do not reason thus coldly about those to whom I owe so much," and abruptly left him.

In bitterness of fear and self-reproach he at once realized his blunder. He followed her, but she was with her father, and he could not speak there. He looked imploringly at her, but could not catch her eye, for she was deeply incensed. Had she not heard him she would not have believed that he could be so ungenerous.

He wrote on a scrap of paper, "Annie, forgive me. I humbly ask your pardon. I'm not myself to-day, and that man's conduct, which you so nobly resented in my behalf, vexed me to that degree that I acted like a fool. I am not worthy of you, but you will perceive that my folly arises from my excess of love for you. I'm going for a walk. Please greet me with pardon in your face on my return."

Impulsive, loving, warm-hearted Annie could not resist such an appeal. She at once relented, and began to make a thousand better excuses for her lover than he could for himself. But she had taught him a lesson, and proved that she was not a weak, willowy creature that would cling to him no matter what he was or did. He saw that he must seem to be worthy of her.

Gregory greeted his partner with a momentary glow of gratitude that he had come so far to see him, and began talking about his business.

"Not a word of that, old fellow," said Mr. Seymour. "Your business is to get well. It seems to me that you have everything here for comfort --good medical attendance, eh?"

"Yes; if anything, too much is done for me."

"I don't understand just how it happened."

Gregory told him briefly.

"By Jove! this Miss Walton ought to be very grateful to you."

"She is too grateful."

"I don't know about that. I met that infernal Hunting downstairs. Of course I couldn't treat him with politeness, and do you know the little lady spunked up about it to that degree that she almost turned her back upon me and left the room."

"Of course," said Gregory, coolly, shielding his secret by a desperate effort; "they are engaged."

"Oh, I understand now. Well, I rather like her spirit. Does she know how accomplished her lover is in Wall Street?"

"No. Hunting is a distant relative of the family. They believe him to be a gentleman, and would not listen to a word against him."

"But they ought to know. He lied like a scoundrel to us, and in your trying all summer to make up the losses, he has nearly been the death of you. I wouldn't let my daughter marry him though he had enough money to break the Street: and it is a pity that a fine girl, as this Miss Walton seems, should throw herself away on him."

"Well, Seymour, that's not our affair," said Gregory, pale and faint from his effort at self-control. "They would listen to nothing."

"Well, good-by, old fellow. I see it won't do to talk with you any more. Get well as soon as you can, for we want you woefully in town. Get well, and carry off this Miss Walton yourself. It would be a neat way of turning the tables on Hunting."

"Don't set your heart on seeing me at the office again," said Gregory, feelingly. "I have a presentiment that I shan't pull through this, and I don't much care. Give my kindest regards to Mr. Burnett, and tell him I shall think of him to the last as among my best friends."

Seymour made a few hearty remonstrances against such a state of mind, and took his departure with many misgivings. Gregory relapsed into his old dreary apathy. Life had so many certain ills that upon the whole he felt he would rather die. But he was too stunned and weak to think much, save when Annie came to him. Her presence was always life, but now it was a sharp revival of the consciousness of his loss. Left to himself, his mind sank down into a sort of painless lethargy, from which he did not wish to be aroused.

Mr. Walton passed a quieter night, but was clearly failing fast. He sent frequent messages of love and sympathy to Gregory, and had an abiding faith that all would be well with him in the next life, if not in this. Annie had not the heart to undeceive him. When he thought it a little strange that Hunting was not with Gregory, Annie explained by saying that the doctor insisted on perfect quiet of mind, and the presence of Hunting might unpleasantly revive old memories, and so unduly excite him.

After the physician saw his patients the following morning, he looked grave and dissatisfied. Annie followed him to the door, and said, "Doctor, I don't like the expression of your face."

"Well, Miss Annie," said the doctor, discontentedly, "I've a difficult task on my hands, in trying to cure two patients that make no effort to live. Your father seems homesick for heaven, and mere drugs can't rouse Mr. Gregory out of his morbid, gloomy apathy. I could get him ashore if he would strike out for himself, but he just floats down stream like driftwood. But really I'm doing all that can be done, I think."

"I believe you are," she said, sadly. "Good-by."

"O merciful God!" she exclaimed when alone. "What shall I do--what shall I do to save him? Father's going to heaven and mother. Where is *he* going?"

CHAPTER XXX
KEPT FROM THE EVIL

With the light of the following day Annie gave up all hope of her father's recovery. He was sinking fast, and conscious himself that death was near. But his end was like the coming into harbor of a stately ship after a long, successful voyage. He looked death in the face with that calmness and dignity, that serene certainty that it was a change for the better, which Christian faith alone can inspire. His only solicitude was for those he was leaving, and yet he had no deep anxiety, for his strong faith committed them trustingly to God.

Annie tried to feel resigned, since it was God's will. But the tie that bound her to him was so tender, so interwoven with every fibre of her heart, that she shrunk with inexpressible pain from its sundering. She knew that she was not losing her father, that the worst before them was but a brief separation, but how could she, who had lived so many happy years at his side, endure even this? It seemed as if she could not let him go, and in the strong, passionate yearning of her heart, she was almost ready to leave youth, friends, lover, and all, to go with him.

She was one who lived in her affections rather than her surroundings. The latter would matter little to her could she keep her heart- treasures. It would have touched the coldest to see how she clung to him toward the last. All else was forgotten, even Gregory, who might be dying also. The instinct of nature was strong, and her father was first.

Moreover, the relation between this parent and child was peculiarly close, for they were not only in perfect sympathy in views, character, and faith, but Annie had stepped to the side of the widowed man years before and sought successfully to fill the place of one who had reached home before him. Though so young, she had been his companion and daily friend, interesting herself in that which interested him, and thus he had been saved from that terrible loneliness which often breaks the heart even in the midst of a household. It was therefore with a love beyond words that his eyes rested most of the time on her and followed her every movement.

She also had a vague and peculiar dread in looking forward to her bereavement. An anticipating sense of isolation and loneliness chilled her heart.

Though she would not openly admit it to herself, Hunting had disappointed her since his return. She did not get from him the support and Christian sympathy she expected. She tried to excuse him, and charged herself with being too exacting, and yet the sense of something wanting pained her. She had hoped that in these dark days he would be serene and strong, and yet abounding in the tenderest sympathy. She had expected words of faith and consolation that would have sustained her spirit, fainting under a double and peculiar sorrow. She had felt sure that before this his just gratitude, like a torrent, would have overwhelmed and destroyed Gregory's enmity. But all had turned out so differently! Instead of being a help, he had almost added to her burden by his hostile feeling toward her preserver, which he had not been able wholly to disguise. Such a feeling on his part seemed both unnatural and wrong. He professed himself ready to do anything she wished for Gregory, but it was in a half-hearted way, to oblige her, and not for the sake of the injured man. When she went to him for Christian consolation, his words, though well-chosen, lacked heartiness and the satisfying power of truth.

Why this was so can be well understood. Hunting could not give what he did not possess. Of necessity there would be a hollow ring when he spoke of that which he did not understand or feel. During his brief visits, and in his carefully written letters, he could appear all she wished. He could honestly show his sincere love for her, and there was no special opportunity to show anything else. In her vivid, loving imagination she supplied all else, and she believed that when they were more together, or in affliction, he would reveal more distinctly his deeper and religious nature, for such a nature he professed to have; and his letters, which could be written deliberately, abounded in Christian sentiment. Self-deceived, he meant to be honestly religious as soon as he could afford to give up his questionable speculations.

But when a man least expects it the test and strain will come, that clearly manifest the character of his moral stamina. It had now come to Hunting, and though he strove with all the force and adroitness of a resolute will and though he was a practiced dissembler, he was not equal to the searching demands of those trying days, and steadily lost ground. The only thing that kept him up was his sincere love for Annie. That was so apparent and honest that, loving him herself, she was able to forgive the rest. But it formed no small part of her sorrow at that dark time, that she must lower her lofty ideal of her lover. Hunting and Gregory seemed nearer together morally than she could have believed possible. Thus she already had the dread that she would not be able to "look up" to Hunting as she had expected, and that it would be her mission to deepen and develop his character instead of "leaning" upon it.

It seemed strange to her as she thought of it, during her long hours of watching, that after all she would have to do for Hunting something like what poor Gregory had asked her to do for him. She prayerfully purposed to do it, for the idea of being disloyal to her engagement never entered her mind.

"Unless men have a Christian home, in which their religious life can be daily strengthened and fostered, they cannot be what they ought," she said to herself. "In continual contact with the world, with nothing to counteract, it's not strange that they act and feel as they do."

Thus she was more disposed to feel sorry for both Hunting and Gregory than to blame them. And yet she looked upon the two men very differently. She regarded Hunting as a true Christian who simply needed warming and quickening into positive life, while she thought of Gregory with only fear and trembling. Her hope for the latter was in the prayers stored up in his behalf.

But now upon this day that would ever be so painfully memorable she had thoughts only for her father, and nothing could tempt her from his side.

Hunting also saw that the crisis was approaching, and made but a formal semblance of a breakfast. He then entered the sick-room, and was thinking how best to broach the subject of an immediate marriage, when a thumping of crutches was heard in the hall.

Miss Eulie entered and said that Daddy Tuggar had managed to hobble over, and had set his heart upon seeing his old friend.

"Certainly," said Mr. Walton; "he shall come in at once."

"Caution him to stay but a few minutes," warned Annie.

Miss Eulie helped the old man in, and he sat down by Mr. Walton's side, with a world of trouble on his quaint, wrinkled face.

But he said abruptly, as if he expected an affirmative answer, "Yer gettin' better this mornin'--yer on the mend?"

"Yes, my kind old neighbor," said Mr. Walton, feebly. "I shall soon be well. It was kind of you, in your crippled state, to come over to see me."

"Well, now," said Mr. Tuggar, greatly relieved, "there *is* use of prayin'. I ain't much of a hand at it, and didn't know how the Lord would take it from me; but when I heard you was sick, I began to feel like prayin', and when I heard you was gettin' wuss, I couldn't help prayin'. When I heard how that city chap as saved the house--(what an old fool I was to cuss him when he first came! The Lord knew what He was doin' when He brought him here)--when I heard how he kept the ladder from falling on Miss Annie, I prayed right out loud. My wife, she thought I was gettin' crazy. But I didn't care what anybody thought. I've been prayin' all night, and it seemed as if the Lord must hear me, and I kinder felt it in my bones that He had. So I expected to hear you say you was goin' to get well; and Mr. Gregory, he's better too--ain't he?"

There was no immediate answer. Neither Miss Eulie nor Annie seemed to know how to reply to the old man at first. But Mr. Walton reached slowly out and took his neighbor's hand, saying, "Your prayers will be answered, my friend. Honest prayer to God always is. I shall be well soon, never to be old, feeble, and sick any more. I'm going where there's 'no more pain.' Perhaps I've seen my last night, for there is 'no night there.'"

"But the Lord knows I didn't mean nothin' of that kind. We need you here, and He orter know it. What's the use of prayin' if you get just the opposite of what you pray for?"

"Suppose the opposite is best? I'm an old man--a shock of corn fully ripe. I'm ready to be gathered."

"Are yer goin' to die?" asked the old man, in an awed whisper.

"No, Mr. Tuggar; I've been growing old and feeble, I've been dying for a long time. Now I'm going to live--to be strong and well, forever and ever. So don't grieve, but rather rejoice with me."

The old man sat musing a moment, and then said softly to himself, "This is what the Scripter means when it tells about the 'death of the righteous.'"

"Yes," continued Mr. Walton, though more feebly; "and the Scripture is true. The dear Lord doesn't desert His people. He who has been my friend and helper so many years now tells me that my sins, which are many, are all forgiven. It seems that I have also heard Him say, 'To- day thou shalt be with me in Paradise.'"

Tears gathered in Daddy Tuggar's eyes, and he said, brokenly, "The Lord knows--I've allers been a sort--of well-meanin' man--but I couldn't talk that way--if I was where you be."

"Mr. Tuggar," said Mr. Walton, "I'm too weak to say much more, but I want to ask you one question. You have read the Bible. Whom did the Lord Jesus come to save?"

"Sinners," was the prompt response.

"Are you one?"

"What else be I?"

"Then, old neighbor, you are safe, if you will just receive Him as your Saviour. If you were sure you were good enough and didn't need any Saviour, I should despair of you. But according to the Bible you are just such as He came after. If you feel that you are a sinner, all you have to do is to trust Him and do the best you can."

"Is that all you did?"

"All. I couldn't do anything more. And now, good-by. Remember my last words--Whom did Jesus come to save?"

"Why, He come to save me," burst out the old man, rising up. "What a cussed old fool I was, not to see it afore! I was allers thinkin' He came after the good folks, and I felt that no matter how I tried I could not be good enough. Good-by, John Walton. If they are goin' to let sinners into heaven who are willin' to come any way the Lord will let 'em come, I'll be yer neighbor again 'fore long;" and with his withered, bronzed visage working with an emotion that he did not seek to control, he wrung the dying man's hand, and hobbled out.

But he pleaded with Miss Eulie to let him stay. "I want to see it out," he said, "for if grim Death ain't goin' to get one square knock- down now, then he never had it, I want to see the victory. 'Pears to me that when the gates open the glory will shine out upon us all."

So she installed him in Mr. Walton's arm-chair by the parlor fire, and made him thoroughly at home.

"I'm a waitin' by the side of the river," he said. "I wish I could go over with him. 'Pears I'd feel sure they wouldn't turn me back then."

"Jesus will go over the river with you," she said, gently, "and then they can't turn you back."

"I hope so, I hope so," said this old, child-like man, "for I'm an awful sinner."

After this interview, which greatly fatigued him, Mr. Walton dozed for an hour, and then brightened up so decidedly that Annie had faint hopes that he was better.

The children were brought to him, and he kissed and fondled them very tenderly. Then, in a way that would make a deep impression on their childish natures, he told them how he was going to see their father and mother, and would tell what good children they had been, and how they always meant to be good, and how all would be waiting for them in heaven.

Thus the little ones received no grim and terrible impressions at that death-bed, but rather memories and hopes that in all their future would hold them back, like angel hands, from evil.

Hunting now believed that the time for him to act had come. He had told Jeff to have the horse and buggy ready so that he might send for the old pastor at once.

He came to Annie's side, and taking her hand and her father's, thus seeming a link between them, said very gently, very tenderly, "Annie, your father has told me that it would be a great consolation to him to leave me in charge of you all as his son, legally and in the eyes of the world, as I feel I am in reality. I could then do everything for you, relieve you of every care, and protect with unquestionable right all the interests of the household. Again, the marriage tie, like that of our betrothal, consummated here at his side, would ever seem to us peculiarly tender and sacred. It will almost literally be a marriage made in heaven. I hope you will feel that you can grant this, your father's last wish."

Annie felt a sudden and strong repugnance to the plan. In that hour of agonized parting she did not wish to think of marriage, even to one she loved. Her thoughts immediately recurred to Gregory, and she felt that such an act might, in his weak state, cause disastrous results. And yet if it were her father's wish--his last wish-- how could she refuse him--how could she refuse him anything? The marriage day would eventually come. If by making this the day she could once more show her filial love and add to his dying peace, did she not owe him her first duty? The dying are omnipotent with us. Who can refuse their last requests?

She looked inquiringly, but with tear-blinded eyes, at her father.

"Yes, Annie," he said, answering her look, "it would be a great consolation to me, because I can see how it will be of much advantage to you--more than you can now understand. It will enable Charles to step in at once as head of the house- hold, and so you will be relieved of many perplexities and details of business which would be very trying to you, as you will feel. I want to spare you and sister all this, and you have no idea how much it will save your feelings, and add to your comfort, to have one like Charles act for you with such power as he would have as your husband. After seeing you all thus provided for, it seems to me that I could depart in perfect peace."

"Dear father," said Annie, tenderly, "how can I deny you anything! This seems to me no time for marriage, but, since you wish it, your will shall be mine. It must be right or you would not ask it; and yet--" She did not finish the sentence, but buried her face in her hands, weeping.

"That's my noble Annie," Hunting exclaimed, with a glad exultation in his voice that he could not disguise; and, hastening out, he told Jeff to bring the minis- ter as speedily as possible.

Miss Eulie was called, and acquiesced in her brother's opinion, and hovered around Annie in a tender flutter of maternal love.

Hunting now felt that he was master of destiny, and in his heart bade defiance to Gregory and all his own fears. His elation and self- applause were great, for had he not snatched the prize out of the hand of death itself, and made events that would have awed and disheartened other men combine for his good? He had schemed, planned, and overreached them all, though, in this case, for their interests as well as his own, he believed. While he would naturally wish the marriage to take place as soon as possible, his chief reason was to forestall any revelations which might come through Gregory; and this motive made his whole course, though apparently dictated by the purest feeling, a crafty trick. Yet such was the complex nature of the man that he honestly meant to fulfil all Mr. Walton's expectations, and become Annie's loving shield from every care and trial, and a faithful guardian of the household. Nay, more, as soon as he was securely intrenched, with all his coveted possessions, he purposed that Annie should help him to be a true, good man--a Christian in reality.

Well may the purest and strongest pray to be kept from the evil of the world. It lurks where least suspected, and can plot its wrongs in the chamber of death, and on the threshold of heaven. Annie and her father might at least suppose themselves safe now. Were they so, with God's minister on his way to join truth with untruth--a pure-hearted maiden to a man from whom she would shrink the moment she came to know him? Not on the human side. They were safe only as God kept them. If Annie Walton had found herself married to a swindler, hers would have been a life-long martyrdom. But unconsciously she drew momentarily nearer the edge of the precipice. Time was passing, and their venerable pastor would soon be present. Annie had welcomed him every day previously, as he came to take sweet counsel with her father rather than prepare him for death, but now she had a strange, secret dread of his coming.

Her father suddenly put his hand to his heart.

"Have you pain there?" asked Annie.

"It's gone," he replied, after a moment. "They will soon be all past, Annie dear. How does Mr. Gregory seem now?" he asked of Miss Eulie.

"Greatly depressed, I'm sorry to say," she answered. "He knows that you are no better, and it seems to distress him very much."

"God bless him for saving my darling's life!" he said, fervently; "and He will bless him. I have a feeling that he will see brighter and better days. I can send him almost a father's love and blessing, for he now seems like a son to me. Say to him that I shall tell his father of his noble deeds. Be a sister to him, Annie. Carry on the good work you have so wisely begun. May the friendship of the parents descend to the children. And you, Charles, my son, will surely feel toward him as a brother, whatever may have been the differences of the past."

Innocent but deeply embarrassing words to both Hunting and Annie.

Again Mr. Walton put his hand to his heart.

Hunting left the room, for it was surely time for Jeff to return. With a gleam of exultant joy he saw him driving toward the house with the white-haired minister at his side. He returned softly to the sick- room.

Mr. Walton had just taken Annie's hands, and after a look of unutterable fondness, said, "Before I give you to another--while you are still my own little girl--let me thank you for having been all and more than a father could ask. How good God was to give me such a comfort in your mother's place!"

"Dear father!" was all that Annie could say.

Even then the minister was entering the house.

"I bless thee, my child," the father continued; then turning his eyes heavenward he reverently closed them in prayer, saying, "and God bless thee also, and keep thee from every evil."

God answered him.

His grasp on Annie's hand relaxed; without even a sigh he passed away.

Annie started up with a look of alarm, and saw the same expression on the faces of her aunt and Hunting. They spoke to him; he did not answer. Hunting felt his pulse. Its throb had ceased forever. The chill of a great dread turned his own face like that of the dead.

Miss Eulie put her hand on her brother's heart. It was at rest. Annie stood motionless with dilating eyes watching them. But when her aunt came toward her with streaming eyes she realized the truth and fell fainting to the floor.

Just then the old minister crossed the threshold, but Hunting said to him, almost savagely, "You are too late."

CHAPTER XXXI
"LIVE! LIVE!"--ANNIE'S APPEAL

Annie's swoon was so prolonged that both her aunt and Hunting were alarmed. It was the reaction from the deep and peculiar excitement of the last few days. Every power of mind and body had been under the severest strain, and nature now gave way.

The doctor, when he came to make his morning call, was most welcome. He said there was nothing alarming about Miss Walton's symptoms, but added very decisively that she would need rest and quiet of mind for a long time in order to regain her former tone and health.

When Annie revived he gave something that would tend to quiet her nervous system and produce sleep.

"I now understand Mr. Walton's case," he said to Miss Eulie. "I could not see why his severe cold, which he had apparently cured, should result as it did. But now it's plain that it was complicated with heart difficulties."

His visit to Gregory was not at all satisfactory, for his patient's depression was so great that he was sinking under it. Mr. Walton's death, leaving Annie defenceless, as it were, in the hands of a man like Hunting, seemed another of the dark and cruel mysteries which to him made up human life. The death that had given Daddy Tuggar such an impulse toward faith and hope only led him to say with intense bitterness, "God has forgotten His world, and the devil rules it."

"Mr. Gregory," said the physician, gravely, "do you know that you are about the same as taking your own life? All the doctors in the world cannot help you unless you try to live. Drugs cannot remove your apathy and morbid depression."

"Very well, doctor," he replied; "do not trouble yourself to come any more. I absolve you from all blame."

"But I cannot absolve myself. Besides, it's not manly to give up in this style."

"I make no pretence of being manly or anything else. I am just what you see. Can a broken reed stand up like a sturdy oak? Can such a thing as I reverse fate?

Thank you, doctor, for all you have done, but waste no more time upon me. I knew, weeks ago, that the end was near, and I would like to die in the old place."

The doctor looked at him a moment in deep perplexity, and then silently left the room.

"Internal injuries that I can't get at," he muttered, as he drove away.

Miss Eulie came to Gregory's side, and laying her hand gently on his brow said, "You are mistaken, my young friend. You are going to live."

"Why do you think so?" he asked.

"The dying often have almost prophetic vision;" and she told him all that Mr. Walton had said, though nothing of the contemplated marriage. She dwelt with special emphasis on the facts that he had told Annie to be a sister to Gregory and had gone to heaven with the assurance to his old friend that his son would join him there.

Gregory was strongly moved, and turning his face upon the pillow, gave way to a passion of tears; but they were despairing, bitter, regretful tears. He soon seemed ashamed of them, and when he again turned his face toward Miss Eulie, it had a hard, stony look.

Almost with sternness he said, "If the dying have supernatural insight, why could not Mr. Walton see what kind of a man Hunting is? Please leave me now. I know how kind and well-meant your words are, but they are mockery to me;" and he turned his face to the wall.

Miss Eulie sighed very deeply, but felt that his case was beyond her skill.

Daddy Tuggar was at first grievously disappointed. He had wrought himself up into the hope of a celestial scene, and the abrupt and quiet termination of Mr. Walton's life seemed inadequate to the occasion. But Miss Eulie comforted him by saying that "the Christian walked by faith, and not by sight--that God knew what was best, better than we, His little children.

"Death had not even the power to cause him a moment's pain," she said. "God gave him a sweet surprise, by letting him through the gates before he was aware."

Thus she led the strange old man to think it was for the best after all. The Rev. Mr. Ames, who had come on such a different mission, also tried to make clearer what Mr. Walton had said to him. But Daddy Tuggar would not permit his mind to wander a moment from the simple truth, which he kept saying over and over to himself, "I'm an awful sinner, and the good Lord come after just such."

Another thing that greatly perplexed the old man was that Mr. Walton had not been permitted to live long enough to see his daughter married. As an old neighbor, and because of his strong attachment to Annie, he had been invited to be present.

"'Pears to me that the Lord might have spared him a few minutes longer," he said.

"It *appears* to you so," replied Mr. Ames, "but the Lord **knows** why he did not."

"Well, parson," said Daddy Tuggar, "I thank you very kindly for what you have said, but John Walton has done the business for me. I'm just goin' to trust--I'm just goin' to let myself go limber and fall right down on the Lord Jesus' word. I don't believe it will break with me. Anyhow, it's all I can do, and John Walton told me to do it and I allers found he was about right." And thus late in the twilight of life the old man took his pilgrim's staff and started homeward.

As soon as Hunting recovered from his bitter disappointment and almost superstitious alarm at the sudden thwarting of his purpose, his wily and scheming mind fell to work on a new combination. If he still could induce Annie to be married almost immediately, as he greatly hoped, all would be well. If not, then he would assume that they were the same as married, and at once take his place so far as possible at the head of the household, in accordance with Mr. Walton's wish. On one hand, by tender care and thoughtfulness for them all, he would place Annie under the deepest obligation; on the other, he would gain, to the extent he could, control of her affairs and property. In the latter purpose Mr. Walton had greatly aided by naming him one of the executors of his will; and only Miss Eulie, the sister-in-law, was united with him as executrix. Thus he would substantially have his own way. Indeed, Mr. Walton, in his perfect trust, meant that he should.

Having seen Annie quietly sleeping, he started for New York to make arrangements for the funeral, and look after some personal matters that had already been neglected too long.

His feelings on the journey were not enviable. He had enough faith to fear God, but not to trust and obey. The thought recurred with disheartening frequency, "If God is against this, He will thwart me every time."

The day had closed in thick darkness and a storm before Annie awoke from the deep sleep which the sedative had prolonged. Though weak and languid, she insisted on getting up. Her aunt almost forced her to take a little supper, and then she went instinctively and naturally to that room which had always been a place of refuge, but which now was the chamber of death.

She turned up the light that she might look at the dear, *dear* face. How calm and noble it was in its deep repose! It did not suggest death--only peaceful sleep.

With a passionate burst of sorrow she moaned, "O father, let me sleep beside you, and be at rest!"

Then she took his cold hand, and sat down mechanically to watch, as in the days and nights just passed. But as she became composed and thought grew busy, the deep peace of the sleeper seemed imparted to her. In vivid imagination she followed him to the home and greetings that he had so joyously anticipated. She saw him meet her mother and sister, and other loved ones who had gone before. She saw him at his Saviour's feet, blessed and crowned. She heard the wild storm raging without in the darkness, and then thought of his words "There is no night there."

"Dear father," she murmured, "I would not call you back if I could. God give me patience to come to you in His own appointed way."

Then she dwelt upon the strange events of the day. How near she had come to being a wife! Why had she not become one? That the marriage should have been so suddenly and unexpectedly prevented on the very eve of consummation, caused some curious thoughts to flit through her mind.

"It is enough to know that it was God's will," she said; "and my future is still in His hands. Poor Charles! it will be a disappointment to him; and yet what difference will a few weeks or months make?"

Then her father's words, "Be a sister to Gregory," recurred to her, and she reproached herself that she had so long forgotten him. "Father is safe home," she said, "and I am leaving him to wander further and further away. Father told me to be a sister to him, and I will. When he gets well and strong, if he ever does, he will feel very differently; and if he is to die (which God forbid), what more sacred duty can I have than to plead with him and for him to the last?"

Pressing a kiss on her father's silent lips, she went to fulfil one of their last requests. She first asked her aunt if it would be prudent to visit Gregory. "I hardly know, Annie, what to say," said Miss Eulie, in deep perplexity; and she told her what had occurred in relation to Gregory, the doctor, and herself, omitting all reference to Hunting. "If he is not roused out of his gloom and apathy, I fear he will die," concluded her aunt; "and if you can't rouse him, I don't know who can."

Annie gave her a quick, questioning glance.

"Yes, Annie, I understand," she said, quietly. "He received his worst injury before the ladder fell."

"O aunty, what shall I do?"

"Indeed, my dear child, I can hardly tell you. You are placed in a difficult and delicate position. Perhaps your father's words were wisest, 'Be a sister to him.' At any rate, you have more power with him than any one else, and you owe it to him to do all you can to save him."

"I am ready to do anything, aunty, for it seems as if I could never be happy if he should die an unbeliever."

Annie stole noiselessly to Gregory's side, and motioned to the young man who was in charge to withdraw to the next room. Gregory was still asleep. She sat down by him and was greatly shocked to see how emaciated and pale he was. It seemed as if he had suffered from an illness of weeks rather than days.

"He will die," she murmured, with all her old terror at the thought returning. "He will die, and for me. Though innocent, I shall always feel that his blood is upon me;" and she buried her face in her hands, and her whole frame shook with a passion of grief.

Her emotion awoke him, and he recognized with something like awe the bowed head at his side.

Her grief for her father, as he supposed it to be, seemed such a sacred thing! And yet he could not bear to see her intense sorrow. His heart ached to comfort her, but what words of consolation could such as he offer? Still, had she not come to him as if for comfort? This thought touched him deeply, and he almost cursed his unbelieving soul that made him dumb at such a time. What could he say but miserable commonplaces in regard to a bereavement like hers?

He did not say anything, but merely reached out his hand and gently stroked her bowed head.

Then she knew he was awake, and she took his hand and bowed her head upon it.

"Miss Walton," he said, in a husky voice, "it cuts me to the heart to see you grieve so. But, alas! I do not know how to comfort you, and I can't say trite words which mean nothing. After losing such a father as yours, what can any one say?"

She raised her head and said, impetuously, "It's not for father I am grieving. He is in heaven--he is not lost to me. It's for you--you. You are breaking my heart."

"Miss Walton," he began, in much surprise, "I don't understand--"

"Why don't you understand?" she interrupted. "What do you think I am made of? Do you think that you can lie here and die for me and I go serenely on? Do you not see that you would blight the life you have saved?"

His apathy was gone now. But he was bewildered, so sudden and overpowering was her emotion. He only found words to say, "Miss Walton, God knows I am yours, body and soul. What can I do?"

"Live! live!" she continued, with the same passionate earnestness. "I impose no conditions, I ask nothing else. Only get well and strong again. If you will do this, I have such confidence in your better nature, and the many prayers laid up for you, as to feel sure that all will come out right. But if you will just lie here and die, you will imbitter my life. What did the doctor tell you this morning? And yet I shall feel that I am partly the cause. O, Mr. Gregory, you may think me foolish, but that strange little omen of the chestnut burr is in my mind so often! I never was superstitious before, but it haunts me. Don't you remember how you stained my hand with your blood? I can't get it out of my mind, and it has for me now a strange significance. If I had to remember through coming years that you died for me all hopeless and unbelieving, do you think so poorly of me as to imagine I could be happy? Why can't you be generous enough to brighten the life you have saved? Among my father's last words he said I must be a sister to you. How can I if you die? You would make this dear old place, that we both love, full of terrible memories."

He was deeply moved, and after a moment said, "I did not know that you felt in this way. I thought the best thing that I could do was to get out of the world and out of the way. I thought I knew you, but I do not half understand your large, generous heart. For your sake I will try and get well, nor will I impose any conditions whatever. But pardon me: I am going to ask one thing, which you can grant or not as you choose. Please do not wrong me by thinking that I have any personal end in view. I have given all that up as truly as if I were dead. I ask that you do not speedily marry Charles Hunting--not till you are sure you know him."

"O dear!" exclaimed Annie, in real distress, "this dreadful quarrel! What trouble it makes all around!"

"If your father," continued Gregory, with grave earnestness, "told you to be a sister to me, then I have some right to act as a brother toward you. But as an honest man, with all my faults, and with your interests nearest my heart, I entreat you to heed my request. Nay, more: I am going to seem ungenerous, and refer for the first and last time to the obligation you are under to me. By all the influence I gained by that act, I beg of you to hesitate before you marry Charles Hunting. Believe me, I would not lay a straw in the way of your marrying a good man."

"Your words pain me more than I can tell you," said Annie, sadly. "I do not understand them. Once they would have angered me. But, however mistaken you are, I cannot do injustice to your motive.

"I do not see how your request can injure Charles," she continued, musingly. "I have no wish to marry now for a long time--not till these sad scenes have faded somewhat from memory. If you will only promise to live I will not marry him till you get strong and well--till you can look upon this matter as a man--as a brother ought. But your hostility must not be unreasonable or implacable. I *know* you do Mr. Hunting great injustice. And yet such is my solicitude for you that I will do what seems to me almost disloyal. But I know that I owe a great deal to you as well as Charles."

"What I ask is for your sake, not mine. I only used the obligation as a motive."

"Well," said Annie, "I yield; and surely a sister could do no more than I have done to-night."

"And I have simply done my duty," he answered, quietly. "And yet I thank you truly. You also may see the time when you will thank me more than when I interposed my worthless person between you and danger."

"Please never call yourself 'worthless' to me again. We never did agree, and I fear we shall be gray before we do. But mark this: I am never going to give you up, whatever happens. I shall obey dear father's last words from both duty and inclination. But let us end this painful conversation. What have you eaten to-day?"

"I'm sure I don't know," he said.

"Will you eat something if I bring it?"

"I will do anything you ask."

"Now you give me hope," and she vanished, sending the regular watcher back to his post.

Gregory found it no difficult task to eat the dainty little supper she brought. She had broken the malign spell he was under. As we have seen, his was a physical nature peculiarly subject to mental conditions.

Soon after she said, in a low tone meant only for his ear, "Good-night, my poor suffering brother. We all three shall understand each other better in God's good time."

"I hope so," he said, with a different meaning. "You have made me feel that I am not alone and uncared for in the world, though I cannot call you sister yet. Good-night."

Annie went back to her father's side, and remained till her aunt almost forced her away.

It is not necessary to dwell on the events of the next few days. Such is our earthly lot, nearly all can depict them by recalling their own sad experience: the hushed and solemn household, even the children speaking low and treading softly, as if they might awake one whom only "the last trump" could arouse.

John Walton's funeral was no formal pageant, but an occasion of sincere and general mourning. Even those whose lives and characters were the opposite of his had the profoundest respect for him, and the entire community united in honoring his memory.

Perhaps the most painful time of all to the stricken family was the evening after their slow, dreary ride to the village cemetery. Then, as not before, they realized their loss.

Annie felt that her best solace would be in trying to cheer others. She had seen Gregory but seldom and briefly since the interview last described, but had been greatly comforted by his decided change for the better. He had kept his word. Indeed, it was only the leaden hand of despondency that kept him down, and he rallied from the moment it was lifted. This evening he was dressed and sitting by the fire. As she entered, in her deep mourning, his look was so wistful and kind, so eloquent with sympathy, that instead of cheering him, as she had intended, she sat down on a low ottoman, and burying her face in her hands, cried as if her heart would break.

"Oh that I knew how to comfort you!" said Gregory, in the deepest distress. "I cannot bear to see you suffer."

He rose with difficulty and came to her side, saying, "What can I do, Miss Walton? Would that I could prevent you, at any cost to myself, from ever shedding another tear!"

His sympathy was so true and strong that it was a luxury for her to receive it; and she had kept up so long that tears were nature's own relief.

At last he said timidly, hesitatingly, as if venturing on forbidden ground, "I think the Bible says that in heaven all tears will be wiped away. Your father is surely there."

"Would that I were there with him!" she sobbed.

"Not yet, Annie, not yet," he said, gently. "Think how dark this world would be to more than one if you were not in it."

"But will you never seek this dear home of rest?" she asked.

"The way of life is closed to me," he said, sadly.

"O, Mr. Gregory! Who is it that says, 'I am the way?'"

"But He says to me, 'Depart.'"

"And yet I, knowing all--I, a weak, sinful creature like yourself-- say, Come to Him. I am better and kinder than He who died for us all! What strange, sad logic! Good-night, Walter. You will not always so wrong your best Friend."

Gregory's despairing conviction that his day of mercy was past was hardly proof against her words and manner, but he was in thick darkness and saw no way out.

Annie went down to her aunt and Hunting in the parlor. "Why will Mr. Gregory be so hard and unbelieving?" she said, tearfully.

"If you knew him as well as I do you would understand," said Hunting, politicly, and then changed the conversation.

He was consumed by a jealousy which he dared not show. Annie's manner toward him was all that he could ask, and he felt sure of her now. But it was the future he dreaded, for he was satisfied that Gregory had formed an attachment for Annie, whether she knew it or not, and, unless he could secure her by marriage, the man he had wronged might find means of tearing off his mask. With desperate earnestness he resolved to press his suit.

His course since Mr. Walton's death had been such as to win Annie's sincerest gratitude. When action rather than moral support was required, he was strong, and no one could be more delicately thoughtful of her feelings and kinder than he had been.

"Dear Charles," said Annie, when they were alone. "What should I have done without you in all these dreary days! How you have saved me from all painful contact with the world!"

"And so I ever wish to shield you," said Hunting. "Will you not, as your father purposed, give me the right at once?"

"You have the right, Charles. I ask no more than you have done and are doing. But do not urge marriage now. I yielded then for father's sake, not my own. My heart is too sore and crushed to think of it now. After all, what difference can a few months make to you? Be generous. Give me a respite, and I will make you a better wife and a happier home."

"But it looks, Annie, as if you could not trust me," he said, gloomily.

"No, Charles," she said, gravely, "it looks rather as if you distrusted me; and you must learn to trust me implicitly. Out of both love for you and justice to myself, I exercise my woman's right of naming the day. In the meantime I give you my perfect confidence. No words of others--nothing but your own acts can disturb it, and of this I have no fear."

He did not seek to disguise his deep disappointment. While she felt sorry for him, she remained firm, and he saw that it would not be wise to urge her.

Annie would not carelessly give pain to any one, much less to those she loved. And yet her mind was strong and well-balanced. She knew it was no great misfortune to Hunting to wait a few months when her own feelings and the duty she owed another required it. "When Mr. Gregory gets strong and well and back to business," she thought, "he will wonder at himself. I have no right almost to destroy him now in his weakness by doing that which can be done better at another time; and indeed, for my own sake, I should have required delay."

The next day Hunting was reluctantly compelled to go to the city. Somewhat to Annie's surprise, Gregory made no effort to secure her society. In her frank, sisterly regard she was slow in understanding that her presence caused regretful pain to him. But he seemed resolutely bent upon getting well, and was gaining rapidly.

He walked out a little while during the middle of the day, and her eyes followed him wistfully as he moved slowly and feebly along the garden walk. She saw, with quickly starting tears, that he went to the rustic seat by the brook where they had spent that memorable Sunday afternoon, and that he stood in long, deep thought.

When he came back she offered to read to him.

"Not now--not yet," he said, sadly. "I know my own weakness, and would be true to my word."

"Why do you shun me?" she asked.

"May you never understand from experience," he said with a smile that was sadder than tears, and passed on up to his room.

And yet, though he did not know it, his course was the best policy, for it awakened stronger respect and sympathy on her part.

The next morning ushered in the first of the dreamy Indian-summer days, when Nature, as if grieved over the havoc of the frost, would hide the dismantled trees and dead flowers by a purple haze, and seek as do fading beauties to disguise the ravages of time by drawing over her withered face a deceptive veil.

Gregory felt so much better that he thought he could venture to make a parting call on Daddy Tuggar. He found the old man smoking on his porch, and his reception was as warm and demonstrative as his first had been a month ago, though of a different nature. Gregory lighted a cigar and sat down beside him.

"I'm wonderful glad to see you," said Mr. Tuggar. "To think that I should have cussed you when it was the good Lord that brought you here!"

"Do you think so?" asked Gregory.

"Certain I do. Would that house be there? Wouldn't all our hearts be broke for Miss Annie if it wasn't for you?"

Gregory felt that his heart was "broke" for her as it was, but he said, "It was my taking her out to walk that caused her danger. So you wouldn't have lost her if I had not come."

"You didn't knowin'ly git her in danger, and you did knowin'ly git her out, and that's enough for me," said the old man.

"Well, well, Mr. Tuggar, if I had broken my neck it would have been a little thing compared with saving the life of such a woman as Miss Walton. Still, I fear the Lord has not much to do with me."

"And have you been all this time with John Walton and Miss Annie and still feel that way?"

"It's not their fault."

"I believe that. Are you willin' to say you are a great sinner?"

"Of course. What else am I?"

"That's it--that's it," cried the old man, delightedly. "Now you're all right. That's just where I was. When John Walton bid me good-by, he asked me one question that let more light into my thick head than all the readin' and preachin' and prayin' I ever heard. He asked, 'Whom did Jesus Christ come to save?' Answer that."

"The Bible says He came to save sinners," replied Gregory, now deeply interested.

"Well, I should think that meant you and me," said Mr. Tuggar, emphatically. "Anyhow, I know it means me. John Walton told me that all I had to do was to just trust the Saviour--not of good people--but of sinners, and do the best I could; and I have just done it, and I'm all right, Mr. Gregory, I'm all right. I don't know whether I can stop swearin', but I'm a tryin'. I don't know whether I can ever get under my old ugly temper, but I'm a tryin' and a prayin'. But whether I can or not, I'm all right, for the good Lord came to save sinners; and if that don't mean me, what's the use of words?"

"But can you trust Him?" asked Gregory.

"Certain I can. Wasn't John Walton an honest man? Wasn't Jesus Christ honest? Didn't he know what He come for?"

"Admitting that He came to save sinners, how can you be sure He will save all? He might save you and not me."

"Well," said Mr. Tuggar, "I hadn't been home long before that question come up to me, and I thought on it a long time. I smoked wellnigh a hundred pipes on it afore I got it settled, but 'tis settled, and when I settle a thing I don't go botherin' back about it. But like enough 'twon't satisfy you."

"At any rate, I should like to hear your conclusion."

"Well, I argued it out to myself. I says, 'Suppose there's some sinners too bad, or too somethin' or other, for the Lord to save, and suppose you are one of them, ain't ''lected,' as my wife says. If I could be an unbelievin' sinner for eighty years, it seemed to me that if anybody wasn't 'lected I wasn't. I was dreadfully down, I tell yer, for I'd set my heart on bein' John Walton's neighbor again. After I'd smoked a good many pipes, I cussed myself for an old fool. 'There, you've brought your case into court,' I says, 'and you're goin' to give it up afore it's argued.' Then I argued it. I was honest, you may be sure. It wouldn't do me any good to pettifog in this matter. First I says, if there was any doubt about the Lord savin' all sinners who wanted Him to, John Walton orter have spoken of it, and from what I know of the man he would. Then I says, arter all, it's the Lord I've got to deal with. Now what kind of a Lord is He? Then I commenced rememberin' all that Miss Eulie and Miss Annie had read to me about Him, and all I'd heard, and I got my wife to read some, and my hopes grew every minute. I tell you what, Mr. Gregory, it was a queer crowd He often had around Him. I'd kinder felt at home among 'em, 'specially with that swearin' fisherman Peter.

"Well, the upshot of it was, I couldn't find that He ever turned one sinner away. Then why should He me? Then my wife, as she was readin', come across the words, 'Him that cometh to Me I will in no wise cast out.' I had heard them words afore often, but it seemed now as the first time, and I just shouted, 'I've got His word for it,' and my wife thought I was crazy, sure 'nuff, for she didn't know what I was drivin' at. And now, Mr. Gregory, you're just shut up to two things, just two things. Either the Lord Jesus will save every sinner that comes to Him, or he ain't honest, and don't mean what he says, and won't do as he used to. I tell yer I'm settled, better settled than yonder mountain. I just let myself go limber right down upon the promise, and it's all right. I'm going to be John Walton's neighbor again."

Gregory was more affected by the old man's quaint talk than he would have believed possible. It seemed true that he was "shut up" to one or the other of the alternatives presented. He commenced pacing up and down the little porch in deep thought. Mr. Tuggar puffed away at his pipe with such vigor that he was exceedingly beclouded, however clear his mind. At last Gregory said, "I shall think over what you have said, very carefully, for I admit it has a great deal of force to my mind."

"That's right," said Mr. Tuggar; "argue it out, just as I did. Show yourself no favors, and be fair to yourself, and you can't get away from my conclusion. You've got to come to it."

"I should be very glad to come to it," said Gregory, gravely.

"I should think you would. There'll be some good neighbors up there, Mr.

Gregory; these Waltons are all bound to be there. Miss Annie would be kinder good company--eh, Mr. Gregory?"

In spite of himself he flushed deeply under the old man's keen scrutiny.

"There's one thing that's mighty 'plexing to me," said Mr. Tuggar, led to the subject by its subtle connection with Gregory's blush, "and that's why the Lord didn't keep John Walton alive a few minutes longer, so that the marriage could take place."

Gregory gave a great start. "What marriage?" he asked.

"Why, don't you know about it?" said Mr. Tuggar, in much surprise.

"No, nothing at all."

"Then perhaps I ortn't ter speak of it."

"Certainly not, if you don't think it right."

"Well, I've said so much I might as well say it all," said the old man, musingly. "It's no secret, as I knows of;" and he told Gregory how near Annie came to being a wife.

Gregory drew a long breath and looked deathly pale and faint.

"Well, now, I'd no idea that you'd be so struck of a heap," said the old man, in still deeper surprise.

"God's hand was in that," murmured Gregory; "God's hand was in that."

"Do you think so, now? Well, it does seem kinder cur'us, and per'aps it was, for somehow I never took to that Hunting, though he seems all right."

"Good-by, Mr. Tuggar," said Gregory, rising; "you have given me a good deal to think about, and I'm going to think, and act, too, if I can. I am going to New York to-morrow, and one of the first things I do will be to fill your pipe for a long time;" and he pressed the old man's hand most cordially.

"Let yourself go limber when you come to trust, and it will be all right," were Daddy Tuggar's last words, as he balanced himself on his crutches in parting.

Gregory found Annie in the parlor, and he said, "I have good news for you; Daddy Tuggar is a Christian."

Annie sprang joyfully up and said, "I'm going over to see him at once."

When she returned, Gregory was quietly reading in the parlor, showing thus that he had no wish to avoid her.

She came directly to him and said, "Daddy Tuggar says that you propose going home to-morrow."

"Well, really, Miss Walton, I have no home to go to; but I expect to return to the city."

"Now I protest against it."

"I'm glad you do."

"Then you won't go?"

"Yes, I must; but I'm glad you don't wish me to go"

"Why need you go yet? You ought not. You should wait till you are strong."

"That is just why I go--to get *strong*. I never could here, with you looking so kindly at me as you do now. You see I am as frank as I promised to be. So please say no more, for you cannot and you ought not to change my purpose."

"O dear!" cried Annie, "how one's faith is tried! Why need this be so?"

"On the contrary," he said, "what little faith I ever had has been quite revived this afternoon. Daddy Tuggar has been 'talking religion' to me, and, pardon me for saying it, I found his words more convincing than even yours."

"I am not jealous of him," said Annie, gladly.

"I can't help thinking that God does see and care, in that He prevented your marriage."

Annie blushed deeply, and said, coldly, "I am sorry you touched upon that subject," and she left the room.

Gregory went quietly on with his reading, or seemed to do so. Indeed, he made a strong effort, and succeeded, for he was determined to master himself outwardly.

She soon relented and came back. When she saw him apparently so undisturbed, the thought came to her, "He has truly given me up. There is nothing of the lover in that calmness, and he makes no effort to win my favor," but she said, "Mr. Gregory, I fear I hurt your feelings. You certainly did mine. I cannot endure the injustice you persist in doing Mr. Hunting."

"I only repeat your own words, 'We all three shall understand each other in God's good time'; and after what I heard to-day, I have the feeling that He is watching over you."

"Won't you promise not to speak any more on this subject?"

"Yes, for I have done my duty."

She took up his book and read to him, thus giving one more hour of mingled pain and pleasure; though when he thought how long it would be before he heard that sweet voice again, if ever, his pain almost reached the point of anguish. As she turned toward him and saw his look of suffering, she realized somewhat the effort he had made to keep up before her.

She came to him and said, "I was about to ask a favor, but perhaps it's hardly right."

"Ask it, anyway," he said, with a smile.

"I don't urge it, but I expect Mr. Hunting this evening. Won't you come down to supper and meet him?"

"For your sake I will, now that I have gained some self-control. I am not one to quarrel in a lady's parlor under any provocation. For your sake I will treat Mr. Hunting like a gentleman, and make my last evening with you as little of a restraint as possible."

"Thank you--thank you. You now promise to make it one of peculiar happiness."

Annie drove to the depot for Hunting, and told of Gregory's consent to meet him. She said, "Now is your opportunity, Charles. Meet him in such a way as to make enmity impossible."

His manner was not very reassuring, but, in his pleasure at hearing that Gregory was soon to depart, and that in his absence Annie's confidence in him had not been disturbed, he promised to do the best he could. She was nervously excited as the moment of meeting approached, and, somewhat to her surprise, Hunting seemed to share her uneasiness.

Gregory did not come down till the family were all in the supper-room. Annie was struck with his appearance as he entered. Though his left arm was in a sling, there was a graceful and almost courtly dignity in his bearing, a brilliancy in his eyes and a firmness, about his mouth, which proved that he had nerved himself for the ordeal and would maintain himself. Instantly she thought of the time when he had first appeared in that room, a half-wrecked, blase man of the world. Now he looked and acted like a nobleman.

Hunting, on the contrary, had a shuffling and embarrassed manner; but he approached Gregory and held out his hand, saying, "Come, Mr. Gregory, let by-gones be by-gones."

But Gregory only bowed with the perfection of distant courtesy, and said, "Good-evening, Mr. Hunting," and took his seat.

Both Hunting and Annie blushed deeply and resentfully. After they were seated, Annie looked toward Hunting to say "grace" as usual, but he could not before the man who knew him so well, and there was another moment of deep embarrassment, while a sudden satirical light gleamed from Gregory's eyes. Annie saw it, and it angered her.

Then Gregory broke the ice with quiet, well-bred ease. In natural tones he commenced conversation, addressing now one, now another, in such a way that they were forced to answer him in like manner. He asked Hunting about the news and gossip of the city as naturally as if they had met that evening for the first time. He even had pleasant repartee with Johnny and Susie, who had now come to like him very much, and his manner toward Miss Eulie was peculiarly gentle and respectful, for he was deeply grateful to her. Indeed, that good lady could scarcely believe her eyes and ears; but Gregory had always been an enigma to her. At first he spoke to Annie less frequently than to any one else, for he dreaded the cloud upon her brow and her outspoken truthfulness, and he was determined the evening should pass off as he had planned. Though so crippled that his food had to be prepared for him, he only made it a matter of graceful jest, and gave ample proof that a highly bred and cultivated man can be elegant in manners under circumstances the most adverse.

Even Annie thawed and relented under his graceful tact, and felt that perhaps he was doing all she could expect in view of the simple promise to "treat Hunting like a gentleman, for her sake." But it had pained her deeply that he had not met Hunting's advances; and she saw that, though perfectly courteous, he was not committing himself in the slightest degree toward reconciliation.

Moreover, she was excessively annoyed that Hunting acted so poor a part. It is as natural for a woman to take pride in her lover as to breathe, but she could have no pride in Hunting that evening. He seemed annoyed beyond endurance with both himself and Gregory, though he strove to disguise it. He knew that he was appearing to disadvantage, and this increased his embarrassment, and he was most unhappy in his words and manner. Yet he could take exception at nothing, for Gregory, secure in his polished armor, grew more brilliant and entertaining as he saw his adversary losing ground.

All were glad when he supper-hour was over and they could adjourn to the parlor. Here Gregory changed his tactics, and drawing the children aside, told them a marvellous tale as a good-by souvenir, thus causing them to feel deep regret for his departure. He next drew Miss Eulie into an animated discussion upon a subject he knew her to be interested in. From this he made the conversation general, and continued to speak to Hunting as naturally as if there were no differences between them. But all saw that he was growing very weary, and early in the evening he quietly rose and excused himself, saying that he needed rest for his journey on the morrow. There was the same polite, distant bow to Hunting as at first, and in deep disappointment Annie admitted that nothing had been gained by the interview from which she had hoped so much. They were no nearer reconciliation. While Gregory's manner had compelled respect and even admiration, it had annoyed her excessively, for he had made her lover appear to disadvantage, and she was almost vexed with Hunting that he had not been equal to the occasion. She was sorry that she had asked Gregory to come down while Hunting was present, and yet courtesy seemed to require that he should be with them, since he was now sufficiently well. Altogether it was a silent little group that Gregory left in the parlor, as all were busy with their own thoughts.

Hunting determined to remain the following day and see Gregory off and out of the way forever, he hoped.

The next morning Gregory did not come down to breakfast. But at about ten o'clock he started for a short farewell stroll about the old place. Annie joined him in the garden.

"I do not think you were generous last evening," she said. "Mr. Hunting met you half-way."

"Did I not do just what I promised?"

"But I was in hopes you would do more, especially when the way was opened."

"Do you think, Miss Walton, that Mr. Hunting's manner and feelings toward me were sincerely cordial and friendly? Was it the prompting of his heart, or your influence, that led him to put out his hand?"

Annie blushed, in conscious confusion. "I fear I shall never reconcile you," she said, sadly.

"I fear not," he replied. "There must be a great change in us both before you can. Though the reason I give you was a sufficient one for not taking his hand in friendly feeling, it was not the one that influenced me. I would not have taken it under any circumstances."

"Mr. Gregory, you grieve me most deeply," she said, in a tone of real distress. "Won't you, when you come to part, take his hand for my sake, and let a little of the ice thaw?"

"No," he said, almost sternly; "not even for your sake, for whom I would die, will I be dishonest with myself or him; and you are not one to ask me to act a lie."

"You wound me deeply, sir!" she said, coldly.

"Faithful are the wounds of a friend," he replied. She did not answer.

"We shall not part in this way, Annie," he said, in a low, troubled voice.

"The best I can do is to give you credit for very mistaken sincerity," she answered, sadly.

"That is all now, I fear," replied he, gently. "Good-by, Annie Walton. We are really parting now. My mission to you is past, and we go our different ways. You will never believe anything I can say on this painful subject, and I would not have spoken of it again of my own accord. Keep your promise to me, and all will yet be well, I believe. As that poor woman who saved us in the mountains said, 'There will at least be one good thing about me. Whether I can pray for myself or not, I shall daily pray for you'; and I feel that God who shielded you so strangely once, will still guard you. Do not grieve because I go away with pain in my heart. It's a better kind of suffering than that with which I came, and lasting good may come out of it, for my old reckless despair is gone. If I ever do become a good man--a Christian --I shall have you to thank; and even heaven would be happier if you were the means of bringing me there."

"When you speak that way, Walter," she said, tears starting to her eyes, "I must forgive everything; and when you become a Christian you will love even your enemy. Please take this little package from me, but do not open it till you reach the quiet and seclusion of your own rooms. Good-by, my brother, for as such my father told me to act and feel toward you, and from my heart I obey."

He looked at her with moistened eyes, but did not trust himself to answer, and without another word they returned to the house.

Gregory's leave-taking from the rest of the household was no mere form. Especially was this true of Miss Eulie, to whom he said most feelingly, "Miss Morton, my mother could not have been kinder or more patient with me."

When he pressed Zibbie's hand and left a banknote in it, she broke out in the broadest Scotch, "Maister Gregory, an' when I think me auld gray head would ha' been oot in the stourm wi' na hame to cover it, I pray the gude God to shelter yours fra a' the cauld blasts o' the wourld."

Silent Hannah, alike favored, seemed afflicted with a sudden attack of St. Vitus's dance, so indefinite was the number of her courtesies; while Jeff, on the driver's seat, looked as solemn as if he were to drive Gregory to the cemetery instead of the depot.

At the moment of final parting, Gregory merely took Annie's hand and looked into her eyes with an expression that caused them speedily to droop, tear-blinded.

To Hunting he had bowed his farewell in the parlor.

When the last object connected with his old home was hidden from his wistful, lingering gaze, he said, with the sorrow of one who watches the sod placed above the grave of his dearest, "So it all ends."

But when in his city apartments, which never before had seemed such a cheerless mockery of the idea of home, he opened the package Annie had given him-- when he found a small, worn Bible, inscribed with the words, "To my dear little daughter Annie, from mother," and written beneath, in a child's hand, "I thank you, dear mother. I will read it every day"--he sprang up, and exclaimed it strongest feeling, "No, all has not ended yet."

When he became sufficiently calm he again took up the Bible, and found the leaves turned down at the 14th chapter of St. John, with the words, "Begin here."

He read, "Let not your heart be troubled: ye believe in God, believe also in me.

"In my Father's house are many mansions: if it were not so, I would have told you. I go to prepare a place for you."

"How sweetly--with what exquisite delicacy--she points me beyond the shadows of time!" he said, musingly. "I believe in God. I ever have. Then why not *trust* the 'Man of Sorrows,' who also must be God? Both Annie and her quaint old friend are right. He never turned one away who came sincerely. In Him who forgave the outcast and thief there glimmers hope for me. How thick the darkness as I look elsewhere. Lord Jesus," he cried, with a rush of tears, "I am palsied through sin: lift me up, that I may come to Thee."

Better for him that night than a glowing hearth with genial friends around it was Annie's Bible.

Looking at it fondly, he said, "It links me to her happy childhood before that false man came, and it may join me to her in the 'place' which God is preparing, when he who now deceives her is as far removed as sin."

CHAPTER XXXII
AT SEA--A MYSTERIOUS PASSENGER

Immediately after Mr. Walton's funeral Miss Eulie had written to a brother-in-law, then, in Europe, full particulars of all that had occurred. This gentleman's name was Kemp, and he had originally married a sister of Miss Eulie and Mrs. Walton. But she had died some years since, and he had married as his second wife one who was an entire stranger to the Walton family, and with whom there could be but little sympathy. For this reason, though no unfriendliness existed, there had been a natural falling-off of the old cordial intimacy. Mr. Walton had respected Mr. Kemp as a man of sterling worth and unimpeachable integrity, and his feelings were shared by Miss Eulie and Annie, while Mr. Kemp himself secretly cherished a tender and regretful memory of his earlier marriage connection. When he heard that his niece, Annie, was orphaned, his heart yearned toward her, for he had always been fond of her as a child. But when he came to read of her relations with Hunting, and that this man was in charge of her property, he was in deep distress. He would have returned home immediately, but his wife's health would not permit his leaving her. He wrote to Miss Eulie a long letter of honest sympathy, urging her and Annie to come to him at Paris, saying that the change would be of great benefit to both.

This letter was expressed in such a way that it could be shown to Annie. But he inclosed another under seal to the aunt, marked private, in which by strong and guarded language he warned her against Hunting. He did not dare commit definite charges to writing, not knowing how much influence Hunting had over Miss Eulie. He felt sure that Annie would not listen to anything against her lover, and justly feared that she would inform him of what she heard, thus putting him on his guard, and increasing his power for mischief. Mr. Kemp's hope was to act through Miss Eulie, and get both her and Annie under his protection as soon as possible. He knew that when he was face to face with Annie he could prove to her the character of her lover, and through her compel him to resign his executorship. Therefore he solemnly charged Miss Eulie, as she loved Annie, not to permit her marriage with Hunting, and, as executrix, to watch his financial management closely.

Miss Eulie was greatly distressed by the contents of this letter. Mr. Kemp's words, combined with Gregory's manner, destroyed her confidence in Hunting, and made her feel that he might cause them irretrievable disaster. She knew her brother to be a man of honor, and when he wrote such words as these, "If Mr. Walton had known Hunting as I do he would rather have buried his daughter than permit her to marry him," she was sure that he did not speak unadvisedly.

"Moreover," Mr. Kemp wrote, "I am not giving my mere opinion of Hunting. I have absolute proof of what he is and has done."

But it was his opinion that it would not be safe to reveal to Annie the contents of this letter, as Hunting, in the desperation of his fears, might find means to compass a hasty marriage, or disastrously use his power over her property.

As we have seen, in quiet home-ministerings Miss Eulie had no superior, but she felt peculiarly timid and self-distrustful in dealing with matters like these. Her first impulse and her growing desire were that she and Annie might reach the shelter and protection of her brother. She did not understand business, and felt powerless to thwart Hunting.

Annie's spirits greatly flagged after her father's death. Hunting did not seem to have the power to comfort and help her that she had expected to find in him. She could not definitely find fault with a single act, save his treatment of Gregory; he was devotion itself to her, but it was to her alone. He proved no link between her and God. Even when in careful phrases he sought to use the "language of Canaan," he did not speak it as a native, and ever left a vague, unsatisfied pain in her heart. He was true and strong when he spoke of his own love. He was eloquent and glowing when his fancy painted their future home, but cold and formal in comparison when he dwelt on that which her Christian nature most needed in her deep affliction.

When Annie found that she could leave the children in charge of a careful, trustworthy relative, she was readily persuaded into the plan of going abroad. She felt the need of change, for her health had begun to fail, and she was sinking into one of those morbid states which are partly physical and partly mental.

Hunting, also, strongly approved of the project. Business would require him to visit Europe during the winter, and in having Annie as a companion he thought himself fortunate indeed. He felt sure that as soon as she regained her health and spirits she would consent to their marriage; moreover, it would place the sea between her and Gregory, thus averting all danger of disclosure. A trip abroad promised to further his interests in all respects. He knew nothing of Mr. Kemp save as a New York business man, and supposed that Mr. Kemp had only a general and favorable knowledge of himself.

For Annie's sake and her own Miss Eulie tried to prevent any marked change in her manner toward Hunting, and though she was not a very good actress he did not care enough about her to notice her occasional restraints and formality of manner. But Annie did, and it was another source of vague uneasiness and pain, though the causes were too intangible to speak of. She thought it possible that Gregory had prejudiced her aunt slightly. But it was her nature to prove all the more loyal to Hunting, especially when he was so devoted to her.

Before they could complete arrangements for departure, Annie was taken seriously ill, and January of the ensuing year had nearly passed before she was strong enough for the journey. During her illness no one could have been more kind and attentive than Hunting, and Annie felt exceedingly grateful. Still, in their prolonged and close intimacy since her father's death, something in the man himself had caused her love for him to wane. She had a growing consciousness that he was not what she had supposed. She reproached herself bitterly for this, and under the sense of the wrong she felt herself doing him, was disposed to show more deference to his wishes, and in justice to him to try to make amends. When, therefore, he again urged that the marriage take place before they sailed, giving as his reasons that he could take better care of her, and that henceforth she could be with him, and that he would not be compelled to leave her so often on account of his business, she was half inclined to yield. She felt that the marriage-tie would confirm her true feelings as a wife, and that it was hardly fair to ask him to be away from his large and exacting business so much, especially when he had appeared so generous in the time he had given her, which must have involved to him serious loss and inconvenience. She said to herself, "I shall be better and happier, and so will Charles, when I cease secretly finding fault with him, and devote myself unselfishly to making a good wife and a good home."

Hunting exultantly thought that he would carry his point, but Miss Eulie proved she was not that nonentity which, in his polite and attentive indifference, he had secretly considered her. With quiet firmness she said that, as Annie's natural guardian, she would not give her consent to the marriage. As a reason she said, "I think it would show a great lack of respect and courtesy to Annie's uncle and my brother, who is so fond of her, and has been so kind. I see no pressing need for the marriage now, for I am going with Annie and can take care of her as I have done. If it seems best, you can be married over there, and I know that Mr. Kemp would feel greatly hurt if we acted as if we were indifferent to his presence at the ceremony."

The moment her aunt expressed this view Annie agreed with her, and Hunting felt that he could not greatly complain, as the marriage would be delayed but a few weeks.

Annie felt absolved from her promise to Gregory by an event that occurred not very long after his departure. Gregory had sent a box, directed to Miss Eulie's care, containing some toys and books for the children, and the promised tobacco for Daddy Tuggar, also a note for Annie, inclosed in one to Miss Eulie, in which were these words only, "If you had searched the world you could not have given me anything that I would value more."

In his self-distrust, and in his purpose not to give the slightest ground for the imputation that he had sought her promise of delay to obtain time to gain a hearing himself, he had said no more. But Annie thought that he might have said more. The note seemed cold and brief in view of all that had passed between them. Still, she hoped much from the influence of her Bible.

One evening Hunting came up from the city evidently much disturbed. To her expressions of natural solicitude he replied, "I don't like to speak of it, for you seem to think that I ought to stand everything from Mr. Gregory. And so I suppose

I ought, and indeed I was grateful, but one can't help having the natural feelings of a man. I was with some friends and met him face to face in an omnibus. Knowing how great was your wish that we should be friendly, I spoke courteously to him, but he looked at me as if I were a dog. He might as well have struck me. I saw that my friends were greatly surprised, but of course I could not explain there, and yet it's not pleasant to be treated like a pickpocket, with no redress. I defy him," continued Hunting, assuming the tone and manner of one greatly wronged, "to prove anything worse against me than that I compelled him and his partners to pay money to which I had a legal right, and which I could have collected in a court of law."

The politic Hunting said nothing of moral right, and innocent Annie was not on the lookout for such quibbles.

Her quick feelings were strongly stirred, and on the impulse of the moment she sat down and wrote:

"Mr. Gregory--I think your course toward Mr. Hunting to-day was not only unjust, but even ungentlemanly. You cannot hurt his feelings without wounding mine. I cannot help feeling that your hostility is both 'unreasonable and implacable.' In sadness and disappointment, "Annie Walton."

"There," she said, "read that, and please mail it for me."

"That's my noble Annie," he said, gratefully. "Now you prove your love anew, and show you will not stand quietly by and see me insulted."

"You may rest assured I will not," she said, promptly; adding very sadly after a moment, "I cannot understand how Mr. Gregory, with all his good qualities, can act so."

"You do not know him so well as I do," said Hunting; "and yet even I feel grateful to him for his services to you, and would show it if he would treat me decently."

"He shall treat you decently, and politely too, if he wishes to keep my favor," said she, hotly.

But the next day, when she thought it all over quietly, she regretted that she had written so harshly. "My words will not help my Bible's influence," she thought in self-reproach, "and only when he becomes a Christian will he show a different disposition."

Her regret would have been still deeper, if she had known that Hunting had sent her note with one from himself to this effect:

"You perceive from the inclosed that you cannot insult me as you did yesterday and still retain the favor of one whose esteem you value *too highly* perhaps. My only regret is that you were not a witness to the words and manner which accompanied the act of writing."

Still stronger would have been her indignation had she known that Hunting had greatly exaggerated his insult. Gregory had merely acted as if unconscious of his presence, and there had been no look of scorn.

When Gregory received the missives he tossed Hunting's contemptuously into the fire, but read Annie's more than once, sighed deeply, and said, "He keeps his ascendency over her. O God! quench not my spark of faith by permitting this great wrong to be consummated." Then he indorsed on her note, "Forgiven, my dear, deceived sister. You will understand in God's good time."

But he felt that God must unravel the problem, for Annie would listen to nothing against her lover.

She hoped that Gregory would write an explanation, or at least some words in self-defence, and then she meant to soften her hasty note, but no answer came. This increased her depression, and she was surprised at her strong and abiding interest in him. She could not understand how their eventful acquaintance should end as it promised to. Then came her illness, and through many long, sleepless hours, she thought of the painful mystery.

As she recovered strength of body and mind she felt that it was one of those things that she must trustingly put in God's hands and leave there. This she did, and resolutely and patiently addressed herself to the duties of her lot.

As for Gregory, from the first evening of his return to the city, he adopted the resolution in regard to Annie's Bible which she, as a little child, had written in it so many years ago, "I will read it every day."

It became his shrine and constant solace. Instead of going to his club, as was his former custom, he spent the long, quiet evenings in its study. The more he read the more fascinated he became by its rich and varied truths. Sometimes as he was tracing up a line of thought through its pages, so luminously and beautifully would it develop that it seemed to him that Annie and his mother, with unseen hands, were pointing the way. Though almost alone in the great city, he grew less and less lonely, and welcomed the shades of evening, that he might return to a place now sacred to him, where the gift Bible, like a living presence, awaited him.

His doubts and fears vanished slowly. His faith kindled even more slowly; but the teachings of that inspired Book gave him principle, true manhood, and strength to do right, no matter how he felt. He had honestly and sturdily resolved to be guided by it, and it did guide him. He was a Christian, though he did not know it, and would not presume to call himself such even to himself. In view of his evil past he was exceedingly humble and self-distrustful. As Mr. Walton had told poor old Daddy Tuggar, he was simply trying to "trust Jesus Christ and do the best he could."

But those associated with him in business, and many others, wondered at the change in him. Old Mr. Burnett, his senior partner, was especially delighted, and would often say to him, "I thank God, Mr. Gregory, that you nearly had your neck broken last October"; for the good old man associated this accident with the change.

Gregory also began attending church--not a gorgeous temple on Fifth Avenue, where he was not needed; but he hunted up an obscure and struggling mission, and said to the minister, "I am little better than a heathen, but if you will trust me I will do the best I can to help you."

Within a month, through his liberal gifts and energetic labors, the usefulness of the mission was almost doubled. It was touching to see him humbly and patiently doing the Lord's lowliest work, as if he were not worthy. He hoped that in time he might receive the glad assurance that he was accepted; but whether it came or not, he purposed to do the best he could, and leave his fate in God's hands. At any rate God seemed not against him, for both his business and his Christian work prospered.

One bright morning late in January, Annie, Miss Eulie, and Hunting were driven down, to the steamer, and having gone to their state-rooms and seen that their luggage was properly stowed away, they came up on deck to watch the scenes attending the departure of the great ship, and observe the views as they sailed down the bay. Hunting had told them to make the most of this part of the voyage, for in a winter passage it might be long before they could enjoy another promenade.

Annie was intensely interested, for all was new and strange. She had a keen, quick eye for character, and a human interest in humanity, even though those around her did not belong to her "set." Therefore it was with appreciative eyes that she watched the motley groups of her fellow-passengers waving handkerchiefs and exchanging farewells with equally diversified groups on the wharf.

"It seems," she said to her aunt, "as if all the world had sent their representatives here. It makes me almost sad that there is no one to see us off."

Then her eye rested upon a gentleman who evidently had no one to see him off. He was leaning on the railing upon the opposite side of the ship, smoking a cigar. His back was toward all this bustle and confusion, and he seemed to have an air of isolation and of indifference to what was going on about him. His tall person was clad in a heavy overcoat, which seemed to combine comfort with elegance, and gave to him, even in his leaning posture, a distingue air. But that which drew Annie's attention was the difference of his manner from that of all others, who were either excited by their surroundings, or were turning wistfully and eagerly toward friends whom it might be long before they saw again. The motionless, apathetic figure, smoking quietly, with his hat drawn down over his eyes, and looking away from everything and everybody, came to have a fascination for her.

The steamer slowly and majestically moved out into the stream. Shouts, cries, final words, hoarse orders from the officers--a perfect babel of sounds--filled the air, but the silently-curling smoke-wreaths were the only suggestion of life from that strangely indifferent form. He seemed like one so deeply absorbed in his own thoughts that he would have to be awakened as from sleep.

Suddenly he turned and came toward them with the air of one who feels himself alone, though jostled in a crowd, and instantly, with a strange thrill at heart, Annie recognized Walter Gregory.

Hunting saw him also, and Annie noted that, while the blackest frown gathered on his brow, he grew very pale.

In his absorption, Gregory would have passed by them, but Annie said, "Mr. Gregory, are you not going to speak to us?"

He started violently, and his face mantled with hot blood, and Annie also felt that she was blushing unaccountably. But he recovered instantly, and came and shook her hand most cordially, saying, "This is a strangely unexpected pleasure. And Miss Morton, also! When was I ever so fortunate before?"

Then he saw Hunting, to whom he bowed with his old, distant manner, and Hunting returned the acknowledgment in the most stiff and formal way.

"Do you know," said Annie, "I have been watching you with curiosity for some time past, though I did not know who you were till you turned. I could not account for your apathy and indifference to this scene, which to me is so novel and exciting, and which seems to find every one interested save yourself. I should hardly have thought you alive if you had not been smoking."

"Well," he said, "I have been abroad so often that it has become like crossing the ferry, and I was expecting no one down to see me off. But you do not look well;" and both she and Miss Eulie noticed that he glanced uneasily from her to Hunting, and did not seem sure how he should address her.

"Miss Walton has just recovered from a long illness," said Miss Eulie, quietly.

His face instantly brightened, and as quickly changed to an expression of sincerest sympathy.

"Not seriously ill, I hope," he said, earnestly.

"I'm afraid I was," replied Annie, adding, cheerfully, "I am quite well now, though."

His face became as pale as it had been flushed a moment before, and he said, in a low tone, "I did not know it."

His manner touched her, and proved that there was no indifference on his part toward her, though there might be to the bustling world around him.

Then he inquired particularly after each member of the household, and especially after old Daddy Tuggar.

Annie told him how delighted the children had been with the toys and books. "And as for Daddy Tuggar," she said, smiling, "he has been in the clouds, literally and metaphorically, ever since you sent him the tobacco. Whenever I go to see him he says, most cheerfully, 'It's all settled, Miss Annie. It grows clearer with every pipe' (while I can scarcely see him), 'I'm all right, 'cause I'm an awful sinner.'"

She was rather surprised at the look of glad sympathy which Gregory gave her, but he only said, "He is to be envied."

Then at her request he began to point out the objects of interest they were passing, and with quiet courtesy drew Hunting into the conversation, who rather ungraciously permitted it because he could not help himself.

Annie again, with pain, saw the unfavorable contrast of her lover with this man, who certainly proved himself the more finished gentleman, if nothing else.

With almost a child's delight she said, "You have no idea how novel and interesting all this is to me, though so old and matter-of-fact to you. I have always wanted to cross the ocean, and look forward to this voyage with unmingled pleasure."

"I'm sincerely sorry such a disastrous change is so soon to take place in your sensations, for it will be rough outside to-day, and I fear you and Miss Morton will soon be suffering from the most forlorn and prosaic of maladies."

"I won't give up to it," said Annie, resolutely.

"I have no doubt," he replied, humorously, "as our quaint old friend used to say, that you are 'well meanin',' but we must all submit to fate. I fear you will soon be confined to the dismal lower regions."

"Are you sick?"

"I was at first."

His prediction was soon verified. From almost a feeling of rapture and a sense of the sublime as they looked out upon the broad Atlantic with its tumultuous waves, the ladies suddenly became silent, and glanced nervously toward the stairway that led to the cabin.

Gregory promptly gave his arm to Miss Eulie, while Hunting followed with Annie, and that was the last appearance of the ladies for three days.

CHAPTER XXXIII
COLLISION AT SEA--WHAT A
CHRISTIAN COULD DO

On the morning of the fourth day, as the sea had become more calm, the ladies ventured upon deck for a short time. Gregory immediately joined them and complimented their courage in coming out during a winter voyage.

"Nature and I are friends all the year round," said Annie, with a faint attempt at a smile, for she was still sick and faint. "I rather like her wild, rough moods. It has been a great trial to my patience to lie in my berth, helpless and miserable from what you well term a 'prosaic malady,' when I was longing to see the ocean. Now that we have made a desperate attempt to reach deck, there is nothing to see. Do you think this dense fog will last long?"

"I hope not, especially for your sake. But do not regret coming out, for you will soon feel better for it."

"I do already; I believe I could live out of doors. Have you been ill?"

"O no; I should have been a sailor."

"Mr. Hunting has fared almost as badly as we," said Annie, determined that they should make one group.

"Indeed! I'm sorry," said Gregory, quietly.

"I hate the ocean," snarled Hunting, with a grim, white face; "I'm always sick."

"And I'm afraid of it," said Miss Eulie. "How can they find their way through such a mist? Then, we might run into something."

"In any case you are safe, Miss Morton," said Gregory, with a smile.

She gave him a bright look and replied, "I trust we all are. But the sea is rough, boisterous, treacherous, and mysterious, just the qualities I don't like. What a perfect emblem of mystery this fog is through which we are going so rapidly!"

"Well," said Gregory, with one of his expressive shrugs, "I find all these experiences equally on the land, especially the latter."

Annie gave him a quick, inquiring look, while color came into even Hunting's pale face.

Annie felt no little curiosity as to Gregory's developing character, for though he had said nothing definite, his softened manner and quiet dignity made him seem very unlike his old self.

"How do you pass your time?" she asked.

"Well, I read a great deal, and I take considerable exercise, for I wish fully to regain my health."

She gave him a grateful look. He was keeping his promise. She said, "You look very much better than I expected to see you, and I'm very glad, for you were almost ghostly when you left us. What do you find so interesting to read?"

His color rose instantly, but he said with a smile, "A good old book that I brought with me."

The expression of his face answered her swift, questioning look. It was her Bible. Neither Miss Eulie nor Hunting understood why she became so quiet; but the latter, who was watching them closely, thought he detected some secret understanding. In his jealous egotism it could only mean what was adverse to himself, and he had an attack of something worse than sea-sickness.

Gregory quietly turned the conversation upon ocean travel, and for a half-hour entertained the ladies without any effort on their part, and then they went back to their state-rooms.

By evening the ship was running so steadily that they all came out to supper. Gregory, who was a personal friend of the captain, had secured them a place near the head of the table, where they received the best of attention. Annie, evidently, was recovering rapidly, and took a genuine interest in the novel life and scenes around her. She found herself vis-a-vis and side by side with great diversities of character, and listened with an amused, intelligent face to the brisk conversation. She noted with surprise that Gregory seemed quite a favorite, but soon saw the reason in his effort to make the hour pass pleasantly to his fellow-passengers. The captain had given him a seat at his right hand, and appealed to him on every disputed point that was outside of his special province.

She was also pleased to see how Gregory toned up the table-talk and skilfully led it away from disagreeable topics. But he had a rather difficult task, for, sitting near her, was a man whose ostentatious dress reflected his character and words.

Some one was relating an anecdote of a narrow escape, and another remarked, "That's what I should call a special Providence."

"Special Providence!" said Annie's loud neighbor, contemptuously. "A grown man is very weak-minded to believe in any Providence whatever."

There was a shocked, pained expression on many faces, and Annie's eyes flashed with indignation. She turned to Hunting, expecting him to resent such an insult to their faith, but saw only a cold sneer on his face. Hunting was decidedly English in his style, and would travel around the world and never speak to a stranger, or make an acquaintance, if he could help it. Then, instinctively, she turned to Gregory. He was looking fixedly at the man, whose manner had attracted general attention. But he only said, "Then I am very weak-minded."

There was a general expression of pleased surprise and sympathy on the faces

of those who understood his reply, while the captain stared at him in some astonishment.

"I beg your pardon, sir," said the man; "I meant nothing personal. It was only a
rather blunt way of saying that I didn't believe in any such things myself."

"I give you credit for your honesty, but some of us do."

"Then you pretend to be a Christian?"

"I should not ***pretend*** to be one under any circumstances," said Gregory, with
the perfection of quiet dignity, "and I am very sorry to say that I am not so favored.
But I have full belief in a Providence, both special and general."

"I like your honesty, too," said the man, seemingly anxious for an argument.
"By the word 'pretend' I only meant claim, or assert. But it seems to me that the
facts in the case are all against your belief. I find nothing but law in the universe.
You might as well say that this ship is run by special Providence, when, in fact, it is
run by accurately gauged machinery, system, and rules."

"Now your argument is lame," said the captain, laughing. "We have plenty of
good machinery, system, and rules aboard, but if I wasn't around, looking after everything all the time, as a special Providence, I'm afraid you'd find salt water before
Liverpool."

A general laugh followed this sally, and Gregory said: "And so I believe that the
Divine Providence superintends His own laws and system. I think my friend the
captain has given a most happy illustration of the truth, and I had no idea he was so
good a theologian."

"That's not an argument," said the man, considerably crestfallen. "That's only
a joke."

"By the way, Mr. Gregory, it seems to me that your views have changed since
you crossed with me last," remarked the captain.

"I frankly admit they have," was the prompt reply. "Perhaps I can explain myself by the following question: If you find, by a careful observation, that you are
heading your ship the wrong way, what do you do?"

"Put her about on the right course."

"That is just what I have tried to do, sir. I think my meaning is plain?"

"Nothing could be clearer, and I'd rather be aboard now than when you were
on the old tack."

Annie gave Gregory a glance of glad, grateful approval that warmed his heart like sunshine.

Hunting said, enviously, **sotto voce**, "I think such conversation at a public table wretched taste."

"I cannot agree with you," said Annie, decidedly; "but, granting it, Mr. Gregory did not introduce the subject, and I wish you had spoken as he did when every Christian at the table was insulted."

He colored deeply, but judiciously said nothing.

With increasing pain she thought, "He who says he is not a Christian acts more like one than he who claims the character."

But she now had the strongest hopes for Gregory, and longed for a private talk with him.

The next day it blew quite a gale, and Hunting and Miss Eulie were helplessly confined to their staterooms. But Annie had become a sailor, and having done all she could for her aunt, came upon deck, where she saw Gregory walking back and forth with almost the steadiness of one of the ship's officers.

She tried to go to him, but would have fallen had he not seen her and reached her side almost at a bound. With a gentleness and tenderness as real as delicate, he placed her in a sheltered nook where she could see the waves in their mad sport, and said, "Now you can see old ocean in one of his best moods. The wind, though strong, is right abaft, filling all the sails they dare carry, and we are making grand progress."

"How wonderful it is!" cried Annie, looking with a child's interest upon the scene. "Just see those briny mountains, with foam and spray for foliage. If our own Highlands with their mingled evergreens and snow were changed from granite to water, and set in this wild motion, it could hardly seem more strange and sublime. Look at that great monster coming so threateningly toward us. It seems as if we should be engulfed beyond a chance."

"Now see how gracefully the ship will surmount it," said Gregory, smiling.

"O dear!" said she, sighing, "if we could only rise above our troubles in the same way!" Then, feeling that she had touched on delicate ground, she hastened to add, "This boundless waste increases my old childish wonder how people ever find their way across the ocean."

"The captain is even now illustrating your own teaching and practice in regard to the longer and more difficult voyage of life," said Gregory, meaningly. "He is 'looking up'--taking an observation of the heavens, and will soon know just where we are and how to steer."

Annie looked at him wistfully, and said, in a low tone, "I was so glad to learn, last evening, that you had taken an observation also, and I was so very grateful, too, that you had the courage to defend our faith."

"I have to thank you that I could do either. It was really you who spoke."

"No, Mr. Gregory," she said, gently, "my work for you reached its limit. God is leading you now."

"I try to hope so," he said; "but it was your hand that placed in mine that by which He is leading me. He surely must have put it into your heart to give me that Bible. When I reached my cheerless rooms in New York I felt so lonely and low-spirited that I had not the courage to go a single step further. But your Bible became a living, comforting presence from that night. What exquisite tact you showed in giving me that little worn companion of your childhood, instead of a new gilt-leaved one, with no associations. I first hoped that you might with it give me also something of your childhood's faith. But that does not come yet. That does not come."

"It will," said she, earnestly, and with moistened eyes.

"That, now, is one of my dearest hopes. But after what I have been, I am not worthy that it should come soon. But if I perish myself I want to try to help others."

Then he asked, in honest distrustfulness, "Do you think it right for one who is not a Christian to try to teach others?"

"Before I answer that question I wish to ask a little more about yourself;" and she skilfully drew him out, he speaking more openly in view of the question to be decided than he would otherwise have done. He told of the long evenings spent over her Bible; of his mission work, and of his honest effort to deal justly with all; at the same time dwelling strongly on his doubts and spiritual darkness, and the unspent influences of his old evil life.

The answer was different from what he expected; for she said: "Mr. Gregory, why do you say that you are not a Christian?"

"Because I feel that I am not."

"Does feeling merely make a Christian?" she asked. "Is not action more than feeling? Do not trusting, following, serving, and seeking to obey, make a Christian? But suppose that even with your present *feeling* you were living at the time of Christ's visible presence on earth, would you be hostile or indifferent, or would you join His band even though small and despised?"

"I think I would do the latter, if permitted."

"I know you would, from your course last night. And do you think Jesus would say, 'Because you are not an emotional man like Peter, you are no friend of mine'? Why, Mr. Gregory, He let even Judas Iscariot, though with unworthy motive, follow Him as long as he would, giving him a chance to become true."

"Miss Walton, do not mislead me in this matter. You know how implicitly I trust you."

"And I would rather cast myself over into those waves than deceive you," she said; "and if I saw them swallowing you up I should as confidently expect to meet you again, as my father. How strange it is you can believe that Jesus died for you and yet will not receive you when you are doing just that which He died to accomplish."

He took a few rapid turns up and down the deck and then leaned over the railing. She saw that he brushed more than one tear into the waves. At last he turned and gave his hand in warm pressure, saying, "I cannot doubt you, and I will doubt Him no longer. I see that I have wronged Him, and the thought causes me sorrow even in my joy."

"Now you are my brother in very truth," she said, gently, with glad tears in her own eyes. "All that we have passed through has not been in vain. How wonderfully God has led us!"

It was a long time before either spoke again.

At last he said, with a strange, wondering smile, "To think that such as I should ever reach heaven! As Daddy Tuggar says, 'there will be good neighbors there.'"

She answered him by a happy smile, and then both were busy with their own thoughts again. Annie was thinking how best to introduce the subject so near her heart, his reconciliation with Hunting.

But that gentleman had become so tortured with jealousy and so alarmed at the thought of any prolonged conference between Annie and Gregory, that he dragged himself on deck. As he watched them a moment before they saw him, he was quite reassured. Gregory was merely standing near Annie, and both were looking away to sea, as if they had nothing special to say to each other. Annie was pained to see that Gregory's manner did not change toward Hunting. He was perfectly polite, but nothing more; soon he excused himself, thinking they would like to be alone.

In the afternoon she found a moment to say, "Mr. Gregory, will you never become reconciled to Mr. Hunting? You surely cannot hate him now?"

He replied, gravely, "I do not hate him any longer. I would do him any kindness in my power, and that is a great deal for me to say. But Mr. Hunting has no real wish for reconciliation."

In bitter sorrow she was compelled to admit to herself the truth of his words. After a moment he added, "If he does he knows the exact terms on which it can be effected."

She could not understand it, and reproached herself bitterly that so many doubts in regard to her affianced would come unbidden, and force themselves on her mind. The feeling grew stronger that there was wrong on both sides, and perhaps the more on Hunting's.

That was a memorable day to Gregory. It seemed to him that Annie's hand had drawn aside the sombre curtain of his unbelief, and shown the path of light shining more and more unto the perfect day. Though comparatively lonely, he felt that his pilgrimage could not now be unhappy, and that every sorrow would at last find its cure. In regard to her earthly future he could only hope and trust. It would be a terrible trial to his faith if she were permitted to marry Hunting, and yet he was sure it would all be well at last; for was it not said that God's people would come to their rest out of "great tribulation"? She had given him the impression that, under any circumstances, her love for him could only be sisterly in its character.

But he was too happy in his new-born hope to think of much else that day; and, finding a secluded nook, he searched Annie's Bible for truths confirmatory of her words. On every side they glowed as in letters of light. Then late that night he went on deck, and in his strong excitement felt as if walking on air in his long, glad vigil.

At last, growing wearied, he leaned upon the railing and looked out upon the dark waves--not dark to him, for the wanderer at last had seen the light of his heavenly home, and felt that it would cheer his way till the portals opened and received him into rest.

Suddenly, upon the top of a distant wave, something large and white appeared, and then sank into an ocean valley. Again it rose--a sail, then the dark hull of a ship.

In dreamy musing he began, wondering how, in mid-ocean, with so many leagues of space, two vessels should cross each other's track so near. "It's just the same with human lives," he thought. "A few months or years ago, people that I never knew, and might have passed on the wider ocean of life, unknowing and uncaring, have now come so near! Why is it? Why does that ship, with the whole Atlantic before it, come so steadily toward us?"

It did come so steadily and so near that a feeling of uneasiness troubled him, but he thought that those in charge knew their business better than he.

A moment later he started forward. The ship that had come so silently and phantom-like across the waves seemed right in the path of the steamer.

Was it not a phantom?

No; there's a white face at the wheel--the man is making a sudden, desperate effort--it's too late.

With a crash like thunder the seeming phantom ship plows into the steamer's side.

For a moment Gregory was appalled, stunned; and stared at the fatal intruder that fell back in strong rebound, and dropped astern.

Then he became conscious of the confusion, and awakening uproar on both vessels. Cries of agony, shouts of alarm, and hoarse orders pierced the midnight air. He ran forward and saw the yawning cavern which the blow had made in the ship's side, and heard the rush of water into the hold. Across the chasm he saw the captain's pale face looking down with a dismay like his own.

"The ship will sink, and soon," Gregory shouted.

There was no denial.

Down to the startled passengers he rushed, crying, "Awake! Escape for your lives!"

His words were taken up and echoed in every part of the ship.

He struck a heavy blow upon the door of Annie's stateroom. "Miss Walton!"

"Oh, what has happened?" she asked.

"You and Miss Morton come on deck, instantly; don't stop to dress; snatch a shawl--anything. Lose not a moment. What is Hunting's number?"

"Forty, on the opposite side."

"I will be back in a moment; be ready."

Hunting's state-room was so near where the steamer had been struck that its door was jammed and could not be opened.

"Help! help! I can't get out," shrieked the terrified man.

Gregory wrenched a leaf from a dining-room table and pried the door open.

"Come," he said, "you've no time to dress."

Hunting wrapped his trembling form in a blanket and gasped, as he followed, "I'll pay you back every cent of that money with interest."

"Make your peace with God. We may soon be before Him," was the awful response.

Miss Eulie and Annie stood waiting, draped in heavy shawls.

"I'm sorry for the delay; Hunting's door was jammed and had to be broken open. Come;" and putting his arm around Miss Eulie and taking Annie's hand, he forced them rapidly through the increasing throng of terror-stricken passengers that were rushing in all directions.

Even then, with a strange thrill at heart, Annie thought, "He has saved his enemy's life."

He took them well aft, and said, "Don't move; stand just here until I return," and then pushed his way to the point where a frantic crowd were snatching for the life preservers which were being given out. The officer, knowing him, tossed him four as requested.

Coming back, he said to Hunting, "Fasten that one on Miss Morton and keep the other." Throwing down his own for a moment, he proceeded to fasten Annie's. He would not trust the demoralized Hunting to do anything for her, and he was right, for Hunting's hands so trembled that he was helpless. Having seen that Annie's was secured beyond a doubt, Gregory also tied on Miss Eulie's.

In the meantime a passenger snatched his own preserving-belt, which he had been trying to keep by placing his foot upon it.

"Stop," Annie cried. "O Mr. Gregory! he has taken it and you have none. You shall have mine;" and she was about to unfasten it.

He laid a strong grasp upon her hands. "Stop such folly," he said, sternly. "Come to where they are launching that boat. You have no choice;" and he forced her forward while Hunting followed with Miss Eulie.

They stood waiting where the lantern's glare fell upon their faces, with many others more pale and agonized.

Annie clung to him as her only hope (for Hunting seemed almost paralyzed with fear), and whispered, "Will you the same as die for me again?"

"Yes, God bless you! a thousand times if there were need," he said, in tones whose gentleness equalled the harshness of his former words.

She looked at him wonderingly. There was no fear upon his face, only unspeakable love for her.

"Are you not afraid?" she asked.

"You said I was a Christian to-day, and your Bible and God's voice in my heart have confirmed your words. No, I am at peace in all this uproar, save anxiety for you."

She buried her face upon his shoulder.

"My darling sister!" he murmured in her ear. "How can I ever thank you enough?"

Then he started suddenly, and tearing off the cape of his coat, said to Hunting, "Fasten that around Miss Morton;" and before Annie quite knew what he was doing he had taken off the body part and incased her in it.

"Here, Hunting, your belt is not secure"; and he tightened the straps.

"Pass the women forward," shouted the captain.

Of course those nearest were embarked first. The ladies in Gregory's charge had to take their turn, and the boat was about full when Miss Eulie was lowered over the side.

At that moment the increasing throng, with a deeper realization of danger, as the truth of their situation grew plainer, felt the first mad impulse of panic, and there was a rush toward the boat. Hunting felt the awful contagion. His face had the look of a hunted wild beast. Annie gazed wonderingly at him, but as he half-started with the others for the boat she understood him. Laying a restraining hand upon his arm, she said, in a low tone, "If you leave my side now, you leave it forever."

He cowered back in shame.

The officer in charge of the boat had shouted, "This boat is for women and children; as you are men and not brutes, stand back."

This checked the desperate mob for a moment, and Gregory was about to pass Annie down when there was another mad rush led by the blatant individual who had scouted the idea of Providence.

"Cut away all," shouted the captain from the bridge, and the boat dropped astern.

It was only by fierce effort that Gregory kept himself and Annie from being carried over the side by the surging mass, many of whom leaped blindly over, supposing the boat to be still there.

Pressing their way out they went where another boat was being launched. Hunting followed them like a child, and was as helpless. He now commenced moaning, "O God! what shall I do? what shall I do?"

"Trust Him, and be a man. What else should you do?" said Gregory, sternly, for he was deeply disgusted at Hunting's behavior.

Around this boat the officer in charge had placed a cordon of men to keep the crowd away, and stood pistol in hand to enforce his orders. But the boat was scarcely lowered before there was the same wild rush, mostly on the part of the crew and steerage passengers. The officer fired and brought down the foremost, but the frenzied wretches trampled him down with those helping, together with women and children, as a herd of buffaloes might have done. They poured over into the boat, swamped it, and as the steamer moved slowly ahead, were left struggling and perishing in the waves.

Gregory had put his arm around Annie and drawn her out of the crush. Fortunately they had been at one side, so that this was possible.

"The boats are useless," he said, sadly. "There will be the same suicidal folly at every one, even if they have time to lower any more. Come aft. That part will sink last, and there will be less suction there when the ship goes down. We may find something that will keep us afloat."

Annie clung to his arm and said, quietly, "I will do just as you say," while Hunting followed in the same maze of terror.

They had hardly got well away before a mast, with its rigging, fell where they had stood, crushing many and maiming others, rendering them helpless.

"Awful! awful" shuddered Hunting, and Annie put her hands before her eyes.

An officer, with some men, now came toward them with axes, and commenced breaking up the after wheelhouse.

"Here is our best chance," said Gregory. "Let us calmly await the final moment and then do the best we can. All this broken timber will float, and we can cling to it."

The ship was settling fast, and had become like a log upon the water, responding slowly and heavily to the action of the waves. But under the cold, pitiless starlight of that winter night, what heartrending scenes were witnessed upon her sinking deck! Death had already laid its icy finger on many, and many more were grouped near in despairing expectation of the same fate.

While many, like Hunting, were almost paralyzed with fear, and others shrieked and cried aloud in agony--while some prayed incoherently, and others rushed back and forth as if demented--there were not wanting numerous noble examples of faith and courage. Fortunately, there were not many ladies on board, and most of these proved that woman's fortitude is not a poetic fiction. One or two family groups stood near in close embrace, and some men calmly folded their arms across their breasts, and met their fate as God would have them.

Annie was conscious of a strange peace and hopefulness. She thrilled with the thought which she expressed to Gregory--"How soon I may see father and mother!"

She stood now with one hand on Hunting's trembling arm, for at that supreme moment her heart was very tender, and she pitied while she wondered at him. But Gregory was a tower of strength. He took her hand in both his own, and said, "I can say the same, and more. Both father and mother are awaiting me--and, Annie," he whispered, tenderly, "you, too, will be there. So, courage! 'Good neighbors,' soon."

Why did her heart beat so strangely at his words?

"O God! have mercy on me!" groaned the man who had *seemed*, but was not.

"Amen!" breathed both Annie and Gregory, fervently.

Suddenly they felt themselves lifted in the air, and, looking toward the bow, saw it going under, while what seemed a great wave came rolling toward them, bearing upon its dark crest white, agonized faces and struggling forms.

Annie gave a swift, inquiring look to Gregory. His face was turned heavenward, in calm and noble trust.

Hunting's wild cry mingled with the despairing shriek of many others, but ended in a gurgling groan as he and all sank beneath the waters.

CHAPTER XXXIV
UNMASKED

It seemed that they passed through miles of water that roared around them like a cataract. But Annie and Gregory held to each other in their strong, convulsive grasp, and her belt caused him to rise with her to the surface again. A piece of the wheelhouse floated near; Gregory swam for it, and pushing it to Annie helped her upon it. Hunting also grasped it. But it would not sustain the weight of all three, especially as Gregory had no preserver on.

One must leave it that the other two might escape.

"Good-by, Annie, darling," said Gregory. "We will meet again in heaven if not on earth. Cling to your plank as long as you can, and a boat may pick you up. Good-by, poor Hunting, I'm sorry for you."

"What are you going to do?" gasped Annie.

"Don't you see that this won't float all three? I shall try to find something else."

"No, no," cried Annie, "don't leave me: you have no belt on. If you go I will too."

"I once lived for your sake; now you must for mine. I may save myself; but if you leave we shall both drown. Good-by, dearest. If I reach home first, I'll watch and wait till you come."

She felt him kiss her hand where she clung to her frail support, and then he disappeared in the darkness.

"Why did you let him go?" she said to Hunting--"you who have a preserver on?"

"O God, have mercy on me!" groaned the wretched man.

Annie now gave up all hope of escape, and indeed wished to die. She was almost sure that Gregory had perished, and she felt that her best- loved ones were in heaven.

She would have permitted herself to be washed away had not a sense of duty to live until God took her life kept her firm. But every moment it seemed that her failing strength would give way, and her benumbed hands loosen their hold.

"But," she murmured in the noblest triumph of faith, "I shall sink, not in these cold depths, but into my Saviour's arms."

Toward the last, when alone in the very presence of death, He seemed nearest and dearest. She could not bear to look at the dark, angry waters strewn with floating corpses. She had a sickening dread that Gregory's white face might float by. So she closed her eyes, and only thought of heaven, which was so near that its music seemed to mingle with the surging of the waves.

She tried to say a comforting word to Hunting, but the terror-stricken man could only groan mechanically, "God have mercy on me!"

Soon she began to grow numb all over. A dreamy peace pervaded her mind, and she was but partially conscious.

She was aroused by hearing her name called. Did the voice come from that shore beyond all dark waves of earthly trouble? At first she was not sure.

Again and louder came the cry, but too full of human agony to be a heavenly voice--

"Annie! Annie!"

"Here!" she cried, faintly, while Hunting, helpful for once, shrieked aloud above the roar of the waves.

Then she heard the sound of oars, and a moment later strong hands lifted her into the boat, and she found herself in Gregory's arms, her head pillowed on his breast. Then all grew dark.

When she again became conscious she found herself in a small cabin, with many others in like pitiable plight. Her aunt was bending over her on one side and Gregory on the other, chafing her hands. At first she could not remember or understand, and stared vacantly at them.

"Annie, darling," said Miss Eulie, "don't you know me?"

Then glad intelligence dawned in her face, and she reached out her arms, and each clasped the other as one might receive the dead back to life.

But quickly she turned and asked, "Where is Mr. Gregory?"

"Here, safe and sound," he said, joyously, "and Hunting, too. I shall bless him all the days of my life, for his cries drowned old ocean's hoarse voice and brought us right to you."

Hunting looked as if he did not exactly relish the tribute, but he stooped down and kissed Annie, who permitted rather than received the caress.

"How did you escape?" she asked Gregory, eagerly.

"Well, I swam toward the ship that struck us, whose lights I saw twinkling in the distance, till almost exhausted. I was on the point of giving up, when a small piece of the wreck floated near. By a great effort I succeeded in reaching it. Then a little later a boat from this ship picked me up and we started after you or any others that could be found. I am glad to say that quite a number that went down with the ship were saved."

She looked at him in a way to bring the warm blood into his face, and said, in a low tone, "How can I ever repay yon?"

"By doing as you once said to me, 'Live! get strong and well.' Good-by now. Miss Morton will take care of you."

Her eyes followed him till he disappeared, then she turned and hid her face on Miss Eulie's shoulder. The good old lady was a little puzzled, and so was Hunting, though he had dismal forebodings. But he was so glad to have escaped that he could not indulge in very bitter regrets just then. As his mind recovered its poise, however, and he had time to think it all over, there came a sickening sense of humiliation.

In a few minutes Gregory returned and said to Annie, "See how honored you are. I've been so lucky as to get the captain's best coat for you, and those wet things that would chill you to death can be taken off. You can give my coat to Hunting. You see I was up at the time of the accident, and so am dressed."

"If I am to wear the captain's coat," said Annie, "then, with some of his authority, I order you to go and take care of yourself. You have done enough for others for a little while."

"Ay, ay, captain," said Gregory, smiling, as he again vanished.

It would only be painful to dwell on the dreary days and nights during which the comparatively small sailing vessel was beating back against a stormy wind to the port from which she had sailed. She had been much injured by the collision, and many were doubtful whether, after all, they would ever see land. Thus, to the mani- fold miseries of the rescued passengers, was added continued anxiety as to their fate. It was, indeed, a sad company that was crowded in that small cabin, half- clothed, bruised, sick, and fearful. What seemed to them an endless experience was but a long nightmare of trouble, while some, who had lost their best and dearest, refused to be comforted and almost wished they had perished also.

Annie's gratitude that their little party had all been spared grew stronger every hour, and the one through whose efforts they had been saved grew daily dearer.

At first she let her strong affection go out to him unchecked, not realizing whither she was drifting; but a little characteristic event occurred which revealed her to herself.

Her exposure had again caused quite a serious illness, and she saw little of Gregory for a few days. Hunting claimed his right to be with her as far as it was possible. Though she would not admit it to herself, she almost shrunk from him. Of course the sailing ship had been provisioned for only a comparatively small crew, and the sudden and large accession to the number threatened to add the terrors of famine to their other misfortunes.

Annie had given almost all of her allowance away. Indeed she had no appetite, and revolted at the coarse food served. But she noticed that Hunting ate all of his, or else put some quietly away, in view of future need. She said to him, upon this occasion, "Can't you spare a little of your portion for those poor people over there? They look half-famished."

"I will do so if you wish," he replied, "but it would hardly be wise. Think what tremendous business interests I represent, and it is of the first importance that I keep up."

"Mr. Gregory is almost starving himself," said Miss Eulie, quietly. "I feel very anxious about him."

"I represent a business of thousands where Mr. Gregory does hundreds," said Hunting, complacently.

"I wish you represented something else," said Annie, bitterly, turning away.

Her words and manner jostled him out of himself. A principle that seemed to him so sound and generally accepted appeared sordid and selfish calculation to Annie and she felt that Gregory represented infinitely greater riches in his self-denial for others.

Hunting saw his blunder and instantly carried all his portion to those whom Annie had pointed out. But it was too late. He had shown his inner nature again in a way that repelled Annie's very soul. She turned sick at the thought of being bound to such a man.

At first she had tried to excuse his helpless terror on the ship by thinking it a physical trait; but this was a moral trait. It gave a sudden insight into the cold, dark depths of his nature.

Immediately after the disaster she had been too sick and bewildered to realize her situation. Her engagement was such an old and accepted fact that at first no thought of any other termination of it than by marriage entered her mind. Yet she already looked forward to it only as a duty, and she felt that her love for Hunting would be that of pity rather than trust and honor. But she was so truthful--so chained by her promises--that her engagement rested upon her like a solemn obligation. Again, it had been entered into under circumstances so tenderly sacred that even the wish to escape from it seemed like sacrilege. Still, she said, in intense bitterness, "Dear father was deceived also. We did not know him as we should."

Yet she had nothing against Hunting, save a growing lack of congeniality and his cowardice at a time when few men could be heroic. In her strong sense of justice she felt that she should not condemn a man for an infirmity. But her cheeks tingled with shame as she remembered his weakness, and she felt that a Christian ought to have done a little better under any circumstances. When, in the event above described, she saw his hard, calculating spirit, her whole nature revolted from him almost in loathing.

After a brief time she told him that she wanted to be alone, and he went away cursing his own folly. Miss Eulie, thinking she wished to sleep, also left her.

"How can I marry him?" she groaned; "and yet how can I escape such an engagement?"

When her aunt returned she found her sobbing as if her heart would break.

"Why, Annie, dear, what is the matter?" she asked.

"Don't ask me," she moaned, and buried her face in her pillow.

Then that judicious lady looked very intelligent, but said nothing more. She sat down and began to stroke Annie's brown, dishevelled hair. But instead of showing very great sympathy for her niece, she had an unusually complacent expression. Gregory had a strong but discreet friend in the camp.

When Annie became calmer, she said, hesitatingly, "Do you think--is Mr. Gregory--doesn't he eat anything?"

"No; he is really wronging himself. I heard it said that the captain had threatened, jokingly, to put him in irons if he did not obey orders and eat his allowance."

"Do you think I could make--do you think he would do better if I should ask him?" inquired Annie, with her face buried in her pillow.

"Well," said Miss Eulie, gravely, though with a smile upon her face, "Mr. Gregory is very self-willed, especially about some things, but I do think that you have more power over him than any one else."

"Won't you tell him that I want to see him?"

He was very glad to come. Annie tried hard to be very firm and composed, but, with her red eyes and full heart, did not succeed very well.

At first he was a little embarrassed by her close scrutiny, for she had wrought herself up into the expectation of seeing a gaunt, famine- stricken man. But his cheeks, though somewhat hollow, were ruddy, and his face was bronzed by exposure. Instead of being pained by his cadaverous aspect, she was impressed by his manly beauty; but she said, "I have sent for you that I might give you a scolding."

"I'm all meekness," he said, a little wonderingly.

"Aunty tells me that you don't eat anything."

"That is just what she says of you."

"But I'm ill and can't eat."

"Neither can I."

"Why not?"

"How can a man eat when there are hungry women aboard? It would choke me."

Instead of scolding him, she again buried her face in her pillow, and burst into tears.

He was a little perplexed, but said, gently, "Come, my dear little sister, I hope you are not worrying about me. I assure you there is no cause. I never felt better, and the worst that can happen is a famine in England when I reach. It grieves me to the heart to see you so pale and weak. The captain says I have a bad conscience, but it's only anxiety for you that makes me so restless."

"Do you stay upon deck all night this bitter weather?"

"Well, I want to be ready if anything should happen."

"O Walter, Walter! how I have wronged you!"

"No, beg your pardon, you have righted me. What was I when I first knew you, Annie Walton? There is some chance of my being a man now. But come, let me cheer you up. I have good news for you. If I had lost every dollar on that ship I should still be rich, for your little Bible (I shall always call it yours) remained safe in my overcoat pocket, and you brought it aboard. Now let me read you something that will comfort you. I find a place where it is written, 'Begin here.' Can you account for that?"

And he read that chapter, so old but inexhaustible, beginning, "Let not your heart be troubled."

Having finished it, he said, "I will leave my treasure with you, as you may wish to read some yourself. In regard to the subject of the 'scolding,' which, by the way, I have not yet received, if Miss Morton here can tell me that you are eating more, I will. Good-by."

Annie's appetite improved from that hour. She seized upon the old Bible and turned its stained leaves with the tenderest interest. As she did so, her harsh note to Gregory, written when Hunting complained that he had been insulted, dropped out. How doubly harsh and unjust her words seemed now! Then she read his words, "Forgiven, my dear, deceived sister." She kissed them passionately, then tore the note to fragments.

Miss Eulie watched her curiously, then stole away with another smile. She liked the spell that was acting now, but knew Annie too well to say much. Miss Eulie was one of those rare women who could let a good work of this kind go on without meddling.

Annie did not read the Bible, but only laid it against her cheek. Then Hunting came back looking very discontented, for he had managed to catch glimpses of her interview with Gregory.

"Shall I read to you from that book?" he said.

She shook her head.

"You seemed to enjoy having Mr. Gregory read it to you," he said, meaningly.

Color came into her pale face, but she only said, "He did not stay long. I'm ill and tired."

"It's rather hard, Annie," he continued, with a deeply injured air, "to see another more welcome at your side than I am."

"What do you mean?" she asked, in a sudden passion. "How much time has Mr. Gregory been with me since he saved both our lives? You heard my father say that I should be a sister to him; and yet I believe that you would like me to become a stranger. Have you forgotten that but for him you would have been at the bottom of the Atlantic? There, there, leave me now, I'm weak and ill--leave me till we both can get into better moods."

Pale with suppressed shame and anger, he went away, wishing in the depth of his soul that Gregory was at the bottom of the Atlantic.

Again she buried her face in her pillow and sobbed and moaned, "How can I marry that man! He makes my very flesh creep."

Then for the first time came the swift thought, "I could marry Gregory; I'm happy the moment I'm near him;" and her face burned as did the thought in her heart.

Then she turned pale with fear at herself. A sudden sense of guilt alarmed her, for she had the feeling that she belonged to Hunting. So solemn had been her engagement that the thought of loving another seemed almost like disloyalty to the marriage-tie. With a despairing sigh, she murmured, "Chained, chained."

Then strongly arose the womanly instinct of self-shielding, and the purpose to hide her secret. An hour before, Gregory could not come too often. He might have stooped down and as a brother kissed her lips, and she would not have thought it strange or unnatural. Now she dreaded to see him. And yet when would he be out of her thoughts? She hoped and half-believed that he was beginning to regard her as a sister, and still, deep in her soul, this thought had an added sting of pain.

Ah, Annie! you thought you loved before, but a master-spirit has now come who will stir depths in your nature of which neither you nor Hunting dreamed.

Hunting, seemingly, had no further cause to be jealous of Gregory during the rest of the voyage. With the whole strength of her proud, resolute nature, Annie guarded her secret. She sent kind messages to Gregory, and returned the Bible, but did not ask him to visit her again. Neither did she come on deck herself till they were entering the harbor of an English port.

When Gregory came eagerly toward her, though her face flushed deeply, she greeted him with a kind and gentle dignity, which, nevertheless, threw a chill upon his heart. All the earnest words he meant to say died upon his lips, and gave way to mere commonplaces. Drawing her heavy shawl about her, she sat down and looked back toward the sea as if regretting leaving it with all its horrors. He thought, "When have I seen such a look of patient sorrow on any human face? She saw the love I could not hide at our last interview. I did not deceive her by calling her 'sister.' Her great, generous heart is grieving because of my hopeless love, while in the most delicate manner she reminds me how vain it is. Now I know why she did not send for me again."

He walked away from the little group pale and faint, and she could not keep back the hot tears as she watched him. Miss Eulie was also observant, and saw how they misunderstood each other. But she acted as if blind, feeling that quickly coming events would right everything better than any words of hers.

Gregory went to another part of the vessel, and leaned over the railing. Annie noticed with an absorbing interest that he seemed as indifferent to the delight of the passengers at the prospect of soon being on land, and the bustle on the wharf, as he had appeared at the commencement of the voyage. But she rightly guessed that there was tumult at his heart. There certainly was at hers. When the vessel dropped anchor and they would soon go ashore, he turned with the resolve, "I will show her that I can bear my hard lot like a man," and again came toward them, a proud and courteous gentleman.

Annie saw and understood the change, and her heart was chilled by a sense of loneliness and isolation greater than if the stormy Atlantic had rolled between them. And yet his manner toward her was very gentle, very considerate.

He took charge of Miss Eulie, and soon they were at the best hotel in the place. The advent of the survivors caused great excitement in the city, and they were all overwhelmed with kindness and sympathy.

After a few hours Gregory returned to the hotel, dressed in quiet elegance, and he seemed to Annie the very ideal of manhood; while she, in her mourning robes, seemed to him the perfection of womankind. But their manner toward each other was very quiet, and only Miss Eulie guessed the subterranean fires that were burning in each heart.

"Are you sure that you will be perfectly comfortable here?" he asked.

"Entirely so," Annie replied. "Mr. Hunting has telegraphed to my uncle, and we will await him here. I do not feel quite strong enough to travel yet."

"Then I can leave you for a day or two with a quiet mind. I must go to Liverpool."

She turned a shade paler, but only said, "I am very sorry you must leave us so soon."

"I missed a note from your Bible," he said, in a low tone.

"Forgive me! I destroyed it," and she turned and walked to the window to hide her burning face.

Just then Hunting entered, and a few moments later Gregory bade them a quiet farewell.

"How wonderful is her constancy!" he sighed as he went away. "How can she love and cling to that man after what he has shown himself!"

He had utterly misunderstood her and believed that she had destroyed the note, not because of her own harsh words, but of his reflecting on Hunting.

Annie thought she knew what sorrow was, but confessed to herself in bitterness, after he had gone, that such had not been the case before.

If Hunting secretly exulted that Gregory was out of the way, and had been taught by Annie that he must keep his distance, as he would express it, he was also secretly uneasy at her manner toward him. She merely endured his lavish attentions, and seemed relieved when he was compelled to leave her for a time. "She will feel and act differently," he thought, "when she gets well and strong, and will be the same as before." Thus the harassing fears and jealousy that had tortured him at sea gave way to complacent confidence. But he was greatly provoked that he could scarcely ever see Annie without the embarrassing presence of Miss Eulie.

He had a growing antipathy for that lady, while he felt sure that she did not like him. Annie was very grateful to her aunt for quietly shielding her from caresses that every hour grew more unendurable.

Gregory was detained for some time in Liverpool, and on his return to the city where he had left Annie and Miss Eulie he met Mr. Kemp, whom he had known well in New York, also seeking them. This gentleman greeted him most warmly, for he had read in the papers good accounts of Gregory's behavior. In a few moments they entered the hotel together. Fortunately, as Gregory thought, but most unfortunately, has he learned afterward, Hunting was out at the time.

The warm color came into Annie's face as he greeted her, and she seemed so honestly and eagerly glad to see him that his sore heart was comforted.

Mr. Kemp's manner toward his niece and sister was affectionate in the extreme. Indeed, the good old man seemed quite overcome by his feelings, and Gregory was about to retire, but he said, "No, please stay, sir. Forgive my weakness, if it is such. You don't know how dear these people are to me, and when I think of all they have passed through I can hardly control myself."

"We should not be here, uncle," said Annie, in a low, thrilling voice, "had it not been for Mr. Gregory."

Then the old gentleman came and gave Gregory's hand such a grasp that it ached for hours after. "I have been reading," he said, "warm tributes to his conduct in the papers, but I did not know that we were all under such deep personal obligations to him. Come, Annie, you must tell me all about it."

"Not now, please," said Gregory. "I start in a few moments for Paris, and must even now say good-by for a little time. I warn you, Mr. Kemp, that Miss Walton will exaggerate my services. She has a way of overvaluing what is done for her, and undervaluing what she does for others."

"Well," said Mr. Kemp, with a significant nod, "that's a trait that runs in the Walton blood."

"I long ago came to regard their blood as of the truest blue," said Gregory, laughing.

"Must you leave us again so soon?" said Annie, with a slight tremble in her voice.

"Yes, Miss Walton, even now I should be on the way to the train. But you are surrounded by those who can best take care of you. Still I earnestly hope that, before many days, I shall see you in Paris, and in greatly improved health. So I won't say good-by, but only good- morning."

Ah, he did not know, or he would have said "farewell" with a heavy heart.

His parting from her was most friendly, and the pressure of his hand warm and strong, but Annie felt, with a deep, unsatisfied pain at heart, that it was all too formal. Mr. Kemp was exceedingly demonstrative, and said, "Wait till I see you in Paris, and I will overwhelm you with questions, especially about your partner, my dear old friend, Mr. Burnett."

But staid, quiet Miss Eulie surprised them all. She just put her arms about his neck, and gave him a hearty kiss, saying, "Take that, Mr. Gregory, from one who loves you like a mother."

He returned the caress most tenderly, and hastened away to hide his emotion.

Then envious Annie bitterly reproached herself that she had been so cold, and, to make amends, began giving a glowing account of all that Gregory had done for them.

The old gentleman listened with an amused twinkle in his eyes, secretly exulting over the thought, "It is not going to break her heart to part with Hunting."

In the midst of her graphic story that unfortunate man entered, and her words died upon her lips. She rose quietly, and said, "Charles, this is my uncle, Mr. Kemp."

But she was amazed to see Mr. Kemp, who thus far had seemed geniality itself, acknowledge her affianced with freezing coldness, and Hunting turned deathly pale with a presentiment of disaster.

"Be seated, sir," said Mr. Kemp, stiffly; "I wish to make a brief explanation, and after that will relieve you of the care of these ladies."

Hunting sank into a chair, and Annie saw something of the same terror on his face which had sickened her on the sinking ship. "Annie," said her uncle, very gravely, "have you entire confidence in me? Your father had."

"Certainly," said Annie, wondering beyond measure at this most unaccountable scene.

"Will you take my word for it, that this man, who seems most conscious of his guilt, deceived--yes, lied to Burnett & Co., and swindled them out of so large a sum of money that the firm would have failed but for me? Because, if you cannot take my word, I can give you absolute proof."

Annie buried her face in her hands and said, "Now I understand all this wretched mystery. How I have wronged Mr. Gregory!"

"You could not do other than wrong him while Mr. Hunting had any influence over you. I know Mr. Gregory well. He is an honorable business man, and always was, with all his faults. And now, sir, for your satisfaction, let me inform you that Mr. Burnett is one of my most intimate friends. He told me all about it, and gave ample proof of the nature of the entire transaction. I am connected with the bank with which the firm deposited, and through my influence I secured them such accommodation as tided them over the critical time in their affairs which your villany had occasioned."

Hunting now recovered himself sufficiently to say, "I did nothing different from what often occurs in business. I had a legal right to every cent that I collected from Burnett & Co."

"But how about *moral right?* Do we not all know that often the most barefaced robberies take place within the limits of the law? And such was your act. Even the hardened gamblers of the Street were disgusted."

"You have no right to speak to me in this way, sir," said Hunting, trying to work up a little indignation. "Mr. Walton trusted me, and I became engaged to Miss Walton under circumstances the most solemn and sacred; we are the same as married."

"Come, sir," interrupted Mr. Kemp, hotly, "don't make me lose my temper. John Walton was the soul of Christian honor. He would have buried his daughter rather than have her marry you, if he had known you as I do. I now insist that you resign your executorship and relieve us of your presence."

"Annie," cried Hunting, in a voice of anguish, "can you sit quietly by and hear me so insulted?"

She sat motionless--her face, burning with shame, buried in her hands. With her intense Walton hatred of deceit, the thought that she had come so near marrying a swindler and liar scorched her very soul.

He came to her side and tried to take her hand, but she shrunk from him in loathing, and, springing up, said passionately, "When I think, sir, that with this guilty secret you would have tricked me into marriage by my father's death-bed, I am perfectly appalled at your wickedness. God in mercy snatched me then from a fate worse than death."

She turned away for a moment and pressed her hands upon her throbbing heart. Then turning her dark and flashing eyes to where he stood, pale, speechless, and trembling, she said, more calmly, "May God forgive you. I will when I can. Go."

She proved what is often true, that the gentle, when desperately wronged, are the most terrible.

He slunk cowering away without a word, and to avoid exposure Mr. Kemp at once compelled him to sign papers that took from him all further power of mischief. Mr. Kemp eventually became executor in his stead.

As soon as Annie grew calmer she had a glad sense of escape greater than that which had followed her rescue from the wrecked ship. Her heart sprung up within her bosom and sung for joy. Then again she would shudder deeply at what she had so narrowly avoided. Stronger than her gratitude for life twice saved was her feeling of obligation to Gregory for his persistent effort to shield her from this marriage. She was eager to start for Paris at once that she might ask forgiveness for all her injustice toward him. But in the excess of her feelings she was far more unjust toward herself, as he would have told her.

Still, even if Hunting's dishonesty had not been revealed to her, Annie would have broken with him. As soon as she gained her mental strength and poise--as soon as she realized that her love was hopelessly gone from him--her true, strong nature would have revolted from the marriage as from a crime, and she would have told him, in deepest pity, but with rock-like firmness, that it could not be.

The next day she greatly relented toward him, and, in her deep pity, sent a kind farewell message which it would nave been well for him to heed.

CHAPTER XXXV
A CHESTNUT BURR AND A HOME

When Gregory reached Paris, to his grief and consternation he found a despatch informing him of the sudden death of old Mr. Burnett, and the illness of Mr. Seymour, the other partner. "Return instantly," it read; "the senior clerk is coming out to take your place."

At first it appeared a double grief that he could scarcely endure, for it seemed that if he went back now Annie would be lost to him beyond hope. But after thinking it all over he became calmer, "It may be best after all, for as my wife she is lost to me beyond hope, and God sees that I am not strong enough to meet her often yet and sustain myself, and so snatches me from the temptation."

Thus little children guess at the meaning of an earthly father, but Gregory did what a child should--he trusted.

He wrote a warm but hasty note to Annie, which through some carelessness was never delivered, attended to some necessary matters, and was just in time to catch the French steamer outward bound.

When Annie reached Paris, she learned in dismay that he had sailed for New York. Seemingly he had left no message, no explanation; all they could learn at his hotel was that he had received a despatch summoning him instantly home. Annie was deeply wounded, though she tried to believe that he had written and that the letter had been missent or lost. A thousand conjectures of evil ran in her mind, and the thought of his being again on the ocean, which she now so dreaded, at the stormiest season of the year, was a source of deep anxiety. In her morbid fears she even thought that the scheming Hunting might have something to do with it. She gave way to despondency. Then her aunt tried to comfort her by saying, "Annie, I am sure I understand you both better than you do each other, and I think I can write Mr. Gregory a line which will clear up everything."

But the quiet little lady was quite frightened by the way in which Annie turned upon her.

"As you love me, aunty," she said, "never write a line on this subject. I am not one to seek, but must be sought, even by Gregory. Not one line, I charge you, containing a hint of my feelings."

"Well, Annie, darling," she said, gently, "it's all going to come out right."

But Annie, in her weak, depressed state, saw only the dark side. As with Gregory there was nothing for her but patient trust.

But when, in due time, there came a despatch from him announcing his safe arrival, she was greatly reassured. The light came back into her eyes and the color to her cheeks.

"What kind of medicine have you been taking to-day?" asked her uncle, slyly.

"She has been treated with electricity," Miss Eulie remarked, quietly.

"O, aunty!" said Annie, with a deep blush, "when did I ever hear you indulge in such a witticism before?"

And when, some days later, she received a cordial, brotherly letter from Gregory, relating all that had occurred, a deep content stole into her heart, and she felt, with Miss Eulie, that all would eventually be well. She replied scrupulously, in like vein with himself, and thus began a correspondence that to each became a source of the truest happiness. Their letters were intensely brotherly and sisterly in character, but Annie felt almost sure that, under his fraternal disguise, she detected the warmth and glow of a far stronger affection; and, before many months had passed, he hoped the same of her dainty letters, though he could not lay his finger on a single word and say, "This proves it." But Annie's warm heart unconsciously colored the pages, nevertheless.

Of Hunting he briefly wrote, "God pity him."

In May, Gregory was glad to find that he would have to go to Europe again, and purposed to give Annie a surprise. But he received only a very sad one himself, for, on arriving at Paris, he learned, to his intense disappointment, that Mr. Kemp and his party had suddenly decided to return home. He was eventually comforted by receiving a letter from Annie, showing clearly that she had been as greatly disappointed as himself; but, woman-like, most of the letter was an effort to cheer him.

Still he was growing almost superstitious at the manner in which she seemed to elude his loving grasp, and sighed, "I fear she will always prove to me a spirit of the air."

One bright morning, in the ensuing October, Gregory again greeted, like the face of a friend, the shores of his native country, and the thought that Annie was beyond that blue line of land thrilled his heart with impatient expectation.

As they approached Sandy Hook, the pilot brought abroad a New York paper, and as he was carelessly glancing over it, his eyes were caught by an advertisement of the sale by auction of the Walton estate, his old home. He saw by the date that the sale would not take place till the following day, and he now felt sure that he could give Annie a double surprise, for he had not written of his return. He had learned from Annie that her father must have intrusted large sums to Hunting which could not be accounted for, and that beyond the country-place not much had been left.

He rightly guessed that this place was about to be sold to provide means for the support of the family. He was surprised that Annie had not written to him about the sale, and indeed she had wished to, thinking that he might like to buy it. But Mr. Kemp had dissuaded her, saying that it was not at all probable that Gregory had the means to buy so large a property, and judging Gregory by himself, he added, "A business man does not want a country-place anyway. Besides, Annie, if you should suggest it, it might be a source of much pain to him to feel that he could not."

But as soon as Gregory was ashore he hunted up one of his senior clerks, and instructed him to go up the following morning and buy the place at any cost, but not to let any one know it was for him. He also told him to assure the family that they need not vacate the place in any haste.

It soon became evident at the sale that the stranger from the city was determined to have the property, and the other bidders gave way.

When the clerk returned that evening Gregory plied him with questions, and learned that Miss Walton seemed to have great regret at leaving, and was very grateful when told that she could take her own time for departure. In fact, Annie grudged every October day at the old place, that brought back the past so vividly. Gregory could not forbear asking, with a slight flush, "How did Miss Walton look?"

"Like her surroundings," said the clerk, politely blind, "and not like a city belle. Mr. Gregory, I congratulate you on possessing the most home-like place on the river."

Gregory took the earliest train the following morning, and at noon found himself by the cedar thicket again, with a strange thrill, as he recalled all that had occurred there and since. He sat down to rest for a moment on the rock where Annie had first found him more than a year before. Beneath him lay his home--his now in truth--embowered in crimson and golden foliage, that seemed doubly bright in the genial October sunlight, while at his very feet were the orchard's laden boughs, beneath which he had proved to Annie the reality and depth of his love; and there beyond was the cottage of Daddy Tuggar, with that old man smoking upon the porch. But, chief of all, he could mark the very spot by the brook in the garden where Annie's hand, like an angel's, had plucked him from the brink of despair, and given the first faint hope of immortal life. Tears blinded his eyes, but the bow of promise shone in them as he looked heavenward, and said, "Merciful Father! how kind of Thee, in view of my past, to give me this dear earnest of my heavenly home!"

The sound of approaching steps aroused him, and springing up he saw through the thicket, with an emotion so deep that it made him tremble, the one woman of the world to him.

With an expression of deep sadness, and the manner of one taking a lingering leave of a very dear friend, Annie came slowly toward him along the brow of the hill. He tried to still even the beating of his heart, for he would not lose one moment of exquisite anticipation. And yet he was deeply agitated, for he knew that he could not maintain the brotherly disguise an hour longer.

Suddenly she looked toward the cedar thicket, and, as if recalling what had occurred there, covered her face with her hands, to hide the painful scene. Then he saw that she would not even come to the place, but was turning to go to the house by another way.

He darted out from his concealment and rushed toward her. At first, in wild alarm, she put her hand to her side, and leaned against a chestnut-tree for support. Then recognizing him, with a glad cry, she permitted him to take her in his arms, while she hid her face on his shoulder. A moment later they recoiled from each other in blushing confusion.

"Well?" said Gregory, stupidly.

She was the first to recover herself, and said, "O, Walter, I'm so--so glad you have come at last!"

"Do I look sorry?" he asked, taking her hand.

"Oh!" she exclaimed; "this is too good to be true!"

"That's what I think, I feared you would take flight the moment I appeared."

"When did you arrive? Come, tell me everything."

"Not all at once, dear--Annie. But let me give you a seat on the rock by the thicket, and then I will say the catechism."

"Please, no, Walter; not there," she said, drawing back.

"Yes, there; we will give that place a new association."

But she was glad to reach the seat, for she trembled so she could hardly stand.

Then he told her how he purposed to surprise her, and answered every eager question.

"O, Annie!" he concluded, "how I have longed for this hour! Never did that dreadful ocean seem so wide before."

She looked at him more fondly than she knew, and said, "Ah, Walter! your blood is not on my hands after all."

"Let me see," he said.

"I know it is not," she replied, putting them behind her back; "don't I see you there well and happy?"

"I don't know but it will be on your hands yet," he said, half- tragically, springing up.

She gave him a swift look of inquiry, but her eyes dropped as quickly beneath his eager gaze, while her deep blush caused her to vie with the sugar-maple on the lawn in very truth. But he said after a moment, "Annie, dear, won't you let me interpret another chestnut burr for you?"

"Certainly, Walter," she tried to say innocently, "all that are on the tree."

"Now don't make fun of me, because I'm desperately in earnest. I don't want one like that I chose with a great lonely worm-infested chestnut in it. What a good, wholesome lesson you gave me then! Thank you, Annie, darling."

"Brothers don't use such strong language toward their sisters," said Annie, looking on the ground.

"I can't help it. To tell the honest truth I'm not much of a brother. Neither do I want one like that which you chose with three chestnuts in it. *Three*, faugh! I've had enough of that. I want to find one like that which you brought me the first day I met you here."

"You will never find it if you stand talking forever."

"You won't go away?"

"Perhaps not."

He looked at her doubtfully, but she would not meet his eye. Then he started on his search, but kept looking back so often that she laughed, and said, "I'm not a chestnut burr."

"I'm afraid of you."

"Then you had better run away."

"Sisters shouldn't tease their brothers."

"Well, forgive me this time."

He caught a branch full of half-open burrs, and peered eagerly in them till he found one to his mind, and pulled it off regardless of the pricking spines, then came and kneeled at her side, and said, "Now, Annie, dear, look into it carefully. This is nature's oracle. You see two solid, plump chestnuts."

"Well?" she said, faintly.

"And you see this false, empty form of shell between them?"

"Yes"--with a touch of sadness.

"That's Hunting, poor wretch! How unspeakable was his loss!" and he tossed the worthless emblem away.

"And now, Annie, loved beyond all words I can ever find to tell you, see how near these two chestnuts are together--as near as you and I are in heart, I trust. Surely my poor pretence of brotherly character has not deceived you for a moment. Won't you please put your dainty fingers down into the burr and join the two together?"

She lifted her drooping eyes a moment to the more eloquent pleading of his face, but they fell as speedily.

In a low, thrilling tone she said, "No, Walter, but you may."

He dropped the burr and sealed the unspoken covenant upon her lips.

After a few moments he said, very gently and gravely, "Annie, do you remember when my arm last encircled you?"

The crimson face turned pale as she recalled that awful midnight when he rescued her from death.

Both breathed fervently, "How good God has been to us!"

In their joy, as in fear and sorrow, they remembered Him.

"O, see!" cried Annie, "your hands are bleeding where the burr pricked them, and you have stained my hands again. Your blood is on them," she added, almost in fear.

"Yes, and the best blood of my heart ever will be. Is not the 'blood upon us' the deepest and most sacred hope of our hearts? Is it not the proof of the strongest love the world has known? Let mine there be the pledge that my life is as nothing when it can shield and shelter you."

And so he changed the meaning of the omen.

The hours passed unheeded. At last they went across the orchard as before, and stopped and looked at the place where the ladder fell, and then at each other.

"Walter," said Annie, shyly, "I gave you my first kiss here."

"I am repaid then."

Before going to the house, they called on Daddy Tuggar. He was so amazed that he could only ejaculate, "Evenin'."

"Mr. Tuggar, I have acted on your suggestion," said Gregory. "I thought Miss Walton would be good company forever, and I have the promise of it."

"To think that I should have cussed you!" said the old man, in an awed tone.

"But you will give us your blessing, now?" said Annie, smiling.

"My blessin' ain't worth nothin'; but I know the good Lord will bless you both, even if Miss Annie never was an awful sinner."

"Mr. Tuggar," said Gregory, "I own that place over there. Will you take me for a neighbor till you are ready to be Mr. Walton's?"

"O, Walter!" said Annie, with a glad cry, "is that really true?"

"Yes, it became mine yesterday; or, rather, it remained yours."

"Mr. Gregory," said Daddy Tuggar, his quaint face twitching strangely, "if anybody steals your apples, I'm afraid I'll swear at 'em, even yet."

"No, you won't, Daddy," said he. "But I'm going to bring you over to spend an evening with us soon. Good-by!"

They found Miss Eulie in the parlor, pensively packing up some dear little relics of a home she supposed lost. Gregory put his arm around her and said, "Aunty, I'm going to claim relationship right away; put those things back where you found them, and sit down here in the cosiest corner of the hearth, your place from this time forth."

"How is this?" she exclaimed, in breathless astonishment.

"Well, Annie owns me, and therefore this place."

Johnny came bounding in, and Gregory caught him, and said, "Here is the prophet of my fate. How did you tell me your Aunt Annie managed people, the morning after my first arrival here?"

"I said she kinder made people love her, and then they wanted to do as she said," replied the boy, timidly.

"Let me tell you a secret," and he drew the boy and whispered in his ear, "she is going to manage me on just those terms."

Then little Susie came sidling in, and Gregory took her in his arms, saying, "So dimpled, yet so false, you renounced me for a chipmonk; and now I am going to be Aunt Annie's beau till I'm gray."

Jeff next appeared with a basket of wood. Gregory gave his black hand an honest shake, and said, "Why, Jeff, old fellow, what is the matter with you to-night? The last time I saw you you looked as if you were driving me to the cemetery."

"Well, Misser Gregory," said Jeff, ducking and shuffling. "Ise did come mighty neah takin' de turnin' to de cem'try dat day. I tho't you looked as if you wanted to go dar."

As they sat down to tea, Zibbie put her head in at the door, and said, "The gude God bless ye, for ye ha' kept the auld 'ooman fra the cauld wourld yet."

Delighted Hannah could not pass a biscuit without a courtesy.

That evening the hickory fire glowed and turned to bright and fragrant coals as in the days past, but Annie looked wistfully toward her father's vacant chair, and sighed, "If father were only here!"

"Don't grieve, darling," said Gregory, tenderly. "He is at home, as we are."

A few evenings later Gregory brought up from the city a large, square bundle.

"What have you there?" said Annie, greeting him as the reader can imagine.

"Your epitaph."

"O, Walter! so soon?"

His answer was a smile, and quickly opening the pack age, he showed a rich, quaint frame containing some lines in illuminated text. Placing it where the light fell clearly, he drew her to him and said, "Read that."

> "God sent His messenger of faith,
> And whispered in the maiden's heart,
> 'Rise up and look from where thou art,
> And scatter with unselfish hands
> Thy freshness on the barren sands
> And solitudes of death.'"
>
> "O beauty of holiness,
> Of self-forgetfulness!"

With a caress of unspeakable tenderness he said, "You are the maiden, and God sent you to me."

THE END

The Codes Of Hammurabi And Moses
W. W. Davies

QTY

The discovery of the Hammurabi Code is one of the greatest achievements of archaeology, and is of paramount interest, not only to the student of the Bible, but also to all those interested in ancient history...

Religion   **ISBN:** *1-59462-338-4*   **Pages:132**
MSRP $12.95

The Theory of Moral Sentiments
Adam Smith

QTY

This work from 1749. contains original theories of conscience amd moral judgment and it is the foundation for systemof morals.

Philosophy **ISBN:** *1-59462-777-0*   **Pages:536**
MSRP $19.95

Jessica's First Prayer
Hesba Stretton

QTY

In a screened and secluded corner of one of the many railway-bridges which span the streets of London there could be seen a few years ago, from five o'clock every morning until half past eight, a tidily set-out coffee-stall, consisting of a trestle and board, upon which stood two large tin cans, with a small fire of charcoal burning under each so as to keep the coffee boiling during the early hours of the morning when the work-people were thronging into the city on their way to their daily toil...

Childrens   **ISBN:** *1-59462-373-2*   **Pages:84**
MSRP $9.95

My Life and Work
Henry Ford

QTY

Henry Ford revolutionized the world with his implementation of mass production for the Model T automobile. Gain valuable business insight into his life and work with his own auto-biography... "We have only started on our development of our country we have not as yet, with all our talk of wonderful progress, done more than scratch the surface. The progress has been wonderful enough but..."

Biographies/   **ISBN:** *1-59462-198-5*   **Pages:300**
MSRP $21.95

The Art of Cross-Examination
Francis Wellman

QTY

I presume it is the experience of every author, after his first book is published upon an important subject, to be almost overwhelmed with a wealth of ideas and illustrations which could readily have been included in his book, and which to his own mind, at least, seem to make a second edition inevitable. Such certainly was the case with me; and when the first edition had reached its sixth impression in five months, I rejoiced to learn that it seemed to my publishers that the book had met with a sufficiently favorable reception to justify a second and considerably enlarged edition. ..

Reference   ISBN: *1-59462-647-2*

Pages:412

MSRP $19.95

On the Duty of Civil Disobedience
Henry David Thoreau

QTY

Thoreau wrote his famous essay, On the Duty of Civil Disobedience, as a protest against an unjust but popular war and the immoral but popular institution of slave-owning. He did more than write—he declined to pay his taxes, and was hauled off to gaol in consequence. Who can say how much this refusal of his hastened the end of the war and of slavery ?

Law   ISBN: *1-59462-747-9*

Pages:48

MSRP $7.45

Dream Psychology Psychoanalysis for Beginners
Sigmund Freud

QTY

Sigmund Freud, born Sigismund Schlomo Freud (May 6, 1856 - September 23, 1939), was a Jewish-Austrian neurologist and psychiatrist who co-founded the psychoanalytic school of psychology. Freud is best known for his theories of the unconscious mind, especially involving the mechanism of repression; his redefinition of sexual desire as mobile and directed towards a wide variety of objects; and his therapeutic techniques, especially his understanding of transference in the therapeutic relationship and the presumed value of dreams as sources of insight into unconscious desires.

Psychology   ISBN: *1-59462-905-6*

Pages:196

MSRP $15.45

The Miracle of Right Thought
Orison Swett Marden

QTY

Believe with all of your heart that you will do what you were made to do. When the mind has once formed the habit of holding cheerful, happy, prosperous pictures, it will not be easy to form the opposite habit. It does not matter how improbable or how far away this realization may see, or how dark the prospects may be, if we visualize them as best we can, as vividly as possible, hold tenaciously to them and vigorously struggle to attain them, they will gradually become actualized, realized in the life. But a desire, a longing without endeavor, a yearning abandoned or held indifferently will vanish without realization.

Self Help   ISBN: *1-59462-644-8*

Pages:360

MSRP $25.45

QTY

The Rosicrucian Cosmo-Conception Mystic Christianity *by Max Heindel*   ISBN: *1-59462-188-8* **$38.95**
The Rosicrucian Cosmo-conception is not dogmatic, neither does it appeal to any other authority than the reason of the student. It is; not controversial, but is: sent forth in the, hope that it may help to clear...   New Age/Religion Pages 646

Abandonment To Divine Providence *by Jean-Pierre de Caussade*   ISBN: *1-59462-228-0* **$25.95**
"The Rev. Jean Pierre de Caussade was one of the most remarkable spiritual writers of the Society of Jesus in France in the 18th Century. His death took place at Toulouse in 1751. His works have gone through many editions and have been republished...   Inspirational/Religion Pages 400

Mental Chemistry *by Charles Haanel*   ISBN: *1-59462-192-6* **$23.95**
Mental Chemistry allows the change of material conditions by combining and appropriately utilizing the power of the mind. Much like applied chemistry creates something new and unique out of careful combinations of chemicals the mastery of mental chemistry...   New Age Pages 354

The Letters of Robert Browning and Elizabeth Barret Barrett 1845-1846 vol II   ISBN: *1-59462-193-4* **$35.95**
by Robert Browning and Elizabeth Barrett   Biographies Pages 596

Gleanings In Genesis (volume I) *by Arthur W. Pink*   ISBN: *1-59462-130-6* **$27.45**
Appropriately has Genesis been termed "the seed plot of the Bible" for in it we have, in germ form, almost all of the great doctrines which are afterwards fully developed in the books of Scripture which follow...   Religion/Inspirational Pages 420

The Master Key *by L. W. de Laurence*   ISBN: *1-59462-001-6* **$30.95**
In no branch of human knowledge has there been a more lively increase of the spirit of research during the past few years than in the study of Psychology, Concentration and Mental Discipline. The requests for authentic lessons in Thought Control, Mental Discipline and...   New Age/Business Pages 422

The Lesser Key Of Solomon Goetia *by L. W. de Laurence*   ISBN: *1-59462-092-X* **$9.95**
This translation of the first book of the "Lemegton" which is now for the first time made accessible to students of Talismanic Magic was done, after careful collation and edition, from numerous Ancient Manuscripts in Hebrew, Latin, and French...   New Age/Occult Pages 92

Rubaiyat Of Omar Khayyam *by Edward Fitzgerald*   ISBN: *1-59462-332-5* **$13.95**
Edward Fitzgerald, whom the world has already learned, in spite of his own efforts to remain within the shadow of anonymity, to look upon as one of the rarest poets of the century, was born at Bredfield, in Suffolk, on the 31st of March, 1809. He was the third son of John Purcell...   Music Pages 172

Ancient Law *by Henry Maine*   ISBN: *1-59462-128-4* **$29.95**
The chief object of the following pages is to indicate some of the earliest ideas of mankind, as they are reflected in Ancient Law, and to point out the relation of those ideas to modern thought.   Religion/History Pages 452

Far-Away Stories *by William J. Locke*   ISBN: *1-59462-129-2* **$19.45**
"Good wine needs no bush, but a collection of mixed vintages does. And this book is just such a collection. Some of the stories I do not want to remain buried for ever in the museum files of dead magazine-numbers an author's not unpardonable vanity..."   Fiction Pages 272

Life of David Crockett *by David Crockett*   ISBN: *1-59462-250-7* **$27.45**
"Colonel David Crockett was one of the most remarkable men of the times in which he lived. Born in humble life, but gifted with a strong will, an indomitable courage, and unremitting perseverance...   Biographies/New Age Pages 424

Lip-Reading *by Edward Nitchie*   ISBN: *1-59462-206-X* **$25.95**
Edward B. Nitchie, founder of the New York School for the Hard of Hearing, now the Nitchie School of Lip-Reading, Inc, wrote "LIP-READING Principles and Practice". The development and perfecting of his meritorious work on lip-reading was an undertaking...   How-to Pages 400

A Handbook of Suggestive Therapeutics, Applied Hypnotism, Psychic Science   ISBN: *1-59462-214-0* **$24.95**
by Henry Munro   Health/New Age/Health/Self-help Pages 376

A Doll's House: and Two Other Plays *by Henrik Ibsen*   ISBN: *1-59462-112-8* **$19.95**
Henrik Ibsen created this classic when in revolutionary 1848 Rome. Introducing some striking concepts in playwriting for the realist genre, this play has been studied the world over.   Fiction/Classics/Plays 308

The Light of Asia *by sir Edwin Arnold*   ISBN: *1-59462-204-3* **$13.95**
In this poetic masterpiece, Edwin Arnold describes the life and teachings of Buddha. The man who was to become known as Buddha to the world was born as Prince Gautama of India but he rejected the worldly riches and abandoned the reigns of power when...   Religion/History/Biographies Pages 170

The Complete Works of Guy de Maupassant *by Guy de Maupassant*   ISBN: *1-59462-157-8* **$16.95**
"For days and days, nights and nights, I had dreamed of that first kiss which was to consecrate our engagement, and I knew not on what spot I should put my lips..."   Fiction/Classics Pages 240

The Art of Cross-Examination *by Francis L. Wellman*   ISBN: *1-59462-309-0* **$26.95**
Written by a renowned trial lawyer, Wellman imparts his experience and uses case studies to explain how to use psychology to extract desired information through questioning.   How-to/Science/Reference Pages 408

Answered or Unanswered? *by Louisa Vaughan*   ISBN: *1-59462-248-5* **$10.95**
Miracles of Faith in China   Religion Pages 112

The Edinburgh Lectures on Mental Science (1909) *by Thomas*   ISBN: *1-59462-008-3* **$11.95**
This book contains the substance of a course of lectures recently given by the writer in the Queen Street Hail, Edinburgh. Its purpose is to indicate the Natural Principles governing the relation between Mental Action and Material Conditions...   New Age/Psychology Pages 148

Ayesha *by H. Rider Haggard*   ISBN: *1-59462-301-5* **$24.95**
Verily and indeed it is the unexpected that happens! Probably if there was one person upon the earth from whom the Editor of this, and of a certain previous history, did not expect to hear again...   Classics Pages 380

Ayala's Angel *by Anthony Trollope*   ISBN: *1-59462-352-X* **$29.95**
The two girls were both pretty, but Lucy who was twenty-one who supposed to be simple and comparatively unattractive, whereas Ayala was credited, as her Bombwhat romantic name might show, with poetic charm and a taste for romance. Ayala when her father died was nineteen...   Fiction Pages 484

The American Commonwealth *by James Bryce*   ISBN: *1-59462-286-8* **$34.45**
An interpretation of American democratic political theory. It examines political mechanics and society from the perspective of Scotsman James Bryce   Politics Pages 572

Stories of the Pilgrims *by Margaret P. Pumphrey*   ISBN: *1-59462-116-0* **$17.95**
This book explores pilgrims religious oppression in England as well as their escape to Holland and eventual crossing to America on the Mayflower, and their early days in New England...   History Pages 268

QTY

The Fasting Cure *by Sinclair Upton*   ISBN: *1-59462-222-1*   **$13.95**
In the Cosmopolitan Magazine for May, 1910, and in the Contemporary Review (London) for April, 1910, I published an article dealing with my experiences in fasting. I have written a great many magazine articles, but never one which attracted so much attention...   New Age/Self Help/Health Pages 164

Hebrew Astrology *by Sepharial*   ISBN: *1-59462-308-2*   **$13.45**
In these days of advanced thinking it is a matter of common observation that we have left many of the old landmarks behind and that we are now pressing forward to greater heights and to a wider horizon than that which represented the mind-content of our progenitors...   Astrology Pages 144

Thought Vibration or The Law of Attraction in the Thought World   ISBN: *1-59462-127-6*   **$12.95**
by William Walker Atkinson   *Psychology/Religion Pages 144*

Optimism *by Helen Keller*   ISBN: *1-59462-108-X*   **$15.95**
Helen Keller was blind, deaf, and mute since 19 months old, yet famously learned how to overcome these handicaps, communicate with the world, and spread her lectures promoting optimism. An inspiring read for everyone...   Biographies/Inspirational Pages 84

Sara Crewe *by Frances Burnett*   ISBN: *1-59462-360-0*   **$9.45**
In the first place, Miss Minchin lived in London. Her home was a large, dull, tall one, in a large, dull square, where all the houses were alike, and all the sparrows were alike, and where all the door-knockers made the same heavy sound...   Childrens/Classic Pages 88

The Autobiography of Benjamin Franklin *by Benjamin Franklin*   ISBN: *1-59462-135-7*   **$24.95**
The Autobiography of Benjamin Franklin has probably been more extensively read than any other American historical work, and no other book of its kind has had such ups and downs of fortune. Franklin lived for many years in England, where he was agent...   Biographies/History Pages 332

Name	
Email	
Telephone	
Address	
City, State ZIP	

☐ **Credit Card**   ☐ **Check / Money Order**

Credit Card Number	
Expiration Date	
Signature	

Please Mail to: Book Jungle
PO Box 2226
Champaign, IL 61825
or Fax to: 630-214-0564

ORDERING INFORMATION
web*: www.bookjungle.com*
email*: sales@bookjungle.com*
fax*: 630-214-0564*
mail*: Book Jungle PO Box 2226 Champaign, IL 61825*
or PayPal *to sales@bookjungle.com*

Please contact us for bulk discounts

DIRECT-ORDER TERMS

**20% Discount if You Order
Two or More Books**
Free Domestic Shipping!
Accepted: Master Card, Visa,
Discover, American Express